M000209795

BOOK FOUR

RUTHLESS ENDS

KATIE WISMER

RUTHLESS ENDS

Copyright © 2023 by Katie Wismer

All rights reserved. Printed in the United States of America. No part of this book may be used or reproduced in any manner whatsoever without written permission of the publisher, except in the case of brief quotations embodied in critical articles and certain other noncommercial uses permitted by copyright law.

For more information visit: www.katiewismer.com

Cover design by Seventhstar Art
Proofreading by Beth Attwood

Paperback ISBN: 978-1958458037

Hardcover ISBN: 978-1958458044

First Edition: October 2023

10 9 8 7 6 5 4 3 2 1

This one's for you, Paige!

ALSO BY KATIE WISMER

Find your next read here: https://www.katiewismer.com/books

THE ESTATES

New York City, United States
Carrington Estate

Prince Rupert, Canada
Auclair Estate

São Joaquim, Brazil
Queirós Estate

Stockholm, Sweden
Olofsson Estate

Rjukan, Norway
Botner Estate

Dikson, Russia
Vasiliev Estate

Utqiagvik, United States
Locklear Estate

Chongqing, China
Wénběn Estate

Tórshavn, Faroe Islands
Jógvan Estate

Hat Yai, Thailand
Suksai Estate

PLAYLIST

Listen on Spotify: https://shorturl.at/BDKQ0

Killer — The Ready Set

don't sleep, repeat — 44phantom, Machine Gun Kelly

Die For Me — Post Malone, Halsey, Future

Robbery — DREAMERS, Sueco

Welcome To The Jungle — Tommee Profitt, Fleurie

Misery — The Maine

I am not a woman, I'm a god — Halsey

Anti-Hero — Taylor Swift

R U Mine? — Arctic Monkeys

Mother's Daughter — Miley Cyrus

Karma — Taylor Swift

Like People, Like Plastic — AWOLNATION

My Way — PVRIS

It's Not My Time — 3 Doors Down

When I Come Around — Green Day

Bring Me To Life — Evanescence

Tripping Over Air — Aidan Bissett

NYC's better off without u — Libby Larkin

Lose Control — Barcelona

Midnight City — M83

Guilty Filthy Soul — AWOLNATION

Slide — The Goo Goo Dolls

Loved You A Little — The Maine, Taking Back Sunday,
Charlotte Sands

Midnight Rain — Taylor Swift

Happy — The Maine

Only Place I Call Home — Every Avenue

Lavender Haze — Taylor Swift

Any Other Way — We The Kings

Lonely — Palace Royale

Kiss My Scars — August Royals

Box in a Heart — The Maine, renforshort

Fought for Me — Paradise Fears

Would've, Could've, Should've — Taylor Swift

FUCK ABOUT IT — Waterparks, blackberry

SELF-SABOTAGE — Waterparks

Maybe You Saved Me — Bad Suns, PVRIS

WE MADE PLANS & GOD LAUGHS — Beauty School

Dropout

ANIMAL— PVRIS

you're not special — Maggie Lindemann

Kryptonite — 3 Doors Down

Numb — Linkin Park

Addicted — Saving Abel

I Love This Part — The Wrecks

Sleepwalking — All Time Low

Heaven, We're Already Here — The Maine

Another Night on Mars — The Maine

My Own Worst Enemy — Lit

Four Letter Words — K.Flay

The Great War — Taylor Swift

Temporary Bliss — The Cab

Candle (Sick and Tired) — The White Tie Affair

Harder To Breathe — Maroon 5

How Far We've Come — Matchbox Twenty
My Heroine — The Maine
Shiver Shiver — WALK THE MOON
Ring — Selena Gomez
Lock Me Up — The Cab
Smells Like Teen Spirit — Nirvana
I Don't Wanna Live Forever — ZAYN, Taylor Swift

This book contains material that may be triggering for some readers. Reader discretion is advised. For a complete list of trigger warnings, please visit katiewismer.com/trigger-warnings

CHAPTER ONE

NOW

Mirrors, I've found, are the most satisfying for punching. Because of the shattering, yes, but also because of the pain. It's unique. Dynamic. It's different every time, depending on how many shards pierce your skin and where. It can be especially exquisite if you manage to break a bone, but that's more difficult than you might think.

I stare at the blood, the red vibrant and dramatic as it runs down the pale skin of my forearm. Maybe, finally, this time it will scar. This time, it'll leave a mark. This time, it won't just disappear like nothing ever happened.

Along with the blood comes the familiar burn of magic on my skin. The heat builds hotter, sharper, almost to the point of pain, the fire blurring from orange to white to blue. It's dizzying, intoxicating, *devastating*. Somehow…*more* than it's ever been before.

"Fuck, Val, not again."

I huff as Adrienne hurries across the room and needlessly

fusses over my arm. It's not like it won't heal. My blood pools in the bathroom sink, a mosaic of broken glass and spots of crimson decorating the counter. The mirror itself is mostly intact—a few fissures and cracks with a single hole toward the center.

Underwhelming.

If she hadn't walked in, I probably would've tried again.

She says something else as she grabs tweezers from a drawer, but I'm not listening.

It's my fault, really, for doing this in her room. Not that I have anywhere else to go. But she wasn't supposed to be here today.

"Let me see it."

"It's fine." I try to pull away, but her grip on my shoulder is hard enough to bruise.

"What the hell do you think you're accomplishing with this?" she mutters under her breath as she gets to work extracting the tiny shards from my skin. "I thought we were past this. Are you *drunk*? It's not even midnight."

"Of course not." I sway on my feet.

"Come on. Sit down." She ushers me to her bed, her voice gentler now, and I hate it.

I hate the careful way she's holding my arm, the worry creasing her forehead, the way her eyes keep flicking up to inspect my face.

I hate the way she's tried to take on Mom's role at eighteen.

I hate that she never gets mad at me, never raises her voice, no matter what I do.

I wrench away as she pulls out another piece of glass.

"Valerie——"

"Leave it," I snap, but she's right. The whiskey is catching up to me, and I blink, trying to force the room to right itself.

The whiskey was the first mistake. Nasty, barbaric stuff. But it was all I'd been able to find.

She wrangles me onto the bed again, though she's given up on tending to the wound. Instead, she grabs both sides of my face.

She looks tired. There are dark circles under her eyes, and her hair is unwashed and pinned up with clips. The hard set of her jaw doesn't relent. "I did not just get you back to watch you kill yourself like this." Her voice is lethally quiet, and her grip tightens on my skull.

"Don't be so dramatic."

She couldn't be more wrong. I haven't fought so hard to escape death this many times just to go running into its waiting arms. The bleeding, the pain, it's not killing me. It's saving me. It's so much easier to hold on to the anger, the fight, with it buzzing through my veins. Without it, the darkness threatens to creep in, the sadness.

And I'm sure as hell not going to sit around and waste time feeling sorry for myself, not after clawing myself back here.

I want this anchor. *I need it.*

"You've spent the last three years hating me anyway," I mutter.

"That's not fair."

I snort. *Fair.* Since when has any of this been fair?

Somewhere in the back of my mind, a different version of me knows she's right, that I'm being a bitch to her for no reason. But I can't stop, and that version of me is currently

3

drowning in whiskey and self-pity, and it's all too easy to block her out.

I push to my feet. Adrienne reaches out as if to catch me, but I keep moving.

"Where are you going?"

"Training." I swing the door open.

"I—*training*? You can't show up like this."

"Like he'll care."

"You know what? Fine." Adrienne throws her hands up, then stomps out ahead of me. I expect her to keep going, but she stops in the middle of the hall, crosses her arms over her chest, and taps her foot.

"I really don't need an escort."

"Think of me as a babysitter then."

I push past her, the gashes in my hand burning as they heal. Blood dribbles along my path as I head for the sprawling grounds behind the estate.

Despite being here for weeks, the winding corridors of Auclair haven't gotten any more familiar. Or maybe it's because I've spent little time navigating them sober.

Adrienne breathes down my neck the entire way, her body heat rolling off her in waves. The scent is too appetizing for comfort. I clear my throat and loosen my collar. As irritating as she's been, I don't think sinking my fangs into her jugular would improve the situation.

Especially with how much my body remembers how good her blood tasted, even if my mind can't.

"Shouldn't you be at school?" I ask.

"It's Saturday."

"Shouldn't you at least be at the academy then? Socialize.

You'll never make friends if you keep coming back here all the time."

"I have friends," she says with an indignant lift of her nose.

I grunt to refrain from saying something I'll regret later.

My shoulders hunch as we step outside. The wind's had a bite to it most days now with winter rolling in. I'm just grateful we haven't seen any snow yet. Harsh white stadium lights illuminate the grounds, blotting out the stars and moon overhead.

A single man stands in the center of the field, his sleeves pushed up to his elbows. He lifts his chin an inch to acknowledge my approach.

"Took you long enough," says Cam.

CHAPTER TWO

TWO WEEKS EARLIER

THE BLOOD LOOKS different in the sunlight. It darkens as it dries like ink splotches against the tarmac, more than I'd thought there'd be with the number of casualties.

But then comes the crowd. So many people, voices, hands pulling me this way and that, car headlights as SUVs blur before me. I don't resist as I'm shoved into a back seat.

None of the Russians who'd been trying to kidnap me are in sight.

Because they're all dead.

The others talk among themselves, their voices not registering enough to process the words.

Or maybe it's because a different word is playing on a loop in my head.

Fiancée. Fiancée. Fiancée.

I blink, coming back to the car, but the rest of the back seat is empty. I don't know either of the Marionettes in the front.

And Reid isn't here.

They probably had different protocols to get the vampires out of the sun, which is rapidly rising in the distance.

Right. That must be it.

But that doesn't even begin to address the question of who *the fuck* is Anya?

Did he bring her here? Was that part of his plan? Or was she with the brothers who were trying to kidnap me tonight? And why has he never so much as mentioned her name?

I'm yours, Valerie. Completely. And I'm hoping that you want to be mine.

I'll never want that with anyone else.

I've definitely never loved anyone the way I love you.

My eyes burn, and I clench my teeth, fighting the stupid impulse to cry. Because this doesn't make any sense.

I couldn't have been that wrong about him. Not him.

Once we're back at the estate, there's still no sign of him. Not as I follow the Marionettes out of the car, and not as the corridors fill with people, all heading to the same place, but then they disappear into a room, pointedly not letting me follow.

The clang of the door closing echoes in the empty hall.

I stumble back a step, then another, unsure of where to go, what to do. What is the appropriate reaction to nearly being kidnapped by psychos trying to raise their brother from the dead and then getting accosted by the fiancée of your boyfriend?

"Hey, princess."

My spine stiffens, my heart skittering in my chest.

Am I dreaming? Is that why nothing makes sense?

He looks the same as the last time I saw him, when he dropped me and Reid off at a motel. Though now there's a gash from his cheek to his forehead, deep enough that it probably needs stitches. Blood saturates his blond hair, darkening it several shades, and there's a bite mark on the side of his throat, the puncture wounds jagged and wide.

The momentary spark of relief turns to ice as I meet Cam's eyes. "What the hell are you doing here? If they see you…"

"You worried about me?" The light, teasing tone of his voice is a direct contrast to the intensity in his expression.

We stare at each other, and a million emotions I don't want to acknowledge war in my chest. Because, well, yes. One of them is definitely worry, made only worse by how beaten up he looks.

Finally, he adds, "Nothing to worry about, princess. I've had an agreement with the Auclair estate for years. They know I'm here."

The words shouldn't be a surprise—plenty of the other estates are more welcoming toward weres than the Carrington —but I can't imagine Cam cooperating with the royal vampires in any capacity, especially given his blood deal with James Westcott.

"Do they—"

"They know about the deal," he says lowly, then wraps his fingers above my elbow, urging me to follow him. The heat of his skin sinks into me, and I pull away.

"What are you doing here?"

He lets out a short breath through his nose and mutters

something I don't catch. "Are you going to walk with me or not?"

For some reason, I do.

Because I have nowhere else to be and it's pathetic to wait outside this room they locked me out of, I tell myself.

The corridors are eerily empty as I follow Cam. In the short time I've been at Auclair, I've never seen it this quiet.

"The other wolf…"

"Leif. He's fine. A few of the others are here too. They might get on my fucking nerves, but they're loyal, I'll give them that. Didn't even hesitate to follow me once Nina took over the pack—"

"Wait, *what?*"

An involuntary shudder rolls through me at Nina's name. Despite spending however many weeks in the woods surrounded by wolves, being in her presence was the first time I'd felt that primal fear. The very cells in my body recognized her as a threat.

She'd been so insistent in Cam's tent about Reid's punishment after the two of us were caught, going on and on about how his pack wouldn't respect him anymore, how there could be a usurper…a situation she clearly took full advantage of.

"What? You thought I came here just for you?"

My face burns as he turns for the exit that leads to the grounds.

"What happened with Nina?"

He sighs. "She saw an opportunity and took it. Everyone was already on edge after Terrence. I wish I could say we'd put up a more united front but…"

The sun is sharp and blinding as it crests the horizon, and

I hold back my wince as we step outside. Cam nudges me to the shade on the other side of him as we walk, the touch tender in a way.

"I'm sorry, Cam. About the pack. I know it was your dad's."

He turns so I can't see his face as he nods, and a knot of guilt twists in my stomach. Would the same have happened if it hadn't been for me? If him helping me hadn't pissed off so many of his wolves?

"Pack masters come and go, packs merge. It isn't unusual."

It's a clear attempt to shut down the topic, so instead, I ask, "Where are the others now?"

"With the healer, last I checked. Patching up some minor stuff. They're being dramatic, honestly. They just like the infirmary because the beds are more comfortable than in our quarters."

I smirk. That does sound like them. "How did you even know...?"

Did Reid reach out? I can't bring myself to ask. Just thinking his name hits like a punch to the chest.

Something shifts in Cam's eyes, a wall coming down. Our steps slow as we come to a patch of shrubs surrounding a small fountain. He takes a seat on the bench and waits until I sink beside him, leaving a healthy amount of space between us.

He wets his lips and considers his words before saying, "I felt that you needed help. It was like it was in my bones or something. I think, maybe, well..." His gaze drifts to where the black mark had been on my wrist.

I blink at him, stunned, but the shock lasts only a second. "You don't mean...we're not..."

He scratches the back of his neck.

I swat his arm hard enough that he lets out a noise of protest.

"You let me *bind* myself to you? You didn't think that would be something to mention?"

"I didn't know!" He shrinks away before I can hit him again, and his shoulders creep up to his ears in a gesture that looks distinctly guilty and entirely foreign on him. "And it's not…I don't know. I just felt that I needed to be here. I didn't know why. I didn't know what was going on. There was nothing keeping me in the barrens anyway."

My fingers drift to my wrist even though they won't find what they're looking for. I should be disturbed by the thought of somehow being connected to Cam. Horrified, even. And I am. *I am.*

"I can't feel you" is all I manage. At least, I don't think I can. Would I have noticed with all the other chaos going on? Would it feel different than the bond with—

"I can't feel you either. Not now. And not since that one time. And it wasn't that I could feel you, exactly. I didn't realize you were the reason until I got here."

"Does that usually happen after transferring a blood deal?"

"I wouldn't have the first idea. Are you okay?"

I jump at the pressure of his fingers on my arm. The touch lingers for only a moment as he inspects the dried blood on my skin before he pulls away.

"I should be asking you that." The cuts on his face look even worse from this distance, and there's an angry rash on his cheek like his face dragged across the concrete.

"I meant about the Russian chick."

My eyes cut to his. "How did you know about that?"

"I was there, remember?"

I look away, the words sending an unwelcome jolt of ice through my system. "Here to gloat?"

"Do I look like I'm gloating?"

The grounds disappear around us, and I search for a smug glint in his eyes, but there's nothing of the sort. There's no softness or kindness, not that there usually is with him—just a firm sincerity.

"I'm not trying to be a dick. And I'm not trying to come on to you—well, maybe I am a little—but I'm asking if you're okay because I care if you are. And I want to make sure someone is asking you."

I don't know what he knows, what he overheard, but I guess it doesn't matter. I focus on my hands, somehow feeling every emotion at once and nothing at all.

"Why are they letting you be here?" I ask instead of answering his question. "Don't they see you as a liability if you're indebted to Westcott?"

He lets out a slow exhale and stretches his legs in front of him. "My original deal with him is null."

My eyes snap to his face, but there's no relief there.

"Apparently, my deal was contingent on me being the leader of that pack, which I no longer am." A faint smirk tugs at his lips. "A loophole. Irony's a bitch, huh?"

"But my deal?"

"If Westcott gave me a direct order, I'd have to follow it. But he'd have to find me to contact me first. I'm in his service until he releases me—those were your terms. But he hasn't set those parameters for me since I've taken your deal. So until then, we're playing it by ear. If that changes and I become a liability, we've already discussed I'll need to leave."

"That seems risky. What if the deal makes you do something you don't want to or it won't let you warn them first or—"

"Take a breath." I scowl, but he presses on. "Okay, so 'playing it by ear' is putting it mildly. I submitted to a truth spell, and I have regular check-ins with the king's Marionette, and there seems to be a few others unofficially keeping tabs on everything I do while I'm here. Right now, Auclair must see me as more of a liability outside his walls than in, and I'll be here as long as that remains true."

The look in his eyes sinks all the way to my bones, so much *more* than it had been a moment ago.

Quietly, he says, "To be clear, princess, nothing's changed for me."

I shake my head, my throat tight. "Cam…"

"I get it. If it had been Rea who came back… But just because he's alive, it doesn't mean you'll always want to be with him. It doesn't mean that's the life that's best for you. I think it's supposed to be you and me. And it's okay if I can see that before you can."

I swallow hard, at a loss for how to respond. A few weeks ago, everything was different. When I looked at him, I saw the future he's talking about. At least the potential of it.

But a few weeks ago, I thought Reid was dead. I thought I'd never come back here. That I'd never be this version of myself again.

"Miss…Miss Darkmore?" A spindly human servant pauses

a few feet away, wringing his hands together. "Queen Carrington has requested I escort you to her room."

Tension seizes my muscles, but I give the man a curt nod. Cam rises from the bench with me, saying nothing else as I follow the human inside.

The corridors are just as abandoned as we wind our way to the queen's guest room, where the human doesn't meet my eyes before he bows and scurries away.

The queen flashes a smile full of teeth as I step into the room, nothing about it warm. I'm surprised she's not in the meeting down the hall, especially considering her son's involvement.

Thinking of Reid threatens to let the spiraling thoughts resurface, so I take the seat she gestures to, fold my hands tightly in my lap, and focus on the light reflecting off the teeth in her crown as she takes the seat across from me.

"Tea?" she offers.

I resist the urge to ask what's in it, considering last time she was using it to test me for Wendigo Psychosis. I shake my head as she pours herself a cup.

"Now, the two of us are overdue for a chat, don't you think?"

I sit up straighter. "I'm not sure I know what you're referring to."

"Oh, Valerie." She sighs as she plops a sugar cube in her tea. "I'm on your side. Your mother leaving so abruptly, and after you just returned, I can't even imagine."

The fake sympathy on her face brings a sour taste to the back of my mouth. We both know she couldn't care less about how I'm doing, or motherly duties, for that matter, given her own children. She's not even trying to be subtle about her phishing.

"Rosemarie was so good to me for decades," she continues. "The best Marionette I've had, I'd say. It's a true loss."

"I don't know where she is, if that's what you're wondering."

The queen leans back, blinking rapidly for a moment, but I'm too exhausted to play whatever game she's looking for here.

"She must have said something to you before she left."

I shake my head. "Truly. I was as shocked as anyone."

I refrain from asking how *she* doesn't know more, seeing as she's the one bonded to my mother. Do they still have that connection? Did my mother break it before leaving?

Does she know more about what happened than she's saying?

"Well, as you saw, Princess Anya Vasilieva just arrived. I'll admit, we weren't expecting her, but she'll now be one of the representatives for the Russian estate as we navigate through all of this...unpleasantness."

The queen must see the confusion on my face because she adds, "Anya has always been more...*free-spirited* than the rest of the Vasiliev family. Her stowing away on a plane isn't unusual for her, trust me. I do feel a need to apologize for her escorts though. The Russians have always been so...primitive."

My eyes flick to the teeth in her crown that she apparently considers civilized.

Stowed away? So the brothers hadn't known she was there? Or is that her story now to save face? That's an awfully long flight to stay hidden.

But if that's not true, and she was somehow in on the plans

those brothers had for me, does that mean she knows the truth about my necromancy?

She ripped Mikhail's spine straight out of his body, for fuck's sake. If she'd been in on their plan, why would she save me?

"You'll have to forgive their manners," continues the queen, and my eyes refocus on the displeased scrunch of her nose. "Though I am curious as to why they took such an interest in you."

I stifle a hiss as I pick the skin around my nails hard enough to draw blood. The queen's attention shoots to my hand, her pupils dilating.

"I believe they were trying to get back at Reid. They had a...history."

"And why would they think targeting you would be the best way to do that?"

The knowing lilt of her voice grates on my nerves, but all I say is "You know how loyal he is to his partners."

She gives me a small smile like she's humoring me. "Well, as I'm sure you know, Anya Vasilieva is betrothed to my son." Her smile grows like she is fully aware that I didn't know. "And what Reginald does behind closed doors is his own business. But make no mistake." She leans forward, slashing the distance between us in half, all pleasantries and fake smiles gone. "This betrothal will go through. Strong alliances between the estates are more important now than ever until we deal with this Westcott situation, and the union of Reginald and Anya will help mend the rocky relationship Vasiliev has had with the other estates for the past several years. Not to mention, my son will one day take the Carrington crown, and the woman at his side will be one fitting for his station." She looks me up and down. "His judgment is unsurprising, given his father, but a witch, Marionette or not, will never be anything more than his whore." She smiles and leans back in her seat. "Just so we're clear."

I don't even have time to dissect what she means about Reid's dad—he died before Reid left the estate as a child, before I could even *talk*—my brain getting caught on how casually the word *whore* rolls off her tongue.

I know what she expects. For me to sit here quietly, chagrined. As if I'm a child cowering beneath her authority as she looks down at me from her throne.

But this isn't her throne room, and I'm not that child anymore.

If anyone needs a reality check here, it's her. She's acting like nothing's changed, as if she hasn't taken up residence in another region, one where she has virtually no authority. As if she isn't under the protection of a different estate because she failed to hold her own. As if her estate isn't the first to have fallen.

The thought makes me sit up a little straighter, as if another following suit is a certainty.

But then why had she been so insistent that Reid and I get paired in the first place if she was just going to turn around and usher me out the door when the time came?

Her eyes harden at my hesitation.

There are a million things I'd like to say to her, maybe starting with the son she's suddenly so concerned about. The one she's always seen as expendable and threatened to kill if he stepped too far out of line. And now she's talking about him one day taking over her legacy? As if she'd ever willingly forfeit that crown. She'd sooner see the estate go up in flames.

One of these days, you psychotic bitch. But not here, and not now.

Instead, my jaw tightens as I force my own smile and say, "Perfectly."

CHAPTER THREE

AUCLAIR IS BURSTING at the seams, well past capacity as it struggles to accommodate its usual inhabitants and the refugees from the Carrington estate. Too many bodies, not enough beds, enough food, enough *blood*. I heard it's gotten bad enough for them to start relocating people to their emergency bunker. It wasn't a problem when we first got here and I was staying with Reid, but now as I step out of Queen Carrington's room, I realize I have nowhere to go.

Of all the conversations the queen could have wanted to have with me, her son's sex life hadn't been what I expected.

But the information about Anya...I need to find out why she's really here. What she knows. Why she was willing to kill her brother's friends to save my life when she'd never even met me.

And it's a stupid, inconsequential comment to get caught up on in light of everything else, but my body flushes with heat that I wish I could pass off as anger, hatred, rage—anything, *anything* but this shame.

You'll never be anything more than his whore.

Because twenty-four hours ago, I never would've doubted him. I never would've believed it.

But then Anya showed up, and now he's nowhere to be found.

"Val?"

Adrienne stands at the other end of the hall in navy blue pajamas decorated with tiny stars, her feet bare. I'm rushing toward her before I realize it, almost taking the two of us down as I throw my arms around her shoulders.

"Oh!" she grunts as she hugs me back. "I heard about what happened, are you okay?"

Yes, but also not at all.

She doesn't wait for a response before untangling from me and guiding us down a few doors to the room she's been staying in.

"You were with the queen?" she asks. "Was it about Mom?"

"Did she talk to you too?"

"No, but I've been thinking it's just a matter of time." She rifles through her drawers until she finds me something clean to wear. I'm out of my body as she helps me redress, barely feeling her touch, hearing her voice. The combination of the past few days weighs so heavily on my chest I feel like I can't breathe.

The fiancée.

The kidnapping.

Reid dead. Then not dead.

Cam.

My mother...

I blink back to the room. "Did she tell you where she was going? Have you heard from her?"

Adrienne digs in her eyebrows and ushers me under the covers. "No. She just disappeared. Did she tell you?"

I shake my head then grab her hand before she can leave. She squeezes my fingers. "I'm not going anywhere," she murmurs, then slides into bed behind me, her arms locking me in a protective embrace. "Okay, now start at the beginning."

THE KNOCK COMES the following evening shortly after I climb out of the shower and pull on a pair of Adrienne's sweats. My muscles go frigid at the small tug in my core, the first thing I've felt from the bond since I left the tarmac. Slowly, I hang the towel I'd been using to dry my hair on the hook as I hear Adrienne swing the front door open.

"You have a lot of nerve."

Reid sighs, and a shock runs down the length of my spine at the sound. "Can I come in?"

"No, you definitely can the fuck not."

"Adrienne—"

"Don't *Adrienne* me!"

My reflection stares back at me, wide-eyed, as I lean my ear toward the door. I don't think I've ever heard that kind of power in Adrienne's voice before.

"I don't know what you've heard—"

"Everything. I've heard everything! That's my sister. *My*

sister, you asshole." There's a thump, another, and then a dozen more in rapid succession, and it takes me a moment to realize she's hitting him.

"Valerie," he says, his voice low, and it's like he's standing right beside me. "I know you're in there, and I know you can hear me. Please."

"Haven't you done enough?" demands Adrienne. "You worthless, spineless, lying piece of—"

Her words cut off as I crack the door open. I give her a small nod, and she whips toward Reid, a single finger pointing at his face like a weapon. "I'll be just down the hall," she warns, then slips past him.

I stare at the place she'd been longer than necessary, bracing myself to look at him. To see his face, his eyes. He takes a step into the room, letting the door close behind him.

He didn't sleep at all, if the bags under his eyes are any indication. He's in the same clothes he was wearing on the tarmac, now torn and stained with blood and dirt, though if he sustained any injuries during the fight, it looks like they've healed by now. His eyes scan me from head to toe as if searching for damage before finally finding my face.

He lifts the blood bag in his hand an inch. "I thought you might be hungry. I'm sorry I couldn't get here sooner. How are you?"

I stare at him, unable to respond. Such a simple question. But it feels like it's from a different life, and there's nothing easy about the answer now.

"They're all dead," he adds. "Mikhail, Viktor, and the others they hired. Auclair has assured me he's looking into it to see if anyone else was working with them. But apparently they weren't expected in the region at all, so it looks like they were working alone."

"Is it true?"

His mouth freezes around whatever he was going to say next. Judging by the light dimming in his eyes, I don't need to elaborate. His jaw works as he sets the blood on the bed. "Yes."

It was different hearing it from some woman I'd never seen before, even from the queen, but from him? To have him look me in the eyes and confirm it?

"How could you do that?" I ask, my voice lethally quiet. "All those things you said to me—how could you—"

"Valerie." He takes another step forward, reaching for me, and I jerk back.

"Don't you dare touch me."

He takes my face between his hands anyway, and I try to yank away, but he holds firm.

"Don't touch me!"

"Listen to me." He leans his face close, forcing me to meet his eyes. "I need you to let me explain. Five minutes. And if you want me to leave after that, I will. Okay?"

I harden my jaw, the bone threatening to tear through skin, but I give a stiff nod.

When it's clear I'm not going to make a break for it, he releases my face and takes a step back. "It's true. Anya and I are betrothed, but I swear I've never lied to you. And I swear I've meant every word I've said.

"Betrothals with the royals are common, especially for political alliances. And they don't have the same expectations human engagements have. I've had other relationships in my life, as I'm sure she has. But it's never been much of a concern to me, because until you, I've never had someone that I...I've never..." He swallows hard like he's fighting to find the right words.

"My mother and King Vasiliev made the agreement when Anya was born. I was seven years old. I've met her twice. Once after her birth, and once when she was three and I was ten. I have never intended on going through with it. Half of my siblings have had similar betrothals that never turned into marriages because the political landscape changed by then or they negotiated something different with the other estate. And as ridiculous as it seems, it's not something I've given much thought to over the years aside from paying extra attention to maintaining a decent relationship with Vasiliev. It's just some-thing that's always been there, like some third cousin you've never met before."

I balk. "You're really comparing not mentioning an engagement to—"

"No, no." He rubs his eyes then runs his hands through his hair. "What I mean is, since you and I have been paired, there's been so much going on. First with you turning, then your final trial and Connor, the psychosis, Westcott, trying to find you—it never seemed like the right time to tell you. And God, I—I didn't plan on falling in love with you!" The words sit in the air for what feels like a lifetime before he continues. "I didn't plan on getting involved with you at all beyond our partnership because I knew what kind of target that would put on you. But I—"

"But you did. You did get *involved* with me. And you never thought to say, *Hey, by the way, I'm engaged?*"

"Valerie." He spreads his hands wide, his voice coming out like a plea.

"When were you going to tell me? Because it wasn't before you slept with me. It wasn't before you told me you loved me. It wasn't before you asked me to be with you and no one else. Were you just planning on riding this out with me for as long as you could until you had to turn around and marry her instead?"

My voice spikes up an octave by the end, and I hold up a shaking hand, not wanting to hear his response. Not wanting to have this conversation at all. I just want to go back to twenty-four hours ago before this entire fucking mess.

"I know I should've told you sooner—"

"How the fuck did you expect me to react to this?" I try desperately to hold on to the anger, but my voice is quivering, and now that the tears have started flowing, I know there's no stopping them. "How did you...how could you..." I hiccup, cover my face with my hands, and turn away from him.

He doesn't get to see me cry. Not over this.

Because I have been wrong about so many things in my life, so many people, but this? *Him?*

It feels like the floor has been ripped out from under me and the walls have been torn from the building around us, exposing not the estate grounds, but limitless, dark outer space, and there's no gravity tethering me to the floor anymore.

"You have every right to be angry with me," he says, his words coming out rushed and desperate. "I can't tell you how sorry I am for the way you found out."

His hands brush my arms from behind, and I jerk away,

hating the way warmth soars through me, how my body still reacts to his touch.

"I love you," he all but whispers. "I love you so goddamn much, and I am so sorry." The bond warms in my chest, and a small shiver runs down it like fingers stroking skin.

"Did you know…that she…"

"I had no idea she was coming. Valerie, I swear."

I hold up a hand to stop him before he can touch me again. "I believe you," I force out through the lump in my throat and lift my arms out to the sides. "But I don't know what you want me to say. It's still true. And she's still here."

"I know," he says roughly.

"So what are you asking me? Am I supposed to be okay with this? You want me to slip in and out of your room in the middle of the day when no one can see me like I'm your dirty little secret?"

"God, of course not."

I shake my head, fighting another wave of tears, and turn away.

"I will fix this. I swear to you—"

"So what happens if you don't marry her? If you break the agreement with Vasiliev?"

A muscle feathers along his jaw. "With the current state of things, they wouldn't take it lightly. And with the Carrington estate in such a vulnerable position right now…."

I pace to the opposite side of the room.

"I'm not going through with it," he insists.

"So then, what? I get to blame myself for whatever happens if you don't? I get to spend my whole life knowing it's my fault? All the people who die, that blood would be on my hands just as much as yours."

"No—"

"Then what do you want me to say, Reid?"

"I want you to say that you trust me!" he shouts. His chest rises and falls rapidly with his breath as he shoves a hand through his hair, fighting to rein himself back in. "I want you to say that you trust me to fix this. I don't know how yet, but I want you to say you have faith in me to figure it out. I will not let all those people die, but I will not lose you either. I need you to believe me when I tell you that I love you. More than I've ever loved anything, I love you."

He pulls in a sharp breath and runs a hand along the bottom of his jaw. Quieter, he adds, "I never asked for this, Valerie. I never had a say in any of it. You are the only thing in my life that I have ever chosen for myself."

I sink onto the edge of the bed, no longer able to hold myself up, and swipe the tears from my cheeks with the back of my hand. "Why is she here?" I whisper.

"I don't know."

I do the math. Seven years younger than Reid...so she must be eighteen now, or close to it. She's a goddamn child. But it's the age I'm willing to bet was in the agreement for them to marry.

I hang my head and press my fingers into my temples.

An eternity passes, our hearts racing in sync and echoing in my head. The bond is pulled taut, like we're each gripping one end and holding on for dear life.

His next words come out thick. "I understand if you can't get past it. But I hope one day you can forgive me." Tentatively, he kneels in front of me and pushes my hair behind my ears.

I should pull back, shove his hands away, but instead, my eyes flutter shut.

"I promise you I will fix this."

I lay my hands over his and bring them down from my face. "Reid, I can't...I can't do this with you while she's... while I know..."

"I know. I would never ask you to. But I am asking you not to give up on me in the meantime."

Then all too soon, he pulls away to leave.

My hand shoots out, and I grab his shirt in my fist, my gaze trained on my fingers instead of his face because I will lose what little self-preservation I'm clinging to right now if I look into his eyes.

"I'm trusting you," I whisper. "And I'm asking you, please don't break my heart."

His lips are on mine before I finish the words, and it feels like drowning, like staying here will kill me, but pulling away will just push me farther under.

I close my eyes as he leans his forehead against mine. His breath washes over my cheek as he whispers, "My heart belongs to you, Valerie, and you alone. And I will treat yours like the most precious thing I have. Always."

His gaze is steady on mine, determined in a way it wasn't before. He studies my face like he's committing every detail to memory. I force my hand to release his shirt with a shuddering breath, and then I let him go.

CHAPTER FOUR

HE ISN'T hard to find. The extravagance of the estate goes against everything I know about Cam, so I start my search outside. Sure enough, despite the cold, he's the only person in the expanse of grass beside the gardens.

Sweat drips from his bare chest as he does a series of push-ups, and there's training equipment scattered around him that he must have taken from the gym.

He doesn't acknowledge my approach, but I know he knows I'm here.

To be clear, princess, nothing's changed for me.

I think it's supposed to be you and me. And it's okay if I can see that before you can.

The words churn in the pit of my stomach.

I wait until he's finished with his push-ups, and he wipes the sweat from his face with a white towel as he returns to his feet.

I cross my arms, bristling under his stare. "Sorry to interrupt your workout."

"What can I do for you?" he asks as he retrieves his water bottle, and it's strikingly normal. No humor, no smirk, no annoying nicknames.

"I need you to tell me everything you know."

"A fairly vague request. Might be a long chat then."

"Cam," I say, my voice sounding like a plea. "You're not bound by your deal to Westcott now. Just tell me how fucked we are. What do you know that we don't?"

"Funny," he says, though he doesn't sound amused. "I had a similar conversation with Auclair earlier. Where do you want me to start?"

A million things I could ask are on the tip of my tongue, but strangely, the one thing I can't get over is *why*. Cam's no saint, but even when I thought the worst of him, it never made sense for him to side with someone like Westcott. There has to be something I don't understand.

"When did you start working with Westcott? You must have known him before your deal."

He lets out a slow breath and squints at something off in the distance. "I was young when we met. Not even thirteen. Naïve. He said all the right things, made all the right promises. My dad believed in him. Believed he could change things. And I believed in my dad. But then my dad died, and I took over the pack, and Rea… It took me too long to realize who he really was. But by then I'd made the deal, and…" He trails off, his brows knitting together as he shakes his head.

"And the estates? You said you have an agreement with Auclair? Why?"

"I've always kept as decent of relationships with the estates as I could. Keeping your enemies close and all that. Whether I want to work with either of them is beside the point. They hold the power, and whatever happens next to the rest of us will come down to them. So I could either be a bystander and wait and see, or I could put myself in the thick of it. Westcott thought I was a spy for him, the vamps think I'm a spy for them, and at least I have somewhat of an idea of what the hell is going on."

I narrow my eyes when he doesn't continue. "And which are you?"

He shrugs, a ghost of his familiar, cocky smile making an appearance. "Neither."

"And why should I trust you?"

His smile falls, something that looks like hurt flashing behind his eyes, but then it's gone just as quickly. "I've already had plenty of witches rummaging around in my head since I got here. If you wanted to have a go too, all you had to do was ask."

My skin crawls at the thought of sifting through his memories. I can see why Auclair would do it—the smartest course of action, really—but there's a part of me that's afraid of what I'd find.

I break the eye contact and turn to stare at the mountains in the distance. "You must have proved your loyalty one way or another for either of them to trust you."

"Westcott forced my loyalty. He made sure of that. And I don't work for Auclair. We just have an understanding. He's known me since I was a kid. My father was far more diplomatic than I'll ever be, but I've tried to maintain the relationships he had. Auclair being one of them. And his region has always been more welcoming of weres in general. Treats them like citizens instead of criminals. Employs them. I've kept him updated on what's happening outside of his region, giving him a heads-up if I've heard anything he might need to know. But he's known about my deal with Westcott since it happened—known he could only trust me so much after that."

I nod slowly, taking all of this in. There's no affection in his voice when he talks about Auclair, but there isn't the blatant disdain he gets on his face whenever Westcott's name comes up.

"What *do* you do for Westcott then?"

"It changes. For a while, it was recruiting people outside the estates' regions, pointing people to him who seemed like a good candidate for his cause. Usually people who formerly lived in one of the regions and escaped. And whatever task he ordered me to do—making the cuffs and babysitting you, for example."

"Is that what you were doing when you left the camp?"

His eyes cut to mine for a moment then quickly flick away. "No."

"Then what—"

"Ask me a different question."

I balk. "Cam."

"*Ask* me a different question, Darkmore." His voice isn't hard or commanding, and that may be what's most startling. He says it softly, like a plea.

I cross my arms over my chest, but there's something about the look in his eyes that stops me from pushing further.

"It has nothing to do with what's been going on, okay?" he says quietly. "I promise."

Nothing to do with what's been going on? So if he wasn't out running errands or whatever for Westcott and he wasn't helping the estates in some way…what the hell was he doing? I know at least part of the time was for making trips to town and getting supplies for the camp, but there's no way that's the full extent of it.

I narrow my eyes, but now's not the time to get swept up in my curiosity. If I keep pushing at what's apparently a sensitive topic, he might not answer anything else. "What are the cuffs for?" I finally ask.

Cam bobs his head a few times, visibly relieved. "Based on what he had us put in them, they seemed like they were for protection."

"Protection?" I'd assumed they were like mine—a punishment, a sign of imprisonment—even if the effects weren't the same.

"There were a lot of ingredients that usually help ward off vampires, make you less susceptible to glamours, that kind of thing. My guess was always he was putting them on his people —as many as he could, at least—to take away that advantage. Any other questions for your interview, princess? Or should I say interrogation?"

Ignoring that, I ask, "Why are you here now? What's in it for you?"

He weighs his answer for a few moments before responding. "Westcott is out of his goddamn mind, and it's only gotten worse over the years I've known him. I might not like the way the vamps run things, but I can't imagine giving that prick

33

more power than he already has would be much of an improvement. And if no one's here to be a voice for everyone outside of those boundaries, they'll get more fucked over than they already have been."

Cam has a certain talent for tiptoeing around what he actually means, disguising it in harsher words as if that will distract from what he's saying.

He cares about the people outside of these estates. Outside of the regions. He's here for them.

Even after his pack went behind his back, he's looking out for them and people like them. And despite how hard he fights to keep up this image of someone else, it doesn't surprise me at all.

"I've told them everything I could," he continues. "I didn't have access to much information, just a few different pieces that didn't make any sense together, but hopefully some of it will build on what they already knew." He grabs a set of dumbbells and starts doing biceps curls as he talks. "He's big on making connections, that much was always clear. Whether it was voluntary or not." He gives me a meaningful look. "I have a feeling that's why a few of your estates dropped off the map."

"Wait, some of the estates are working *with* him?"

"I don't know for sure." He exhales heavily and sets the weights at his feet. "But you've had some pulling out of your alliance for years now, haven't you? Seems like something he would do—swoop in and collect the people pissed off enough to work together, even if it is only over a common enemy."

That would make how many estates on his side? China and Brazil have been out for as long as I can remember, and the Faroe Islands and Sweden pulled out this year. Vasiliev has never been reliable. I can't even begin to estimate how much that would increase his numbers if that were true.

"You heard about the wendigo attacks all those years ago, didn't you?" he continues. "It's been decades at this point. I don't know much, but with how similar it sounds to what's happening now, I think Westcott tried to make his move back then, and it didn't work out. So he's been revising his plans and biding his time. I don't think he'll accept failure this time around."

"What do you know about the wendigo experiments he has going on in the basement of his compounds?"

His expression noticeably darkens. "Just that the people who went down to that lab never came back. Not the same, at least. Apparently they were all voluntary, but from what I've gathered, the process requires something similar to a blood deal, so once they're in, they're in."

That would explain how Westcott has managed to keep control over them all.

He shakes his head again. "I was never involved in that side of things. He didn't tell me much, and I don't understand the science behind it. But those experiments have been going on for as long as I've known him. But back then, I don't think he'd figured out how to do whatever the hell he's doing now yet, because it didn't seem like many people who went down to those labs survived. I was with my dad at one of his compounds—I think I was fourteen?—as they brought a new group of humans in. When I asked Westcott why they were all tied up and being forced downstairs, he'd said they were sick. They needed his help." He looks away as a muscle jumps in his jaw. "I saw their bodies getting taken out in trash bags later that night as my dad and I were leaving."

I can't help it. A shiver runs up my spine, a million images I don't want to remember flashing behind my eyes.

Fog and cloaks and claws ripping through flesh.

I chew on my lip as I look down at my feet. There are plenty of more important things to talk about right now, but I can't help but play back the moment Cam and I met after I'd killed Rome in the control room. I hadn't thought much of it at the time, far too preoccupied with needing to warn Reid and being caught red-handed.

Halfling. A daughter then, I'm assuming.

"Out with it, princess."

My eyes snap to his, and he raises his eyebrows.

"You knew who I was the second you saw me. You knew *what* I was, and you knew I was Westcott's daughter."

His shoulders slump with his exhale.

"What do you know about us—all of us? Why does he have so many halfling daughters?"

"I can't imagine any scenario where it's not on purpose. Just statistically, it should be impossible how many he has. Halflings are so rare, let alone a single bloodline having them so frequently. And they're all daughters, as far as I know. Maybe he has other children that aren't halflings that we don't know about, but I think it's telling that he's been gathering you all like collectibles and keeping you close." He frowns as he meets my eyes. "I wish I had more for you, I really do. But I *do* know that your mother is the only mother of his children that he was ever married to. Whether that was because they were in love or for some other purpose, your guess is as good as mine. Your mother doesn't seem like the type to be easily manipulated though. Are you sure she's not in on his plans?"

I open my mouth to deny it, but something stops me. *Am I sure?* I'm not sure of much of anything these days. I was too young to remember much from before Westcott left us, to remember if my mother has always been like this, or this is what she became after being betrayed and abandoned by someone she thought was the love of her life.

A door flies open behind me and slams against the side of the estate with a bang. I jump as a few Marionettes in uniform cut across the field in the opposite direction, clamoring voices inside the hall spilling out until the door shuts again.

I crane my neck, trying to see what's going on in there. I'm not even sure where that hallway goes, let alone why it would be so packed at this time of day.

"Valerie."

I blink back to Cam, the sound of my name in his voice a bit startling. His eyebrows are dug in, a muscle in his jaw jumping as he looks from me to that door.

"I wouldn't…if I were you."

Well, now I'm *really* curious.

He sighs and shakes his head a little as he retrieves the dumbbells from the ground.

The door swings open again as a few more Marionettes step out, revealing a line that snakes all the way down the hall. My feet carry me forward, and a few vampires I don't recognize shoot me dirty looks as I slip past them.

We're all practically shoulder to shoulder in this hall, and I strain my neck to see what everyone is in line for. There's a metal door at the end, and I think through what I know about Auclair, about what's on this side of the estate...

The blood drains from my face as my steps slow.

The basement.

The voices around me buzz and blur together.

"—this is a waste of time—"

"—they're refusing to even acknowledge the shortage—"

"—there won't be any left by the time we get to the front—"

"—I don't see why they're not roping in the servants, at least for a few servings' worth—"

There must be a blood farm down there, and with this many people flocking this way, the usual supply near the kitchens must already be out.

My gums throb, as if being in such close proximity to this many hungry vampires is contagious, though I already fed from the bag Reid brought me.

I push my way through the crowd, trying to get out, but the line curves around the corner like it'll never end.

It shouldn't be surprising. Of course the usual system wouldn't be able to keep up with the demand of double the number of vampires, the same way they're struggling to find accommodations for everyone.

But there's a big difference between vampires without a bed and vampires without blood.

And I have a sinking feeling this is just the beginning.

CHAPTER FIVE

"Just five more minutes, Aid! I'm almost done!" I unwind the towel from my hair and toss it on the hook behind the bathroom door, double-checking the time on my phone to ensure I'm not running late, but I'm good. I have over an hour.

Adrienne pounds on the door again, and I sigh. She must *really* need to go to the bathroom. Thank God we never had to share one growing up. I gather the products I need and tuck them against my chest so I can keep getting ready at the mirror by the bed. "Okay! Okay! I'm coming out!"

I swing the door open to find *Connor* standing there. To be honest, I wasn't sure he was still at Auclair. I haven't seen him around aside from the night I arrived and he came to see me in Reid's room. Though with the entirety of the first region evacuated right now, I suppose he can't go to his apartment in the city.

"I—oh." The bottle of leave-in conditioner tumbles free,

and Connor's hand shoots out, catching it before it can hit the ground. "Thanks," I mutter, glimpsing over his shoulder for my sister, but the rest of the room is empty.

"Adrienne's not here. She said she'll be back in a bit, and that you and I should...talk."

"She asked you to come here?"

He nods, helping me unload the bundle in my arms onto the counter. "I've been wanting to come by anyway to see how you were doing. I've only heard bits and pieces about what happened with those Russian guys, and you know how rumors spread around here. But I guess the fiancée part is true, right? That's why she...well, she came to me with an idea."

"She came to you with an idea about Anya," I parrot.

What the hell does Adrienne think Connor could do about this situation? And how could she think it's appropriate after he and I broke up? I could *strangle* her. She is utterly incapable of minding her own business.

"She thinks we should pretend to be back together."

"Look, I'm sorry. She never should have—she thinks we should *what*?"

He runs a hand along the back of his neck, his usual *I'm uncomfortable* tell. "She said the queen was on your case about it and is already unhappy since your mom left. And it would probably be best if Anya doesn't know. She's worried that... we're *both* worried that if the wrong people think the two of you are together, if they see your relationship as a threat, something might happen to you."

"I—" I hadn't thought that far ahead, to be honest. My mind's still reeling from the fiancée reveal, not quite getting around to what other implications there might be.

But the worst part is, he's not wrong. No matter what they say about how being a Marionette offers you protection, if they saw me as an obstacle, a complication, I have no doubt they'd happily dispose of me.

"I would never ask you to do that."

"You're not asking. I'm offering. And if anyone's gonna know how to play the part, it's me, right?"

I give him what I'm sure is an unconvincing smile. I have no doubt he'd do a damn good job of selling it. And that's exactly the problem. This breakup still feels fresh to me, and that's with me having already moved on. For him...

"I just mean...Connor, I just...I don't want you to—"

"I know what you're trying to say. And I'm not doing this because I think I'm gonna win you back by the end of it. I know this is over for you no matter what. For us. But that doesn't mean I stopped caring about you. There's been a lot that's happened to you in the last year that I haven't been able to do anything about. I haven't been able to help you. Hell, our whole lives I haven't been able to help you."

"That's not true," I say quietly, meaning it. "You've helped me more than anyone, Connor."

Maybe he didn't have the power or the influence or the physical strength when he was human. But that never stopped him. Not from comforting me, not from standing up to my mother even when he knew she could have destroyed him. It never stopped him from listening to my problems even when his were so much worse. From showing me compassion and empathy even when I didn't deserve it.

Reid talks about me turning out a decent person despite my circumstances as if it's my own personal accomplishment.

But I think a lot of my kindness and goodness came from knowing Connor.

He gives me a sad smile like he doesn't believe me. "Let me help you now, Valerie."

There are so many things about him that are the same as they've always been—his eyes, the unruly curls in his hair, the warmth in his voice.

But the differences are impossible to miss. He stands taller now, like he's no longer afraid to be seen. I never realized how much he used to collapse in on himself to draw the least amount of attention possible. There's also less tension in his shoulders, less stress, less worry.

"I wouldn't even know how to..." I trail off and vaguely wave a hand between us.

He cracks a half smile. "Is that a yes? Valerie Darkmore, are you agreeing to be my fake girlfriend?"

I snort out a laugh, though I can't help but get transported to the moment he first asked me to be his girlfriend. He'd been so nervous that time, barely able to hold eye contact with me. Nothing like the calm, confident man standing in front of me now.

When I hesitate, he crosses the rest of the distance between us and takes my face in his hands, forcing me to look at him.

"I already spent months trying to grieve you, and that was when there was a chance you were alive. If there's any chance this will keep you safe—please don't make me go through that again, Valerie." My eyes fill with tears at the crack in his voice. "I know you and I are never getting back together. I know that. But I want you as my friend again. I *need* you as my friend again."

"I've really missed you," I whisper.

He pulls me into his chest, and I hug him back just as tightly. "I've missed you too."

PULLING on my Marionettes uniform feels more like stepping into a costume. The soft black material hangs looser than it used to, and I tuck the tank top into the pants to make it less noticeable.

"Did they say what the meeting's about?" Adrienne asks behind me.

I meet her eyes in the mirror. She's sitting on the edge of the bed, hands twisting nervously in her lap.

"They never do." I'm just glad they're not locking me out of this one.

I talked with Connor longer than I realized. There's not enough time to do anything with my hair, so I gather it into a ponytail.

"Do you think...do you think they're looking for Mom?"

I pause with the rubber band stretched between my fingers. I have no idea. The queen obviously wants to know where she is, but will she sacrifice the resources needed to look for her in the middle of this mess? I doubt Auclair would even *allow* her to do so if this blood shortage is as serious as it seems when he's already stretched thin because of Westcott.

But if my mother left willingly, although considered highly shameful, abandoning your duties in the Marionettes is not unheard of. Enough to prevent you from ever working for the vampire industries again, but not illegal. So what grounds would they have, really?

All I can do is shake my head in response—as a *No* or *I don't know*, I'm not sure.

My eyes flick to the clock on the nightstand. "You should get going if you're going to make the train back to the academy."

She shrugs. "Thought I'd teleport instead." She keeps her voice light, casual, though the spark of pride in her eyes is unmistakable.

I smirk, that pride mirrored in my own eyes, not that I'd let her see that. Teleporting is one of the more difficult spells a blood witch can attempt, and one that has far too many ways it could go wrong. The worst part is trying it for the first time, like leaping off the edge of a cliff, hoping something will catch you on the other side.

After successfully pulling one off when she'd heard the news I arrived at Auclair—alive—she's been determined to master it, never staying in one place for too long.

"How are things at the academy?" I ask.

"Fine, I guess. It's just weird not being at York, you know? The other students are welcoming enough, but you can tell who's from Radmore and who's not."

I nod. York academy was evacuated shortly after the Carrington estate, its students relocated to neighboring academies—like Radmore, the one closest to Auclair—until the situation is *handled*.

Most of the others are at Radmore as well. Kirby, Monroe, Daniel, Wes, Beth, Andie.

But not me. Everyone here decided it would be best to

keep me close by considering the likelihood of Westcott taking me again. Which I guess shouldn't bother me. I've already missed half of senior year. I'm not exactly missing exams and classrooms and curfews.

And yet.

A roof over my head and the extravagances of the estate aside, am I really any less of a prisoner here than I'd been at the wolf camp?

Would anywhere *not* feel like a prison at this point?

"Is...um..." Adrienne sighs as she crosses her arms. "Is *he* coming to pick you up?"

"No," I say, turning away from the mirror. "I'm meeting him there."

Relief softens Adrienne's features, though she coughs to cover it. Just because I've forgiven Reid doesn't mean she has.

And just because I've forgiven him doesn't mean the thought of seeing him today doesn't feel like someone shoved their hand into my chest, twisting my heart like they're wringing out the blood inside.

Because I will walk into that room as his partner, his Marionette, and nothing more. I will look his fiancée in the eye and have no reaction. I will pretend his mother didn't feel the need to pull me aside and tell me how I'm not good enough for him.

And he will let me.

"Connor's going to walk with me," I add, shooting Adrienne a meaningful look.

She blushes and ducks her head. She'd returned to the room shortly after Connor left, playing innocent.

"So you agreed to it then?" she asks, her voice all high-pitched and hopeful.

"It wasn't a terrible idea," I mumble.

She beams and gives my hand a quick squeeze as I head out. Connor meets me halfway to the conference room and takes my hand as we walk. It feels nothing like the millions of times we've held hands before. Now we're both stiff and awkward. I hope it's not obvious to anyone else.

Connor follows me into the room, just enough for people to see him. A few others are already seated, but not many. A couple Marionettes I don't know, though one I recognize as King Auclair's partner, as well as Reid and Headmistress Coderre.

I pause in the doorway, and she gives me a small nod. "Glad to see you doing well, Valerie."

If she's surprised I'm alive, she doesn't show it. But none of the other academy heads are here, so why...?

But then it hits me. She's not here as York's headmistress. She's taken over as the queen's right hand. Which means Queen Carrington must be certain my mom is not coming back.

Does she know something I don't?

The vampire beside Reid has his hand casually thrown over the back of Reid's chair, an easy, familiar smile on his face as they talk, like they've been friends for years.

Reid turns at my name. Connor gives my hand a quick squeeze before releasing me and disappearing into the hall.

I don't miss the way Reid's eyes zero in on the contact. A terrible, petty part of me finds satisfaction in that, only for a moment. But no matter how confused and angry I am, I don't want to hurt him. I open the bond enough to let my earlier conversation with Connor pass through.

Reid remains expressionless as he pulls out the seat on the other side of him, but I feel his side of the bond relax like a muscle.

Queen Carrington joins the room next, followed by King Auclair, the crown prince of Auclair—Shane, I think, is his name—along with several Marionettes and advisors...and *Cam*.

I stare at him as he takes the seat across from me. What the hell is he doing here? He notices my attention and winks. Once all the seats are filled, I relax against my chair. Maybe I won't have to be in the same room as—

"What a maze it is around here!" The door flies open and bangs against the wall as Anya Vasilieva struts inside.

The brief memory I have from that night casts her as this shiny, sparkling creature kneeling on the step above me. I'd chalked it up to oxygen deprivation from getting strangled, but no, as her golden hair billows out behind her shoulders, she seems to glow from within. She's in formfitting riding pants and a high-neck tunic like she's prepared to step into battle. She smiles sweetly, meeting the eyes of the others in the room one by one, her smile growing an inch as she finishes with me.

"I do hope you haven't started yet. I wasn't certain on the time since my invitation seems to have gotten lost."

King Auclair gives her a pleasant smile and waves at the human servant beside the door. "If you'll grab another chair for—"

"Oh, that won't be necessary!" Anya's high heels click menacingly against the floor as she approaches. "I'll just take the one beside my fiancé, if you don't mind. I did not realize

Auclair was so...*progressive*. At Vasiliev, the Marionettes stand along the outskirts of the room."

The tips of my ears burn, my heart beating harder in my chest.

"You can have mine," Reid says, already pushing back from the table.

"Oh, don't be ridiculous. You're far too important to this meeting, I'm sure. And it's fitting for us to sit together, is it not? Your partner won't mind."

My nails bite into my palms as I clench my fists. *So this is how it's going to be.* It's clear no one is going to tell her no. No one gives a shit if some teenage princess stomps her foot until I go stand in the back of the room.

If only no one would give a shit if I burned her from the inside out, melting her internal organs one by one, raising her body temperature until her blood boiled inside of her, like pumping the sun that's so deadly to them directly into her veins.

I blink, the image a little too clear in my head. Where the hell did that come from?

"Of course not," I say, not because I want to give her my seat, but if moving gets me farther away from her jugular right now, it's probably for the best.

"No." Reid grabs the arm of my chair before I can stand. "My partner is as important to this meeting as everyone else. Considering she's one of the only people at this table who has seen Westcott in the last decade, I'd argue she's even *more* important. We can bring in another chair."

"There's hardly room for another, Reginald," says Queen Carrington, flicking her wrist with an unmistakable gleam in her eye. She's *enjoying* this. "And I think we've wasted enough time on this, haven't we? No one is denying Valerie's invaluable knowledge, but with all things considered, perhaps her role may look different now."

"What are you suggesting?" Reid demands.

Queen Carrington shrugs. "Partnerships change, Reginald, as you well know, for many reasons. One being if the Marionette in question is no longer the best fit for their partner. And after all she's been through, Valerie's certainly not in the expected physical shape for her position anymore. She didn't finish her final year at the academy. I'm merely suggesting we consider a reassignment."

I suck in a sharp breath. *Reassignment.* I just got back, and she's already trying to get rid of me. First with the meeting, now this. She doesn't just want me to stay out of Reid's engagement. She wants me out of his life entirely.

But why? Why keep my family close all these years like she was building a blood witch collection just to cast me out now?

Maybe you didn't turn out to be as valuable as she thought, a small voice whispers in the back of my mind.

Or something else has changed.

"First of all, that's absolutely not happening." Reid's fist tightens around my chair in a death grip. "And that's hardly the most pressing matter right now."

"I disagree. Royals are being targeted. Killed in the streets, kidnapped. There are bounties out for bringing them back alive. Having the best protection for you, and all royal vampires, should be one of our top priorities right now."

All eyes in the room are on me, and every nerve in my body flames with heat.

Stinging, sinking, shameful heat.

Because she's not wrong. I'm *not* at my best right now to protect him, and he *is* in more danger than ever.

"Here, Princess," Cam grunts as he stands and pulls his chair back. Though the words are directed at Anya, his gaze is solely on me. Anya opens her mouth to protest, but he cuts her off. "I insist. Chairs are far too civilized for us wolf folk anyway. Much prefer the corner."

She relents and heads for the other side of the table, but not before shooting a curious look between me and Cam.

I meet Cam's eyes for a split second as he leans against the wall, shoves his hands in his pockets, and crosses one ankle over the other. He winks, though his smile is too soft to be the smirk I'm sure he's going for.

"Why *is* the wolf here?" Queen Carrington asks.

"I'll thank you to speak to my guests with respect," says King Auclair pleasantly. "*All* of my guests. And I'd assume you'd welcome any allies we can get, considering your position."

Her position?

The condescension leeches from her expression as she sits up straighter.

"If you're really that concerned about the qualifications of our Marionettes, I'm sure Camden would be happy to aid with their training. He's been incredibly helpful in a similar position for me before," continues King Auclair, folding his hands on the table. "And if you're quite through wasting all of our time, shall we get to the purpose of this meeting? The Carrington estate was seized yesterday, along with the entire territory of the first region."

The news shouldn't be surprising considering the state of the city a few days ago. It had been abandoned, a ghost town ripe for the taking.

And yet...

So many memories on those grounds, in those halls. The room I lived in for most of my life. To think of someone else in there, going through the things I'd left behind...

"...a scouting team has reported back there's a magical barrier around the region. No one can cross the line. Not from the outside, at least."

"And our people on the inside?" Reid asks tightly.

His mother sighs. "We haven't been able to make contact with anyone."

Grief, humming and low, flashes through the bond before Reid slams the door between us, cutting me off. I peek at him out of the corner of my eye. His hands are fisted tightly in his lap, the line of his jaw sharp enough to cut glass.

He's probably blaming himself for leaving them behind. We were *just* there.

"It's clear what he's doing," says Shane. "Using the wendigos to create chaos, lower our numbers, clear out the region. And we did exactly what he wanted by evacuating. Leaving the territory open for him to swoop in and claim it. The Carrington estate won't be the last."

I glance at Cam, and Anya doesn't bother being subtle as she turns around in her chair. "Have you asked him? He's Westcott's lapdog, is he not? Did you know about this? What is he planning next?"

"You overestimate his trust in me," Cam mutters. "I've never been privy to the details of his plans."

"So you say," says Anya.

He meets her gaze, unflinching. "Yes. So I say."

"We should be focusing our Marionettes on getting through the boundary," says Shane, ignoring Anya beside him.

"There's no guarantee Westcott is there," offers one of the Auclair advisors, an older man with graying hair tied in a low ponytail. "He could be planning another attack elsewhere as we speak."

"So we do nothing?" counters Shane. "Let them have the first region?"

"Of course not," snaps Queen Carrington.

"Officials from the other estates in the alliance should be arriving later tonight," cuts in King Auclair, his eyes briefly flitting to Anya, and he bows his head. "Vasiliev has already sent their representative."

Anya straightens, her smile sharp as the room's attention falls on her. But it's the look in her eyes that has the hair standing up on the back of my neck. Like maybe what Auclair is saying isn't quite true, and that's not why she came at all.

According to Queen Carrington, they hadn't been expecting her.

"…all of whom have agreed to offer aid in whatever way they can," continues the king. "No one wants to see this man's plans succeed. They all know it's only a matter of time before he comes knocking on their doors."

"And the estates that left the alliance?" Anya asks.

There's a crack in King Auclair's calm exterior. "We haven't been able to get ahold of them."

What if Cam's right and the reason we can't get ahold of the other estates is because they've already flipped sides?

"What's this I've been hearing about a blood shortage?" the man on Reid's other side asks.

All eyes turn to Auclair. The younger advisor beside him shifts in his seat and loosens his tie as Auclair sighs and braces his forearms on the table.

"We're trying to keep it under wraps to avoid panic, but I'm sure you've all heard the rumors circulating. We weren't prepared for the sudden demand increase, and pairing that with the recent mass loss of humans in the estate—"

Reid sits up taller. "What mass loss?"

"Earlier this week we had large groups quit and leave the region. We currently are down about half of our employees."

Silence settles over the table as I chew on the inside of my cheek.

The humans working at the estate all leaving at once—either they got scared after seeing what happened at the Carrington estate or they realized the other side would be better for their own interests.

"Have you considered the potential security breach?" I find myself saying, then immediately regret it as everyone turns to me.

"Security breach?" Queen Carrington repeats, her voice sounding like a laugh.

I hold her gaze, refusing to let her make me feel small. "If those humans left to join Westcott, the first thing they probably did was tell them everything they knew about the estate, the region. Anything that could help him."

"As if humans would be privy to anything of importance," scoffs the queen.

I cock my head. Does she actually believe that? Are these

people really that naïve? When Connor was working for the Carrington estate, he wasn't trusted with any information, sure, but that didn't stop him from knowing everything about everything that went on under that roof.

"But they're observant. And they listen," I insist. "I'm sure they know more than you're aware of."

"We'll need to take extra precautions," agrees King Auclair, rubbing the space between his eyebrows with two fingers.

"If we don't find a solution to this blood shortage quickly," murmurs the younger advisor, "I'm willing to bet our guests will start taking out what little staff we have left."

Maybe that had been Westcott's plan for Auclair all along. Everyone has been looking at the attack as a failure because he didn't seize the estate, but trapping us inside and leaving us to starve and turn on each other will be plenty effective too.

"We've contacted the other blood farms in the region and are expecting shipments shortly, and some of the representatives from the other estates are graciously bringing prisoners with them, so we're hopeful we'll be able to get this under control soon," says Auclair.

"This is ridiculous," exclaims a woman at the far end as she slams her hands on the table and rises to her feet. She's built like a mountain, and judging by her uniform, she's part of Auclair's security. The head, if I had to guess. "Does no one else see an issue here? No one else has a problem with her being in this room?"

To my shock, she points at me.

"She's Westcott's *daughter*, for fuck's sake. Talk about needing to take precautions. We're supposed to take her word that she's not a spy for him? Or that he is, for that matter?" She pivots toward Cam, whose mouth is now set in a firm line.

Anya scoffs. "Did he not infect her with the psychosis, kidnap her, then dump her in the woods with a bunch of were-wolves? And you think she's *loyal* to him? Are you out of your goddamn mind? Blood doesn't run *that* deep."

I blink. Is she...sticking up for me? What's even more shocking, however, is the next person who comes to my defense is Queen Carrington.

"I've looked through Valerie's memories myself. And I was present for Camden's questioning," she adds, though her upper lip curls as she says his name. "I don't question the loyalty of anyone in this room."

"Nor do I," says Auclair. "And given the lack of intel from our teams on the ground lately, we'll take all of the assets we can get. I'm an understanding man, Sawyer, but question my judgment again, and there will be no place for you here."

The moment goes on forever as her hands remained curled into fists on the table. But then she bows her head almost imperceptibly and lowers into her seat.

"Has there been any news?" Anya asks.

"News?" repeats Auclair.

Anya spreads her hands wide as if her meaning was obvi-ous. "From Westcott. Has he made demands? Offered negotia-tion terms?"

Auclair's eyes darken, and the queen sits up straighter, lifting her chin as she does.

If what Westcott told me at the compound was true, he *did* try to negotiate with them a long time ago. Considering they stabbed him in the back and tried to execute him instead, it's safe to say they weren't interested.

And from everything I know, everything I've seen, I think he's past that point. He wants reform, yes, but there's a personal angle to this.

Part of this is merely about revenge.

Finally, the Auclair advisor says, "He's made it clear there will be no peaceful resolution to this. He won't be satisfied until everyone he considers an enemy is dead."

"I advise none of you leave the region," says Auclair. "Our Marionettes have created a boundary to keep the wendigos out, but that hasn't stopped their numbers from gathering on the other side. Our scouting teams will report should they find Westcott's other compounds. We know of a few." He dips his head toward Cam then me. "In the meantime, our team will review the recent attacks that have been documented, see if we can find any patterns, anything we've missed. Any hints as to what he might do next. We'll reconvene when the other officials have arrived."

One by one, the others filter from the room, but I'm glued to my chair, unable to move.

I don't know what I'd been expecting from this meeting, but it hadn't been my own competence as Reid's partner and trustworthiness getting called into question.

"See you tomorrow for training, princess?" Cam offers casually as he slips from the room.

CHAPTER SIX

MY FEET CARRY me forward of their own accord. At this point, I don't care where they take me as long as it's far away from here. Energy buzzes in my veins, begging to convert to magic, to let hot blood spill over my fingers, to let it take over, to let it take, take—

I shake my hands out, squeezing my eyes shut until Anya's smug face fades from my memory. The lift of her chin, the pointed look she'd cast at me over her nose.

I've never considered myself to be a jealous or insecure person. But the sheer rage I'd felt upon seeing her, at the stupid games she tried to play with me in there. They were nothing other than a transparent attempt to get under my skin, to see how far she could push me. Logically, I know this. I *know* I'm giving her exactly what she wants.

But it's this *other* feeling inside of me that has my stomach in knots, my throat tightening to the brink of suffocation. Because those fantasies had sprung to my mind as if they were their own living things. That wasn't petty anger or a thirst for revenge—it was cold, hard bloodlust.

I wanted to kill her. I wanted to *destroy* her.

My steps slow as I reach an archway eerily similar to the one outside the infirmary at the Carrington estate. The walkway is framed with walls of floor-to-ceiling windows and towering beams scattered in between.

I've been meaning to come by and see the other wolves since Cam told me where they were, but it's been an overwhelming few days. Even that feels like a pathetic excuse considering they helped save my life.

I push through the double doors. Hopefully they're still around.

Half the beds are full of sleeping people when I step inside, and there's no healer in sight. Most of the inhabitants don't look sick or injured—at least not visibly so; maybe they're so short on beds they've started relocating people here. I tread quietly through the aisle, searching each spot for a familiar face.

"Darkmore," someone hisses.

Leif smirks at me from the bed on the far left. My heart somehow warms and drops into my stomach at the same time, happy to see him again, but also...he looks a lot worse than Cam led me to believe.

I hurry down to his station, unable to keep the surprise from my face at the bandages wrapped around his head, stained red and clearly needing replacing. There are puncture marks all over his throat, and his left hand is wrapped in so much gauze only his fingertips are visible.

"Leif," I breathe. "Oh my God, I had no idea—"

"It looks worse than it is," he assures me, though he winces as he props himself into a seated position. "Promise."

"If I hug you am I going to hurt you?"

He holds out his right arm before I even finish the sentence. I carefully wrap my arms around his waist and rest my forehead on his shoulder, fighting the sudden urge to cry.

"I'm not the best at healing," I say, flipping the blade out of my ring. "But I—"

"I'm fine, Valerie."

I give him a stern look. "Just sit back and let me return the favor, would you?"

His smirk returns as I examine his injuries, trying not to let my thoughts play out on my face. If this is how bad it looks with his accelerated wolf healing *and* another witch clearly did a few healing treatments on him...I'm going to *kill* Cam for downplaying it so much. If Leif were human, he'd be dead. Even as a wolf, it looks like it's a miracle he's not.

"I would've been here a lot faster if I'd known it was this bad," I whisper.

I draw blood from my wrist, then intertwine my fingers with his, focusing on the warmth growing in my palm, imagining it sinking through my skin, into his, and traveling into his blood, repairing the damage as it goes.

He lets out a surprised sigh, the tension easing from his shoulders.

"Cam said Saint and Jones are here too?" I ask as I finish and set his hand on his lap.

He nods, eyes closed as he pulls a deep breath through his nose, probably still coming down from the healing. It can make you pretty dizzy. "They went to get food."

At least if they're up and moving, they're probably in better shape than Leif was.

I catch movement out of the corner of my eye and turn as the vampire in the bed across from Leif sits up, his nostrils flaring as he sniffs the air. The disgust on his face as he looks Leif up and down is obvious even beneath the layer of bandages around his head. I don't recognize him, but he must be one of the Carrington estate refugees. When he catches me glaring at him, he doesn't even have the decency to look away. If anything, his face contorts more.

Sawyer's voice resurfaces in the back of my mind.

She's Westcott's daughter, for fuck's sake.

We're supposed to take her word that she's not a spy for him?

Maybe she's not the only person here thinking that way.

"Do you feel any better now?" I ask, fighting to keep my voice light as I turn to Leif.

"Much. Thank you."

"No, thank *you*. I don't know what would have happened if you guys didn't show up."

"Nah, you would've flipped the script somehow. You're like a cockroach. Nothing can take you out." His smile turns crooked, but his usual ease is missing from his eyes. "I mean that as a compliment."

I chew on the inside of my cheek, debating if bringing it up would only make it worse. "How are you, really?" I ask softly. "With being here."

I don't have to elaborate because his smile fades and he gives me a small nod. Even if we're not at the Carrington estate, the queen is here. I can't imagine being under the same roof as the woman responsible for your parents' execution and just being okay with it, let alone surrounded by other vampires who might hold the same views. The Auclair region is more accepting of weres, but there's pretty much an equal ratio of Auclair to Carrington vampires in this estate right now.

Exhibit: the guy across from us who I'm pretty sure still hasn't blinked.

"I'm fine," he insists as footsteps sound behind me.

"Well hell, we should've brought more back."

Saint has me crushed to his chest in a hug before I can register what's happening, smelling like greasy French fries and onion rings.

"Don't drop the tots!" cries Jones as he pulls a paper tray from Saint's hand.

"Shh," Leif hisses. "People are sleeping."

"Right." Saint ducks his head as he pulls back, his smile almost shy. "Still not used to the vamp schedule."

"It's good to see you guys," I say, going in to hug Jones next, the heaviness that settled in my chest easing at their presence. To think in a matter of months I've become more comfortable around *werewolves* than my own kind. Jones props his armful of appetizers on the foot of Leif's bed, then hugs me so tightly I can barely breathe.

Neither of them looks much worse than they usually do— smeared with dirt and their hair looking like they just rolled out of bed, but no visible injuries comparable to Leif's.

"Is it insensitive if we ask about the Russian fiancée?" Jones mumbles out of the side of his mouth.

Saint smacks his shoulder. "You're such a gossip."

"Like you don't want to know!"

I smirk and situate myself on the end of Leif's bed. Whatever strange fire that had been raging inside of me on the subject of Anya seems to have fizzled out. The mention of her now only elicits a slight pang in my stomach. "I'll tell you, but I have two conditions."

"Name your price," says Saint.

"Can you use your gossiping powers for good and let me know if you hear anything about her? I just…something feels off. I don't think she's telling anyone the full story about why she's here."

"And the second condition?" asks Jones.

I snatch the onion rings into my lap. "You share some of these with me."

"Deal," Saint and Jones say at the same time.

I'M NOT ready to return to Adrienne's room after I leave the wolves, to sit alone in silence as those four walls close in on me. So not knowing where else to go, I explore. Upon first glance, the Auclair estate has countless similarities with the Carrington, but the more I walk, the more differences I notice. Everything here is so much…*bigger*.

A shaky breath passes my lips as I crest a set of stairs leading to the roof. The tower is on the south end of the property, so it has a nice vantage point overlooking the estate, a full expanse of mountains and trees set out below.

The gardens, for example, are farther out on the property here than at the Carrington estate, so looking at them from the yard made them seem much smaller than they are. Looking at them from above gives a much better view. They stretch on for acres, separated into a few different levels with grassy stairs, benches, and water features intermixed with the rows of plants and flowers.

I think of the new violin Reid got me, discarded somewhere in his room now. As much as I'd like to find a place to camp out down there, I don't think I could bring myself to play it. It wouldn't clear my mind. It would just remind me of everything that's too painful to think about right now.

I fiddle with my ring, flipping the blade in and out. After a few cycles of it, the knife pricks the side of my finger. A single drop of blood wells, but you'd think by the amount of power that surges through me that I was close to bleeding out, using every last ounce of magic in my blood that I have. My breath catches in my throat, the heat building, tingling, expanding in my chest, the magic ready to *go, go, go.* Ready to claim, to kill, to conquer. Nothing would be too much. Nothing would be too hard if I just let it *go.*

I smear the blood away with the pad of my thumb and force down a deep breath.

What the hell is going on?

"Valerie Darkmore."

I gasp and spin around, steadying myself against the stone railing.

A dark-haired man I don't recognize stands at the door to the stairs. An Auclair Marionette, judging by his uniform. He stares at me with a dazed look in his eyes, like he's not seeing me at all.

Like he's been glamoured.

I can't believe I let my guard down so much that I didn't

hear him come up. All those years of training…I should know better than that.

"I come with a message," he says before I can make a move for the door.

The dried blood lingering on my skin pulses, my skin warming as if my magic is reminding me it's there, urging me to make another cut. My finger remains poised over the blade. "What message?"

"From your father."

I tense, casting a quick glance around the rest of the roof. But of course Westcott isn't *here*. He wouldn't expose himself, put himself at risk like that. Using others to do his dirty work has always been more his style.

It's unsurprising that he knows I'm here, given the state of the Carrington estate and how most people were brought here after evacuating.

"He wanted to say he's sorry for how things have played out. Certain events have been regrettable, and he wants you to know you will still have a place with him when you decide to return."

I scoff. *When.*

You will still have a place with him—as if he hadn't kicked me out and sent me to live with a bunch of wolves who spent the last few months relishing in tormenting me. As if I'd left of my own volition instead of being drugged and smuggled into the back of a van.

"Your mother and sister are anxiously waiting for your return, so if not for him, think about their sake, as well as your own. The Auclair estate will not be a safe haven for much longer. None of the estates will be. But he recognizes he cannot save someone who does not want to be saved. The choice must be yours. But know this: this is only the beginning. This is only the first."

Only the first? Before I can puzzle out the meaning, the man walks forward. I shrink away, but he's not heading toward me. He's not looking at me at all anymore.

And there's not a single moment of hesitation as he crests the railing at the edge and jumps.

A scream gets caught in my throat, and it takes several seconds before the shock releases my limbs. I hurry to the railing, my hand covering my mouth as I brace myself and look down. The man is splayed out on his stomach on the concrete, a halo of blood already spreading around him. Voices echo somewhere below me, and I hit the stairs at a run.

Others are crowded around when I reach the ground, craning their necks to see where he'd jumped from. I kneel at his side, his blood soaking through my pants, and press my fingers to his throat.

But there's no pulse. No breathing.

At least it was a quick death.

When I pull my hand back, it's shaking.

How had Westcott gotten to him? *Who* glamoured him in the first place? Is it someone on the inside? Someone here working with Westcott?

This is only the first.

The first to die, he'd meant.

He's going to keep killing until I come back to him.

The tremble in my fingers spreads up my arms, down my chest, engulfing the rest of my body. I push to my feet and take several steps back, each breath I pull in shallower than the last.

I'm back in Central Park covered in blood. The city is deserted. Death is everywhere I go, at my hands. Just killing and blood and bodies. *My fault. My fault. My fault.*

I run into something hard, then fingers grip my arms.

My vision blurs around the edges, blackening, the world going dark.

"Come on." The hands pull me back.

"What happened here?" a voice booms behind me. "What—"

Doors creak, footsteps echo, and then I'm in darkness.

"Take a deep breath. Look at me."

Hands frame my face.

"Come on. Breathe."

I blink several times, Reid finally coming into focus.

Every line of his face is hard, a crease running deep between his eyebrows as he studies my face. "There you go," he murmurs. "Breathe."

The rest of our surroundings register—a supply closet, a single naked bulb hanging overhead.

"Tell me what happened." He drops his hands once it's clear I'm no longer on the brink of hysteria, but he's still standing inches away.

"That man," I whisper, "he came and found me on the tower. He'd been glamoured to deliver a message from West-cott, and when he was done, he jumped."

"Are you all right? Did he hurt you?"

I shake my head.

Reid exhales and runs a hand over his face. "What was the message?"

I recount as much as I can remember, freezing as something finally sinks in. My mother. He'd said my sister *and* my mother were waiting for me.

Is that where she disappeared to when she left here? Did she go there by choice or did Westcott abduct her and stage the entire thing like he did for me?

Or was that another lie?

"He's going to keep killing people. As long as I'm here—"

"He's going to keep killing people whether you do what he wants or not. Taking the Carrington estate won't be the end of it." Quieter, he adds, "He knows your heart. Your conscience. He's trying to prey on your best qualities to lure you back." I startle as he takes my chin in his hand, forcing me to meet his eyes. The hardness of his expression is gone now. "Don't you dare let him."

Silence falls between us as he takes a step back, and I look down at my hands. I'm coated in that man's blood.

I don't even know his name.

"I'm sure they'll have some Marionettes see what they can find from the body," says Reid. "If we can figure out who glamoured him, track his recent movements. They won't take this security breach lightly."

"He said Auclair won't be a safe haven for much longer."

Reid shakes his head. "He's already attacked here once and was unsuccessful. And I don't see a point in announcing this as his next target beforehand instead of capitalizing on the element of surprise, but I'll speak with the king about what you heard." He extends his hand. "Come on. I'll take you back so we can get you cleaned up."

"I don't need an escort." I mean for the words to come out light, but there's an unexpected bite to them.

Reid rocks back on his heels and nods, the earlier familiarity between us rapidly dissipating. Because for a moment, I'd forgotten everything that happened in the past few days, and we were *us* again.

"I'm sorry," I say after a beat, hating the way he won't look at me now. He was doing something nice, trying to help. "I— I'm not trying to punish you, Reid. It's just hard to be around you right now."

His eyes soften as they meet mine again, and he nods. He steps to the side and lets me pass without another word.

The storage closet is just inside the main corridor beside the grounds. A crowd is still collected around the body, and I keep my head down as I head in the opposite direction toward the living quarters, the blood hardening against my skin.

I squeeze my eyes shut as I slip inside Adrienne's room and close the door behind me, the moment before he fell playing on repeat, the sound he'd made as he hit the ground...

I scrub at my arms until my skin feels raw, but the blood doesn't budge.

I should've tried to stop him. To help him. Maybe if I'd gotten down there faster, I could've saved him. He might not have died on impact. I should've done more. Maybe I could have used magic to neutralize whatever order made him jump.

Maybe, maybe, maybe.

This is only the first.

CHAPTER SEVEN

NOW

OVER A WEEK PASSES, but clarity doesn't follow, and neither does relief. If anything, my muscles are wound tighter, my brain spiraling faster, never resting enough to let me sleep, let me *breathe*. Maybe it was foolish to think things would calm down after I escaped the wolf camp. I hadn't been naïve enough to expect normalcy, but somehow the stress and chaos is even worse here.

More deaths on my hands. My partnership with Reid at risk. My home estate under siege. An out-of-the-blue fiancée who's looking at me like a small creature she'd like to torture for entertainment. And now I'm parading around in a fake relationship with my ex-boyfriend.

The nights have started to blur together since the tarmac. But maybe that's the alcohol, or maybe it's the bloodletting. Either way, I haven't seen Reid since the night that man killed himself in front of me, and I know it isn't an accident. I've been attending my training sessions with Cam, as King Auclair officially decided was best, which means I haven't been included in any usual Marionettes duties in the meantime.

Leaving me with nothing but a hell of a lot of time to overthink.

Cam's nose twitches like he can smell the alcohol on me as I stop a few paces away and sway on my feet.

I can't decide if him getting assigned to my training was a special, deliberate kind of torture, or if the universe just has a really shitty sense of humor.

He glances at my injured hand. "You couldn't have at least wrapped that first? I don't want your blood on me."

I scowl. "It's dried."

"I hope you're not injuring yourself to get out of our trainings. Because it won't work."

"Are we just going to stand here talking all night?"

His gaze drifts somewhere over my head, and his lips press together in a hard line. I don't have to turn. King Auclair may have agreed to let a few of the wolves stay, but his trust only goes so far. A Marionette—or three—has been trailing Cam's every move since he got here, though they haven't admitted as much, always keeping a careful distance.

Maybe they would've backed off already if not for the security breach with the glamoured Marionette.

Although I'm pretty convinced whatever made him jump off the tower was no simple glamour. There were so many magical triggers left in his brain that any attempts to gather information from his corpse activated the spells, accelerating the decomposing process of his body until there was nothing left for them to use.

Security camera footage and interviews with everyone who

came in contact with him days leading up to his death also proved fruitless.

Because there wasn't a single hair out of place.

He hadn't left the estate, not once. He had no ties to Westcott. He'd attended to all of his usual duties. Friends reported his behavior to be completely normal. Even the vampire partnered with him hadn't sensed anything off.

The king has downplayed the situation, trying to avoid panic. But everyone is on edge, and anyone can see it.

"Tell me you at least had something to eat with that whiskey." Cam's frown deepens when I hesitate. "I can only do so much to build up your strength if you don't give your body the fuel it needs."

"Last I checked, lecturing wasn't a part of your job description."

I expect more pushback, but he just waves his hand. "Give me two laps around the field to warm up."

I let out a huff of protest as I wind my hair into a ponytail. Apparently Adrienne deemed Cam a worthy enough replacement babysitter because she's conveniently nowhere to be seen now. I think he scares the hell out of her.

I take off at a slow jog, but instead of criticizing my pace, Cam falls into step beside me. I peer at him sideways, wondering if he's tagging along to continue lecturing me, but he says nothing as we make our way around the field.

I make it through a full lap and a half before hunching over the bushes and emptying the contents of my stomach. Cam sighs, as if expecting this, but still says nothing as he holds my hair with one hand and braces the other on my back.

"Stop being nice to me," I snap as I wipe my hand across my mouth.

"You're punishing yourself enough. You don't need it from me too."

The nausea in my stomach surges up and settles behind my jaw. He said something like that to me once before. Standing outside my tent, a fire roaring in the background, my body feeling even weaker than it does right now.

The only person you're punishing is yourself, and maybe that's what you're trying to do.

I don't want him to be right. But the guilt that sparks in my chest every time I replay that man jumping off the building does ease when I let myself bleed.

I retch again, hoping the tears on my cheeks look like my eyes watering from vomiting. Cam's hand rubs gentle circles on my back, and I let myself, just for a moment, find comfort in it.

"Come on," he says once it's clear I'm not going to start again. "Let's get you something to eat."

"You're supposed to be my trainer, not my personal chef."

"I'm supposed to help you get your strength back. And right now, your body doesn't need a workout, so shut up and follow me before I throw you over my shoulder and carry you there. And I want your vomit on me even less than I wanted your blood, so please don't make me do that."

I also know he won't hesitate in doing it, seeing as that's how he carried me into the wolf camp that first day. I scowl, but like my stomach is agreeing with him, it takes the opportunity to let out a weird gurgle.

Cam's eyebrow hikes up.

"Fine," I grumble. "But I'm not drinking one of those disgusting protein shakes again."

He flashes me a satisfied smile, then nudges me forward. "You'll take what I give you and you'll like it."

───────

WHEN I GET BACK to Adrienne's room, my stomach is full, my buzz has all but worn off, and I'm desperately in need of a nap. But as soon as I open the door, my eyes fall on a package sitting in the center of the bed. It's small, barely larger than an envelope, and wrapped in white paper and twine.

Adrienne's bags are gone, so she must have already left for school. I take a cautious step forward, every hair on my body standing at attention.

Because I can feel the current of magic lingering on the package even from several feet away. For some reason, it feels familiar. Not quite the way my magic feels, but adjacent. Related.

Adrienne?

A shock of electricity courses through my fingers as I pick it up, and I let out a low hiss, but the sting subsides quickly. I unwrap it slowly in case it does it again. Inside, there's a sheet of thick cardstock. Something clatters to the ground as I pull the note from the envelope.

I gasp at the flash of pain as whatever it is ricochets off my foot. A bead of blood wells to the surface of my skin, and I squat, searching the ground—there.

My hand freezes midway.

A pointed fingernail painted midnight black.

With a razorblade lining the side.

My mother's.

My gaze darts to the note. There's a bloody fingerprint smeared across the top of the page, and it sings with the hum of magic as I run my finger over it.

I don't recognize the handwriting—all caps and jagged lines.

BREAK THE TEETH
313 VOLUME 12
IN THE MIRROR
DESTROY THIS

CHAPTER EIGHT

RADMORE IS nothing like York academy. Sleek, modern architecture replaces the gothic style I've grown accustomed to. Moonlight reflects off the dizzyingly tall buildings covered in so many windows they look like mirrors. The student body here is more than twice our size, so I guess they need the extra space.

The teleportation spell doesn't take as much out of me as I'd been preparing for, though I do end up near the entrance gates rather than Adrienne's dorm by accident. It's always tricky with places you've never been before, going off an address rather than a concrete image in your head.

Towering, snowcapped mountains loom behind the school. Objectively, they're beautiful, but the sight of them does little more than summon memories I don't want to remember.

Snow and gravel crunch underfoot as I trek up the path. The campus is relatively quiet, only a smattering of people out and about. It must be the middle of a class block.

I don't let myself picture what it would be like to finish my last semester here with my friends. To lounge on this quad, gaze at the view of mountains from those high floors while I study, my biggest worry of the week being what outfit I'd wear out on the weekend or exactly what grade point average I'd need to scrape by and keep my assigned partnership without trying *too* hard because that's what senior year's for.

What it was supposed to be for.

As I follow the wide sidewalks through the buildings, it occurs to me I have no idea where I'm going or what Adrienne's dorm even looks like. I check the note on my phone again.

Astor Hall.

I squint at the buildings, my frown deepening with each golden sign I pass that's not it.

"You lost?"

It takes me a moment to recognize him. And it isn't because his hair is longer or because he's lost weight. It's his demeanor. He leaves several feet of space between us, his hands in his pockets and his face lacking his trademark care-free grin. Instead, he's looking at me like he's not sure if I'm really there.

"You're just going to stand there?" I mean for it to sound light, teasing, but my voice comes out thin.

Finally, Daniel breaks out of whatever trance had been holding him back, crosses the distance between us, and throws his arms around my shoulders. I hug him back tightly and bury my face against his shoulder.

"You asshole," he murmurs.

"I know."

"You really had to steal my thunder, huh? Had to one-up my almost dying by going full out?"

I jab him in the stomach, and he lets me go with a breathy laugh. His eyes search my face, the amusement fading.

"How are you? We heard a lot of rumors. And you look terrible."

I can't even pretend to take offense to that because I know I do. "So do you."

He tilts his head, acknowledging this.

"Is it true your rise-from-the-dead return to the Auclair estate was riding a werewolf?"

I let out a choked laugh.

"It's not even the weirdest rumor, believe it or not."

I shake my head. Who comes up with this stuff? "I'm looking for Adrienne's dorm. Astor Hall?"

He juts his chin to the path behind me. "I'll walk with you. You're not coming back to school, are you?"

"I don't know," I admit. "How do you like it here?"

He shrugs and tucks his hands in his pockets. "It's not home, you know? Everything feels temporary. How do you like staying at Auclair?"

I smirk. "Feels temporary."

A loud bell drones, and shortly after, streams of people join the paths from all directions. The uniform at Radmore is slightly different than ours—the blazers navy blue instead of red, the plaid skirts green and blue.

Daniel steps closer to me so we don't get separated, his shoulder bumping mine. He clears his throat. "It's really good to see you, Valerie—"

"Please don't get sappy on me."

"If being sappy was ever justified, I think this is it—"

"Of course it is," I snap, looping my arms through one of his and leaning against him as we walk. "But if you keep it up, I'll start crying, then I'll have to hurt you."

A corner of his mouth kicks up, and he squeezes my arm. "Here we are."

There's nothing that sets this building apart from the others, all shiny windows and just as tall. For being in the middle of nowhere, Radmore does a good job of making you feel like you're in the heart of a city. Maybe that's the appeal, why it's one of the more popular academies.

Daniel checks his watch and presses his lips into a thin line. "I have to get going, but can we catch up later?"

"We better."

"We'll get dinner," he decides, pointing a finger at me as he jogs away backward.

I wave as he disappears into the crowd.

Like York's buildings, the doors won't open without a key card. Sighing, I lean against a column by the entrance and send a quick text to Adrienne, waiting for someone to come or go so I can slip inside.

My fingers skim the outline of the note in my jeans pocket. Now that Daniel's gone and the overwhelm has subsided, the heavy dread returns to the center of my chest, accompanied by something…else. Something not as easy to identify. Or maybe it is. The lump in the back of my throat, it's been there since the moment I saw that fingernail.

The magic inside of me warms at the thought, like it remembers once being hers. Another unnecessary reminder that the only reason I'm still breathing is because of my mother.

My mother who wished me dead, then turned around and sacrificed the thing she loved most to save me.

My brain can't make sense of it, especially not as my stupid, traitorous heart and desperate-for-affection inner child are vying to take over control.

I suck in a deep breath and force the line of thinking away with my exhale. Whatever her reasoning might have been, if she'd gone to such lengths to save me, I don't see why she'd lead me astray with this note now. Whatever it means, it must be important.

Maybe I should have gone to Reid. But I just…couldn't. At some point, even a saint would get exhausted with the same person always coming to them with a problem. Especially when we're barely speaking, our partnership is hanging on by a thread, and he has more than enough on his plate already. I did send him a quick text to let him know where I'd be, though, so he wouldn't worry.

"I got here as fast as I could." Adrienne jogs up the stairs, her backpack hung over one shoulder and her short hair pulled back in a haphazard ponytail. She's out of breath by the time she reaches me. "What is it? Are you okay? What's wrong?"

I should tell her everything's fine to get her to calm down, but is it? My panic might not be as obvious as hers, but that doesn't mean it's not singing in my veins just as clearly. The note burns against my leg.

"Can we talk inside?"

Unlike the rest of the campus, there are no noticeable

differences to the inside of York's dorms. The rooms are the same small size, same furniture—though the window is larger and the view nicer.

"Are you going to tell me what this is about now, or are you trying to see if I have a heart attack?"

Adrienne stomps into her room ahead of me and drops her backpack on the twin mattress. Her roommate isn't home, thankfully. I fish out the note, and she reaches for it but yanks her hand back with a hiss the second her fingers make contact.

"Ow, it shocked me." She shakes out her hand. "Is that magic?"

"It did the same to me."

Tentatively, she tries a second time. I glance at the rest of the room as she looks at the note, though there's not much to see. Her roommate is clearly a fan of pink, but Adrienne's side has no embellishments, no decorations. My heart sinks a little. There's nothing in here that looks like her.

"Break the teeth? In the mirror? What the hell is this? Where'd you get it?"

"It was on your bed when I went back to your room. It also…it also came with this." I hold the nail out in the palm of my hand.

Her eyes snap to mine, then the nail, then the note.

"…and Westcott sort of glamoured a Marionette to deliver a message to me, insinuating Mom and Calla were with him, trying to get me to go back, then made the guy jump off the roof," I add in a rush.

Adrienne's eyes bulge, and she slowly backtracks until she hits her bed and sits. "You should have started with that. You think this is from them?"

"Do those numbers mean anything to you?"

She frowns. "Volume—like Mom's spell books?"

"That's what I was thinking."

She flips the note around her fingers then squints at the bloody fingerprint. "What was on this page?"

"Who knows?" I cross my arms and lean against the opposite wall. "The books are at the Carrington estate. At least, I think they are. They're not at Auclair. Mom cleared out her stuff when she took off. Westcott has control of the entire first region now, and there's a magical boundary up that no one can pass through."

"Fuck," she breathes. "And the teeth part?"

"Your guess is as good as mine."

Silence falls between us, and she runs her fingers over the blood on the card again. "It feels like Calla's magic," she whispers.

"I know."

She holds my eyes, a determined line forming between her eyebrows. "So how the hell are we going to get this book?"

———

By the time dinner rolls around, catching up with Daniel turns into a group event. There's a diner not far from the academy, about the same distance as Main Street from York.

I walk there with Adrienne, and the others are already waiting for us at a booth in the back. Daniel offers a wave as we approach, and Kirby and Monroe smile, but everything about it looks off, forced.

Adrienne and I slide into the remaining corner seats of the

booth, though two chairs on the opposite side of the table are still empty.

"Beth and Wes said they'd swing by," Daniel explains.

I try to catch Monroe's attention, but she's pointedly not looking at me. I catch the red rims of her eyes before she tilts her head, letting her hair obscure her face, and Kirby protectively grips her leg beneath the table.

"Is everything okay?" I murmur.

There's an edge to Kirby's round features I don't think I've ever seen before, and she gives a minute shake of her head, the message in her eyes clear. *Not now.*

I nod slowly and lean back in my chair, my stomach twisting at Monroe's body language—the rounded set of her shoulders and bowed head. What the hell could have happened to have her of all people looking like that?

The diner around us is quiet with only a few other patrons. The entire place is drenched in a red tint from the neon signs along the walls advertising things like *actually* Bloody Marys and spiked milkshakes.

"Have you guys been here before?" I ask, trying for a light-hearted, casual tone, but I think we all see through it.

"The hash browns are good," offers Kirby.

I glance around the diner again. The closest person is sitting on one of the padded stools along the countertop, and there's a booth of people along the smudged windows.

"They can't hear us," says Adrienne. I lift an eyebrow, and she opens her hand, revealing the blood pooled in her palm. "And if they look this way, they will feel an inexplicable urge to look somewhere else."

A slow smile creeps onto my face. I've never underestimated Adrienne, exactly. Even as kids, her power was undeniable, let alone her work ethic. Her desire to keep up with me and Calla was unyielding, even though our lessons were several years more advanced than hers. Even now, as she's moved on to her own time at the academy, and in just a matter of years she'll get her own pairing, part of me will always see her as the baby of the family. My little sister.

"Did you guys hear about the Carrington estate?" asks Monroe. "I don't know how much of it is gossip."

"It's true," I say. "There was a meeting before I left Auclair."

A waitress with a bright red Bonnie name tag comes by for our drink orders, smacking her gum and humming after each of our responses. When she walks away, I set the note on the table.

"What's this—ow!" Kirby drops it, shakes out her fingers, then leans forward to squint at it. "I don't see anything."

"You can't read that?" Adrienne asks.

"Read what?" Monroe nudges it hesitantly and lets out a soft hiss as it shocks her too. "It's blank."

I meet Adrienne's eyes.

"A security system?" she murmurs.

I nod. The shock, it must be vetting who's touching it. But it allowed Adrienne *and* me to see it. Because we're family? Because we're blood witches?

Adrienne explains the contents of the note as I twist it around in my hands, inspecting it again.

"Please tell me you're not planning on breaking into the Carrington estate for the book," Daniel mutters.

"Supposedly there's a magical barrier around the entire region that no one can cross," I say.

"Supposedly," echoes Monroe.

I shrug. "Westcott glamoured someone to tell me to come back...I think he'll let me through."

"Yeah, and then never let you leave again," scoffs Adrienne. "That's not an option."

"I—" Kirby stops short and offers the waitress a thin-lipped smile as she sets our drinks on the table.

"Just some onion rings and nachos to share for now," says Daniel.

She pops her gum and turns away. "Whatever."

"Have you tried contacting your sister again?" Monroe asks, staring at the note on the table.

I shake my head but stop myself before I can say what I'm thinking.

Yes, I want to know what's on that page. Yes, I want to make sure Calla and Mom are okay.

But no, I don't trust her. Not anymore.

Not after Reid.

Adrienne shifts in the seat next to me but says nothing. She'd suggested the same thing earlier.

I sigh and stuff the note in my pocket. "I don't even know for sure if the book is there. If Westcott has control of the place, I'm sure he's already gone through our family's things. We should probably just forget about it."

"You'll never be able to do that," mutters Daniel.

I kick him under the table, and he smirks.

A bell rings over the front door as Wes and Beth duck inside and beeline toward us.

"I'm so sorry we're late!" says Beth, throwing her arms around my shoulders and pulling me into a suffocating hug. "We lost track of time."

"You're going to behead her," says Wes, pulling her off.

"Sorry! Sorry! It's just so good to see you. You have no idea."

Wes leans in for a hug next, though his is much less painful, then pulls out the remaining chairs, keeping one hand on the small of Beth's back as they sit. I know I'm staring, but I can't stop.

"When did…uh…"

"Oh." Wes grins, the pride clear on his face as they intertwine their hands on the table. "A few months ago."

"Wow." I blink, my smile kicking in a beat too late. "That's so…great. I'm happy for you guys."

Beth beams, her eyes shining as she looks at Wes, and I peek at Daniel out of the corner of my eye. He's smiling, though his gaze is pointedly on his menu.

Daniel and Wes never crossed that friendship line, as far as I know, but I think we were all expecting them to at some point.

"It really is good to have you back, Val," Wes adds, quieter now, his smile softening. "Never felt right without you. Now"—he grabs one of the menus from the center of the table and pries the sticky pages apart—"why the hell are you guys looking so serious over here at our welcome home party?"

I snort. "I didn't realize this was a party."

"Hell yeah, it's a party!" Daniel jostles my shoulder. "We got our blood bitch back!"

"Figure out what the hell this note means, then we'll talk parties," I mutter.

Wes shoots a curious look around the table, and Kirby leans over to fill them in.

"In the mirror...as in the shadow realm?" Beth asks, cocking her head. "So it could mean shadow projecting." She looks to Wes. "That was one of the other terms for it, right?"

"Oh yeah, that's right. We had a lesson on that a few weeks ago," says Wes, but the rest of his words get lost in the static filling my ears.

Shadow projecting.

"We took that class last semester," Monroe is saying, and she winces as she chews on the inside of her cheek. "That was some serious shit though. Our professor made it seem like one of the riskiest kinds of magic you could do. Said they stopped teaching the advanced version of the class decades ago because of how many...incidents there were."

Kirby shivers and shakes her head a few times as if remembering something unpleasant.

"Well, that's if you try to do it alone, for sure," says Beth, her voice matter-of-fact. "The process can be too much for a single person to handle. Not necessarily because of the power needed, but because there are so many things that can go wrong, so you need someone else there to make sure you don't flame out or go too far into the dark to find your way back."

My gaze bounces between them as they discuss this magic I've never heard of before, feeling more on the outside than I ever have. My blood magic gave me a leg up in a lot of ways going through school, and as flawed as my mother's methods were, she did prepare me well.

But I should have known nothing would compensate from missing an entire year of school, and the one with the most advanced classes offered, at that.

I've missed out on enough that I couldn't even figure out what the damn note meant.

Queen Carrington's words echo in my head yet again.

Valerie's certainly not in the expected physical shape for her position anymore. She didn't finish her final year at the academy. I'm merely suggesting we consider a reassignment.

Adrienne meets my eyes, and there's something about the look on her face that's grim, resigned.

It's Kirby, though, who says, "So are we doing this tonight or what?"

CHAPTER NINE

"THIS IS SO EMBARRASSING. I wasn't expecting visitors!" Kirby torpedoes through the house, picking up dirty clothes and old dishes as the rest of us shuffle through the door.

"Kirby, it's fine——" Monroe starts.

Kirby's head shoots around the corner, a strand of pink hair stuck to her cheek and murder in her eyes. "Help. Me."

Monroe sighs and follows her down the hall.

The senior housing is a collection of townhomes, each big enough for three people. Kirby and Monroe's third roommate is nowhere to be seen though.

"It would probably be best to do it outside anyway!" Beth calls. "With the moon and everything."

"Oh, I know!" Kirby reappears, all smiles now, and gestures for us to follow. "I was just clearing the path there. We can set up out back while we wait for Daniel to get the supplies."

The hall runs alongside the stairs and leads to a small living area, the kitchen tucked off to the right. Monroe pushes the sliding glass door aside and leads us to a patio. Their backyard is little more than a sliver of grass between the deck and the fence, but it's certainly nicer than living in the dorms. They have a small bistro table and three folding chairs set up, along with a few lines of twinkle lights strung overhead.

I press my lips together to hold back my smirk at the row of dead plants. Kirby's doing, if I had to guess. A wiz with poisons for sure, but keeping things alive is another story.

I flip the page of the textbook Monroe offered me, rereading the section on shadow projecting, trying to catch myself up. The spell itself doesn't look too complicated, but the Risks and Warnings part of the chapter goes on for a good twenty pages.

Beth stops in the middle of the grass, hands on her hips, and cranes her neck back to look at the moon. "This should work!"

Monroe steps up beside me and lays a hand on my shoulder. "Val," she says under her breath, "let one of us do it. Tell us what we're looking for, tell us what to do, and let one of us go."

I shake my head. "Absolutely not. If something goes wrong—"

"Exactly," she says, her voice suddenly hard. "You've already been through hell, and we're not going to lose you again. At least let one of us come with you."

"I'll be fine." I don't know if I'm trying to convince her or me, but I put as much confidence into the words as I can manage. Besides, if none of them were able to read the note, I'm willing to bet similar security measures have been taken to protect the book. It *has* to be me. "The more of you holding the line here, the better anyway. With this much power on this side, it'll be fine."

I squint, trying to inspect her face now that I can actually see it. It's not just the redness in her eyes—her entire face is puffy like she's been crying. "What's going on with you? Did something happen?"

For what feels like the first time tonight, she looks me in the eye. She opens her mouth like she wants to say something, then casts a glance at the others. They're occupied setting up for the spell, paying us no mind. I take her arm and guide her a few more steps away until we're against the side of the house.

"It's Nathan," she finally says.

I wait for her to continue, and she lets several moments pass, long enough that I lay a hand on her arm in a sad attempt at comforting her.

"He's always been a flirty drunk," she all but whispers, "but I thought it was harmless. Especially once he knew I was with Kirby, I figured it was how he was with everyone. But then a few weeks ago, he really wasn't taking the hint, and we got into this huge fight. But then the next time I saw him, he pretended like nothing happened, so I figured I'd let it go too."

I stiffen, bracing myself for wherever this is going.

"Apparently he hadn't let it go like I thought. That or he does shit like this for fun—" She breaks off, and I can't tell if it's tears or fury that has her breathing quickening. "He—he put a fucking camera in my room. And he recorded us, well, you know. Which would be bad enough, but apparently he's had a great time showing it around to all of his friends the past few weeks. I'm guessing it's probably online somewhere too."

"I'll kill him," I say immediately, my fingers tightening around the book in a death grip. "I swear to God, I can make it look like an accident."

The rage bleeds from her expression, leaving nothing but that godawful haunted look she'd had at the diner.

"Can't you at least get reassigned?" I add.

No fucking wonder Avery kicked Nathan to the curb if he pulled some shit like this with her. How many other girls has he done this to? And to his *partners*? Even if their bond isn't as intimate as mine and Reid's, I can't imagine being that cruel to someone period, let alone someone you're bound to in that way.

Monroe lifts her hands and gestures around us. "It's not exactly a top priority of the estates." She barks out a bitter laugh. "Hell, we don't even *have* an estate right now. And I know it's something small in comparison to everything else, but..." She trails off, her eyes catching on Kirby across the lawn.

If she did get reassigned, she'd have no say in her new partner, meaning she could end up halfway across the world.

I force my jaw to unclench. She's right. We'd be hard-pressed to find anyone who cared enough with everything else going on.

But she can't stay paired to him. Especially not now. We're supposed to believe he'll have her back and keep her safe if it comes down to it?

"Have you confronted him?"

That sparks another hard laugh out of her. "Oh yeah. He seemed thrilled I found out. Told me 'there are plenty more videos where that one came from.'"

I spare a glance at Kirby, but she's staring stoically at the grass as Beth explains something with big hand gestures. I have no idea how she's so calm right now if she's in the videos too.

"I'm so sorry you guys have been dealing with this," I say.

"Such a piece of shit," Monroe mutters. "Didn't you tell us his last partner was all weird about him when she asked for a reassignment and left?"

The image of Avery in the pool room resurfaces in my mind. The way her fingers were shaking around her cigarette, how she wouldn't tell me what happened with Nathan, and that alone should've been the biggest red flag. She always loved to gossip.

"Such a piece of shit," I repeat Monroe's earlier words, shaking my head.

I'm willing to bet Avery wasn't the first and Monroe won't be the last. And he keeps getting away with it.

"Anyway." Monroe forces a smile and squeezes my arm. "I know you have plenty more important things to worry about—"

"This *is* important, Roe," I say quietly. "Thank you for telling me."

She blinks away tears and nods a few too many times. "I'm so fucking angry, but I also *hate* myself right now."

"What? Why? Roe, this isn't your fault."

She sniffles and crosses her arms. "Because it's not just me in the videos," she whispers. "And I feel like—I feel like I let her down, you know? She's been the strong one through all of this—"

I throw my arms around her shoulders and pull her close, tightening my hold until she finally relaxes against me. "No part of this is your fault," I insist. "Don't you dare let that bastard make you feel guilty on top of everything else. He won't get away with this, and we're going to get you out of this partnership. No matter what it takes."

She sniffles and nods against my shoulder. "It's really good to have you back, Val."

I hold her tight for another moment and revel in how a few weeks ago, I'd thought I would never have this again. That everything about this life had been stolen from me forever.

"It's really good to be back," I say as I pull away.

She offers a weak smile and quickly wipes the few stray tears from her cheeks. As she joins Beth in the middle of the yard, Adrienne heads toward me, every line of her face hard.

"I'll go with you," she says.

"I need you to stay here."

She shakes her head. "This isn't just about you. This is my family too. That note was left in my room."

"I know this is about you too. And I'm not just asking you to stay to protect you"—even though that's exactly what I'm doing; one look at the risks listed in this book and I knew there was no way in hell I was letting my barely-a-freshman baby sister try this—"I need you on this side because if anything goes wrong, the connection with you is what will call me back. Our magic. Our blood. I need that line."

She searches my eyes for a moment as if trying to read if I'm telling the truth. "Let me go and you stay then."

"I have no doubt in your abilities at all. But I have four years more experience than you do. Let me do this, Adrienne, please."

I don't bother telling her I know as little about this kind of spell as she does. I close the book in my hands for good measure. Doom-reading everything that could go wrong right beforehand probably isn't going to help.

"All right, everybody. Are we good to go?" Daniel and Wes hurry into the yard with their arms full of supplies. Adrienne gives me a long look before nodding and going to join them.

"You sure about this, kid?" Kirby asks, throwing an arm over my shoulder.

"Not you too."

"Hey, I'm not gonna try to talk you out of it. I'm just asking if you're sure about this, because if you have a single doubt in your mind, we can come up with a plan B. Between the seven of us, we're bound to come up with another idea."

"Between the seven of us, we should be able to pull this off no problem, right? Other witches manage to do this with two. Should be a breeze."

She makes a noise in the back of her throat at that but hooks her arm through mine and leads me forward.

"Have any of you done this before?" Adrienne asks as we fan out in a circle, stretching from one end of the grass to the other.

"Nope," Daniel says as he situates a black tarp on the ground then wide black and white candles on top. Beth sprinkles herbs on them as Wes creates a line of ash and black sand by our feet. He pauses as he reaches me.

"If you're the one going, I think your blood needs to be—"

"I know." I flip the blade out of my ring. I make the cut in my wrist for more control of where the blood lands, then follow Wes, allowing it to drip from my fingers to the protective circle, then head for the candles in the middle once the circle is complete. Beth fishes in Daniel's bag for some matches, but I tighten my fist around the blood already pooled inside, eyes leveled on the wicks, and they alight at once.

"You should save your strength," says Wes.

I roll my eyes and let my blood fall onto the flames. "I fake die once and you all think I'm helpless."

"Not funny!" calls Daniel.

"Do you have some kind of vial?" I ask Beth.

"Let me check." She digs around in the bag before pulling out a container no longer than her finger with a stopper in it. "Will this work?"

"Perfect." I take the vial from her and squeeze my fist until a single drop of blood falls inside.

Wes's gulp is audible. "You need ours too, don't you?"

"Just a drop." I extend the container toward him in one hand, the blade from my ring in the order. He pricks his finger and lets his blood join mine. One by one, the rest follow suit, and I stopper the vial as I find my spot in the circle beside Adrienne. She eyes the blood as I tuck the container into my bra, probably putting the pieces together.

A spell like this doesn't need their blood, not if they don't have blood magic. But it's the best safety net I could come up with. A way to anchor myself to all of them if need be.

"Ready to get started?" Beth asks.

"If you're not back in an hour," says Monroe on my other side, "I will yank you back myself."

Energy buzzes between our palms as we join hands, and I give her fingers a squeeze. "I'm counting on it."

———

APPARENTLY, I've been through the shadow world a hundred times. So really, there's nothing to worry about.

Granted, passing through it for a fraction of a second while teleporting is pretty different from trying to keep a foothold for an hour, but teleporting was an impossible, terrifying construct before I tried it for the first time too.

I feel it the moment the spell starts. The chanting around me fades and numbness creeps into my extremities. The color leeches from our surroundings, draining into the ground like water. The air gets thicker like it's filling with smoke, and the outlines of my friends turn blurry, their edges blending in with the haze around them. I take a step forward, and my foot makes no sound against the grass.

Then I turn, taking one last look at my body.

She's standing in her place in the circle, her hands holding Monroe's and Adrienne's. Her eyes are closed, though her mouth is no longer moving along to the incantations. I step out of the circle, my shadow-body passing through her as if she isn't there at all. I pat my chest, making sure the vial of blood is there, then flip the blade out of my ring.

There's no time to waste.

My blood looks black here, dripping down my wrist like

ink. Instead of my magic heating my skin, a chill washes over me. The teleportation actually feels easier here with one fewer barrier to cross.

I don't risk teleporting all the way to the Carrington estate. Not without knowing if I'll be able to get past the boundary first. I don't know where the line is. From the sounds of that meeting, the boundary is not just around the estate, but the entire region. I play it safe by taking myself to the border.

A million memories resurface as I find myself at the checkpoint on the other side of the bridge, the same one Reid and I took after we left the wolf camp.

I had no idea what to expect coming back here, if it would be as deserted as last time, if it would be full of Wescott's people, if there would be death and blood and destruction.

And still, I can't tell because the boundary cuts through the space, reaching up as far as my eyes can see in a solid black wall. I don't know if that's what it looks like normally or if it's because I'm in the shadow world. The edges are misty, like black smoke drifting off.

I can feel the power emanating from it. It chills me to the bone. I don't know who created this boundary, who was powerful enough, what kind of magic they used, but it feels dark. Wrong.

I hesitate inches from the wall. Everyone had been so concerned about me getting stuck in the shadow world, but maybe we should have been more worried about *this*.

I hadn't really given a second thought to the boundary other than whether or not I'd be able to cross it, but what if it doesn't just stop me from moving forward?

What if something *else* happens if I try?

But I didn't come this far just to turn back now.

Before I can talk myself out of it, I push my fingers through the barrier…

…and feel nothing at all.

My entire hand goes through, and still, nothing. I step forward until I'm on the other side and look up at it again, but there's nothing visible from this side. There's a sort of glimmer in the air, a hint that something is out of the ordinary, but you probably wouldn't see it if you weren't looking for it.

Strange, but I don't have time to dwell on it. It may have let me through, but I have no idea if it somehow alerted whoever created it.

I let the next teleportation spell take me all the way to the estate, specifically, to my mother's old room. It's messier than I ever remember seeing it, but that's probably from gathering her things in a hurry when they evacuated. Or someone has scavenged it since.

Clothes and papers are scattered across the floor, candles overturned by the fireplace. I head down the hall to her den first. If someone wanted to steal from her, this would probably be the first place they cleaned out. But when I step through the curtain, the shelves are fully stocked. I head straight for the bookshelf, pushing aside jars and containers until I can see the spines at the back.

Volume 12 . Volume 12…

They're all out of order, some shoved in sideways. I pull out the stack of volumes 3, 7, and 10 in case there's one wedged behind it.

Voices sound on the other side of the wall, too low for me to make out what they're saying. Setting the books down, I dive back into the shelf, desperately searching for number 12. If someone comes in here, they might not be able to see me, but they'll see things moving around. Where is this goddamn book? But even after I go through the entire shelf twice, there's no sign of volume 12.

I swallow a curse and survey the rest of the room. They couldn't have sent more specific instructions? It's not on the altar, not on the other bookcases. But there are all of the needed ingredients for a locator spell in here.

I freeze with my fingers around a jar of raven feathers, then slowly trace them along the grooves in the shelf instead. It couldn't have always been like this. I would have noticed.

The edges—just for a few inches in the back—are blackened, thick, like they're shrouded in shadow.

Like you wouldn't be able to see the abnormality normally, but the shadow world is highlighting it.

I dig my fingers along the edges, trying to find a notch, a button.

"Ow," I hiss and pull my hand away, a drop of blood welling on the tip of my finger. Whatever pricked it was sharp as a blade, way too sharp for a splinter.

Then the slat glides to the side, revealing a hidden compartment in the back of the bookcase. The pocket is deep but only a few inches wide. Just wide enough for a book.

Dust swirls around me as I pull the volume out, this one much heavier than the others. The leather cover is black instead of the faded reds and browns of the others, the spine cracked and barely holding on. The compartment's cover slides back into place the moment the book is removed. The cover is plain, nondescript. But engraved on the spine near the bottom is the number twelve.

I start to flip to page 313, but then voices sound on the other side of the wall again, louder this time. It'll have to wait. Tucking the book under my arm, I hurry out to the main part of the room.

How much time has passed since I crossed over? I know I should head back, not take any unnecessary risks, but it also feels like a missed opportunity to leave without looking around. To see what I can find about what Westcott's up to here. Maybe I can find something useful, something that could help stop him.

I skid to a stop as I reach the main living space. Directly beside the door is a black figure, more shadow than tangible, so dark my eyes nearly can't detect it. It's as tall as a man, though its limbs are thin, spindly. Black mist swirls around its edges. It watches me and cocks its head.

Ice cold fear slithers down my spine. I don't know what it is or what it's doing in my mother's room—on the side of the shadows or not—but I'm not waiting around to find out.

I teleport myself from the room, but not out of the estate. Just to the wing that houses the royal accommodations. With Westcott's ego, if he's staying here, this is where he'll be.

Shadows like fog hang in the air as I wind down the halls. Guards are on patrol, but they can't see me. I can't smell them from this side of the veil, but they seem like vampires, if I had to guess. But there are only a few of them. If Westcott were here, I think he'd have more protection.

My brain must switch to autopilot at some point, because

when I blink, suddenly I'm standing in front of Reid's old room.

I shouldn't go inside. This isn't essential.

I nudge the door open an inch, then all the way when I see it's empty. I should be able to pass through the walls if I concentrate, but I'm not sure how that would work while holding a physical object like the book.

But the guards passed me in the hall without a second glance, so maybe by picking up the book I brought it into the shadow realm with me? Otherwise they would've seen a random floating book in the hall—definitely something attention-catching.

Reid's room is such a disaster, I'm momentarily frozen in place. Every time I was in here it was pristine. Now there are folders and papers covering every table, the bed, the floor. I pace to the seating by the fireplace. A book on wendigos is spread wide, along with a background check printed out about Cam, articles on the barrens, and all the documented attacks within a hundred-mile radius of the estate.

His research. From when he'd been trying to help me. When he'd been trying to find me.

I take in the rest of the room—the hundreds upon hundreds of articles and books and notes. He couldn't have been sleeping. How else would he have found this much time?

There's a picture on the nightstand, one I don't even remember him taking. It's of me on the grounds of the estate. I'm lying on my back in the grass, my books and notes spread around me. From the summer when he'd been helping me study. My eyes are closed, a soft smile on my face as I rested my head in my hands.

A tear runs down my cheek, and I let it fall.

Footsteps clamber in the hall, and I force myself to take a step away from the bed.

I'll do a quick walk-through of the rest of the estate to see what's going on, then I'll get the hell out of here. This time, I try passing through the wall, and there's a slight tug of resistance, but then I'm in the hallway, the book still in my arms.

Good to know.

I pass a dozen guards at most on my way to the main level of the estate, but even once I'm on the ground floor, it doesn't get any more populated. From peeking through the windows, the grounds look deserted, as does the pool room, the dining rooms, the kitchen. I suppose there could be people in the bunker, maybe in the servants' quarters? But overall, it doesn't look much different from the last time I was here. If I didn't know ahead of time, I'd have no reason to suspect Westcott seized it.

I circle through one more time, heading for the throne room. The fog is thicker here, spilling out the open door in waves. A strange sense of déjà vu washes over me, and I shake my head as I shiver, trying to clear it. But then I peer inside the throne room, and that déjà vu turns into a tidal wave.

Because for the first time, one of the rooms isn't empty.

But it's not Westcott or his people I find on the other side of the door.

From one wall to another, the room is packed with wendigos. The darkness seeps from their cloaks and slithers along the floor like tentacles.

My chest burns like I can still feel their claws tearing through me. That day in the field I hadn't been able to figure out how those wendigos had been there but also not, or how I was the only one to see them...had I been in the shadow realm?

I inhale sharply, and every head in the room turns.

I stumble back a step, and their eyes track the movement.

Track *me*.

Which means they can see me.

CHAPTER TEN

TELEPORTING without a clear mind is always a risk. Too much potential for error, to end up in the wrong place at best, or to never arrive at all at worst. But I'm short on other options. I've probably gone over my allotted time as is, and getting from New York to Western Canada without it would be no easy feat.

The wendigos drift toward me, faster than I ever remember them moving before. I run for the front door, digging my blade into my wrist as I go. I close my eyes, imagining the backyard with the others and feeling myself slip from reality between one step and the next—

—only to land on my hands and knees in an unfamiliar expanse of grass. I look around, trying to find something I recognize, but the shadows and fog are so goddamn thick, it's like trying to see in the dead of night before I had my vampire vision. The wind howls beside me, and I feel the chill of their presence before I see them.

They followed me? But *how*?

I scramble to my feet and scoop the book off the ground.

There—lights in the distance. I blink, forcing my vision to focus.

Oh thank God. I'm on the Radmore campus. I'm just a few blocks too far.

I take off at a sprint, not daring to look behind me, not daring to slow no matter how much my lungs ache for air. Shit, which house was theirs? It was somewhere in the middle. I veer right, passing through a gate and plunging into someone else's yard. There—three more down on the left.

I gasp for air, the muscles in my legs cramping. My body is so goddamn *weak* right now. A few more feet. Just a few more.

Something's wrong. The circle is broken, and my friends are gathered where I'd been standing. I pass through the last fence separating us, on the verge of collapsing as I near them.

But it looks like my physical form already beat me to the punch. She's on her back, eyes closed, lines of blood coming out of her nose and ears. I reach up as if I'll be able to feel it on my shadow-realm self, but there's nothing there.

But I hadn't felt anything wrong this whole time. I've been fine.

The figure crouched over my body comes into focus last.

Reid.

"You have to hear me. You have to be able to hear me." He holds my cheeks so our noses are an inch apart, and tears run down his face.

How long have I been like this? Is my heart beating? Am I breathing?

A gust of wind cuts through the yard. Half a dozen wendigos drift forward, straight through the fence.

I crouch beside Reid, pressing my hand to my physical body, but I go right through.

"No, no, no," I whisper.

"Please come back," Reid whispers, his eyes closed and forehead pressed to mine. "Please come back. I love you, Valerie, please come back to me."

"I'm right here." I reach for his face, but my hands go through him too. "Reid, I'm right here," I say, louder this time even though I know he can't hear me.

But then his head lifts an inch.

"Can you hear me?" I demand, frantically grasping for the bond in my chest, but I can't feel it right now. "I can't get through! I'm right here. I'm right here!"

I dig my blade into my wrists, letting my blood fall as I press my hands to my physical form again, but nothing happens.

"I'm right *here*," I grit through my teeth.

"Get back in the circle," Reid barks.

"Reid..." Kirby starts, sniffling and rubbing at her wet eyes.

"Now!" He looks at them over his shoulder. "She's *here*," he insists. "She can't get through."

That, finally, spurs them into motion.

The wendigos circle in, one behind each of my friends. Oh God. *Oh God.* What if they can reach them through the veil?

"Stay away from them!" I shriek.

Adrienne and Monroe kneel so they can grasp my physical

body's hands on the ground, tears flowing down their cheeks as they chant.

The wendigo closest to me turns its head, its cloak flowing behind it as it moves closer. It lifts an arm, its sleeve falling back to reveal its claws.

But the panic bubbling inside of me gives way to determination, to rage.

This is not happening again.

"Use the vial."

My head snaps up. A figure as dark and shadowy as the wendigos stands behind Reid. She cocks her head, studying me, an easy smirk on her face.

On...*my* face.

My head spins. That makes three total *mes* in this yard.

She snaps her fingers, bringing my attention back to her, then points at her own chest. "The bottle. You don't have a lot of time."

With shaking fingers, I pull the vial from my shirt.

"Good. Now, get back in line with her." She points to the unconscious version of me—us.

What the fuck is going on?

But I do what she says, aligning myself with my physical body and lying down.

She nods her approval. "Now break it."

"What are you?" I whisper.

"*Break it.*"

The wendigos inch closer, almost close enough to touch. I crush the glass in my fist, covering my hand in the others' blood. I squeeze my eyes shut, clutching the book to my chest, and chant along with the rest of them.

I just need to wake up. I just need to wake up. I just need to—

I WAKE UP SCREAMING.

Voices surge around me, but I hinge at the waist and spit a mouthful of blood into the grass. Hands pull back the hair from my face, rub circles on my back, clasp my shoulders.

But I'm alive. I'm *alive*. And when I open my eyes, the world is in color again...

I gasp and lurch back into something hard. Hands circle my upper arms as I look around us frantically. But everyone is here. No one seems hurt.

The wendigos are gone.

Or at least, I can't see them anymore.

But the shadow version of me is still there.

She stands behind the others and smiles, flashing bright white teeth.

"Wendigos," I say, or I try to say. My voice cracks, the word scraping along my throat.

Reid's voice, by my ear. The heat of his chest pressing against my back registers next, his hands around my arms. "Let's get her inside," he says. "Come on. You're okay." He scoops me into his arms, and the movement makes the entire world spin and blur and blacken—

SOMETHING SOFT HAS REPLACED the ground when I wake again. A bed—sheets tangled around my legs. I stir, my sharp intake of breath filling the silence. My heart rate jumps as my eyes adjust to the darkness, trying to make sense of where I am. The yard—the wendigos—

"Shh, it's okay. You're safe."

I whip to the side to find Reid's blue eyes staring back at me from a chair beside the bed. I search the rest of the room, but there's no one else here, shadow people or otherwise.

Had I imagined her? Some weird byproduct of the exhaustion and stress?

Slowly, I turn back to Reid. He looks exhausted, like he hasn't slept at all. His hair is tangled like he's run his hands through it a million times, and he's in a wrinkled suit he must have been wearing yesterday, the tie and jacket discarded on the ground beside him.

How long has he been sitting here with me?

God, he must have thought I was dead. I can imagine what he'd been feeling all too well, every moment from the night I found him staked to the floor permanently seared into my memory.

I had no idea something like that would happen. Maybe it was naïve to think we'd be able to pull off a spell of this magnitude without a hitch, that he wouldn't need to know about it until later. But the risk seemed necessary.

"I'm so sorry," I whisper. "I didn't mean to worry you."

"I know." He forces a smile that couldn't be less believable. I don't miss the way he keeps his hands in his lap despite his entire body leaning forward like he wants to reach for me. "How are you feeling now?"

"Not great," I admit. "But not terrible."

He rolls his shirtsleeve up to his elbow. "You should drink some of my blood. It'll help."

There's a moment of hesitation—so brief anyone else probably wouldn't notice—before he extends his arm. The moment my skin touches his as I wrap my fingers around his wrist, electricity flares up my arm, and his eyes meet mine like he feels it too.

I'm the first to look away as I duck my head and bite down on his wrist.

"Adrienne filled me in on what's been going on." His blood has a similar effect on me as his skin, the warmth that floods through me as I drink so much more than just the natural heat of his blood.

I'm *starving*, but the feeling is almost too much, so I only take as much as I need to get by before leaning back against the pillow with an involuntary sigh. There's no pain, exactly. But the exhaustion clings to my every limb, weighing me down, like that place still has its hooks in me, trying to pull me back.

"Did they call you?" I rasp.

"No. I felt it when you crossed over. It was like the bond broke again, but I could also feel you, where you were. It just felt *wrong*." When I let myself look at him again, his brow is knit, his eyes searching my face. "I'm so sorry I made you feel like you couldn't come to me with this."

"Reid, this isn't your fault. I should be the one apologizing. I just...I thought I could handle this one myself."

The tension in his face doesn't ease, and he does not look the least bit convinced. "Are you in pain?"

"I'm okay."

He doesn't look the least bit convinced by that either.

"I promise. I'm just tired."

The way he's looking at me, all I want is to curl myself into it. All I see when I close my eyes are those papers covering every inch of his room, the picture of me beside his bed, the lashes across his back at the wolf camp, him staked to the wall, trying to get to me, his shy smile as he gave me the violin, the smile in his eyes when I woke up to him the next morning.

When he looks at me like this, it's too easy for all the reasons we should be apart to lose their importance. There's no war looming or fiancées or disapproval or danger. It's just him and me and the desire to be close to him is an instinctual need that's physically painful to fight.

Tears get stuck in my throat, and I turn away before he can see it written all over my face in addition to whatever he's undoubtedly getting through the bond. So instead of launching myself into his arms, I roll away and tuck myself beneath the blankets.

"The book, did it—"

"It made it."

"And the others?"

"They're fine. Shaken up and tired, but they'll be all right."

That, at least, calms the tension in my shoulders, at least in part.

"There were wendigos here," I say. "On the other side."

"That's what you said when you first woke up. I checked the area, and Radmore has its own protocols for keeping them off campus. No sign of them, from what I could tell. Not on this side of the veil, at least."

I suppose if the wendigos were able to cause harm on this side, they would have already. I nod slowly, words I know I shouldn't say on the tip of my tongue.

There are a million reasons for me to let him go now that I'm okay.

But even with this distance between us, lying here with him feels so much better than it should. His scent, his skin, his voice —I feel like an addict, unable to tear myself away. Unable to even bear the thought. Just having him in the same room is a comfort I haven't felt in weeks.

"What was it like?" he murmurs. "On the other side?"

"Terrifying," I admit. "It was like being underwater, like being buried alive. There wasn't any color, any light. And I don't know if the things I saw...if I was seeing things or if they were really there. How did you know I made it back? Could you hear me?"

"Not exactly. I think it was the bond, but it didn't feel the way it usually does. I don't know how. I just knew." He sighs. "You should get some rest."

I nod, my heart dropping at what I know comes next. An empty room. That tense silence between us returning.

But then quietly, he adds, "Would it...would it be all right if I stay?"

A tear falls onto my cheek, and I press my lips together to hold back my relief. I nod.

"Okay," he breathes, and his hand searches for mine in the sheets. I don't pull away when we make contact. Instead, I interlace my fingers with his and hold him there like I'm afraid he'll be the one to let go, but he grips my hand just as tightly.

"Did you find what was on that page?" he asks after a moment.

"I haven't looked yet."

He says nothing, but we're both probably thinking the same thing.

Whatever it is, hopefully it was worth it.

CHAPTER ELEVEN

I SHOULDN'T BE DISAPPOINTED Reid's gone when I wake up, but the sight of the empty chair beside the bed feels like a fist squeezing around my heart. I take in the room for the first time —Kirby's, clearly. Everything's pink, the bedspread, the feather decorations on the wall, the lights strung around the vanity mirror. I roll over, my joints aching, and reach for the glass of water on the nightstand. The book is beside it, along with a note.

Sorry to leave before you woke up. Pulled into a meeting. Please call me if you need anything.
Reid

I smirk a little at how formal it sounds. How *regal*. I guess at some point all of the royal training gets so ingrained it becomes a part of your DNA.

I chug the water, then pull the book into my lap. If my exhaustion hadn't won out last night, my curiosity would have. I'd thought it might look different here, but the cover is just as dark, dark enough that *black* doesn't feel like a good enough descriptor. Static electricity sings along my fingertips as I trace the cover, not painful, exactly, but the power is potent enough to raise the hairs on the backs of my arms.

Strange. None of my mother's other books feel like anything but leather and paper and ink. I've never seen this one before. Has Adrienne, Calla? For it to be hidden and away from the rest...

I already have a good idea of what I'll find inside, but the breath still leaves my lungs as I turn to the first page.

Every spell book is unique—often passed down through a bloodline, each volume different in style depending on the witch who added to them. But never, not once, have I seen a book like this.

The illustrations are detailed, as they usually are, the black pen marks heavy and sharp. But the images are grotesque. And a swift glance at the ingredients list is enough to put two and two together without reading the spell.

...an offering of flesh...

...the fingernail of an innocent...

...rib removed while the sacrifice is still living...

...blood of a raven, drained from its still-beating heart...

The drawing depicts a person severing their own hand over a fire.

But what the hell would the caster even get out of a spell like this? I skim the page, not wanting to retain more details than necessary, but find nothing. The line at the top, it's in Latin. That must be it. Latin has never been my strong suit.

Possess another's body seems to be the gist. But not with yourself. With something *else.*

I close the book again and take a deep breath through my nose. I'm not oblivious. The Darkmores have a history with dark magic, though it hasn't shown up in documentation for decades. My mother, for one, always made it clear that we were never to dabble in it. Which was part of the reason she'd gone absolutely berserk the first time she'd found me using necromancy.

So I know she wouldn't direct me to this book lightly. Not if there were any other options.

Maybe it hadn't been her at all, a small voice whispers in the back of my mind.

The magic felt like Calla's, sure, and that nail was definitely Mom's, but Adrienne and I just assumed it was from them. What if that's what the *actual* sender wanted us to think? If for some reason they needed one of us to retrieve the book? The compartment in that bookshelf needed a blood offering to open it. Probably a similar security system to the shock on that note.

Steeling myself, I flip to the page the note specified—313.

At least it's not as gruesome as the last one. There are no illustrations, but the words are cramped. There are so many instructions they struggle to fit on a single page. I stare at the Latin at the top, trying to decode its meaning.

Direction? No, no. More like *manipulation. Control.*

It sounds a lot like glamour, actually. But more.

Like a permanent glamour, giving someone the steering

wheel instead of merely giving directions to the driver. It wouldn't quite possess the target, but it would give you ultimate control over their words and actions.

The ingredients aren't any less disturbing though.

A newborn's tongue, twin bones—one broken, one whole, ground hummingbird wings.

But there's also a folded piece of paper tucked between these two pages. It's in the same handwriting as the note that directed me to this book, but this time it contains an address. Something on Main Street in York.

But if the real message had been this address, why not send that as the first note? Why make me go through the trouble of retrieving the book?

I close the book again, my stomach churning.

You couldn't exactly walk into a shop to pick up those kind of ingredients. Where would you even...*how* would you even...

"Hey, you're awake." Adrienne leans against the door jamb, a steaming mug of coffee in each hand.

"Please tell me that's for me."

She smirks and joins me on the bed. Her eyes flick to the book as I take the second cup.

"Have you looked at it yet?"

"I tried." I nudge it toward her with my knee. "You might want to finish your coffee first."

She's silent as she flips through the pages, her expression stoic. She's always had the best poker face of the three of us. I sip my coffee and wait as she reads, her eyebrows pulling together the only hint at her thoughts.

"We should destroy the note now," she says, almost absent-mindedly.

I'd nearly forgotten about that line of it. So no one could track the magic? Or so no one else would find this spell?

"Maybe we should do a tracing spell first," I say. "To be sure it's from—"

"I already did."

"I—you what? When?"

She spares me a brief glance before going back to the book. "While you were asleep. After seeing the book, I thought I'd double-check."

"And?"

Her nod is nearly imperceptible. "Calla."

The confirmation doesn't bring the kind of relief I'd been hoping for. It doesn't make me feel much of anything at all, besides more confusion.

Why this spell? Why this book? Why now?

She closes the book with a thud. "How are you feeling?"

"Fine," I say, then wave off the unconvinced eyebrow raise she gives me. "I'm tired. I'll take it easy."

"You looked a lot more than tired before. We thought—"

"I'm fine." I scratch at the skin below my ear, still itchy from the dried blood. "It was weird though. I felt perfectly fine the entire time in the shadow world. I never would've known something was wrong if I hadn't come back and seen myself."

"I guess that's one of the dangers, isn't it?" she says softly, leaving the book on the bed and pushing to her feet. "Why so many people get lost there. You lose track of time, you don't realize the extent of the damage you're causing, you think you can push it a little more. And that was with *seven* of us."

A shiver runs down my spine. I don't even want to think about what state I would've been in if I'd tried it on my own.

"I've gotta get to class, but are you sure you'll be okay?"

"Yeah, yeah, I'm fine, I promise."

She points a finger at me. "Don't try to teleport to Auclair. Please."

I raise my palms. "I'll get a car."

She narrows her eyes like she doesn't believe me, but heads out just the same.

The house falls into silence after I hear the front door close downstairs. Kirby and Monroe must have already headed out. What time is it anyway? How long have I been out?

I fish around in the sheets for my phone, then notice it sitting on the dresser on the other side of the room and plugged in. I smile a little. Reid.

I try to remind myself of all the reasons I shouldn't let him make me smile anymore, but the arguments sound weak, even to me. My muscles ache as I move, worse than I'd been expecting. Adrienne didn't need to worry about me trying teleportation. I don't think I could pull off a simple spell right now if I tried.

When I power on the phone, the screen fills with messages —Daniel, Wes, Kirby, Monroe, Beth. Everyone apologizing for having to rush out for classes and whatnot today, they'll be back later, they're so glad I'm okay.

I frown at the screen for a moment, not at all liking the feeling threatening to emerge in my chest, but it's there nonetheless. Because while everyone is carrying on with their lives, finishing their education, learning magic I've never heard of, doing everything I was supposed to do, I'm sitting here, alone, stuck in more of a limbo than even the shadow world had felt.

It's of my own doing, I suppose. I could've pushed harder

about going back to the academy. Reid probably would have found a way to make it work.

But do I *really* want to be here, or do I just hate the idea of all of my friends moving on with their lives without me? That I'm no longer the version of myself who fits alongside them.

THE NOTE SPARKS before it goes up in flames in the fireplace. But after staring at it for an hour, trying to decipher any other meaning or code, I let it go.

My issues with Calla aside, I don't want anything to happen to her. And that note in the right hands would've been a direct map to her.

Auclair is quiet when a car brings me back, and I don't have the energy to do much more than shuffle to Adrienne's room, tuck myself into bed, and request some human food get delivered by one of the servants. And in the meantime, I read the book.

Now that the initial shock has subsided, I can't stop turning the pages. I eye the whiskey I'd left beneath Adrienne's bed—that would certainly make the content more palatable—but talk myself out of it. I'm never going to get my strength back if I keep this up. And I won't give the queen more reasons to call my partnership with Reid into question.

Black magic isn't something taught at the academies other than general warnings, tragic events in history that have happened because of it, that kind of thing. The types of spells in this book, I never would've believed they were possible. I can't even imagine the inner workings of a mind that could create these in the first place.

And yet, they're my ancestors.

Their blood runs through my veins.

What does that say about me?

The thought of performing a spell like this is ludicrous, inconceivable. And yet the feeling clinging to my skin feels much closer to *inevitable.*

I just wish I knew why Calla and Mom pointed me to this spell. Do they want me to perform it? Am I supposed to sit around and wait for another note to arrive with more instructions? Should I figure out a way to send a note back to let them know I got the book?

It's infuriatingly vague. Which I guess isn't unlike a lot of the lessons Mom did with us growing up. They were always under the guise of making us better, helping with problem-solving skills, improving our powers. But no matter how you twist it, the exercises were always cruel.

The spell behind the one she indicated catches my eye because I recognize the illustration in the top left corner. The drawing is faded with time. The edges are feathery and blurry, but I can make out the shape well enough. It looks exactly like the figure I saw in Mom's room in the shadow world.

I run my finger over the text beside it, the Latin not making sense to me. Except for a single word.

Demon.

This spell is just as complicated, the list of ingredients long enough to cover the page. It's an entrapment spell. A way to condemn a soul to a different realm and ensure they could never cross back to ours.

Is that what I'd seen in her room? A soul condemned and stuck on that side?

If that's what it was, what was it doing in my mother's room? Is it someone she used this spell on? Judging by how much dust was coating the book when I pulled it out, if she had, it wasn't any time recently.

And in the cruelest brand of irony, one of the final pages is a spell to break blood deals. However, it's one of the most complicated spells in the book, taking up three entire pages, and there's a symbol drawn all around the top of the first page. It looks like a warning. An upside-down triangle engulfed in flames with a thick X carved through it.

It's not the only spell in here that requires a sacrifice, but the things you'd have to do to the other person while they were alive, and it looks like they *have* to be conscious through it all...

How could you stomach it?

How could you be the same person after you'd done it?

And yet, the things I've done, the countless people I've killed, whether I'd wanted to or not...

I close the book and toss it onto the bed beside me. I can't keep obsessing about this. This book has been in my possession for less than a day and I already feel like I'm losing my mind trying to piece it together.

If Calla and Mom want me to do something with it, they're going to have to be a hell of a lot clearer.

Unable to help myself, I flip back to the entrapment spell.

Would it be the same as killing? Or would it be a mercy, a way to stop someone else from causing so much harm? To protect the people on this side to ensure he couldn't be brought back, that he couldn't survive it this time, that his plans and attacks won't stretch out for even more decades? So yet another Darkmore won't be reading about wendigos and the psychosis a hundred years from now?

You could stop this, whispers a voice in the back of my head.

This isn't the first time he's done this, and if given the chance, this will not be the last.

My fingers still on the page. Is that why they chose the spell before this one? To control Westcott? To control his following?

I slam the book shut with a frustrated huff as there's a loud knock on the door.

"It's open," I call.

Jones pokes his head in, grinning.

"Hey, Jones?"

He practically skips into the room, his cheeks flushed and eyes wide like a child on Christmas or something. "I have a full report," he says, stepping to the foot of my bed, a folder held tightly to his chest. He blinks, the excitement in his face dimming as he takes me in on the bed. "Are you okay?"

"Yeah, yeah, I'm good." I wave my hand, eyeing the folder. "*Oh.*" I point at it. I'd almost forgotten what I'd asked him to do, and I'd pretty much assumed he wouldn't follow through with it.

He grins at what must be a baffled expression on my face as he drums his fingers against the folder. "I'm an eager student, what can I say? And I'm bored here, okay? Fucking rich people have too much downtime. I almost miss Cam barking orders at camp. Don't tell him I said that." He licks his finger then starts flipping through the pages. "Princess Anya Vasilieva…is completely and utterly clean. Seriously. Not a spec of dirt to be found. She is like the Russian estate's sweetheart. There's an online fan club. She's on magazine covers. Runs some charity." He pauses to set some articles and pictures on the bed so I can see.

"If she's here for nefarious reasons, she has a very, very good cover. *But.* That's from all of the official channels." He wiggles his eyebrows and flips to another page. "According to the whispers around *these* halls, she's pretty much kept to herself since she got here aside from official business. I over-heard some of the humans talking about how there's tension whenever she's in the same room as another royal. They kind of treat her like an outcast. Her reputation back home is very bubbly and free-spirited…but here she's been reserved and quiet. She spends a lot of time in the library and the gym, I've heard."

I frown. *Reserved? Quiet?* Since she's been here, she's ripped a man's spine out, then made a scene in a meeting with Auclair's high-ranking officials because she wanted my damn seat. And she hadn't been shy about speaking up in that meeting. But admittedly, I haven't been around her besides those two occasions.

"I can keep digging," Jones insists, shifting his weight side to side.

"No, this is good, Jones. Thank you."

He sets the folder on the bed and heads for the door, but hesitates halfway there, biting his lip.

"What is it?"

He shrugs and shoves his hands in his pockets. "I've only seen her a few times around here, but for what it's worth, to me she just looks…scared."

The word hangs heavily in the air.

He shrugs, and I offer a lame wave as he heads back into the hall, then push myself out of bed for good measure, reaching for my shoes.

I may not have the strength for a jog right now, but the fresh air might do me good. And despite my complaints to Cam, training and getting my physical strength back has me feeling more like myself than I have in a long time.

It's quiet out here today, quiet enough to hear the birds singing in the trees. My breath puffs up in a cloud around me, and a layer of fog clings to the ground.

I pace along the trail on the grounds, never venturing far enough that I lose sight of the estate, drumming my fingers against my phone, resisting the urge to text Reid about all of this.

Whatever meeting he's in, I'm willing to bet a lot of Auclair's important personnel are too. But that would mean his Marionette should be with him, but he hadn't asked me to come.

I'm merely suggesting we consider a reassignment.

Even in my head, Queen Carrington's voice grates on my nerves.

But Reid wouldn't…he wouldn't…

"Do you go running to him for help for *everything?*"

I gasp and whip around, my phone clattering to the gravel. Flapping wings fill the silence as birds in the nearby trees burst into flight.

But the path around me is empty. I turn a full circle, trying to find the origin of the voice, but there's no one else out here.

I'm full-on hallucinating now. Great.

I retrieve my phone and turn to head back to the estate—

the fresh air hasn't been as helpful to clear my head as I'd been hoping anyway—but there's a figure on the path now.

"No," I whisper as she makes her way forward.

The fog drifts straight through her like she's not there, and maybe she's not. Maybe this *is* a hallucination. I haven't seen her since that moment after the shadow projecting spell, and I was hoping that would be the last time.

The shadow-me smirks as she stops a few paces away, like she can tell what I'm thinking. Her hair is slicked back in a high ponytail, accentuating the razor-sharp lines of her cheek-bones and jaw. It makes her look perpetually callous, cold.

Is that really what I look like?

I've always thought my features were the softest and roundest of everyone in my family, always making me look a little out of place alongside them. I knew the past few months had done plenty of unkind things for my appearance, but *this*?

"Don't stop on my account." She gestures to the phone. "Go on, go running to your boyfriend about your latest disaster. Give him more proof that you're utterly incompetent."

I inhale sharply. The jab itself barely stings, but was it a lucky guess that I'd been thinking about Reid, or can she somehow see inside my head?

"He's my partner."

"Hm. Does he know that? Seems pretty one-sided to me."

I stand up straighter, my fist tightening around the phone, but I stop myself before responding again. I'm not going to stand here and have an argument with myself.

She's not real. *She's not real.*

She rolls her eyes with a sigh. "Don't tell me you've gone stupid now too. I'm not a hallucination. You know I'm not."

"Then what the hell are you?" I demand, then pinch my lips together and check our surroundings to make sure we're alone. If I'm the only one who can see her, the last thing I need is news of me talking to no one getting around. The queen would just *love* that.

"Don't they teach you anything at those academies?" she mutters. "Everyone has a shadow self on the other side. I'll admit, meeting each other is rare, but what can I say? I saw the opportunity, and I took it. Thanks for that, by the way. Couldn't have crossed the threshold without you. You can call me V."

I shake my head and take a step away from her, then another. Maybe that spell took more out of me than I realized. I just need to rest.

And to get the hell out of here.

"Why don't you ask me?" she says. "Maybe I can help."

"Why the hell would I trust you?"

"God, you really are the stupid one, aren't you? It's okay, it's okay. We can work with that. I'm *you*. Of course you can trust me."

I let out an unintelligible noise in the back of my throat and turn away, heading for the estate.

"Whatever was in that book must have been pretty important, huh?" she calls after me. "It would sure be nice if you had someone with dark magic experience to help you. Or say...that princess who's engaged to your boyfriend. Sure would be nice if someone around here knew something about *her.* If someone could somehow see what all those books she's been reading in the library are about..."

My steps slow, and I close my eyes as I pull in a deep breath.

Let's say, for argument's sake, I haven't completely lost my mind. This shadow version of me is real and here and talking to me. But I don't believe for one second she wants to help me out of the goodness of her heart or whatever.

"And what would be in it for you?" I ask.

"Oh, I can think of a few ways you could repay me." She steps up beside me, flashing a grin that's more showing me her teeth than a smile. "You know what? Take your time. Think it over. I don't mind waiting until you realize you need me."

Someone with dark magic experience. Admittedly, I don't know much about the shadow realm, how it works, what our shadow versions do on the other side. She could be telling the truth, but she could just as easily be telling me what she thinks I want to hear.

"I'm not touching a single spell in that book," I say, but the words don't have nearly as much conviction to them as they should.

"What's your plan then? Are you going to wait around and hope that someone else fixes this or are you going to step up? Personally, I don't think the damsel in distress life suits you, but you've sure been milking it lately, haven't you?"

"I—I am *not* a damsel in distress."

"Waiting around for his royal highness to rescue you, or these idiots"—she gestures to the estate—"or my personal favorite"—she fans herself and flutters her eyelashes—"the pack master."

I grit my teeth but stop before I respond. Is that what I've been doing? Ever since I made my deal with Westcott, I hit a low I've never experienced before. All of my energy was strictly on survival, on making it through another day. On the outside, maybe that *does* look like doing nothing. But it's felt like I was doing *everything*. Giving everything I had, fighting for every breath, every heartbeat. Maybe I look weaker now, incompetent. But surviving has been the hardest thing I've ever done.

But did I lose a part of myself along the way, the part capable of stepping up? The one who took action without question, without fear. Something aches inside my chest, like a plea for that piece of me to return home.

I'm not delusional enough to think I'm safe here, that I can relax now. But maybe it is time to switch out of survival mode.

To wake back up.

"You might think you're taking the noble route," she continues. "You're *too good* for this kind of magic. Hopefully that clear conscience carries over after the thousands—maybe millions—of innocent deaths that you could have prevented. What's that saying? Sacrifice one for the good of many?"

Her smile shifts from amusement to something softer, almost genuine, at whatever she sees on my face. "So I'll ask you again, Valerie. Do you want my help?"

CHAPTER TWELVE

DESPITE YORK ACADEMY'S recent evacuation, the town itself looks untouched, like a tornado hopped through the area but missed this one spot. Humans are walking down the sidewalk talking, the store windows full of light. A weird shock of vertigo hits my system, transporting me back to last year before initiation when everything was normal. Or at least what passed for it.

How quickly everything can change.

The only shop on the street that doesn't look open is the address written on the note in my hand.

Magnolia's.

The sign on the door is turned to closed. Although the shop windows are dark, a hint of light peeks through the curtains of the apartment above. I raise my fist to knock, but the door swings open before I have the chance.

Only half of her face is visible as Magnolia looks me up and down. Last time I showed up on her doorstep, I had a death sentence on my head. If she's surprised I'm alive, she doesn't show it. If anything, she looks amused.

"I was wondering when I'd see you."

The door closes between us before I can respond. There's a clink as she releases the chain, then opens the door enough for me to follow her inside.

Her eyes flick to the backpack thrown over my shoulders. "You foolish girl," she mutters. "Bringing that book here."

I stiffen. The bag is securely shut, the book not at all visible. "I—"

"Don't waste your breath on lies, my dear. I know why you're here. Come, come."

Instead of leading me to the office in the rear of the shop as she did the last time I was here, I follow her up the back staircase to her apartment.

The space is as crowded and cluttered as the shop below, lit only by candles flickering from every surface, not a single electric light fixture in sight. She grunts and gestures to the small pink table as she ambles to the kitchen and places a kettle on the stove.

"How did you know I was coming?" I ask as I lower myself into a wooden chair.

She snorts like the question is amusing. "I have known I would see you on this day at this time for the past three years, Valerie Darkmore. Your mother made sure of that."

"I—my mother?"

She smirks at me over the counter and pulls some tea bags from the cabinet. "Your mother came to see me three years ago. Not long after the disappearance of her eldest."

Calliope.

I sit up straighter at her word choice. *Disappearance*, not *death*. So she's known Calliope wasn't dead.

Does that mean my mother has known all this time too?

She turns her back to me as the kettle whistles. "I don't think she ever expected one of her daughters to come into their dormant nature. Not when the last Darkmore to do so was so many generations ago." Magnolia shuffles to the seat across from me, setting two mugs of steaming tea between us. "She came to me after Calliope's initiation in order to prevent the same from happening to you."

"She knew what really happened to Calla," I whisper. "And she let us believe she was dead."

Magnolia shakes her head. "She knew your sister had turned. But she did believe her to be dead until recently. Your father made sure of that."

My teeth grind at the word *father*, but I don't correct her. "What do you mean, *dormant nature?*"

She flicks her wrist. "The mutated gene that allows blood witches to tap into their necromancy ancestry through vampirism is unpredictable. It skips generations in the same way the werewolf gene does. Of course, there's minimal documentation of when it *does* happen, for reasons I'm sure you're familiar with by now."

"So she knew this was going to happen to me but didn't bother to warn me." I don't mean to say it aloud, but there it is.

So many secrets. So many lies. And for what?

Magnolia sips her tea, apparently unbothered that it must be scalding. "It wasn't a guarantee it would happen to you too. I'd say statistically, it was quite rare."

"Then what did you tell her when she came to see you three years ago? What does that have to do with this?" I pull the note from my pocket and place it on the table.

Magnolia doesn't acknowledge it. She doesn't even blink.

"We considered the infinite paths your life could take to find which would result in your survival. She chose what she believed to be the best option."

I stare at her, trying to process the words. *Infinite paths your life could take...*

"You're a seer," I breathe.

She says nothing and adds another spoonful of sugar to her tea.

It's one of the rarest forms of lunar magic. Until now, I've never met a witch with the ability before.

But it's also the closest link to dark magic a natural power can have, even more than necromancy. And magic like that always comes with a price.

I swallow hard, my hands tightening around my cup. "What did you see?"

She clucks her tongue. "Many things. Many versions. Many deaths."

A shiver runs down my spine, but I force myself to sit up straight.

"The only solution we saw that would allow you to remain at the academy, at the estate, was to connect you with your anapófefktos. In doing—"

"I'm sorry, my what?"

Her forehead creases as she snaps her fingers, as if searching for the word. "It is believed you and another soul have a string of fate connecting you, an invisible line that has always been there, in this life and every other. The wolves call it mates. Humans, soulmates. You get the idea."

I don't lean back in my chair so much as collapse against it. Because years ago, I might have laughed at the ridiculousness of this conversation. But instead, there's a burning in the backs of my eyes, the truth sitting like a rock in my throat.

A small, knowing smile rises to Magnolia's lips. "Having you paired with Prince Reginald was no accident. Your mother knew he would ensure your survival through initiation, even if in the moment, he didn't understand why." She tilts her head to the side. "He just needed a nudge."

"A nudge?"

She flicks her wrist again. "You can go see for yourself. It'll be in his mind, even if he cannot remember."

"Did you know then? That all of this would happen?"

"Don't be dense, child, of course not. Even seers have their limits. The future is always changing, and if we don't know the right questions to ask, we can't find the right answers."

"But you knew I'd come here today."

She nods even though it clearly wasn't a question.

"Do you know how this situation with Westcott turns out? Have you even tried to look? To *help*?" I glance at her arm, searching for the mark of the blood deal I saw last time, but it's covered by her shirt. "Or would *that* stop you?"

She very calmly rolls up her sleeve, then the other.

Both arms are entirely bare.

She says nothing as the gears spin furiously in my mind. I know what I saw. I *know* it was there. Which means she must have completed whatever her part had been. That, or she'd passed the deal to someone else.

"Was it with him?" My voice is a small, desperate thing as a horrible possibility burrows itself into the back of my mind.

How easily I've trusted her, freely given her information. How easily I've believed every word she's said.

Before, I was desperate. She gave me a spark of hope in an endless sea of death, and I latched on to it without question.

She holds my stare and interlaces her hands on top of the table. "Your father and I struck a deal many years ago. My freedom from his psychosis in exchange for a favor. One he did not come to collect until recently."

I lean back in my chair, putting more distance between us as if already knowing what she'll say next.

For the first time, the coldness in her expression cracks, and I can't quite name the emotion that flits across her eyes. Regret? Remorse?

"I was given no explanation. Only a directive. To create a hole in the security of York Academy during the week of the Marionettes initiation."

"The attacks on campus," I whisper. "The wendigos who attacked *me*." I shove away from the table, hot, angry tears rising to the back of my throat. "It was *you*."

Her eyebrows dig in, but she doesn't deny it. "I only created a gap in the protection spells. I knew not his intentions—"

"But you did it anyway! People *died* in those attacks—"

Ryan, the human who worked in the library, there was barely anything of him left. I can picture the broken pieces of his body lying by the lake just days after I asked him for help. All this time, I'd thought he died because of *me*. And Daniel... he almost...he could have...

She slams her hands against the table and rises to her feet. "And when your father came calling at your darkest moment, how long did you hesitate before blindly agreeing to *your* deal, Valerie Darkmore? You may think the worst of me. And if you do not wish to accept my help now, you may go. Or you can allow me to atone for the hand I've played." She slumps into her chair with a sigh as if exhausted now.

I don't return to mine, but I also make no move for the door. "But you had the mark when I came to see you about the psychosis. That was weeks later."

"I was also not to intervene once his plans were in motion until he'd completed his objective."

"His objective being taking me."

She nods.

I pace around the small space, shaking my head. "But you gave me the herbs. How did you know that wouldn't go against your deal?"

"I didn't."

I freeze.

"I didn't," she repeats quietly. "But I found I could not send you away." Whatever that crinkle in her forehead means, I think it's the most emotion I'm going to get from her. She fiddles with the tea set, resituating each piece even though there was nothing wrong with it.

She'd taken a gamble helping me before. One she could have paid for with her life. And still, she helped me.

"You couldn't *see* that either?" I don't know if I mean it as a joke or a jab; it just comes out flat.

But she answers it anyway. "The Sight is often misunderstood. Visions come and go as they please, and though we can go searching with a question, sometimes the answers do not want to be found. My sight has been…murkier as of late than it ever has been. For this, I cannot see clearly enough for any answers you might seek."

"Murky?"

"As I said, seers have their limits, and there are…*obstacles.* Whatever—or whoever—is blocking my sight, I cannot see around it."

"What could do that? What could block your sight?"

She shrugs. "Many things. Other seers, factors too volatile to predict, certain spells. When we interfere, a domino effect can occur, and sometimes the results are changing too rapidly to catch a glimpse."

Her eyes laser focus on my hands as I slowly return to my seat and dig the book out of my bag. I flip to the spell and push it toward her. "So then tell me why the hell I'm here."

"You are certainly Rosemarie's daughter," she murmurs under her breath as she pulls the book closer to examine the page. "I imagine she suspected you would need help procuring the ingredients."

I shove the tea aside and lean my forearms on the table. The time for word games and vague answers has long since passed. "You must know more than that."

"As I said, when it's time to collect your ingredients, you will find what you need here. Some, but not all."

When it's time. As if me performing that spell is inevitable.

"You will have a choice to make." She pushes the book back, apparently done with it, and gets up to refill her tea. "One life or another. It will be in your hands."

One life or another. She must mean the sacrifice. But then

who is the *other*? As a seer, if anyone would know this outcome, it's her.

"Have you seen the other ways this could play out? If I don't go through with this."

Her smile is thin as she returns to her seat. "You are looking for an easier solution. Something fair and right and just. But war rarely lets us hold on to our humanity. The choice is yours to make. And taking no action is also a choice."

V said something similar to me yesterday. *You might think you're taking the noble route.*

There's a knowing glint in Magnolia's eyes as she says it, but she also always looks like she's seeing directly into my soul. How much has she seen? Does she know about V?

"What can you tell me about the shadow realm, or our shadow selves?"

She shows no reaction to the change in subject, as if this next question was exactly what she'd been expecting.

"The veil between our world and the shadow realm is less concrete for those closer to dark magic. Its essence calls to our blood. Which may make crossing the boundary easier, but it can also suck you in, make it harder to return." She gives me a knowing look. "To use you as a conduit to bring pieces of itself over."

"And if something did?" I whisper. "Cross over with you?"

"Shadow selves are often times the darkest parts of oneself in full expression. And their development hinges on the decisions you've made on this side. The parts of yourself you've suppressed, the choices you've made, your shadow self has experienced the opposite. They are the parts of you that you didn't let yourself become. Because their existence is so dependent on you, they wouldn't do anything to put you in real jeopardy. Not if it could potentially harm them. But..."

"Anything else is fair game."

Any*one* else.

"I would advise you to exercise caution, Valerie Darkmore." There's an unreadable look on her face as she searches mine. "Once a shadow self has a taste of our side, they will show no restraint to prevent going back."

"Why? Why would they even want to be on this side?"

Magnolia shakes her head, the crease between her eyebrows deepening. "Because if they can manage to switch places with you—them on our side, and you in the shadows—they would no longer be at the mercy of the effects of your choices. You would be at the mercy of theirs."

THE AUCLAIR ESTATE library is twice the size of the Carrington's, which gives me twice the chance of finding what I need, but also twice the amount of information to sift through. If nothing else, I have the few books Magnolia lent me tucked under my arm.

I gather books on shadow projection, the shadow world, dark magic, and anything that looks vaguely related, then add a few more to the stack for research on locked memories and spells to retrieve them for good measure. If what Magnolia said is true...I just want to make sure I don't mess it up when the time comes for me to look through Reid's head.

I set up camp in the leather chairs in the corner by the windows, pulling up the shadow realm material first. As much as I want to write off V as a figment of my imagination, I know deep down she's not. If my mind hasn't broken enough to start hallucinating from everything that's happened in the last year, there's no way *this* is what would push me over the edge.

Somehow, my shadow self managed to cross the threshold with me, so I need to know exactly what I'm dealing with.

And how the hell to send her back.

She's out of her mind if she thinks I'm going to agree to some kind of alliance with her, as if the last few deals I've made didn't nearly kill me. I don't need her help.

I don't.

Because if they can manage to switch places with you—them on our side, and you in the shadows—they would no longer be at the mercy of the effects of your choices. You would be at the mercy of theirs.

Is that what she's after? Trying to trick me into switching places with her?

Of the thousand pages in each of the dozen books I found, there's collectively twenty pages on the shadow realm. I take pictures with my phone in case I need to reference them later, though from a quick skim, they seem surface level. I should ask the others more about what they've covered in class.

Magnolia's books have a few helpful sections. Both versions of a person cannot exist on the same plane simultaneously, not fully. But there are in between stages, pockets of space where souls can linger…or get trapped. Which means V might be closer to our side than she ever was before, but she's not fully *here*.

Her essence is on this side, but she has no physical form of her own—*my* physical form. So as long as I'm on this side, she can't be.

But how much power she has in this in-between space, that much the books don't cover. If she can use magic, it wouldn't take a physical form to cause some serious damage.

"I was hoping we'd run into each other." Anya gives me a wide smile as she slides into the seat across from me.

Just what I need today. I scan the rest of the room, looking for an out, a rescue, but we're alone.

"I think we're, well, *I'm* overdue for an apology."

I wait for the punchline, but instead of the haughty look over her nose she'd given me in the meeting, she's slouched low in her chair, her manicured fingers fidgeting with one another.

"The meeting the other day." She flicks her wrist, still not quite looking at me. "It was bitchy. Sorry."

...sorry?

I've always thought I was good at reading people, but with Anya, I have no idea what she's thinking, what angle she's playing. First she saves my life on that tarmac, then in the meeting she demands I stand in the back of the room one moment and defends me the next, and now *this*?

When I don't respond, she adds, "Given the circumstances, you and I are bound to be around each other a lot. You probably think I'm a cunt and want nothing to do with me, and it's probably ridiculous to think that maybe we could be friends. But that was more about Reginald in there than it was about you. Still, I'm sorry."

I stare at her, dumbfounded.

141

"I'm not used to—well." She shifts in her seat, crossing her arms over her chest, then uncrossing them again and sitting up straight. "I'm not used to…not being wanted. And you probably think my head is full of air, but I know when a man wants me. And my fiancé clearly doesn't. I don't think I've ever met a man less interested in me. I'm supposed to spend the rest of my life with this man, and he barely looks at me, and he's always so serious. He only wants to talk business. So I think I got kind of…jealous, maybe? Because you two seem close, and he actually has a personality with you. I have to ask. Is he gay? He doesn't seem the type, but I guess that's stereotyping, right? I don't want to make assumptions."

I stifle a cough, not sure if I'm more relieved or surprised by the accusation.

"I can keep a secret, if that's the case." She flicks her wrist.

I shake my head, unable to find words.

Her shoulders deflate, and she frowns like she's disappointed by the answer. "You're his partner. You must know him better than anyone. Am I not his type or something?" She scoffs the question like it's simply unthinkable.

To be fair, she's beautiful. Hell, if I liked girls, I'd probably be into her. She's all full lips and shiny hair and soft lines. I'm sure boys have been falling at her feet all her life. What I'd thought was cold calculation in her eyes is…insecurity.

She didn't ask for this engagement any more than Reid did. She was shipped off to a place she's never been full of people she doesn't know to marry a man she's basically never met like a piece of property her father could bargain with. Then she shows up here and her fiancé wants nothing to do with her. And she's eighteen, for fuck's sake. She's holding it together a lot better than I would have. In a very weird, round-about way, she reminds me of Adrienne.

How did I find myself wanting to comfort the woman engaged to my boyfriend? And what the hell am I supposed to say to her now?

"I think Reid is really stressed with everything that's been going on," I say slowly. "And you showing up here surprised him."

"What's he like?" She leans her elbows on the table, her face suddenly far too close to me, so I lean back in my chair. "I just want to know what I'm getting into, you know? I've heard all kinds of rumors about him, but he's really fucking hard to read."

I snort. "He's not as broody and mysterious as he first comes across as, promise."

The words do little to calm her restless energy though. She drums her fingers rapidly on the table, her shoulders rounded. *I know that look.* I saw it on Calla, Adrienne, felt it in my own permanently fucked-up posture. The body's way of bracing itself, of protecting itself. Subconsciously hunching in and making yourself a smaller target.

This isn't just about him not liking her.

What had Jones said?

To me she just looks…scared.

Even though this is the most bizarre conversation I've ever had, I soften my voice. "If you're concerned, you don't have anything to worry about. He's kind…and loyal…and thoughtful and…" I clear my throat, my cheeks heating. "He's one of the best people I've ever known. So you don't have to worry."

I swallow hard, worried I've said too much, that she'll be

able to read it all over my face. But she offers a smile, looking kind of shy.

"Thanks, Valerie." She drops her gaze again, taking in the books and papers strewn across the table. "Shadow realm, huh?"

I hum noncommittedly as she pulls one of the pages closer to her and examines it.

"You know, my Marionette back at Vasiliev is into this kind of stuff. I swear he's always reading."

"He didn't come here with you?"

She shakes her head, still looking over the page. "He and my father had something to finish up. He's supposed to get here later this week though. You two should chat! My eyes always glaze over whenever he tries to talk to me about this stuff. I will give you his number. The four of us will probably be spending a lot of time together anyway." She takes one of my pens from the center of the table and jots it on the corner of the page in front of her. "His name is Feddei." She offers a small smile as she nudges the paper to me like it's a peace offering.

"Thanks."

We stare at each other until she jabs a thumb over her shoulder. "Right. I'll just—"

"Anya," I call before she can slip from the library.

She casts an uncertain glance at me over her shoulder, looking young and small and nothing like the glowing, intimidating creature who'd stood over me on the plane stairs.

"Thanks for apologizing. And I don't think it's ridiculous that we could be friends."

A sigh of relief loosens the last of the tension in her shoulders, and she gives me her first real smile since she stepped in here.

CHAPTER THIRTEEN

I EXPECT Auclair to be quiet when I rise well before the sun sets. Aside from the human servants, the corridors at the Carrington estate tended to be empty until the vampire residents rose after dark. I can't tell if the crowd here is usual or a product of the over-occupancy and dire situation that has officials working around the clock.

The gym, however, is mostly vacant when I step inside. Cam and I have trained in here only once since he prefers outdoors. A few Marionettes are by the squat racks, and they pay me no mind as I head for a treadmill to warm up.

I immediately miss my runs with Monroe as I start with a light jog. Her constant conversation was always distracting enough to get me through it, but now all I have is the music in my headphones as my out-of-shape lungs struggle through a mile.

I have half the mind to give myself a little magical aid.

Especially with how much power I have to spare these days, maybe sending a little to my tired muscles...

But then I remember how sudden it feels when it comes on. How overwhelming, like it's out of my control. Just the idea of making the cut has the adrenaline in my blood skyrocketing.

For the first time in my life, I think I might be afraid of my own magic.

The disgusting protein shake I chugged before coming here threatens to make a reappearance as I step off the machine, but I keep it down as I head for the punching bag next. A part of me thinks Cam designed the thing to taste bad, but I've been dutifully drinking them every day.

I run through as many of the combinations that I can remember, starting with punches, then kicks, then a mix of both. Sweat pours down my face, but it's like the harder my heart pumps in my chest, the less my mind spirals, giving me a few minutes of blissful quiet.

And it's not like I haven't done much harder things than getting back in shape.

Damsel in distress my ass.

"What are you doing in here?"

I blink, snapping back to my surroundings as the door clicks shut across the room and Cam steps inside, only now realizing the others must have left at some point. The sky is nearly dark through the windows behind him.

Cam frowns, his arms crossed over his chest. "We weren't scheduled for training today."

"I know." I readjust the Velcro on my glove.

"The rest days are important too."

I shrug, turning to the bag. "We skipped that one workout earlier this week. Figured I'd make up for it."

He says nothing as the smack of my fists against the bag fills the room again, but then his footsteps grow closer behind me. I don't turn, focusing on my punches, but then he sighs somewhere near my ear.

"You're not squaring your hips enough. You'll never get much power that way."

I throw another few punches, focusing more on my form. It's not that I don't know the proper way to do it—we had similar instructions at the academy—my body is *tired*, and it's much easier to throw out a lazy rep than engage all of the necessary muscles.

"I know you can do better than that." His hands land on my hips, forcing me to twist and follow through with each punch.

I drop my fists after a few moments, panting, and it takes Cam a beat too long to release me. It registers then how close he's standing, how clearly I can make out his earthy scent, the elevated rate of his heart in his chest.

I look at him over my shoulder, and his eyes meet mine, guarded, but there's another layer beyond that, a fire burning low.

The hairs on the back of my neck prickle, a million memories I don't want to think about pounding at the walls of my mind, begging to resurface. Glimpses of fingers trailing softly over skin, words murmured low in the dark.

Because if I let myself think about it, if I acknowledge the effect he still has on me, I can't pretend what happened between us was a moment of weakness, a lapse in judgment. A desperate attempt at distraction in a horrible situation.

But even if I manage to keep my mind clear, my body revels in the heat of him standing so close, the feel of his gaze as it drops from my eyes to my lips.

I can't even write it off as lust. There's some of that too, but this overwhelming feeling is *safe*. A silent understanding, *knowing*, in the deepest parts of my soul, that for some reason, I can rely on this man. Trust him.

And even though I know I shouldn't—I *can't*—a part of me still wants to.

The moment is suspended between us, something outside of time and logic. But then he steps away, taking all of the tension with him.

I swallow hard and bend to retrieve my water bottle. "What are you doing here? You hate this place."

He takes another step back, resting his shoulder against the mirrored wall. "I was walking by. Saw you through the window."

"And you were so appalled by my form you had to come intervene?" I say flatly.

He smirks. "What are you doing up so early?"

"What are *you* doing up so early?"

"Doesn't feel early to me," he says with a one-shouldered shrug. "The sun's out. Old habits die hard."

"Early risers, huh?"

I jump as the door clambers shut across the room and Anya steps inside in a matching black workout set and her hair slicked back in a high ponytail. She offers me a smile as she heads toward the weight section, picks up some dumbbells that look like they weigh more than she does, and shuffles toward the benches in front of the mirror.

"Oh, Valerie," she says. "That vampire I saw you at dinner with, is that your boyfriend?"

For a brief, ridiculous moment, a jolt goes through my system, and I think she's talking about Reid. But no, of course not. Good to know the charade we've been putting on is working. It's easy to forget the reason Connor's been tagging along when it just feels like having my old best friend back.

I can feel Cam looking at me, but I refuse to meet his gaze. "Um, yeah. His name is Connor. We've known each other forever."

"Well done. He's *cute.*" Anya snaps her fingers, then calls, "Attendant?" without looking at us. "A towel, if you could?"

"I'm not an attendant," Cam says flatly.

She smiles and bats her eyelashes at him over her shoulder. "My mistake." She situates herself on the bench and hefts the weights into her lap. "A spot then?"

I take slow sips of my water and watch in astonishment as Cam pushes off the wall and heads over to her. It's apparent after the first rep of shoulder presses that she has no need for him, so he drops his arms to his sides and takes a step back. She grins as she finishes and sets the dumbbells at her feet.

My eyes flick from her to Cam's face in the mirror, though Cam's expression gives nothing away, as usual. I raise an eyebrow as I try to catch the number written on the side of those weights. Her warmup weight, apparently. They kind of look like the same ones Cam was using the other day. Maybe heavier.

Anya meets my eyes in the mirror with a smirk. "Dump the wolf. I'd be a way better trainer."

I snort as Cam scowls and mutters, "I'll leave you to it then." He hesitates once he reaches the door. "Just...be careful, Valerie. Your progress has been good, but the strength won't come back overnight. Especially if you overwork yourself."

I nod, and he shoots one last look between me and Anya before opening the door and disappearing into the night.

CHAPTER FOURTEEN

ON THE RARE occasion I don't spend the day restlessly tossing and turning, the dreams that await me make me wish I had. It's a different one every time, but the feeling that lingers long after they're gone is always the same.

Snakes and knives carving into skin, whips and wolf claws tearing through flesh, sobs muffled into pillows and bodies on metal tables, exhaustion as a cuff clangs against my ankle, the sun beating down on my face, wrists bound in rope, bones tearing through skin, staring into the eyes of my mother, my sister, my father, all looking back with cold indifference—

"Hey, you're okay."

I blink, forcing my vision to clear. Reid peers at me from where he kneels beside my bed, forehead wrinkled in concern.

My heavy breathing fills the silence as my surroundings come into focus—bed. I'm in bed. My T-shirt is plastered to my chest with sweat.

What time is it? A sliver of light is glowing around the

outline of the curtains. Still daytime then. "What are you doing here?"

His frown deepens. "You were screaming."

I press the heels of my hands into my eye sockets like I can physically force the images out of my head. "Sorry," I mumble, not looking up. "I'm fine."

That couldn't be further from the truth, and I know he can feel it through the bond and see it in my trembling fingers, but instead of his presence bringing comfort the way it always has before, now it twists the knife deeper.

Because he's here, but he's not. Not really.

The weight of the covers lifts off me, and I snap my head up as Reid inches closer, like he's planning to climb in.

"Reid…"

"Move over," he says, his voice soft but inviting no debate.

I don't know why I oblige. Maybe because even with as much as him being here amplifies the pain in my chest, I know that watching him leave will be twice as bad. I scoot to the far side of the bed, leaving more than enough room for him.

An audible sigh escapes my lips as his body finds mine, my face buried in his chest, his hand in my hair, holding me there, the same way he's done several times in situations nearly identical to this one.

Only with one glaring, insurmountable difference.

Something shoves the thought into the back of my mind, letting it get swallowed by the dark until I forget about it completely.

"Just for today," he whispers. "Can we let it rest, just for today?"

Pretend everything is okay, he means.

Another shove, and it's forgotten.

He's so warm against me, and my body shivers, urging me closer, to intertwine my legs with his, to slide my hands beneath the back of his shirt, searching for skin-to-skin contact.

Just for today.

The last time I was wrapped up with him like this I'd been so stupidly happy. After my birthday dinner, when I told him I loved him for the first time.

Because I do. I love him so much my heart aches with it, trying to claw its way out of my body and into his.

His hand glides up and down my back, the touch only comforting, respectful. Not pushing the boundary of this strange line we've been tiptoeing, not even a little bit. The way he'd touch a friend, family.

Not the way he touches me.

And it makes me burn.

I shouldn't want this. I shouldn't want *him*. Not right now.

Those shadows in the back of my mind drift forward, swallowing everything in their path. Making me relax, making me forget. There's only this and now and him and me.

How could anything about this be wrong?

His smell fills my head with every inhale, and the way his bare skin feels against mine burrows deep past the surface, into my heart, my soul. And still, I want him closer.

His fingers brush the skin exposed between my shirt and underwear, lightly skimming over my hip. He trails to the side, then continues up my ribs, then back over to my spine. My eyes flutter shut, a heat that's not nearly as unwelcome as it should be winding in the pit of my stomach, venturing lower, low enough that my thighs involuntarily press together.

Reid's hand stills in the center of my back.

It occurs to me then that the bond is wide open between us, neither of us blocking the other out. There are no thoughts, no images, just heat rushing both ways, like a hot summer wind, but tight and magnetic. The lust pooling in my stomach coils tighter like an animal with a mind of its own.

Slowly, his hand starts moving again, trailing down to the exposed skin of my lower back, then lower, his fingers barely sliding beneath the elastic band of my underwear. He hesitates there, like he's waiting to see if I'll stop him.

It's so slow. The heat in my blood rages hotter, then I'm pushing Reid back by the chest.

His eyes go wide, but then he's on his back, and I straddle his lap, take his face between my hands, and bring his mouth to mine.

His slow, measured movements are gone the moment our lips touch. He seizes the back of my head with one hand, the other holding me to him as he sits up and presses our chests together. I grind my hips against him, a small moan catching in my throat as I find him already hard.

But as quickly as we'd started, he flips me onto my back, letting just the right amount of his weight press into me, his lips never leaving mine. I can't help but let out a breathless laugh.

"You can't let go of control for even a minute, can you?" I say on an exhale.

He runs his nose along the column of my throat before pressing kisses to my chest, my stomach, working his way down to my hips. I rip my shirt over my head as he slides my panties down and opens my legs wide for him.

"If you want control," he murmurs as his lips trail along my inner thigh, teasing me with his tongue and his teeth as he goes, his breath raising every hair on my body as it ghosts across my skin. "Then take it from me."

The challenge in his voice calls to that heat in my belly, but I can't decide what I'd like more—letting him have his way, or seeing him truly surrender to me for the first time.

He ducks his head between my legs before I have the chance to decide. But aside from a brief sweep of his tongue, he moves on, going lower before leaving the bed completely.

Brows pulling together, I prop myself on my elbows and watch as he rifles through my drawers.

I open my mouth to ask what he's doing, but then he returns with a handful of scraps of fabric, and I realize his intentions. He kneels at the end of the bed and looks up at me through his lashes.

"If you're planning on taking over, here's your last chance." He holds the knee-high sock up for emphasis, and in answer, I extend my leg in offering.

His grin is full of dark and wicked promises, but as he takes my foot in his hand, the kiss he presses to the inside of my ankle is gentle. The heat pooling low in my core blazes impossibly hotter as he binds each of my ankles to the ends of the bed frame, and his words from another night replay in my head.

If I had my way with you, I'd tie you to this bed and touch you and lick you and fuck you until you come so many times you physically can't anymore.

He moves on to my wrists next, securing them together in a single tie and fastening them above my head. He presses a soft kiss to the side of my neck as he tightens the knot. "Too tight?"

I shake my head.

"Last one."

I blink up at him, wondering what other part of me he could possibly tie down, when he pulls out a red scarf and loops it around my head. The moment it cuts off my sight, everything feels different.

The darkness, it leaves me nothing to focus on but myself. My body laid open and bare. The knots on the restraints aren't tight enough to keep me here if I don't want to be, but still. It's vulnerable in a way it's never been before. A shallow breath passes my lips, then another, my chest rising and falling in quick succession.

Warm hands press to either side of my face, and his voice is close when Reid murmurs, "You're safe with me, Valerie. Always. Nothing happens here that you don't want, you understand? You say the word, and everything stops."

I pull in another breath, and his thumb strokes my cheek.

"Do you trust me?" he asks.

I nod.

"Do you want me to stop now?"

I shake my head.

I ignite beneath his touch, heightened now that I've lost one of my senses. His fingers take their time trailing from my face, down my neck, over my collarbones, between my breasts, then back up, lightly circling my nipples. He grazes his knuckles against the sides of my breasts, beneath them, the touch so featherlight my body is already screaming for more.

Which must be exactly what he intends, because he never stays in one place for long, the light touch traveling over every inch of my body until I somehow feel it everywhere at once and nowhere at all.

It's just his fingertips at first, but then I feel his hot breath wash across the skin of my inner thigh as his mouth gets closer, and my muscles tighten in anticipation. But then the heat fades, and he goes back to running his fingers up one thigh, across my hips, and down the other, slowly getting closer and closer to where I want him.

I adjust myself on the bed, shimmying my hips farther down, and a small whine escapes me.

Either not hearing it—or, what's more likely, ignoring me —Reid flattens his palms on the outside of my thighs, his fingers digging in, and then finally, *finally*, I feel his tongue.

He barely brushes my clit, but my hips jolt as the air whooshes from my lungs, the anticipation already having me wound so tight I know it won't take long.

He kisses the insides of my thighs before returning to my core, but again, barely brushes it. I don't even bother trying to disguise the whine this time.

But then he prods at my entrance, a single finger sliding inside, and I sigh, my head tilting back in the pillows. He strokes me gently, slowly, before adding a second finger and curling them both inside me, hitting exactly the right spot to make me moan.

A warm, thudding pleasure radiates down the bond, spreading from my chest to my stomach to between my thighs.

I can't tell if it's mine or his or he's stroking the line connecting us to amplify the sensations coming from his tongue and his fingers.

But still, he says nothing, just works his fingers faster, harder, until I'm panting, my hips struggling to rise from the bed to meet each of his thrusts.

He's not usually this quiet. All I can hear are my own breaths, the slick sound of his fingers pumping in and out of me, my heartbeat pounding in my ears.

"Reid?" I breathe, and it comes out like a question.

A loud buzzing fills the room instead of his reply, and my head jerks up. Is that my...when did he have a chance to find my vibrator?

I open my mouth, but no words come out, only a loud, drawn-out moan as he lowers the vibrator to my clit, and then nothing else exists in this moment. His fingers keep the same pace, and my breathing quickens as blistering, intoxicating heat floods through me.

But then he pulls the vibrator away, and I gasp, my wrists straining against their ties. His tongue takes its place, and I grind my hips, desperately trying to get the lost orgasm back, and he pulls away again.

"Reid," I all but cry, my chest heaving. My inner thighs burn from scratching against his stubble—

"Reid...?" My voice comes out small, uncertain. He's almost always clean-shaven. I would've noticed if...

The large length of him replaces his fingers, nudging at my entrance, but then continuing up, sliding along the slickness between my thighs, and I gasp as he grinds against my clit. He seems to be in no hurry though, languidly stroking himself against me until I'm panting and desperately arching my hips up to meet him.

Before I can let out another plea, he thrusts inside so quickly that my breath catches. With how fucking wet I am at this point, there's no resistance. Instinctively, I try to wrap my legs around him or reach for his arms now braced on either side of my head, but then the restraints register again, leaving me help- less to his thrusts as they slowly increase in speed and force.

Fuck. The heat tears through me as pressure builds in my chest. There have been times with Reid that were rough, but this…this feels like…

Ice floods my veins as the man on top of me leans forward, the scruff on his jaw scraping the side of my neck as he murmurs in my ear, "You're doing so good for me, princess."

Princess.

"C-Cam?"

"That's it." He pounds into me harder, deeper. "God, I almost forgot how fucking good you feel."

Before I can string together a thought, he pulls out, then I feel his fingers working into the knot around my ankle. Once he has one leg free, he situates himself behind me, laying me half on top of his lap.

The pressure in my chest fades, and the fog in my mind clears.

What had I been so surprised by? Of course this is Cam. It's been Cam the whole time.

My head falls back with another moan as his fingers stroke my clit and one of his knees comes up to help support my weight as I lean into him. He hums low in his throat as his mouth trails down my neck, my chest, until he pulls my nipple between his teeth.

He lets out an appreciative groan as he rubs himself along the length of me again, positioning himself at my opening and using one hand to angle my hips.

"You need to come, princess?"

A needy, animal-like noise escapes me.

"Then show me."

With only one unbound leg to work with, I struggle to lower myself onto him, but his hands are there on my hips, guiding me. We both gasp at the same time as I bring every last inch of him in.

"I'm all yours, but you'll have to take what you want."

He doesn't move, just keeps one hand on my hip, the other pressing against my throat as he holds me to him and waits for me to take over.

His groan rumbles in his chest as I grind my hips, slowly at first, then circle, testing different angles, breathless despite barely moving just from how he stretches and fills me almost to a painful degree.

I fall into a rhythm, Cam not moving a single inch, letting me control the depth and speed.

"Does that feel good?" he asks lowly.

I let out an answering moan as the heat in my core winds tighter. It gets harder to keep going, my hips spasming and freezing, desperately needing more but somehow also losing function in my body.

"You think you can stop just because you're going to come?" Cam breathes, his fingers digging into my hip as he guides me back to my original pace, now thrusting up to meet me each time.

I let out a helpless moan, my hands desperately wrapping around their restraints.

"Fuck, princess, you should see yourself," he breathes, then tugs at my blindfold until it releases.

But it's not Cam or our bodies together that my gaze lands on.

It's Reid sitting in a chair in the corner, legs stretched out casually in front of him. His eyes meet mine, but none of the emotions I expect to find are there. Just fiery, untamed desire. As if in agreement, the bond burns in my chest.

Cam loosens his arm around my chest. "It's okay." His lips trail along the side of my throat. "I won't make you choose."

Reid leans his forearms on his thighs, his eyes never leaving mine.

Cam's stubble scrapes along the delicate skin behind my ear. "What'll it be, princess? Would you rather have him in your mouth or me?"

Reid slowly rises from the chair, the extent of his arousal stretching the fabric of his pants. My heart pounds furiously in my chest as he approaches. I can't read his face, can't tell how he feels about seeing me like this with Cam.

But before I can speak, he reaches around the two of us for the discarded vibrator at the end of the bed.

My breaths turn into pants as he kneels beside my face, the anticipation leaving me trembling.

"Keep riding or it stops," Reid rasps, a promise in his eyes.

I don't dare look away but do as he says, lifting my hips and searching for my earlier rhythm.

"Good girl."

A loud buzzing fills the air as he switches the vibrator on and lowers it, not directly onto my clit, but just above, making me struggle to grind myself against it.

The moment it makes contact, I lose all the air in my lungs, my back arching, legs tensing.

But then he pulls back. "What did I say?"

I realize I stopped moving. With a groan, I struggle to get my hips back up, and Cam adjusts himself to better support my weight. He kisses my neck as Reid turns the vibrator on. "That's it."

The pressure mounts inside of me again, and he edges the vibrator away, trailing it along my hips and inner thighs instead. The buzzing cuts off, and he runs the toy between my legs without the vibrations, giving my clit the slightest pressure. I whimper and let out a breathy, pathetic "Please."

"Oh, let her have it," says Cam. "Look how hard she's trying."

One of them pinches my nipple between their fingers, but I'm so close and the world is blurry and I can't breathe—

"I've got it," Cam says near my ear, and it takes me a moment to realize he's not talking to me. He takes the vibrator from Reid with his free hand, making sure it stays firmly in place against me as he turns it back on, and despite the fact I've become leaden with pleasure, barely moving my hips at this point, he thrusts up at just the right angle over and over, his face buried in the crook of my neck as he lets me come.

"Fuck," I cry out, my only free leg locking desperately around Cam as my back arches off the bed. A zipper sounds somewhere on my other side as Reid shoves off his pants, then he brushes the hair from my face as the shaking in my body slows.

"Tell me what you want, Valerie," he says, standing there so perfect and naked and ready.

Without thinking, no matter how lewd it comes across, I turn my head and open my mouth wide for him.

His eyes darken and his nostrils flare as he rakes his fingers through my hair until he reaches the back of my head, cradling where my skulls meets my spine. But he doesn't come any closer.

"I want you, Reid," I breathe. "I want you to use my mouth."

Cam releases my wrists from the headboard so they're no longer secure above my head but still bound together. Then he rolls me onto my side, sinking the rest of the way into me from behind as Reid positions himself at my mouth, running his tip along my tongue and lips. His eyes fall half-closed as he gently pushes inside, just a few inches at first.

Cam stills inside of me as I get used to the feeling of both of them.

"Breathe," Reid commands. I do as he says, breathing through my nose, and he pushes in deeper, past the back of my throat. I gag, and he tightens his grip on my head as he stills again, not pulling out but not going any deeper.

"Breathe."

My lungs ache, an instinctual panic setting in as my body fights the intrusion filling my throat, but I force myself to breathe through my nose again, and he pushes deeper, impossibly deeper.

It somehow feels more vulnerable than anything else,

trusting him completely as he holds my head in place, positioning the angle just right, and orders me again to breathe.

"Relax here," he murmurs, his other hand stroking just behind my jaw. I swallow around him, trying to get my throat to relax, and his eyelids flutter. "That's it," he grits out. "You're doing so well, baby."

Heat sings through my blood like pride, reveling in the look on Reid's face, like he's fighting not to come undone.

Just when I start to feel like I can't take it for a moment longer, Reid pulls out, searching my face as I cough and saliva falls from my lips. I'm sure I look like a flushed, breathless mess, but his eyes darken even more at the sight, and my skin grows hot at the hungry way he takes me in. I nod, letting him know I'm okay, and swallow hard before opening my mouth again.

Cam's arm tightens around my chest, holding me to him. His fist is around the restraints on my wrists, positioning my hands by my stomach but giving me enough slack to move.

"You need to stop, you just tap either of us, okay?" Cam says.

I nod, and the buzz of the vibrator fills the room as Reid slips past my lips and Cam drives in. I moan around Reid as the two work me in tandem and Cam lowers the vibrator back to my clit. No games this time, just exactly where I need it.

I choke as Reid hits the back of my throat, and he pauses, letting me catch my breath before grasping my head with both hands and thrusting in deeper, harder, though his hands on my head keep a gentle hold, stroking my cheeks and brushing my hair out of my face. My throat relaxes a bit more, surrendering to him. Cam finds the same pace behind me.

The slams of Reid against the back of my throat blot out all other sounds, and my chest tightens, fighting for breath, but I can tell that he's close by his increasingly jerky movements and his labored breath above me.

I moan around him, and he sucks in a sharp breath, his fingers in my hair tightening. Cam murmurs something I can't understand in my ear.

The sensations fill me, pleasure twisting into pain into everything into oblivion. It's almost too much, or it is too much. I can't breathe, I can't think, I can't, I can't—

CHAPTER FIFTEEN

COMING out of the dream is violent. I lurch up in bed covered in sweat. I whip my head to both sides, finding the room empty and, horrifyingly, my hand down my pants. I snatch it back like I burned myself, then shove myself out of bed as if I can physically put more distance between me and the dream.

Oh my God. *Oh my God.*

Where the *fuck* did that come from?

I'm still hot and too tightly wound, and when I move, I can feel how wet I am.

God, I hope Reid didn't see any of that down the bond. I check for any emotion in my chest that doesn't belong to me, but it's quiet, calm. Not like he's blocking me out, just like he's asleep.

What was *that*?

Even my subconscious can't be that fucked up. It feels like a betrayal. No matter what Reid's done or the mistakes he's made, I still don't want to do anything that would hurt him.

And this...

I check the clock, realizing I'm due to meet Cam for training in a half hour. And even though I know I'll be sweaty and disgusting after we're done, I jump in the shower now. Showing up in this state is not an option. He'd probably be able to smell it or some other weird wolf-trick.

Cam.

It doesn't occur to me until I'm dressed and halfway to our meeting spot.

But the first conversation we had here...the connection he thought transferring the blood deal left behind.

I shove through the doors with renewed purpose, my hands balled into fists as I search the grounds for him. The sun just set moments ago, leaving behind a hint of the day's heat.

"You're early," Cam observes as I find him setting up weights and resistance bands in the grass. He shoves up the sleeves of his hoodie as he rises back to his full height. "You—"

I slap him across the face.

He stumbles back a step, eyes widening. "What the hell, Darkmore?"

I follow him, getting right in his face as I point a finger. Not at all affected by how gold his eyes are, how I can still remember exactly how those lips, that beard felt against my skin.

"You stay the fuck out of my head," I snap, partially to him, partially to myself. "I don't know what game you're playing—"

His tongue flicks out to wet his lips, and I don't look. I

don't pay attention to his mouth at all. I don't remember the way he held me through my orgasm, how he murmured in my ear, how it—

"Hold on, what are you talking about?"

I can't look him in the eyes. I can't look at his lips, his fingers. And God, being this close to him, I can *smell* him. How did he even manage to get the scent right in the dream? It's full of trees, campfires, and fresh air, something deeper and muskier lingering beyond the surface.

"I mean it, Cam. Whatever this weird connection is between us, find a way to get rid of it. I don't care if I have to take that damn deal back—"

"Princess—"

"*Don't* call me that. And if you pull that shit again, I will kill you." The words don't have nearly as much bite to them as they should. I thrust my finger into his face again. "Stay out of my dreams."

He opens his mouth to respond but stops himself. Something seems to occur to him, because the confusion pinching his brow together softens.

The following silence threatens to swallow me whole as we stare at each other.

But then finally, in a voice far too calm, he says, "I wouldn't know how to get into your head if I tried, Darkmore. And I haven't felt anything from that connection since that one time."

I blink, taking a step back from him. He could be lying, but I don't think he is.

But then...I...that would mean...

Heat creeps up the back of my neck, prickling my scalp, and I wait for him to say something else. A suggestive comment, maybe. To point out that I clearly just revealed something mortifying to him.

But instead, he meets my eyes, holding them for a moment that feels much longer than it is, and juts his chin to the side. "Two laps, then we'll get started."

———

THE NIGHT COMES AND GOES, and still no sign of Reid. No feelings from him through the bond either. If there's been news on the Carrington estate situation—or James Westcott— no one's telling me. A search through news sites and social media for updates proves fruitless as well.

I haven't been back to the tower's roof since the night the Marionette leapt from the edge, the memory too fresh, but it seems no one else has either, leaving it the perfect place to get some peace and quiet.

At the Carrington estate, I'd opt for the garden, but from what I've seen in my short time at Auclair, there's much more foot traffic here than back home. The path from the servants' quarters to the estate cuts directly through the gardens, so there's constant movement back and forth. The view from up here is usually the best on the grounds, but the fog is thick tonight, mingling with the darkness and snuffing out the light from the stars and the moon.

With a moment longer of hesitation than usual, I prick my finger to light the torches along the railing. They ignite at once, the thick flames standing proud against the dark, but thankfully, just as quickly as it'd come, my magic ebbs away again without a fight.

I swing my legs over the side to sit on the ledge, looking out at the never-ending darkness. If it weren't for the flames flickering around me, I might think I was back in the shadow world.

I feel it when he starts looking for me. The bond in my chest rises from sleep. That feeling expands, building and filling the rest of my body until I hear the metallic creak of the door behind me opening.

I don't turn, and he doesn't say anything as he makes his way forward, climbs onto the ledge beside me, and hangs his legs over the side. I haven't seen him since the shadow projecting spell three nights ago. Every one of my senses is hyper alert, like the chemistry in my body has been craving his presence, no matter what my mind has to say on the matter. Now pure instinct is fighting to lean over, to touch him, to let myself fall into him.

But all the recent reminders of our situation are fresh in my mind. The conversation with Anya in the library, seeing her in the gym. What Magnolia told me.

What's also fresh in my mind is that damn dream.

Do I tell him about that? But that would be pointless, wouldn't it? People have weird dreams all the time. They don't mean anything.

"A scouting team reported back about one of Westcott's compounds," Reid finally says. "It's south of here, down in Washington. It's close enough to Locklear to get their attention. They've been in discussions with Auclair and my mother. But even still, they're not confident about the numbers. Especially since we don't know how many other compounds we're dealing with, or where they are."

I nod slowly, a confusing tangle of emotions warring in my chest.

He's here to talk about business. I don't know what I'd been expecting. And I'm his partner. Of course I want to know what's going on.

"The scouts also reported something else. No one knew quite what to make of it, but I thought you might be able to."

That gets me to look at him.

The troubled pinch in his forehead is more pronounced than usual. "They reported seeing people wearing a single shackle, kind of like what you had at the camp."

The cuffs. I can taste the smoke in the blacksmith tent at the memory, feel the cramps in my fingers as I spent hour after hour helping assemble them.

Feel the pain blazing through my arm as Terrence branded me.

"What kind of people?" I murmur.

"Humans, witches, everyone. The scouts said it looked like everyone was going about their day as normal. No signs of distress or anything like that. Not the way someone being forced to wear it would act. Do you know anything about this?"

I shake my head a few times. "I—they were making them at the camp. I helped make them. I don't know what they're for. They aren't the same as mine. It wasn't red salt embedded in there, but there was something. Cam said he thought they might be for protection against vampires."

"Were you looking for me earlier?" he asks suddenly. "I thought I felt something from you, but I wasn't sure."

"I was." An eerie numbness slugs through my veins, and I grasp my hands together in my lap. "I went to see Magnolia, and she told me some things…about you."

"About me? What did she say?"

I dig my nails into my palms and focus on the darkness, my voice nearly getting lost to the wind as I say, "Does the word *anapófefktos* mean anything to you?"

He doesn't respond for what feels like a very long time. Long enough that I peek at him out of the corner of my eye. His gaze is lowered to his hands so I can't quite see his expression.

Finally, he murmurs, "Yes."

We meet each other's eyes, and the intensity there makes my breath hitch. But then the look in his eyes softens like he's smiling, though his mouth doesn't move.

"You knew," I breathe.

"Of course I knew," he whispers. "How could I not?"

"I didn't."

He leans his head to one side, acknowledging this. "You were still just a witch when we met. If you'd already turned, it might have been different. Throw in the bond between a new vampire and their maker *and* our partnership bond, and I imagine it would've been impossible to discern what feeling was what."

A small smirk rises to my lips. "Sounds like you've given this a lot of thought."

A slight red hue touches his cheeks, and he ducks his head. I don't know if I've ever seen him blush before, but I immediately know it's my new favorite sight.

But also...if he thought about this so much, maybe he was worried. That he felt the connection and I didn't. Trying to reason out why. My stomach tightens at the thought.

"How long have you known?"

The curl of his lips is subtle, almost rueful. "I think I knew deep down since the moment I met you. But it was a lot clearer after you turned."

"You never—why didn't you say anything?"

"You've had so much on your plate," he says softly. "And things between us have been complicated from the start, so it never felt like the right time to bring it up. And if you had wanted to be with Connor or Cam instead...I never wanted you to feel obligated. I still don't. The connection might be there, but the choice is yours."

Choice. The word sounds all wrong. "Does it feel like a choice to you?"

Because even in the moments it felt like I was making a choice, it was never really a question, was it? It was always a matter of finding the courage to make the choice I wanted, consequences be damned. But this being the one thing that always felt the most right has never changed.

His fingers brush mine. He waits for me to pull away, but when I don't, he laces his fingers through mine. "It's both," he says. "It's something that feels inevitable, but it's also something I would choose for myself. The connection might have drawn me to you, but that's not what made me fall in love with you."

He brushes his thumb over the bones in my wrist and I exhale a shaky breath.

"I fell in love with you because of the kindness you showed to humans even when it put you at risk. The way you didn't act differently with me because of my title. Even before we'd really gotten to know each other, you were still out here making demands and shoving your nose into my business." He smiles as he says it, shaking his head a little. "I fell in love with the way you care about your friends and how hard you work, how at peace you look when you're playing your violin and the way your face is so expressive that I can always tell exactly what you think about something. How you somehow never turned cold or cruel despite the cards life has dealt you. I love your laugh and the way you scrunch your nose, and I don't believe for a minute that I wouldn't have fallen for you just the same, *anapófefktos* or not."

I fight to blink back tears.

"You might not have known as soon as I did, but can you feel it now?" he whispers.

A vibration sings in my chest, through my blood, like the cells in my body, down to the smallest particles, are answering for me. And looking into his eyes, there's not a doubt in my mind. Not a stray thought or worry or question. Instead, my mind is filled with perfect, blissful silence.

Whatever he sees in my face must be answer enough for him, because he smiles, the expression soft, almost shy, making him look years younger. I'm seized with the urge to trace the lines of his face, the subtle dimple in his cheek, the soft hair falling across his forehead. To memorize every detail of him. To lose myself in this silent language where neither of us has to say anything at all, but somehow, I know we're on exactly the same wavelength.

But I pull back an inch, then another, trying to force the haze away. Because as much as I don't want to, there *are* more important things for us to be talking about right now.

"Magnolia told me something else. She said there was something in your mind that you couldn't remember. I think she meant a magical block."

He leans back, putting another inch between us that feels like a mile as he searches my face. "You think someone planted something in my head that I don't have access to."

"She said…well, she said something about why you and I were paired. That my mother had something to do with it. Something that you can't remember. Does that ring any bells?"

"Actually, yes." There's something uncertain about the crease in his forehead now. "When I told you my mother was the reason we got paired, that wasn't the truth. I asked for you."

We stare at each other as my brain slowly processes the words, and the unease in his expression only seems to grow.

He asked for me. But then he told me it was his mother's decision.

He just needed a nudge, Magnolia had said.

"Why?" I whisper.

"Do you remember what we talked about at the art studio? About why I was looking into Westcott."

"You said you didn't know. That it felt like the idea had been planted in your head by someone else—"

"I don't know how I didn't make the connection before," he says, almost to himself. "I had this feeling that I had to be paired with you for initiation, but I didn't know why. I'd chalked it up to wanting to get to know you. But it's a feeling I've only felt when I got back here and started looking into Westcott." The tension between his eyebrows eases as he puts the pieces together. "You think you can get to it."

I give a slow nod. "I've researched it. But you don't have to. I know it's really invasive."

"Valerie, you're already in my head half the time anyway. I don't have anything to hide from you."

I search his eyes, so open and blue and trusting.

"Okay," I whisper.

It's a spell I've never performed myself, though I've seen it plenty of times—had it used on me once by the queen and my mother. I know how it feels on Reid's side of things, but no way of preparing myself for what's coming for me.

I brace myself for the magic again, but the sting of my blade is almost a relief as I press the tip to my finger. I do the same to Reid's hand, then smear the mixture of our blood between my fingertips before pressing them to Reid's temples.

I let out a long exhale and close my eyes. The darkness is immediate, a different kind than the undersides of my eyelids. And it's also oddly familiar. Like touching Reid's skin or smelling his aftershave. I'd recognize this darkness as his, even if I hadn't known ahead of time. I wonder if it would feel like this with anyone I'm close to, or if it's just him.

At first it feels like I've dropped into the middle of the ocean, frantically spinning with waves crashing, not sure which direction is the surface. But as I focus on the steady heat of the bond in my chest and my breath to ground myself, a flicker of light catches the corner of my eye.

I drift toward it, its presence so clearly foreign here. Everything that makes up Reid's mind—his thoughts, his memories—they *feel* like him. This, however, does not.

Small threads drift past me as I inch toward the light, like trails of smoke. I have no idea what damage I'd cause by interacting with anything in here, so I'm careful to avoid them.

When I reach the light, there's no warmth coming from it despite how much it resembles the sun. It's barely larger than the palm of my hand.

And though it doesn't feel like Reid, for some reason, it feels familiar in its own way.

I catch myself holding my breath as I reach for it. What if this isn't what I think it is? What if touching it somehow permanently screws with something in Reid's head? What if—

A jolt of electricity shoots up my arm at the contact, and in the blink of an eye, the darkness around me disappears, morphing into a different scene entirely.

Suddenly I'm standing in an outdoor corridor that I recognize from pictures of the Russian estate.

I gasp as a flash of movement catches the corner of my eye and whip around to face—

Reid.

He's leaning against the building, gaze focused somewhere out in the distance, a pained look on his face that makes my own chest ache. His breath puffs up in a cloud around him, and it's not until then that I notice the snow on the ground. But when he turns his head, he looks straight through me.

"What are you doing here?" he asks.

High heels click behind me, coming closer, and I turn.

My mother smiles as she approaches, and my breath

hitches, at first thinking she's looking at Reid behind me, but no, her eyes are locked on *me*.

But that's not possible. This is a memory. I'm not really here.

But then she reaches for my hand—and makes contact.

CHAPTER SIXTEEN

I GASP as my mother tightens her fingers around mine and pulls me a step closer, and I realize how tight her smile is, her eyes shifting back and forth as if preparing for a threat to jump out at us.

"We don't have much time," she says.

"How are you—what is this—can Reid see this?"

"No, no." She shakes her head, and every muscle in my body tenses as she cradles both sides of my face, her hands gentle as she looks me over. I can't remember her *ever* touching me like this. "You look better."

"What the hell is going on? You...you're the one who planted the idea in Reid's head to get paired with me."

"Yes," she says, impatiently waving her hand, as if the detail is minor. "Now, did you get the book?"

"Oh my God," I breathe.

It was her.

She went to see Reid in Russia, where he'd been when he was still partnered with Graham.

It's a topic we've never talked much about. Even giving me the smallest details, I could tell how much pain it caused him to recall it.

Graham didn't just die. Someone made him attack Reid relentlessly, and whether it was self-defense or not, I know that guilt weighs heavily on him.

He didn't just lose his best friend that night. He also had to shoulder the burden that it was at his hands.

He'd assumed it was a vampire who glamoured Graham.

I stare at my mother, somehow immediately knowing the truth and desperately trying to bury it in the back of my mind.

Because that would mean that Graham died so I could live.

She shakes me. *"Did you get the book?"*

"Yes, yes, I have it."

"Good." Her fingers tighten on my cheeks. "Now I need you to listen to me very closely."

"No." I take a step back, forcing her to drop her hands, a fire sparking in my chest. "You have kept me in the dark about everything for the past twenty-two years. *Twenty-two years.* If you want me to listen to a word you say, then I need the truth, for once, about what the *fuck* is going on."

I expect her to bulldoze right over that too, but she looks at me for a moment, really looks at me, then sighs. "Where do you want me to start?"

A hysterical laugh gets caught in my throat because where could I possibly start? She's been lying to me for my entire life.

"You're at one of Westcott's compounds now?"

She nods.

"How? How could you possibly join him after everything he's done? After he——"

"There's a lot that you don't know, Valerie. It was safer for you not to know. And I know what you must think of me. I know because that's the way it had to be. If there had been any other way, I would have taken it."

She takes a step closer, and I don't pull away as she wraps a hand around my wrist. "The spell I did to bring you back took a lot of my magic out of me. Not all, but most. Enough that I knew I would no longer be welcome at the estates, certainly not fit in my partnership anymore. Which would lead to questions about *why* it was necessary for me to transfer those powers to you, and that would expose your magic. So I left. As for your father...like it or not, this compound was the one place I knew would be safe. I've made a lot of enemies over the years, Valerie, enemies who would love to jump at this opportunity when I don't have my magic. If I hadn't come here...well, you and I wouldn't be having this conversation. And I came here for Calliope."

"Did you know she was alive?" I demand. "Did you let me and Adrienne think she——"

"No," she insists, her voice firm, and despite the million reasons I shouldn't trust a word she says, I believe her.

And despite the way Calla and I left things, I can't help myself from asking, "Is she okay?"

A softness I've rarely seen descends over Mom's eyes. "Yes. She's fine. She also told me what happened while you were here." I brace myself for a lecture, an insult, an admonishment

—something. But she smiles. "I can't tell you how proud of you I am, Valerie."

"Don't," I snap, ripping my arm out of her grasp, refusing to let the hurt little kid version inside of me glow beneath that praise, because I'm pretty sure that's the first time she's ever said that to me. "Don't pretend to care."

She has the audacity to look hurt. "Valerie."

"You told me I was dead to you, do you remember that?"

Her jaw tightens, but she says nothing.

"Or never mind that, what about the hundreds, maybe thousands, of other insults you've thrown at me over the years? What about you telling me you wish I'd died instead of Calla? Or this?" I yank my sleeve up, showing the scar she purposefully left behind on my forearm. "Or my perfume? You poisoned it, didn't you?"

She doesn't blink, and very calmly, she says, "Yes."

I think I'd already known the truth deep down but hearing her confirm it is still so much worse. I shake my head and turn away from her.

"Valerie—"

"No."

"*Valerie.*" She grabs my arm and yanks me to a stop, then steps around to force herself into my sight. "You have no idea the lengths I've gone to protect you. You hate me because I made sure that you would. Your final trial for initiation was to kill Connor because the queen saw your loyalty to him as a threat. And he was just a boyfriend. How do you think she felt when *her* Marionette went and had children?"

I stumble back a step as if her words physically struck me.

"It started with Calliope, but she was willing to let it slide as long as I performed at the same level I did before. But then I had you, and—" She breaks off and clenches her jaw, an emotion I can't read filling her eyes. "You almost didn't make it," she murmurs. "You were so small, and it took magic practically around the clock to keep you breathing for the first few weeks. You were so…breakable. I knew you would never survive in an environment like ours. Not like that."

I grit my teeth, a tear escaping the corner of my eye.

"But I could feel the power in you, even back then. Even before you were…" She trails off, her hand coming to her stomach. "I knew what you could grow up to be. I just had to make sure you survived that long. But if the queen saw that, that…*attention* on you, she would've taken more notice. And with the two of us bound together, I could never keep that much from her. So yes, I was a monster to you. To all of you. Because if I hadn't been, you would've been too soft to make it. Because if I hadn't been, it would've been the three of you on that throne room floor while she demanded I prove *my* loyalty. So you can hate me all you want, Valerie, but everything I have done has been to keep you alive."

I stop bothering to try keeping the tears back. They stream down my cheeks as a montage of memories plays. Every insult, every hit, every punishment. There had been little pockets though, when the cruelty would subside. When I'd see a glimpse of an entirely different version of her. But then she'd catch herself, and over the years, I convinced myself I'd imagined those better moments, twisted dreams into memories.

"And the poison?" I manage.

She shakes her head. "It was a gamble. Magnolia helped come up with the potion. We'd *hoped* it might suppress your vampire side, or at least the most noticeable aspects of it, until you made it through initiation. At the very least, I thought it might make you stand out less in your tasks so the queen wouldn't notice how much more powerful you were than your peers."

"You could have told me."

The softness in her eyes fades, replaced with a look I'm much more familiar with. "I could have done a lot of things differently, Valerie. But I made the choices I made, and I have to live with them."

"How are you here then? If you don't have your magic?" I gesture around us. "What is *this*?"

"You could feel the difference in this memory, couldn't you? You could tell it didn't belong to him?"

I nod.

"That's because it belongs to me. Magic always leaves a trace, and even if I might not be able to do what I once could, I still have that connection to the traces I've left."

"So, what? You knew I'd come looking for this?"

She blinks like she's surprised by the question. "No. I merely locked it away so *he* wouldn't remember it. So he wouldn't question what happened—anything that might get in the way of the two of you being paired. I had no idea you would come here. But I felt it when you stepped into this memory, like a security system."

A gust of wind rushes past us, the surrounding image of Vasiliev starting to blur. She grabs both of my arms, forcing her face right in front of mine.

"I understand what I'm asking you to do is unthinkable. But it must be done, and I can't help you now. Your father's cause might have been a noble one to begin with, but with all of the magic he's absorbed over the years, tinged with the life forces of their owners, he's changed. It's rewired his brain so much that he's not in his right mind anymore. He can't lead this many people. We can't let him have this kind of power. He's beyond reasoning with."

"So you want me to what, take over his mind so I can give that power to *you?*"

Her lips press into a hard line. "He believes his vision for a more inclusive government can't live if the monarchies do, which means he isn't going to leave a single royal vampire alive. He thinks they'll always pose too much of a threat. The same goes for anyone who sides with them. If we don't stop him, Valerie, he will kill them all—"

CHAPTER SEVENTEEN

I COME BACK to reality like someone physically grabs me by the hair and yanks me out of Reid's head. No, not by my hair, by the bond.

Vertigo tears through my system, the disorientation so strong for a moment I can't tell which way is up. The colors are too bright, the sounds too loud.

"We have to go."

I blink, trying to force my vision to focus. Hands are on my face, my arms.

"Valerie."

The world dips and spins, and it takes me a moment to realize it's because I'm no longer on my feet. Reid takes the stairs at a run, me tucked against his chest. When we reach the main level, the corridors are packed with people. The emergency alarm shrills overhead, drenching the halls in red light.

I tap Reid's arm to let him know I'm okay enough to

stand, and he sets me on my feet but keeps an arm around my waist for support.

"What's happening?" I ask.

Reid shakes his head, eyes locked on the chaos around us.

"Oh, Connor!" He's a few people away, but he turns at my voice and shoulders his way toward us. "What's going on?"

But then I see what everyone's flocking to.

I cover my mouth with my hand. "Oh my God."

Reid follows my gaze and stiffens.

I can barely make out his features, but it's unmistakably King Locklear's head mounted on the wall. His eyes are still open, his hair matted with blood.

I'm no stranger to gore, but the gruesome display makes even my stomach flip. Then there's the message painted on the wall around him in what looks to be blood.

Your days are numbered.

"Clear the halls!" bellows a faceless voice.

A few people scatter like mice, but most don't budge. Even through the ruckus, I can make out the booming footsteps approaching. I get a glimpse of King Auclair, followed by a line of Marionettes, but then someone tugs me back. I search for Connor, but he's lost in the crowd again.

Two Marionettes I've never seen before urge me and Reid down a different corridor until we come to the back door of the throne room. Several other officials are already waiting inside, along with their Marionettes. A few Auclair staff members nod along as Sawyer barks orders at them, demanding answers about the security breach. The voices in the room layer over one another, blending until I can't make out who is saying what.

"One of the security cameras must have caught something—"

"How could they pull this off in the middle of the night without someone seeing—"

"Has anyone been able to contact anyone at Locklear—"

The front door to the throne room bursts open as King Auclair strides inside, his expression remarkably calm given the circumstances.

"The Locklear estate has fallen, and the surrounding region is deserted, just like we saw with the Carrington estate," he says. "We're gathering all nonessential Marionettes, including some volunteers from the other estates. One of our own believes they can take out a good number of their wendigos if they can combine enough power. Since Westcott seems to be using the wendigos to weaken an area before he seizes it, it should at least slow him down. We believe these compounds of his are strategically placed near each of the estates. We've found the exact locations of two and have scouts out to search for the others."

I bite my tongue. *Take out the wendigos.* All I can think about is the people strapped to the metal tables in Westcott's compound for his experiments. Most of them are human. Foolish for trusting Westcott, but innocent.

But that won't matter to anyone in this room.

"How did no one receive word of Locklear's death in the time it took to get the body here—"

"Has the footage been checked yet? How did they get inside—"

"Should we be evacuating to the bunker—"

"*Enough,*" roars King Auclair. The Marionettes behind him

189

fan out, herding groups from the crowd and toward the different doors.

"You two." Queen Carrington approaches and gestures for us to follow her.

I exchange a glance with Reid, and he gives a solemn nod. The halls are buzzing with energy, though they're a little less crowded now as we follow the queen to her guest suite. I expect a few Marionettes to follow—Coderre at the very least —but it's just us three, and she locks the door behind us.

A weird feeling settles in the pit of my stomach as Queen Carrington levels her gaze on me, her stare not cold, exactly. Just...blank.

There's nothing behind her eyes, but I see it the moment that changes, like a light switch flicking on. Slowly, she cocks her head to the side and says, "Have you given my offer any more thought, Valerie?"

Her voice comes out low, not even sounding like her.

No.

"Reid…"

But she is a blur of motion before I manage to get the word out. Instead of lunging for me, she pivots and goes for him.

"No!" I shriek as the two of them crash into the glass coffee table and a million shards scatter through the room. Reid recovers quickly and flips her onto her back. She bears her fangs and hisses.

I carve into my wrist with the blade from my ring, tightening my fist around the blood. I focus on her muscles, trying to freeze her in place. Her movements slow, but she doesn't stop. I dig my nails into my palm, adding more blood to the mix, but now her hands are around Reid's throat, and it dawns on me far too late that this isn't like last time. The last person sent with a message killed himself once he was done.

She's been instructed to kill *Reid*.

No matter how much I bleed, she fights through my restraints. She's too old, too powerful. *How is Westcott even able to control her?*

Glass shatters a second time as Reid smashes the teapot over her head, and she stumbles back a step. Shards catch in her hair, her crown.

Everything in my body goes cold.

Break the teeth.

I don't think. I just move.

If I'm right about this, I have a feeling they won't break easily. She whips around and hisses, giving Reid the chance to push to his feet. Even as facing her feels like staring down death, all I can think is *I can't let Reid go through this again.*

He already feels responsible for Graham. And no matter how horrible she is, she's his mom.

I grab a wooden chair in the sitting area and smash it against the wall, trying to break off a leg to use as a stake. It won't kill her, but I just need to slow her down. There's another crash, a snarl, and then pain explodes in the side of my neck. Nails dig into my throat as she grabs my jugular and sinks her fangs into me from behind. My back hits her chest, and I kick off against the wall, trying to throw her off balance as blood gushes over my shoulder. But the venom is already flooding my system and blurring my vision.

"Valerie!"

Reid's voice is faint, distant. I tighten my fist around the chair leg, focusing on the wood against my palm like an anchor. The queen yanks me back, and I throw a foot between hers and hook it around her ankle. I pivot as we fall, putting all of my weight into the stake.

It pierces through her stomach, far too low to do the kind of damage I need, and she bares her teeth, my blood dripping from her chin. She still has that empty look in her eyes—a mindless, deadly predator.

I stagger to my feet as she wraps her hand around the stake, trying to pull it out. I think Reid's hands are on my arm, but all I can see is that crown. Before she can rise again, I smash my foot down as hard as I can on the teeth, focusing on her blood and mine surrounding us, urging, *begging* for its help.

The impact isn't enough, but it does knock the crown free from her hair.

I can't afford to consider this might not be the saving grace I think it is.

"Keep her down!" I yell.

Queen Carrington seizes my ankle, pulling me back, but Reid rips her hand away from me, and I scramble after the crown on my knees.

If the teeth are sealed with the kind of magic I think they are, force won't be enough to break them. I seize the crown with one hand, blood smearing across the surface, and crawl toward the fireplace, my vision going in and out from the venom and the blood gushing from the wound in my neck.

I toss the crown on top of the logs, and my magic burns hot against the blood on my skin as a fire roars to life. Black smoke fills the room as I let my blood join the fire, my unblinking gaze focused on the crown.

For a moment, I think this isn't going to work either. Reid grunts somewhere behind me, and it takes every ounce of willpower to maintain my focus and not stop to help him.

But then, one by one, the teeth separate from the crown.

The sound the queen lets out is inhuman, shrill.

I turn, clamping a hand over the wound still bleeding in my neck, but the pain goes numb the moment I see that haze over the queen's eyes disappear. She offers a small, weak smile as her skin rapidly ages like the hundreds of extra years she's cheated are catching up to her all at once.

Because my mother had been in charge of freezing her aging, and she must have tied the spell to the teeth as a failsafe.

Reid takes a step away from his mother, then another, but instead of a horrified look as he watches her wither away to wrinkles and bones, then ash and dust, his expression is entirely calm, cold.

When it's over and the room falls into silence again, Reid meets my eyes, then scans the rest of me, stilling at the mess of blood at my throat.

Tentatively, I lower my hand from the wound. Before either of us can say anything, the door bursts open.

CHAPTER EIGHTEEN

"Two ESTATE HEADS dead in the same night," mutters King Auclair as he paces behind his desk.

A hysterical laugh gets caught in the back of my throat. A rather regrettable choice of words seeing as the king of Locklear's head was just used as decor in the hallway.

Or maybe the hysteria is coming from the blood all over my hands. The blood of the queen. Who I just killed. Who also happens to be the mother of my boyfriend.

Who I just killed.

"He's picking us off one by one. A simple glamour or mind compulsion spell never would've been enough to overpower her," he continues, mostly talking to himself. "The security breach alone…"

At least he believed us about the glamour, otherwise I doubt we'd be sitting so cordially in his office chairs, at least not without handcuffs. But that isn't much of a relief, at least not enough to quench the nausea churning in my stomach as I peek at Reid out of the corner of my eye.

He hasn't said a word since it happened, and now he sits with his back straight, hands tightly gripping the arms of the chair, gaze leveled on the king. It took me a moment to realize what this would mean for him, but he must have known right away.

He's the crown prince. Next in line for the throne.

I know he's never wanted the crown, but especially now, when the estate heads are Westcott's targets...

What have I done?

Maybe I should have tried harder to subdue her, to get some answers, to figure out who had influenced her to go after Reid. She could have been more useful to us alive.

I startle as Reid's hand slides into my lap, linking my fingers with his and giving them a reassuring squeeze. A similar sensation registers through the bond next, and I realize how tightly it's strung between us.

I guess it's not worth agonizing over. I can't very well bring her back from a pile of ash.

I just reduced my boyfriend's mother to a pile of ash.

"I'll have my Marionettes see if they can glean anything from her...remains. Would you like to keep them?"

I blink back to the room. King Auclair is focused on Reid, his expression almost remorseful.

"No," Reid says simply.

King Auclair gives a single nod. "A team just left, and we have our strongest Marionettes working on a boundary for the estate for extra protection. The other estate heads have all agreed to get involved at this point."

"That won't be enough," a voice singsongs.

I stiffen in my chair, but no one else in the room reacts.

Because no one else can hear her.

V paces to the desk, stopping directly beside the king. She smiles, but there's nothing warm about it, just sick amusement in watching me squirm.

"You could stop this," she says. "Or maybe you don't want to. Maybe you want to see Daddy Dearest's plans succeed? But in that case, why not take him up on his offer and switch sides?"

I grit my teeth to keep from responding and catch Reid looking at me out of the corner of my eye.

"It's not too late to get ahead of this," she continues. "We can take him out now, or you can come crying to me *after* you find your boyfriend's head somewhere other than his body. If it's the ingredients of that particular spell you're so worried about, I'm sure we could find another that would do the trick. I can even pick out who we sacrifice so you don't have to choose."

My hands clench into fists in my lap, and I let a slow breath out through my nose. *There is no* we. Even if I am contemplating using that damn book, it won't be with her help.

But maybe there's another option. A conversation from a different life drifts back to me. The night I turned and attacked Beth in the woods. The memories are drenched in colors too bright, carrying a frantic energy to them, like my brain could retain only so much information as Reid dropped bomb after bomb on me.

Are you familiar with the legends about half-vampires, half-witches?

How much do you know about the necromancers?

The combination of a blood witch and a vampire is said to manifest the same kind of abilities—not as potent as the original necromancers—but an evolution, if you will.

Do you really think a bunch of vampires weren't threatened by witches who could control the dead? All it would take was a few necromancers to band together…

"We've been on the defensive long enough. It's time to show he hasn't weakened us as much as he wants to believe."

"You want to launch a counterattack," says Reid.

"He's going to keep targeting our estates. Right now, his followers are watching his every move, and they're seeing him win. They're seeing us cower behind our walls. That kind of faith and momentum is dangerous. We need to show them if they want to play this game, we can hit them back just as hard. The compound near the Locklear estate should be our first target. Show the residents of Locklear's region that we're avenging their monarch."

A long beat of silence passes, and I look to Reid out of the corner of my eye, my stomach twisting.

"The threat alone might be enough," says Reid. "Take hostages. Make it very public. See if Westcott will negotiate to save his people."

"And if he's not willing to risk it, the rest of his followers will see that firsthand," muses Auclair. "They'll see who he really is—not a voice for them, just a man who will let an entire compound of them die to further his own agenda. Find some cracks in their loyalty. We'll make it flashy. Something they'll *remember.* A fire. I'll have our Marionettes construct a magical barricade over the exits."

A shiver rolls through me like I can already hear the screams of people being burned alive but unable to escape.

The compounds aren't full of soldiers, that much was clear from what Calla told me and from what I saw firsthand. There were some of those, yes, some of Westcott's advisors and employees and other higher-up personnel.

But they were also full of refugees. Families. Children.

Innocents who turned to Westcott because they dared to hope for a better future.

But I don't voice any of that because I already know what they'll say.

Our estates have innocents too.

Our cities weren't spared.

Children, families—the Wendigo Psychosis didn't discriminate. He showed no mercy for us. Why should we show it to them?

"I want a team sent out tonight," decides Auclair. "I'll make the necessary arrangements. In the meantime, Reginald, how would you feel about moving forward with your coronation? I don't want to leave the seat empty for too long in these conditions. It would be a show of good faith, and ensure Vasiliev's support, if your union with Princess Anya were to follow shortly after, and we need all the numbers we can get right now."

All of the air gets sucked out of the room. I don't look at Reid. I can't. It's taking everything in me not to let my feelings show on my face. The edges of my vision blacken, the room going blurry for a moment, and I blink rapidly to clear it.

Because as unthinkable as it is…he's also right.

Because these are all the smart things to do. The right things. The best political moves.

What had Magnolia said?

War rarely lets us hold on to our humanity.

V smirks and lifts her eyebrows in a clear *See?*

"I'll speak with Anya about it," Reid says.

King Auclair nods. "Very good. Don't stray too far on the grounds. I'll have an update within the hour."

I avoid looking at V as we head for the door, but I feel the heat of her gaze on the back of my neck. And unlike after our previous conversation, she doesn't seem to be going anywhere this time.

"Are you sure you're okay?" Reid asks when we reach the staircase on the main floor.

I give him the most encouraging nod I can muster. "We should go talk to Anya."

His hands squeeze into fists at his sides, like he's holding back from touching me. "I can—you don't have to come with me."

"After two estate heads were just taken out? I'm not letting you out of my sight. It's my job."

His nostrils flare, and it looks like there are a million things he wants to say, but in the end, he nods wordlessly and turns for the stairs. I stay close behind him as we navigate the tightly packed halls. The sharp tang of panic hangs in the air as people hurry back and forth, the estate's staff trying to direct people, but they're outnumbered ten times over.

"Have you seen Princess Anya?" Reid asks over and over,

but each time, people shake their heads, and when we reach her room, it's empty.

"She spends a lot of time in the library and the gym," I offer weakly, though I can't imagine her heading to either place after an event like this.

We check both, but still no sign of her. The more we search and the more people we ask, the heavier the dread in my stomach becomes.

Where the hell is she?

The halls have mostly cleared out by the time we make it to the east wing, and Reid's steps slow, his head cocked to the side like he's listening for something.

"This way," he murmurs, heading for a set of stairs.

I follow, my ears picking up two heartbeats alongside the hollow thuds of our footsteps as we reach the hardwood floor at the bottom. As soon as we turn the corner, rows upon rows of wine bottles encased in wood swim into view, warm lights shining down from the ceiling.

A man in the Vasiliev version of the Marionettes uniform —the cut of the sleeves sharper, the stitching red instead of black—stands beside the door, his back straight and arms crossed tightly over his chest.

"Is she...?" Reid starts, and the man gives him a silent nod. After a quick glance at me over his shoulder, Reid heads toward the sound of clicking high heels on the far side of the cellar.

"You must be Anya's Marionette," I say as I step beside him to wait.

"Feddei." He offers me his hand to shake.

"Valerie."

I can feel his power when our palms meet, like its essence is reaching for me. Judging by the soft upturn of his lips, he wanted me to feel it, like an offering so I'd know I could trust him.

"What are you doing down here?" asks Reid, his voice low.

The clicking high heels resume, followed by a light clank of glass as someone removes a bottle from the wall.

"You heard the alarms," comes Anya's voice. "They're probably going to lock us all down for a bit. Thought I'd grab a few of these first."

Feddei's lips twitch, though he doesn't quite smile. But the fondness in his eyes is impossible to miss. "Anya told me you were researching the shadow realm," he says quietly.

"...there's something we need to talk about..." says Reid.

"I—yeah, I have been."

Feddei bobs his head once, and I can't detect anything other than mild curiosity in his expression. "I don't know much about it, but I read this memoir years ago from a witch who claimed he met his shadow self. Most people thought he was crazy. The book is seen more as a joke than anything, especially with how contradictory his supposed findings were from other research on the shadow realm."

"...Auclair thinks it may be best if we secure our estates' alliance sooner rather than later..." continues Reid, but his voice fades more and more to the background as Feddei's words sink in.

Met his shadow self.

Contradictory to research on the shadow realm.

"Do you remember the name of the memoir?" I ask.

Feddei frowns and shakes his head after a moment. "But I can look it up."

"Sound a little more thrilled about the idea, why don't you?" Anya mutters.

There's another clank of glass, and Reid sighs. "I'll hold that." After a moment, he adds, "Is that something you'd be open to?"

More footsteps echo around the room until Anya paces into view outside the very last row, three bottles of wine tucked in her arms. She looks Reid up and down with narrowed eyes. "On one condition."

Reid shifts the bottle he's already holding for her and offers his other hand as she fishes out another. "Which is?"

She hands him the bottle and lifts a single eyebrow. "Have you ever been in love, Reginald?"

My chest constricts, every ounce of my attention zeroed in on them now.

"I—excuse me?"

Anya walks out of view as she paces down the rest of the aisle. "If you want me to consider tying myself to you for the rest of my life in order to help you all clean up this mess, then what I want in return is for you to answer my question. Have you ever been in love?"

The following silence stretches on forever, or maybe it just feels that way as I hold my breath, my heartbeat twice as loud in my chest.

Finally, Reid murmurs, "Yes."

"Don't worry, I'm not drinking all of these," says Anya. "I just want to taste them. I'm sure Auclair won't mind." Her footsteps stop abruptly, and she softens her voice as she asks, "What's it like?"

Reid doesn't answer right away, and I feel frozen where I stand, unable to blink, to *breathe.*

"The world around you is the same," he says, "but suddenly every experience you have is different. It's more. I imagine it's the closest I'll ever get to feeling the sun. Even the worst days are better as long as she's by your side. It's a kind of peace I've never known elsewhere."

"What happened? Why didn't it work out if you were so in love?"

He's followed Anya far enough down the row that I can't see either of them anymore. Can't see his face as he says, "I messed it up. I did things that I shouldn't have because I was so afraid to lose her. I lied. I kept things from her. I was so desperate to keep her that I stopped being the man she fell for in the first place. And people like us, we don't always get to choose the paths our lives take, do we?"

I press my fingers into my sternum, unsure if the heaviness that's settled behind my ribs belongs to me or him.

"And now you're down here basically asking me to marry you," mutters Anya, the earlier amusement in her voice gone now. "Did you at least tell her? Did you tell her how you felt about her when you had the chance?"

"I—um." I take a step away from the wall, then another. My lungs *ache.* There's not enough air in this room. "I'm going to check the hall upstairs. Are you okay down here with them?"

Feddei searches my face for a moment, and I see it in his eyes the moment the realization hits. It doesn't take vampire senses to hear their conversation, and it doesn't take a genius to figure out why I'd want to leave the room now. But in the end, he only nods.

I hurry from the room, but not before hearing Reid's quiet "I tried" behind me.

CHAPTER NINETEEN

THE HALL IS EERILY quiet when I make it to the top of the stairs, each breath I pull in shorter than the last. I do a quick sweep of my surroundings, straining my senses for a trace of a threat, but finding none, I turn for the side door that leads to the grounds. I just need a minute. Some fresh air. I can't *breathe* in here.

Because he's going to marry her. Until now, I guess I never truly believed it would happen. But now it's the right thing to do. And Reid always does the right thing. And hearing him talk about me like that—*us* like that—in the same goddamn sentence as him asking her to marry him—

I'm going to be standing off to the side with Feddei watching over Reid and Anya for the rest of my life.

I pull in a lungful of air as I step outside, my vision swimming from lack of oxygen. I keep close to the side of the building so I can see the stairwell to the cellar through the window.

"Sending your lover off to be with another woman. Tragic."

I curse as V's reflection appears beside me in the window.

"I'm really not in the mood," I mutter.

"Oh really? So there's nothing you want to ask me? Nothing I might be able to help with? Nothing you think I might know that you don't? My mistake."

I grit my teeth as a group of birds takes off into flight from the trees behind us, the flap of their wings filling the silence. My eyes burn as I stare unblinkingly at the stairs to the cellar through the window.

Numbly, I say, "Tell me everything you know about the Darkmores, the necromancers, and dark magic."

"I knew you'd figure it out eventually."

"Figure *what* out?"

She shrugs then taps her chin with her pointer finger. "If only there were a whole bunch of blood witches who inherited necromancy powers after undergoing the turning process. A mini army perfect for eliminating vampires...oh wait. How many little halfling daughters do you think Daddy Dearest has by now? He's had centuries to spread his seed around."

An involuntary shudder rolls through me at the words.

But she's also right.

Calla has said there were nine of us, and that was just at the one compound. Not only does he have that many out there, but he's also been gathering them. And something tells me he had more than a family reunion on his mind.

"So you're telling me he has a loyal following of all kinds of creatures"—I tick off one finger—"a horde of wendigos basically enslaved to him through blood deals"—a second finger—"*and* a mini army of necromancer children."

"The good news is, I can teach you how to properly use your necromancy powers."

I scoff. "And why would you do that? You still haven't told me what you want."

She shrugs like it's obvious. "I want to stay here. Fully, not just in this in-between space."

"You really think I'm stupid, don't you? You think I don't know that would mean you'd take my place here?"

"That's not the only way," she insists. "I can't exist on your side without a physical body. But that doesn't mean yours is the only one I could take."

"I—of course I'm not going to help you *take*—"

"You're thinking about it all wrong! It doesn't have to be some perfectly well, innocent person. It could be someone on the brink of death who wouldn't survive anyway. It could be someone who deserves it—someone this world would be better off without. Let me show you how valuable your necromancy powers can be. Unless, of course, you'd rather keep pretending they're not there and then impulsively whip them out even though you have no idea how to use them and almost get yourself killed—"

"Enough," I say through my teeth.

"You know what? You're right. I can tell where I'm not wanted. You seem to have this all under control anyway."

She turns, her form blurring as if she'll dissolve into the fog around us, and panic sparks in my chest. Maybe she's bluffing, trying to get me to cave, but what if she's not? What if she disappears for good, and then I really am left to my own devices here? I'm way out of my depth. And if she's right, if all of those people die and *this* was the wrong choice I made that could have prevented it, I'll never be able to live with myself.

My brain feels foggy, hazy, and suddenly her words have less edge to them. *Someone on the brink of death. Someone who deserves it.* Would it be so horrible if it meant ending this war before too much blood is shed?

War rarely lets us hold on to our humanity.

"Wait," I croak, the word painful as I drag it out. A very unsettling sense of déjà vu settles on my skin as I tell her, "You have a deal. But *only* if you can prove you're actually helpful and not full of shit."

She grins, all shiny white teeth and wicked glee in her eyes. "We'll need some time to cover the basics before we can make any progress. I imagine your first mistake has been approaching necromancy the same way you use your blood magic. Am I right?"

I say nothing, figuring that's answer enough, and try to keep the surprise off my face. Magic is magic—how else would I summon my power than from blood?

But then I remember resurrecting Reid and the white light I'd funneled into him. My life force, apparently, not my magic. That clearly hadn't been right. Not unless every necromancer dropped dead if they tried to use their powers.

"Plus, your powers are probably acting a little out of whack now."

My head snaps up. "How did you know that?"

She shrugs. "It was just a guess. Your mom didn't just save your life. She funneled her powers into you. Having two different magics living inside of you—I'd be surprised if you *didn't* feel a difference."

Is that where the anger is coming from? The gruesome images, the thoughts that pop into my head that don't even feel like they're coming from me? My magic feels stronger, yes. Sometimes too strong. But the other side of it? What *is* that?

"So if you've been treating necromancy the same as any old blood spell," V continues, snapping me back to the present, "then we need to start basic. Like, the five year olds I teach basic."

I frown. That's the first tidbit of information she's dropped about her own life. She teaches. *Children.*

"What?" She snorts. "You thought I was just twiddling my thumbs over here for the last twenty-two years and watching *your* life play out? You really don't know anything about the shadow realm, do you? You were *inside* the veil when you crossed over to get the book. Basically tiptoeing along the boundary. You've never crossed all the way through to our side."

"So if I'm not supposed to draw from my magic the way I usually do, what *should* I be doing?" I ask, ignoring her comments because she's right. I hadn't given much thought to what it would be like on the other side, picturing more of a prison or purgatory, not somewhere entirely different lives play out.

"You'll have to learn to compartmentalize. Think of your necromancy magic as something entirely different, like a different muscle. And since you've probably rarely used it properly—if ever—it's weak. You have to stop letting your blood magic overcompensate for it. I'm guessing you feel your magic in your blood when you use it, maybe your skin?"

I nod, hugging my arms around myself, not liking how it feels like she's inside my head.

"When you're pulling from your necromancy powers, it should be coming from a place lower than that, deeper. Like you're pulling it from your own shadow and up through the soles of your feet."

The door swings open behind me, and I stiffen as aware-ness settles in the bond a moment later.

How long has he been here? How much has he heard?

Reid rolls his shirtsleeves up to his elbows as he steps outside and takes in the trees around us. "What are you doing out here?"

"I just needed some air." I pointedly avoid looking at V as she sidles on up next to Reid with doe eyes and batting lashes. "How did it go with Anya?"

My heart swells almost to the point of pain as I look into his eyes.

I imagine it's the closest I'll ever get to feeling the sun.

Then comes the first crack in his demeanor—a slight flare of his nostrils as his eyebrows draw together. "She's...open to it."

"He's even hotter up close," V whispers as she fans herself.

"We agreed to talk more after the coronation—"

"And those *eyes*. They're so *blue*."

"In the meantime, Auclair's informing the other repre-sentatives about the counterattack," Reid continues as he loosens the collar of his shirt and roughs a hand through his hair.

"He could be helpful with our training," muses V. "We can resurrect little creatures all day long…"

"—there's no talking them out of it—"

"But if the end goal is to control a living-not-living vampire, practicing on one would—"

"Elemental Marionettes from Locklear have already agreed to help. They're fresh out of their own attack and angry—"

"—and I sure wouldn't mind having some eye candy for our practice sessions. I mean, those arms, that *ass*—"

"Would you shut up!" I exclaim, my head starting to throb. I can't concentrate on a single word Reid is saying with her nonstop voice grating on my last nerve. And judging by the satisfied smirk on her lips, that's exactly what she wanted.

Fuck.

Reid's mouth is open like I cut him off midword. A trace of hurt flashes behind his eyes, but then he slowly trails his gaze from me to the space I've been looking at beside him.

"Who are you talking to, Valerie?" he asks calmly. Too calmly. Like he's worried I'm losing my mind but trying not to show it, probably.

I force myself not to glare at V the way I want to. "I'm not crazy," I whisper.

He shakes his head and takes a step closer, the look on his face not unkind, but I know he's analyzing me, studying me. "I know that. Tell me what you see. There's someone here with us, right?"

I can't help it. My gaze flickers back to V. She shrugs and mouths *Oops*, though she couldn't look less apologetic.

"I promise I'm not crazy."

"Valerie." He crosses the rest of the distance between us and takes my face in his hands, forcing me to look at him. "I know that. Now tell me what's going on."

"When I crossed back with the book," I murmur, not able to hold his eyes, "someone came with me. My shadow self, or whatever."

He drops his hands and takes a step back, looking to where V stands as if he can see her. "That's what you and Feddei were talking about."

"She—uh—well, she thinks she can help. With the whole Westcott situation."

"*Knows*," V corrects. "Knows she can help."

I expect some exasperation, maybe a lecture to remind me how making a deal worked out last time. That is, if he actually believes me and doesn't try to get me committed to the hospital for observation.

But instead, he turns back to me, the intensity in his eyes smoothing into something closer to curiosity as he shoves his hands into his pockets.

"What did she have in mind?"

CHAPTER TWENTY

I'VE SPENT my life surrounded by power-drunk and bloodthirsty vampires, so it shouldn't come as a shock. I shouldn't be surprised as everyone at the Auclair estate gathers around the TVs to watch news coverage of Westcott's compound burning like it's their most anticipated event of the year. The cheers and satisfied smiles should be expected as impossibly orange flames fill the screen and the camera pans out to show the black smoke billowing up toward the sky.

Even with how far away the shot is taken, I swear you can see hands frantically beating on the windows inside.

The fire was days ago, but all of the news stations have been replaying the footage on a loop ever since.

I'd known Westcott wouldn't negotiate. That no amount of threats or hostages would be enough to make him bend, but watching it play out was an entirely different matter.

Westcott let them all burn.

We let them all burn.

And now that the estates have had a taste of vengeance, they won't stop. I know they won't.

They'll target a different compound.

Westcott will target a different estate.

And on and on the bloodshed will go.

Unless.

Unless.

I let out a frustrated breath through my nose and scan the page of Magnolia's book again. It describes harnessing dark magic much differently than V had. It explains summoning the darkness and letting it in, like it's an external force. Maybe that's what it's like for someone without a natural connection to dark magic.

"You're overthinking it."

Connor slams the book shut.

"I was reading that."

He snatches it off the bench and paces farther into the gardens. With everyone still eagerly watching the news coverage inside, it's quiet out here tonight, the same way it's been for days.

"You didn't get the hang of your blood magic overnight either. You'll get it."

"I don't have *time*," I snap. "If I can't pull this off, this is never going to stop!" I jab my finger back toward the estate.

"Val…you can't take this all on yourself. No single person could."

"At least with my blood magic, I could *feel* it. Things were happening right away. I just had to learn to control it. To shape it. But now, Connor, you don't get it. I don't feel anything. *Nothing* is happening." My voice hitches at the end, and I clench my teeth and look away from him, not wanting to see the pity on his face.

I've read every word in every book I could find on dark magic three times over in the past few days. And when I wasn't reading, I was practicing. And still, no improvement. *None.*

And I want to be able to figure this out on my own. I *have* to.

For all her talk of wanting to help, I haven't seen V since the attack on the Locklear estate. Not that I trust her enough to put my faith in her hands, but if I can't manage to teach myself, there's no one else I can ask. None that I know of. Practicing dark magic isn't exactly something you advertise.

"Maybe you're just tired," Connor offers. "We've been at this for hours."

"You don't have to stay out here with me."

"That's not what I meant. I don't need a break. *You* do."

The tug in the bond comes first, then the crunch of footsteps in the distance. Connor must hear them too, because he sighs and hands the book back to me.

"I'll give you two some space," he says, turning to go, but I grab his sleeve before he can get far.

"Thanks for your help, Connor. Really." Not that I'd ended up needing him. We'd thought by now I'd need a vampire around to practice controlling, but it's been days of struggling —and failing—to even summon the damn magic. But the company has kept me from completely losing my mind.

"You'll get it, Val. I know you will." He gives me a small smile before ducking through the trees and heading back toward the estate.

The stress in my chest amplifies as Reid comes into view,

like the bond is syphoning and combining from us both. He loosens his tie as he paces into the garden.

"Thought I might find you out here," he says, though it doesn't sound nearly as light as I think he intended it.

"How is everything?" I ask, clutching the book to my chest.

"No response from Westcott about the attack, so all the estates are preparing for retaliation, just in case. Auclair wants to move ahead and strike again before Westcott has the chance. And my mother let a lot of things fall through the cracks after Westcott seized our estate. We have emergency protocols, but it looks like they didn't go far beyond the ones meant for estate inhabitants—nothing to help our people living in the region *outside* of the estates. We're supposed to have safe houses, shelters, for them to go to while we deal with the emergency—make sure they have enough supplies, that kind of thing. And no one has been overseeing it. I don't know how—" He stops short, his jaw flexing, and shakes his head. "If Auclair doesn't approve my request to send a team out there, I'm going myself."

The words make my stomach drop, but when I open my mouth, nothing comes out. Because how could I possibly argue? Those are his people, his responsibility now, even if the coronation hasn't made things official yet. And it's about time the people of the first region had someone to stand up for them.

"What do you need from me?" I ask. "How can I help?"

"Nothing right now. There's nothing any of us can do. We're trying to get in contact with the shelters first to see if anyone even survived." He swallows hard and busies himself by rolling his shirtsleeves up to his elbows. "Any luck with the training?"

"Not so much."

"And any sign of—?"

"Not since the attack." I hesitate, not missing the way he's barely looked me in the eye since he stepped out here, how the tension in his shoulders only increases the longer we stand here. "Reid...do you... I've been meaning to talk to you for the past few days. How are you? About your mom? I know it's complicated, but I'm here if you want to talk about it."

His eyes snap to mine, his expression smoothing out as if he's surprised by the question. As if I honestly wouldn't ask how he's doing after getting attacked by his own mother and watching her die right in front of him. He blinks once, twice. "I haven't given it much thought," he admits.

I chew on my lip, knowing there's more to it but not wanting to push him. Even when she was alive, their relationship was a topic we rarely broached.

"I guess—I guess I never really believed the day would come." His shoulders relax by a few degrees as if the words released some of the weight clinging to him. "That she'd die and I'd have to take over. I guess I believed that one way or another, I'd die before she did." He shifts his focus to the mountains in the distance. Quieter, he says, "I can't think of a good memory with her. Not one."

"Have you spoken to any of your siblings?"

He gives a stiff nod. "Jared called. He'll be at the coronation. I know Auclair invited some of the others, but I haven't spoken with them."

I inch closer, my fingers aching with how badly I want to

reach for him, but I don't know if it would make things better or worse. I'm the one who put him in this position.

"We just killed thousands of people in that compound," he whispers.

My heart drops at the anguish in his voice, the low volume somehow making it cut even deeper.

"I know," I say softly.

"We just killed thousands of people, and I helped. That was the first thing I did as the king of the first region."

"Reid—"

He shakes his head and turns away so I can't see his face. Before I can talk myself out of it, I cross the rest of the distance between us and force myself into his line of sight. His lips are pressed tightly together, and he still won't focus on me. I grab his face with both hands, and his eyes flutter closed.

He shakes his head. "This isn't—this isn't what I want to be."

"I know."

"I can't rule like her," he whispers. "I won't."

"I know." I pull him in against my chest, and he gives little resistance, his forehead coming to rest on my shoulder, the last of the tension finally releasing him. "I know."

CHAPTER TWENTY-ONE

THE ESTATES LAUNCH another attack on Westcott's compounds the following night—one they found near the Carrington estate, and not too far from where I'd stayed with the wolves in the barrens.

It feels like I've been pushed out of a plane and I'm barreling toward the ground, everything around me moving faster by the second, but my grasp on dark magic isn't getting any better.

Reid lays a comforting hand on my back as if he can feel the anxiety building inside of me as we reach the area of the garden I've been using to practice the past few days. But as we step through the trees, a figure is already standing among the shadows.

"Where have you been?" I demand through my teeth.

She takes a step forward, enough for the light of the moon to fall on her eerily familiar face, and blinks innocently at me.

"Oh, I'm sorry. Did you find that you want me around? That wasn't really the impression I got last time."

"Is this some kind of game to you?"

"See, that tone isn't exactly screaming, *Thank you, V. I soooo appreciate you offering your time for the help I so desperately need.*"

Sounds drift toward us on the breeze, voices and footsteps and heavy thuds of moving furniture—the servants preparing for the coronation tonight—which serves as a reminder that I won't have nearly as much time for practicing as usual today.

Bickering with myself isn't the most productive use of it.

"Fine," I force out. "Thank you."

She beams and claps her hands like she's preparing to teach a class. "So I vote we practice with Prince Charming over there. It can be easier to summon your power if you have a clear goal for what to do with it. Now, it'll be a lot harder with an unwilling vampire, especially if they've ever trained in mentally shielding themselves from magic, let alone working on large numbers at once. In my experience, it'll be easier to infiltrate their body than their mind. To make them move, speak, that kind of thing. But they'll be aware that you're pulling their strings like a puppet. The next level would be to get inside their mind to make them think it's their idea in the first place. But for today, let's start with something small and just in the body. Might I suggest making him take off his shirt?"

Make them move, speak. I think of the Marionette who jumped from the tower. I assumed he'd been glamoured, but what if it was something else? If someone was using dark magic on him? To *control* him?

I glare at V as Reid watches me, confused since he can't hear a word she's saying. He lifts an eyebrow when I blink back to him.

"She wants me to try something simple on you first," I explain. "Only if you're comfortable with it."

His lips twitch. "I'm guessing that's not all she said."

"I took some creative liberties."

"Practice drawing that energy up first," V suggests. "And try to hold it. You'd use the same method for dark spells too, so it's a good thing to master either way."

"Give it a try," Reid encourages.

I grimace as I squeeze my eyes closed. I've tried this a million times already and always gotten the same result. My magic warms in the center of my chest, ready to help, and I try to ignore it, searching for wherever this second source is. V said to draw up from my shadow, but how am I supposed to connect with something that's not even inside my body?

I grit my teeth as I bunch my hands into fists and let out a frustrated breath through my nose.

"You're trying too hard," says V. "This magic is a part of you. It'll feel natural when done right."

"I can't feel anything," I mutter. "I haven't for days."

"Well, I guess that's that then!" V claps her hands together like she's dusting them off. "Everyone else can suck it because Valerie Darkmore isn't nearly as powerful as she's led everyone to believe."

"You're not helping," I snap.

"You're not helping," she mimics, like we're five fucking years old.

221

I open and close my mouth and fists simultaneously, the frustration threatening to boil over.

"Hey. Hey." Reid's hands land on my shoulders, turning me to him. "Ignore whatever she's saying, okay? Just focus on me. I know you can do this."

He keeps his hands on my shoulders as I let my eyes shut again, and I focus on the warmth of his skin against mine to anchor myself. A deep breath, then another, trying to force my body to relax. To let whatever this power is find me instead of me searching for it.

And like bare feet on ice, a flicker of cold so biting it feels warm appears in my soles.

I inhale sharply, following the string it connects to, that does, indeed, feel like it's coming from just behind me. I breathe deeply, inviting it in, welcoming it.

As it slowly travels up from my feet, it feels nothing like my magic normally does. No heat, no tingling, no electricity.

It's smooth like velvet, quiet like the night. Not cold, exactly, but cooling, soothing.

How can something so dark feel so calm?

As if scared off by my judgmental thoughts, as quickly as it came, the power slithers away.

A noise of frustration sounds in the back of my throat as my eyes open again, immediately locking with Reid's.

"I had it. But I think I…offended it." The possibly nearly makes me laugh.

"If you make it feel unwanted, why the hell would it want to work with you?" V chimes in. "It can sense if you're afraid of it too. If you don't trust it. If you want this to work, you have to embrace it. Completely."

I wince. *Sorry*, I offer lamely. *I'm new at this.*

Apparently a forgiving magic, that strange coldness brushes my feet, this time sweeping up my legs faster, then traveling along my spine. I stretch my awareness to Reid's hands on my shoulders, and the magic follows suit, flowing from my body to his like a shadow.

I urge it to gently lower his arms back to his sides, and judging by the sudden absence of his warmth and the sharp intake of his breath, it worked.

"Try something bigger before you lose your concentration," says V, her voice distant, thin.

Similarly to how I would use my blood magic, I imagine the innerworkings of his body, the structure of muscle and bone and tissue, letting the shadow of magic travel from his arms to his chest, the long column of his throat, his vocal cords.

"Bigger how?" he asks, quickly followed by a breathy "Fuck."

My eyes snap open. "Are you okay?"

But he's grinning at me, the pride shining in his eyes enough to warm my cheeks and to make whatever snarky comment coming from V fade to the background. I smile back, the shadows of magic slithering back the way they came and funneling out through the soles of my feet.

We try a few more times, the summoning of the magic faster now, as if it's now grown familiar with its path, and once I get the hang of it, we have Reid offer up more resistance, fighting back against my magic.

By the end of an hour, I'm covered in a fine layer of sweat, feeling more exhausted than I do after a training session with

Cam. And though he hasn't said a word of complaint, I can tell it's taken a toll on Reid as well.

Despite the improvement, my excitement is short-lived as reality checks back in. Controlling Reid took everything out of me, and even though he said he was fighting back as much as he could, I have a feeling he was going easy on me.

I won't improve fast enough. Not when the death toll rises each day.

Not when Reid's coronation is *tonight*, painting an even larger target on his back than there'd been to begin with.

As if reading my thoughts, Reid lets out a slow breath and glances toward the estate. He'll need to head back and get ready.

"Go ahead," I say. "I'm done for the day."

"You sure?"

"Yeah." I wave him off even though the last thing I want to do is watch him walk away. "I'll see you tonight."

Which is true. As his Marionette, of course I'll be at his coronation, but in all the wrong ways.

Though he looks like he wants to say more, he leaves without another word.

"I wonder how long they'll wait after he's crowned to move ahead with the wedding," V muses behind me. "My guess is a week."

Pain flares up my jaw from clenching it so tightly, but I don't snap at her the way I want to. Because she very well could be right.

All these moments with just the two of us have made it easy to forget what's happening. We're just Valerie and Reid.

Partners. Friends. Our dynamic not quite what everything inside of me is yearning for, but not that different from the way things were before the bunker.

But if this moves forward...if he actually *marries* her...

I swallow hard. Then I couldn't afford to forget anymore.

CHAPTER TWENTY-TWO

TODAY WILL BE one for the history books. Not just because Reid is taking the throne, but as far as I know, this is the first time a coronation has taken place in an estate other than the monarch's own. And with how jam-packed Auclair is these days, it'll probably be the coronation with the largest attendance to date.

There's a different uniform for Marionettes on occasions like these, basically a fancier version of what we usually wear. The black material is nicer, thicker, looking more like a suit than athletic gear. The bodice is tight, the straps thinner, and I wriggle around, trying to shimmy it higher onto my chest, but it still rests lower on my boobs than I'd like, leaving little to the imagination. A long, thin skirt attaches at the waist to make it look more like a dress than a uniform, but the fabric is easy to tear away if need be, the standard formfitting pants beneath.

I check my phone for the hundredth time tonight, but no response from my friends. They're coming in from the academy to attend the coronation, as a lot of the York kids are doing, and I asked a few hours ago if they wanted to swing by early to get ready together.

Anxiety buzzes along my skin at the sight of my blank screen. Not responding is unusual for them, especially Kirby. She usually texts back right away. Even Adrienne isn't here yet, leaving me standing in the middle of her room, alone, wringing my hands and wondering if I should do something different with my hair. It's down in loose curls, my eyeshadow smoky and my lipstick bloodred.

I tug the hoops out of my ears, the tightness in my chest growing, and replace them with small gold balls instead, and it finally occurs to me the anxiety isn't all mine.

Reid.

Of course he's nervous about tonight. He usually cuts the bond off from me when he's feeling this way though, so if it's spilling through, it must be really bad.

Forcing one foot in front of the other, I step into the hall and head for Reid's room. As his partner, it's customary for me to accompany him today, though it'll be nothing like our pairing ceremony had been. Then, our partnership had been the focus. Tonight, I'm little more than an extension of the shadows, there to ensure his safety.

When I knock, the door immediately swings open, Reid standing on the other side in a suit dark as night, his hair disheveled as he runs a hand through it then readjusts the gold crown. It's the last time he'll wear this one.

"I was about to come get you," he says.

I don't know what makes me do it—the unrelenting static in the bond, maybe—but I take a step forward and wrap my arms around his waist. He folds into me like he can barely keep himself upright. I hold my breath so I won't breathe in his scent. I try not to let myself melt into the warmth of his touch or how perfectly I fit against his chest, but I fail. The moment we make contact, I'm already dreading when I'll have to let go.

"It'll be okay," I say.

He nods, arms tightening around me for a moment before we straighten and step away from each other, putting a perfectly professional amount of distance between us. But his gaze lingers on me, slowly dragging from my feet to the top of my head, and I feel it as clearly as his hands against my skin.

Wordlessly, he nods for us to walk, but it's through the bond that he murmurs, *You're breathtaking.*

And you look like a king.

A shuddering breath passes his lips at the word, and he adjusts his tie.

And you'll be a good one too, I add, softening my mental voice. *The kind we need right now.*

He meets my eyes, his forehead creased and the corners of his lips tight. We pause as we near the corridor that leads to the ballroom. Conversation and footsteps already fill the air, along with the humming lilt of the musicians. He lets out another breath and faces forward.

I hope you're right.

THE STREAM of guests comes and goes. If history's any indicator, the celebration will last long after the sunrise, though this is the first coronation I've been alive for. The monarchs from our allying estates attend, as well as a few representatives, though the estates who have pulled out are noticeably absent, leaving the rest of the crowd to be mainly populated by residents of the Carrington and Auclair estates.

Despite the cheers and laughter and dancing and music, I don't know if I've ever felt this miserable at a party. I linger near the dais along with a few other Marionettes, eyes sweeping back and forth for any hint of a threat.

Anyone not up and mingling is seated at the various round tables situated throughout the ballroom. My attention snags on a table in the corner for a beat longer than necessary. A woman I don't know in powder pink is in the seat directly next to Nathan Van Doren, and judging by the way he's blatantly ogling her chest in that lowcut gown, I'd say her flirting is going well. She throws her head back in a laugh at whatever he says, and he beams and puffs out his chest.

I can't believe I'd let him fool me into thinking he's *not that bad*, even if only for a second. But he'd fooled all of us, hadn't he? Avery, Monroe, hell, even Reid had seemed to come around to him in the bunker.

Isn't that a telltale sign of a sociopath? Someone who can charm anyone?

I force myself to unclench my jaw for the millionth time tonight.

I blink back to the room, the Marionettes lingering in the shadows coming into focus, their expressions grim because we're all probably thinking the same thing. Auclair wanted to make a big show of tonight, to show we're not scared, we're still in charge. But if I were Westcott, having a gathering of this magnitude would be an awfully opportune time to strike.

Reid's passed around the room like a shiny new toy, shaking hands, mingling, and looking perfectly at ease navigating it all. Like he was born for this.

Because he was.

Anya hangs on his side with her arms wrapped around one of his, laughing along in conversations and leaning her head against his shoulder.

She's glowing tonight. She's in a gold gown that flows like water, the back dipping all the way to her hips. Matching gold makeup shimmers on her cheeks, and her hair is twisted into an elaborate updo, a dainty golden tiara balanced on her brow.

The way she floats through the room, posture perfect, charming anyone who gets near her—she and Reid make a perfect match.

Reid's entire demeanor shifts as he reaches a group of vampires near the door. A man with the same dark hair and crinkles by his eyes grins and throws his arms around Reid's shoulders, roughly tugging him into a hug—one of Reid's brothers. Jared, I think his name is. A small Chinese woman stands behind him, her nostrils flared and eyes bright and alert as she takes in her surroundings, like she's prepared for an attack. But as Reid pulls away from Jared, she offers him a smile and hugs him next.

When she steps aside, I realize a second woman was lingering behind her.

I don't blink. I don't *breathe*.

Reid releases the first woman, and everything about the

way he goes in to hug Quinn is different. He pulls her in gently, one hand holding the back of her head like it's a delicate, breakable thing.

He'd told me she was alive, that he'd run into her while he was looking for me. But he'd also said she was...*different* now. Being human, the psychosis had affected her in a way we'd never seen before.

But now as she holds on to his arms, steps back, and cranes her neck to get a good look at him, that proud, motherly glint in her eye, she looks exactly how I remembered her. At least, before we'd spread what we believed to be her ashes.

Reid looks years younger as he smiles and says something in her ear, the weight of the day momentarily lifting from his shoulders.

"You haven't blinked in several minutes," V says out of the corner of her mouth beside me. "And you're so tense my shoulders hurt just looking at you. Maybe you should have a drink."

I turn away from her, saying nothing, and catch the eye of Feddei beside me. He looks a lot like Anya, like they're siblings. Same tall, slender frame, golden hair. He offers a polite smile before returning to his surveying of the room.

I never reached out to him after Anya gave me his number, even though he did go out of his way to find the name of that memoir for me. Not because I'm not interested in what else he might know, but I don't know how close the two of them are. I have to assume anything I speak with him about could get back to Anya. Though I might be less mistrustful of her now, that only goes so far.

Servants slide through the room in white uniforms offering

blood-laced champagne on their trays, and the music shifts to something more upbeat as pairs head for the dance floor. Reid's made it to the far end of the room now, head ducked to hear whatever King Vasiliev is saying as Anya shifts at his side. Her demeanor is noticeably different around her father. She's no longer hanging off Reid's arm. Instead, she's standing silently behind him, her hands tucked together behind her back.

Admittedly, I don't know much about the Vasiliev family or their monarch, what he's like as a ruler, as a father. Only that Anya and her older brother, Alexei, are his only remaining heirs despite at one point having three other siblings.

"Care to dance?"

I spare Cam a sideways glance as he appears on my left, then do a double take when I notice he's in a black tuxedo, his hair carefully styled away from his face instead of its usual wild mess, and his face is freshly shaved.

He gives me a lopsided smirk. "I think the words you're looking for are *You clean up nice, Cam.*"

I snap my jaw shut and face forward again. "I'm not dancing. I'm working." Not that I couldn't dance if I wanted to, but I'm not going to tell him that.

"Actually, right now you're gazing longingly at his royal highness across the room," quips V. "Anyone can see it."

As she says it, Anya departs from their group and heads toward us. I stiffen, but then remember I'm standing next to her partner. She's probably coming over to him.

"Valerie!" She beams as she approaches like we're old friends. "Wow, black is definitely your color."

I blink stupidly at her.

Feddei drifts forward a step but stops himself as Anya's eyes cut to him, that smile still in place. She just looks…tense. I peek at Feddei sideways, and his lips are folded tightly together, his brow pinched in a cross between anger and concern.

"Seems the two of you might have more in common than you thought," mutters V.

I frown, and she nods toward Anya's father, who is currently glaring daggers at his daughter's back. She didn't come over here for a friendly chat. She was trying to get away from him.

Cam, either oblivious to the tension or not caring, says, "How generous of you to slum it with your lowly subjects over here, Your Highness."

Anya's eyes flash to his. "I'm surprised they even let you in the door. Shouldn't you be outside howling on all fours?"

"Oh, don't worry. I'll get to that later. Care to join me?"

I tune out whatever she says next, my gaze drifting back to Reid. He's been passed from King Vasiliev to Queen Suksai, and he's listening intently while she talks with her hands.

The door at the back of the throne room creaks open as more guests enter, and flashes of red and pink grab my attention.

Finally.

I unconsciously take a step toward my friends but freeze as I take in their grim expressions. Kirby has one hand on Monroe's back, the other on her elbow, and she leads her toward a human servant with regular champagne. Monroe's head is down, her hair obscuring her face, but her posture is all wrong. Shoulders slumped, chin dipped.

They each grab a drink, then retreat to the outskirts of the room, blending in with the other black uniforms of the Marionettes. Kirby's partner is already spinning around on the dance floor with a woman I don't recognize, and Nathan, apparently bored with the woman in pink, is now sauntering around the room and laughing with a few of his royal friends.

"Excuse me," I mutter, though Cam and Anya seem too engrossed in their verbal sparring match to notice.

Kirby sees me coming first, and her smile is lightless. "Hi, Val," she sighs. "I'm sorry about—"

"Don't worry about it." I wave her off. "What's wrong?"

"Nothing new," Monroe bites out. I follow her gaze to Nathan on the other side of the room. Two friends lean over each of his shoulders, gathering around as he shows something on his phone, all of them shaking with laughter.

"Rumors spread fast," Kirby says. "I don't know how many people have seen the videos—"

"But everyone knows they exist," I say.

She gives a stiff nod.

The music cuts off, and an eerie hush falls over the room as King Auclair steps onto the dais.

"Thank you all for coming to celebrate the coronation of the newest Carrington monarch, Reginald Evander Carrington." A few of the other monarchs usher Reid onto the stage as he says it, and he ducks his head at the polite applause that fills the room.

"Although we have important matters to attend to, I thought we all could use a dose of normalcy," continues Auclair. "This whole ordeal has been so uncivilized." He says *uncivilized* with a pointed lift of his chin, as if genuinely offended by it all.

I like Auclair. As far as the monarchs go, he's one of the better ones. He's a fair leader, he cares about his people, and for a royal vampire, he's always seemed one of the most open-minded. Not to mention he's taken us all in when he easily could have turned the Carrington refugees away, me especially. Many of the other estates wouldn't have extended the same generosity, and most wouldn't look down at him if he left us all out to die.

So sometimes it's easy to forget who he is—what he is. A vampire who's walked this earth far longer than he should have. One who views the deaths of thousands to be unfortunate, but more inconvenient than anything as it interferes with the extravagance and refinery he's accustomed to. One who's had a hand in every law running this corrupt system, has allowed every injustice, maybe even come up with some of the ideas himself.

This uprising isn't a serious threat to him, just an aggravated nuisance that's cutting into his social calendar and upsetting his routine.

"But please, please, before we get into the ceremony and the feast tonight, let us propose a cheers to our Marionettes who have worked so hard to keep us all safe during these trying times."

"Hear, hear!" calls a faceless voice, and I have to physically pinch myself to hold back from rolling my eyes. If the other Marionettes hear how empty his words sound, they don't show it.

Reid raises his head and meets my eyes across the room for what feels like the first time tonight. The tension in his expression eases as a single corner of his mouth lifts. The bond shivers between us like fingers gently plucking the strings of a violin.

Hear, hear.

THE CEREMONY itself doesn't take long, nor does the pledging of fealty from the first region residents. Reid's discomfort through the whole thing is palpable through the bond, but you'd never be able to tell from looking at him.

No, not only does he look perfectly calm through the whole precession, he looks regal. Like kneeling on that dais while accepting his new crown is exactly where he was always supposed to be.

When it all dims away, the bows and the applause and the formalities, the vows and the cheers and the traditions, he rises back to his full height, head held high, shoulders thrown back, and for a moment, I hardly recognize him at all.

Then he turns his head, his eyes searching the crowd until they land on me, and he smiles. The kind that brings his entire face to life, and I find myself smiling back.

But then the orchestra music for the first dance begins, and Anya steps up beside him, beaming as she extends her hand.

And he takes it.

As the swell of music and conversation returns to the air, I turn back to Kirby and Monroe, telling myself it's to pick up where we left off before the ceremony and not because I can't stand to watch him take her waist, to see how perfect they look together, to see how Anya blends in with this scene far more than I ever will.

Kirby gives a minute shake of her head, but it's Monroe who says, "Not here."

It's the tone of her voice, cold and unfeeling, more than anything else that stops me from asking any follow-up questions. But I do seek out Nathan in the crowd again.

He's dancing with another girl I don't know, some vampire from the Auclair estate in a floor-length blue sequined gown, Nathan's hands blatantly gripping any curve he can reach as they spin in a slow circle.

I can't help but think of a conversation from a lifetime ago —Avery and I in the pool room before initiation. I'd chalked up her leaving and getting reassigned to some personal difference with Nathan, especially once I saw Monroe all buddy-buddy with him, laughing and calling him *Nate*.

Maybe I should've done more. Dug deeper with Avery for more answers. Tried harder to warn Monroe. Tried harder to protect her, even if I didn't know what I was protecting her from.

The music screeches to a halt as a loud clang echoes through the room, followed by shattering glass. My muscles seize, and I whip my head up to find Reid, but he's still in the middle of the dance floor, unharmed. Behind him, a vampire in a bloodred suit scolds a human servant, whose face is flushed a near identical shade, head ducked low. His uniform is dripping wet with champagne, and a visibly intoxicated vampire woman staggers to her feet behind him, her golden dress covered in food.

By the looks of it, the spectacle is her fault, but she glares at the human when she rights herself again.

King Auclair shouts something about getting back to the

celebration from the dais, a fake smile plastered on his face, and the music starts up again as the servant is escorted from the room, a vampire holding each of his arms.

My teeth grind so hard together I'm sure the people around me can hear it.

"Have you tried these?" Daniel appears on my left as he pops a hors d'oeuvre into his mouth—something that looks like bread and salmon. "I've already had six," he says around his mouthful.

I snort. "You're late."

He shrugs, surveying the table behind us for something else to eat. "Not really my scene."

"Me neither," I mutter, shifting my weight as my heels cut into the sides of my feet.

"I do, however, enjoy the drama of watching a real-time love story play out."

"Are you drunk?"

He gives me an unamused look, then nods to the dance floor. "His royal highness has been shooting you *longing* and *pining* glances all night."

I roll my eyes, though the words make my face heat. *I've* been watching Reid all night—for my job, naturally—and I've only caught him looking back at me once, something I've been mentally scolding myself not to read into all night.

"Now I see why you're all over here! You're hiding the food!" Leif bounds up to us, grin covering his entire face, which is still bruised and cut up, but he looks a lot better than the last time I saw him.

"I didn't know they discharged you," I say as he heads for whatever Daniel was eating a moment ago.

"They didn't." He winks. "Don't tell anyone."

Daniel shifts beside me, and my eyes widen. "Sorry. Rude. Leif, this is Daniel. Daniel, this is—"

"Leif." He extends his hand, eyes locked on Daniel. "Skin-walker, right?"

I realize a beat too late there might be some weird skin-walker-werewolf bad blood scenario about to go down, but Daniel nods as he offers his hand, eyes just as laser-focused on Leif.

Leif ducks his head a little at my questioning glance. "Don't look at me. *You* let Saint and Jones off their leashes."

"I—I didn't tell them to look into *me*."

Leif shrugs, unperturbed, still holding Daniel's hand. "They were curious." He turns back to Daniel, blatantly looking him up and down. "And so was I. Would you like to dance?"

I'm totally staring, but I can't help myself as a blush rushes to Daniel's cheeks, and he nods silently, almost looking...*shy*?

Leif's grin returns, though there's a twinkle in his eye that wasn't there before, and he tugs Daniel after him as he heads for the dance floor.

Kirby lets out a little chuckle beside me. "I give it an hour before they *casually slip out of here.*"

I smile as Leif spins Daniel around and tilts him back in a dip, laughing all the while. Daniel's returning smile is slower, hesitant, but there's a lightness to it that I haven't seen in a while. After everything he's been through—we've *all* been through—someone like Leif is probably exactly what he needs.

The music shifts, one song blending into another, and I eye a nearby servant with the blood champagne. It would be stupid to drink it here in plain sight, but my gums are starting to ache every time I catch sight of some in the corner of my vision.

"Dance with me?"

I blink back to the room, to Reid's deep blue eyes gazing down at me, a single corner of his mouth lifted. The buzzing in my mind quiets at his proximity, the closest we've been since we entered the throne room. I smile back as he takes my hand and leads me onto the floor where several other Marionette pairings are dancing.

"It suits you." I touch the new crown on his temple. It's larger than his old one but much subtler than his mother's had been. There are rubies, diamonds, and obsidians embedded among the gold, along with a few pieces of bloodstone.

He smirks and tightens his arm around my waist, pulling me flush against his chest. "It's heavy."

I chuckle and step back, returning a respectful amount of distance between us no matter how much my body protests the loss of his warmth. His smile dims, and he gives a subtle nod before tightening his fingers around mine.

How are you holding up? I ask through the bond. *Really?*

He caresses the back of my hand with his thumb. *Just trying to get through tonight.*

Was that Quinn I saw you with earlier?

His entire face softens around his smile. *Yeah. I didn't know she'd be here. She seems to be doing a lot better. My brother Jared and his wife brought her.*

"Can I cut in?" Anya's face appears behind Reid's shoulder, her smile small, unsure.

"Of course," I say automatically, dropping Reid's hand as

if it burned me, but he's not so quick to release my waist. In fact, as I go to take a step away, his hold tightens on me, keeping me in place.

I shoot a questioning glance up at him, but he's frowning at something over my head, eyebrows tugging together. Then as if in slow motion, his eyes widen.

"Reid—?"

The absolute horror in his expression makes my blood run cold, and then we're falling. The noise registers somewhere between Reid throwing his body in front of mine, tackling us both to the side, and my shoulder striking the hard floor with agonizing force.

The explosion is first, the noise so *full* and dense, layered and complex, it makes every one of my senses reset before I can process what's happening.

My vision blurs and is marred with black splotches, and my lungs struggle to fill with air. After a moment, I realize it's because Reid's on top of me, his weight pressing into my chest.

Reid.

The back of his suit is shredded, blood covering his neck and the side of his face.

"Reid," I try to say, but I can't hear my own voice over the ringing in my ears.

Smoke fills the room, too thick for me to see farther than a few feet. Tables and chairs are flipped over, bodies lying on the ground, mouths open in silent screams.

My skin burns with magic, healing injuries I haven't registered yet. I'm far too preoccupied with Reid's closed eyes. No matter how much I shake his shoulders, I can't wake him up. With how much energy my body is expending trying to heal itself, I can't try to heal him now. Not without feeding.

Gently rolling him onto his back, I push to my feet, eyes burning as I squint through the smoke.

Oh God. The others—

A few figures materialize as the smoke dissipates. I see a flash of pink hair, then red, both on their feet, helping others on the ground. I let out a shaky breath and nearly trip as I take a step to the side, my heel catching on the fabric of another gown.

Shit. Anya had been standing right next to us.

I kneel, bracing myself, but her golden eyes stare up at me, her chin trembling as she mouths words I can't hear. Shards of silver and glass are lodged into her face, her neck, her chest.

I reach a hand for her, helping her into a seated position, then climb shakily to my feet, searching the room for the origin of the explosion.

What happened? Is another one coming? Is whoever set it off still here? Was this Westcott? Was Reid the target?

I clench and unclench my fists, debating between trying to help and not wanting to leave Reid. Not when he's this hurt and unconscious.

Anya's hand brushes my arm from behind, and she sways in her heels. "Go." She nods, glancing from me to Reid. "I'll find Feddei, and we'll both stay with him."

I push through the smoke, surveying the rest of the room. Enough other Marionettes are up and moving to help the injured that it lessens the fist squeezing around my heart.

"Secure the perimeter!" shouts a voice somewhere in the

distance, followed by pounding footsteps. "No one goes in or out."

I stumble to a halt as I reach the throne room doors, one side blown off its hinges. Even through the haze of the smoke, the display on the wall is all too clear.

The blood rains onto the floor in a never-ending flow, King Vasiliev's eyes open and unseeing, nearly the exact expression King Locklear wore. But there's a second head on a spike directly next to him—his son, Prince Alexei.

And standing in front of them with a vacant look in his eyes and blood dripping from both hands is Nathan.

I slap a hand over my mouth as a figure materializes out of the shadows beside him.

V grins. "You're welcome."

CHAPTER TWENTY-THREE

AMID THE CHAOS of the explosion and the nearby Marionettes tackling Nathan to the ground, no one notices me slip into a supply closet, yanking an invisible person behind me as I go.

And that damn smug look on V's face only grows as I close the door behind us and flick on the overhead light. My hands are shaking, and my mind is only half in this closet with her, the rest of my awareness checking in the bond, making sure Reid is okay.

"What the hell did you do?" I whisper.

She frowns. "What we agreed on—"

"This is not what we agreed on!"

"I said I would help you. And that's exactly what I did. We both know you wouldn't have the balls to get rid of them. But it needed to be done. So I think the words you're looking for are *thank you*."

"How is slaughtering the Vasilievs possibly helping me?"

"Isn't it obvious? Come on, Valerie, keep up with me. Who

were the people who made the deal for Reid and Anya to marry? Queen Carrington and King Vasiliev." She ticks them off on her fingers. "Who were most invested to enforce that betrothal?" She wiggles her two fingers now representing the dead monarchs. "You'd have a much better chance of negotiating with Anya than her father."

"And the prince?"

"Well, Anya wouldn't have any power if her brother took the throne, now would she? And considering the company Prince Alexei used to keep, I figured it was safe to assume he needed to go. Not to mention, if his friends shared their theories about your necromancy with anyone, it was probably him." She gives me a knowing look, and I shiver despite myself.

The Russians who had been after Reid—and had their fun with me—were friends with Prince Alexei. No one decent makes friends like that.

"So now you have Reid on the throne, and Anya on the throne. If they can come to some agreement without marrying, there's no one above them they need to convince. Brilliant, isn't it?"

I narrow my eyes. I don't believe for a second her only motive was to stop Reid's marriage for me.

"Except now you have this entire estate even more panicked than it already was. They were so sure nothing could breach security. What if Auclair decides we need to relocate?"

"That would be inconvenient," she admits. "But as much as I hate to admit it, I think he's smarter than that. The Vasiliev deaths look similar to the attack on Locklear, but not identical. Once his Marionettes examine the bodies and question Nathan, he'll realize the attacks aren't the same."

"But when they look through his head, they'll see that *you* made him do this."

She shrugs, that unhinged smile returning. "Oh, I doubt it. He may have had one of the weakest minds I've ever seen. Controlling him didn't even break a sweat. He one hundred percent believes it was his idea to kill them. They'll find it suspicious, probably, but it won't link back to me."

I sputter, my face getting hot, and a spark of fear ignites in the center of my chest as the full reality of what happened sinks in. Not only can she use magic without a physical form on this side, but she's *strong.* "You can't just go off controlling people—*killing* people! Queen Carrington—that was you too?"

"Ugh, she was a real bitch, wasn't she? Wish I could take credit for that one, but no. Daddy Westcott pulled that one off on his own. But I *can* tell you it was dark magic that did it, so he must have someone else with that skillset working for him. Same person who got that Marionette to nosedive into the pavement, I'm guessing."

"Who would have that kind of power?" I push.

She shrugs. "Anyone, really. Certain witches have a more natural inclination toward dark magic, sure, and it might come easier to them, but that doesn't mean they're the only ones who can do it. It's only rare magic on your side of the veil now because the vamps were so vigilant about destroying all of the books and instructions they could get their hands on back when they tried to eradicate the necromancers. But just because information is hard to come by doesn't mean it doesn't exist. Hell, your dad's been shooting up on stolen powers for so long, maybe he's doing it himself."

"And I'm just supposed to take your word for it? How am I ever supposed to trust you after this?"

"Ungrateful, much? I did this for *you.*"

I shake my head and raise my hands to put some kind of barrier between us. Because the worst part of all of this is, she's right. I asked for her help. I let her in. I convinced myself that I needed her help when I should've been putting my energy into finding a way to send her back.

I did this. I did this. I did this.

If I don't fix this, and soon, who knows what else will happen. What bodies we'll find next, or worse.

Why had I even trusted her in the first place? Looking back on it, I can't believe I ever agreed to it. Sure, I was panicked, but—

Slowly, I raise my eyes to meet hers.

The next level would be to get inside their mind to make them think it's their idea in the first place.

He one hundred percent believes it was his idea to kill them.

Did I decide to work with her, or did she make me *think* it was my decision? She's been working with dark magic her entire life. Who knows how strong she is, what she's capable of? I'd assumed not fully being on this side would limit her abilities, but if tonight's any indication, even if she's not as strong this way, she's strong enough.

I'd known since the start that she was using me, but I thought I'd be able to outsmart her, to see through her plans. She waited until I was exhausted after training with Reid, my mind and body weak and ripe for the taking.

Magnolia had tried to warn me. But I'd been so fucking cocky that I could handle it. That I would have the upper hand. Then I handed over the keys to the estate on a goddamn silver platter.

I bite my tongue hard enough that I taste blood, forcing myself to swallow everything I want to say. She's been ten steps ahead of me this entire time, and for now, I need to let her think that she still is.

Because if she's not going to tell me what she's up to, I'll have to figure it out myself. Afterall, if her life is a byproduct of every choice I've made, of who I've become, then I should know her brain inside and out, right?

———

THE ESTATE IS NOT EQUIPPED to handle this many injuries, especially with the hospital already so overrun. After giving Reid some blood, painkilling potions, and the first wave of healing magic, I help him back to his room where I've been instructed not to leave his side—*don't even blink*, I believe had been the exact directive—until the healers finish their rounds and come back to see if he needs a second wave of healing, or if his body will be able to manage from here with blood and rest.

Aside from King Vasiliev and his son—his *heir*—no deaths have been reported, none that I've heard. Just an enormously inconvenient number of injuries.

They've taken Nathan to the dungeons for questioning, and if his mind is as weak as V described, it shouldn't take long for them to find their answers. And if they decide he's guilty, if they choose to prosecute him to placate everyone's nerves, he could burn for this.

And the way my body reacts to that thought is...annoying. Because he isn't a good person. He's hurt the people I love and probably countless others. But this...this he didn't do.

Reid's half asleep, half high-off-his-ass from the painkillers as I help him to bed, his eyes shut but his lips turned up in a smile. He's still in his suit from the celebration, the fabric torn and covered in blood and debris.

He flops onto the bed on his back, legs dangling off the end, and I kneel to start untying his shoes. He lets out a small hum as the first drops to the ground with a soft thud, then the second.

He shielded me from the worst of the blow, and after a few bags of blood, my body made short work of the healing. Too short of work, but that's a detail I don't have time to get hung up on. I rise onto the bed beside him, and he blinks up at me with wide blue eyes, brighter than usual in contrast to the blood and dirt on his face.

"You're the prettiest girl in the world," he whispers.

I let out something between a scoff and a laugh even as his words travel like a chill down my spine. "You're on drugs."

"Especially when you laugh." Even quieter, he murmurs, "I love it when you laugh." He smiles as his eyes shut, and he makes a hum in the back of his throat as I work my fingers into the knot of his tie. "I'd say the same sober. I've always thought so." His fingers skim my arm, and when I look back at his face, his eyes are open, the goofy, sleepy smile still in place. "I also like it when you undress me."

I do my best to scowl at him, but my lips roll together,

fighting back another laugh. "Stop making me laugh. I'm mad at you."

"No you're not."

"Yes I am."

"No, you're not." His fingers skim my cheek as he tucks my hair behind my ear, and my breath catches. He tightens his hand, pulling my face closer to his.

"Reid…"

His other hand finds my waist.

"Reid, I don't want to hurt you," I murmur, careful of where I put my hands, how much weight I let press into him.

But he pulls me back in, his lips brushing mine as he whispers, "Hurt me."

I already have. The only reason he's even in this bed right now is me. I pull back, looking away before I see his reaction. "You should rest."

"What's wrong?"

"Nothing."

He cups the side of my face, forcing me to meet his eyes, and beyond the haze in his, there's a striking clarity fighting to reach the surface.

I sigh and lay my hand over his. "We can talk about it when you're not high."

"I'm not that high," he slurs, and his lips twitch like he hears it too and is trying not to smile.

"The explosion tonight," I say, folding a leg to sit beside him, "it was V. Apparently she was strong enough to control a vampire to make him kill the Vasilievs."

He searches my face. "Why?"

"She *says* it was so both you and Anya would be on the

thrones now instead of your parents, and you two would have a better chance of negotiating without having to marry, but I doubt that's all there was to it."

"And the vampire she made kill them?"

I can't help the scowl that takes over my face. "Nathan Van Doren."

"Monroe's partner?"

I nod and break the eye contact. I haven't filled him in yet on what Nathan's been up to either, but in part, it doesn't feel like my story to share. "But the point is, even without a physical body on this side, she's strong. Stronger than I realized. Stronger than maybe even *she* realized. But if she didn't know what she was capable of before, she's figured it out now."

My phone chimes in my pocket, and when I pull it out, the screen is unsurprisingly shattered. I can still make out the text waiting for me.

Connor: *Can I come in? The guards won't even let me knock.*

I hurry toward the door, checking through the peephole before unlocking it. Connor stands on the other side, bloody and dirty but in one piece. My stomach drops. I'd been so focused on everyone else, I hadn't even realized he'd been at the coronation.

Two Marionettes are stationed outside as an additional layer of protection for Reid, and they dip their chins to me as I open the door and usher Connor inside. In the meantime, it seems Reid has fallen asleep, his soft snores filling the room.

My chest pinches. Is there something wrong with his lungs? He never snores.

But then I take in the book tucked under Connor's arm

and the determined look on his face, and I wave him over to the chairs by the fireplace.

"Are you okay?" I ask. "Why didn't you tell me you were coming tonight?"

"I wasn't planning on it." He holds up the book. "But I was going through that memoir that Russian Marionette recommended, and I found something."

"Something you think could help send her back?"

"Not exactly…" He flips to a page he has bookmarked, his gaze drifting to Reid on the bed. "Is he okay enough to wake up? He'll want to hear this."

"I'm awake," Reid calls, his voice low and raspy. "What did you find, Connor?"

"A lot of what this guy talks about sounds like insanity and rambles, but there was a detail that I couldn't shake. When describing what it was like coming into contact with shadow selves, he describes them as having no heartbeat." He stares at me expectantly as if this is some grand revelation.

I try to think back to the times I've interacted with V— would I have noticed if she didn't have a pulse? It would be odd for sure, but I don't know if—

The sheets rustle behind us as Reid sits up, and I open my mouth to protest him moving around too much, but the intensity in his eyes as he and Connor exchange a look stops me cold.

"No heartbeat," Reid repeats.

Connor nods.

"What is going on?" I demand. "What does that mean?"

"It means someone needs to go find Quinn," says Reid. "Now."

CHAPTER TWENTY-FOUR

The longer it takes Connor to find Quinn, the more my anxiety grows. She's *human*. I barely survived that explosion, and that was with Reid acting like a body shield, my blood magic, *and* my half-vampire healing. If she'd been close to the blast...

Reid can't lose her a second time. *I* can't watch Reid lose her a second time.

Enough time passes that the healers come back around for Reid's second wave of healing, but he declines the extra painkillers they offer.

"Reid—" I try to protest.

"I need to be awake," he insists quietly. "The pain isn't bad. I promise."

He and I both know he's lying, but I get him another blood bag and help him into a seated position against the headboard.

Just when I start to feel like I can't take it anymore and I'll find someone else to sit with Reid for a few minutes so I can track down Quinn myself, the door opens.

Reid's sigh of relief is audible as I jump up from the bed and hurry toward them. Despite my barely knowing her, Quinn seems unsurprised when I pull her into a hug, then hold her at arm's length checking for injury, but she doesn't have a scratch on her.

"I left to go to the bathroom," she explains. "I don't—I don't even want to think about what could have happened…" She trails off as she takes in Reid on the bed.

Despite looking infinitely better than he had a few hours ago, Quinn's face falls, and I don't think I've ever seen someone cross a room faster.

"It's not as bad as it looks," he assures her, but his voice is weak and low.

She presses the back of her hand to his forehead, murmuring something too low for me to hear, and I can't help but smile at the humanness of it all.

He gives her a smile as weak as his voice. "You sound better," he says.

"The village healer had seen something similar before," she explains. "The first few remedies didn't work, but we kept trying."

I have no idea what he means by *sound better*.

"The village is actually what we wanted to talk to you about," says Connor behind me before I can ask.

The village?

"No one there had a heartbeat," continues Connor. "Why?"

"Wait, what?" I demand.

Quinn's brow furrows as every eye in the room focuses on her. "Shadow selves that have crossed over tend to gravitate toward each other," she says slowly. "The village has always been a safe place for them."

An entire *village* of shadow selves?

"What do you know about shadow selves, Quinn?" says Reid, sounding utterly perplexed. "You said…you said those people were your family."

"They are," she insists. "At least in the important ways. They took me in and raised me after my parents died. At least I think they're dead. I was so young when it happened, I don't remember them at all. My parents—my adoptive parents— said they found me wandering the barrens all alone. I was four. They took me in and waited for my parents to coming looking for me, but they never did. By the time I was seventeen, I moved into New York with the hopes of getting into the vampire industries. Not many opportunities in the barrens, and the risks as a human are…higher. Anyway, by eighteen, I was with Reid." Her smile softens as she lays a hand on his shoulder.

"Do you know how they came over to this side? Or what happened to the versions of them who used to be here?" asks Connor.

"Or do you know how to send a shadow self back?" I add. "One who doesn't have a physical form yet."

Quinn's head ping-pongs between us, the line between her eyebrows deepening. "It was different for each of them, the circumstances that allowed them to cross over. As for sending them back…I don't know. It's rare for one to exist on this plane if not in the full capacity. They would've needed something to latch on to to cross."

"Or someone," murmurs Connor, glancing at me out of the corner of his eye.

Quinn follows his gaze. "It's yours."

I nod.

"And she's made contact with you?"

"That's putting it mildly."

She chews on her lip, worry dampening the light in her eyes. "I've never seen it done before, and with no magic of my own, I've never learned how to do it. Someone back home may know."

But would they willingly give up that information? Something that could be used against them?

"Can you get in touch with them from here?" Reid asks. He leans forward but comes to a sudden stop after a few inches, his wince evident despite how hard he tries to hide it.

"You need to rest," I say. "We can talk about this tomorrow."

"I'll see if I can get ahold of them," says Quinn. "But I agree with Valerie. For now, you just focus on healing."

"Connor, I need to stay here with him, but can you go check that everyone else is okay?"

He nods and heads for the door, Quinn close behind. "I'll keep you updated."

The door clicks shut as I grab a washcloth to wet in the bathroom sink. The healers have been in such a hurry with all the injuries, so they tended to Reid's wounds but didn't have time for much else. His eyes are closed and his head tipped back against the wall as I sit beside him, bringing the wet cloth up to get some of the dirt and blood off his face.

"You don't have to do that," he says softly.

"Stop talking." I move on to his chin, then his jaw, careful to avoid anything that might be painful. Even with all the help he's received and his accelerated vampire healing, he looks so...*human* right now. That blast could've killed him. A second longer standing there and it probably would have.

His hand finds my knee, the touch light. "I really am feeling better already."

I nod, focused on scrubbing the blood from his hairline, but the strands are entirely coated in blood and dirt. I don't think I'll be able to get it out without a full shampoo. Every time I blink, I see him staked to the floor when the Russians were testing if I could bring him back. Coming home to find him not moving, not breathing. Not even a whisper of life left inside him.

His fingers flex against my leg. "Valerie."

Westcott's words—*He's already dead*—echo in my head. Walking into that cold room where his body was so still on a metal table.

"Valerie."

His arms bound to the post as the whip sliced through his flesh, the air filled with jeers and slurs, and he'd just taken it. He'd just put his head down and taken it.

"Please look at me," he whispers.

"Don't ever do that again."

"Valerie—"

"*I* am supposed to protect *you*. Don't *ever* do that—"

"Come here." His other hand finds the side of my neck,

and he tugs me against his side and tucks my head beneath his chin, but I resist from leaning my weight into him.

"I don't want to hurt you." I sniffle, only now noticing the tears on my cheeks.

"You won't."

"You can't do things like this, Reid. Not with so many people counting on you now. You can get another partner. But the region needs you. No one who could take your place will care for them the way I know you will. You are the only hope they have for change. You are the only hope they have for something better."

He presses his lips to the top of my head. "You're not just my partner, Valerie. You know that. And I will never apologize for doing everything I can to protect you. So please, I don't want to argue. Just sit here with me."

Once it's clear I really won't hurt him, I let myself relax against his chest, which is where I stay even long after he falls back asleep.

CHAPTER TWENTY-FIVE

THERE ARE two noticeably empty seats in the conference room the following night. They could've easily been filled with other officials or Marionettes who are standing among the outskirts of the room, but I have a feeling Auclair's using them as a visual reminder of the two deceased royals to sway the vote.

Especially since they're right beside Anya.

She seems mostly healed now, but faint pink scars on her face catch the light as she turns her head. Her hands are tightly grasped together on the table, but her expression is impassive as we walk inside, a flick of her eyes the only sign she notices us.

After a full day's rest and two additional feeding and healing sessions, Reid manages to walk on his own, the slight wince as he sits down the only indication he's in pain.

"My people are starting to panic," says Queen Suksai near the head of the table. "If Westcott breached security here, we can't stay. And I don't want to leave my estate unprepared if we're one of his next targets—"

"This wasn't him," Auclair insists, rising to his feet and raising his palms for the rest of the side conversations in the room to quiet. "I will make an announcement shortly after this meeting to put minds at ease. This was an isolated attack, and Nathan Van Doren was working alone. An altercation over a personal matter with Alexei Vasiliev escalated, and when his father stepped in to break it up, he was also killed." His words are matter-of-fact, but he at least has the decency to pause and bow his head in acknowledgment to Anya. "The suspect has been thoroughly questioned, and his blood tests showed a significant level of alcohol and other illegal substances, which we believe contributed to his lapse in judgment that allowed his vampiric instincts to take over to such a violent degree. This was a tragic accident, and we need to take immediate action before rumors and panic spreads. I've gathered you all to put his fate to a vote. We have our own procedures here, but given the severity of the crime and the unusual circumstances, I wanted all of your voices to be heard."

It takes everything in me to keep my face in check. Is he *serious*? He honestly believes this was some drunken frat boy fight gone wrong? Both of the Vasilievs were *beheaded* and mounted on the wall.

"If we're all in agreement, the lunar Marionettes have requested we wait until the full moon on Saturday so they can harness the energy from his death to strengthen the wards around the estates. I'll make the announcement today, and he'll publicly confess to his crimes prior to his execution."

Reid's brow is furrowed as he watches Auclair. This seems too good to be true.

I'd been worried I'd have to tell Auclair the truth about what happened with V. They were so certain nothing could breach the boundary they erected, that security was impenetrable. If they blamed this on Westcott and assumed he somehow broke through, they might have relocated everyone to somewhere not as safe. There are too many people here to fit in the bunker.

But for him to so readily believe Westcott has nothing to do with this, especially after several displays of mind manipulation that we don't fully understand—like what happened with Reid's mother—Auclair is smarter than that.

Unless.

My blood runs cold.

Unless he's been manipulated too.

The other officials, at least, seem more skeptical as they look around the table.

"Are we certain his memories hadn't been tampered with?" offers an advisor.

"I looked through his mind myself," says Auclair, "along with half a dozen Marionettes, but you're all welcome to do the same. All security systems have been analyzed as well. I can assure you I would not guarantee your safety here lightly given the stakes."

I feel for the bond in my chest and give it a tentative pull. Reid sits up straighter but doesn't look at me.

I think V got to him too.

"All in favor of moving forward with the execution this Saturday?"

You can't tell him the truth, says Reid. *It's too dangerous. If they find out the full extent of it—that you've been practicing dark magic and can control vampires, they'll execute you too, Valerie. They won't leave anything to chance, especially not right now.*

One by one, murmurs of agreement fill the room.

"This show of strength is what we need right now," continues Auclair. "Put our people's minds at ease."

So you're saying we should just let Nathan take the fall for this?

"Reginald."

I blink back to the room as Auclair levels his gaze on Reid.

"The attack happened on Auclair property, but Nathan Van Doren is your subject. We will only move ahead for his execution with your approval. But people want answers. We need to give them something. Are we in agreement?"

All attention lands on Reid—the only other person in this room who knows what really happened. The veins in his hands stand out as he tightens his fists against his thighs. He looks from Auclair to Anya.

The people of the Carrington estate will see this as his first decision as their king. If they believe Nathan broke their sacred law against killing other vampires, they'll be satisfied with nothing less than his death. If Reid shows too much mercy, they might find him weak, incompetent to rule.

There's no way to spare Nathan and satisfy his subjects without outing me.

He'd been so broken up over the attack on Westcott's compound, over the thousands of people he helped kill. And that had been an act of war, one with a chance—no matter how small it might have been—that Westcott would have negotiated instead.

I can't rule like her. I won't.

But this…forcing him to execute a man he knows to be innocent just to save me…

I can't. I can't let him. I can't watch what that will do to him.

I clear my throat, and it sounds too loud in the silence of the room, but he speaks before I can.

"Yes."

REID's entire demeanor changes once we're behind the closed doors of his room again. His limp becomes significantly more pronounced, his shoulders slumped, and he all but drags himself across the room before collapsing into bed. I say nothing, just resituate the pillows and grab him another blood bag and healing potion.

"I'm fine," he murmurs. "I just need rest. You were here all day. You should get some sleep."

As much as I don't want to leave his side, I could desperately use a few hours of sleep…and a shower. I bite my lip, feeling like we should talk about what happened, but his eyes are closed, and God, the bags under them are so dark they look like bruises. It can wait.

Adrienne's not in her room when I step inside, leaving me with only my thoughts for company as I hop in the shower. After voting on Nathan's fate, the officials agreed to hold off on another attack against Westcott's compounds until the Marionettes are able to use the sacrifice to strengthen the wards, not just at this estate, but all of them. That way we'll be more prepared for Westcott's next move.

But a break from the violence for few days doesn't bring much comfort.

I climb straight into bed with my hair still wet. I just need to close my eyes for a few minutes, then I'll be fine—

I WAKE to someone violently shaking my shoulders. I slam my hand up, instincts taking over, and something hard crunches against my palm.

"Ow! Fuck, Val!"

My eyes fly open as Adrienne stumbles back a step, a hand covering her nose.

"Oh my God. Sorry. Is it broken?"

Her fingers come away bloody, but the damage looks minimal. At least, until I take in the smeared makeup. Tracks of mascara run down her face like she's been crying.

I bolt upright. How long was I asleep? "What happened? Are you okay?"

Still holding her nose with one hand, she fishes in her pocket with the other until she produces a scrap of paper. Her fingers tremble as she hands it over.

My stomach drops.

Spill any more of their blood, and I spill hers.

Attached is a picture of my mother hunched in a dimly lit dungeon cell.

"When did—"

"A few hours ago. In my dorm room. He's going to kill her," she whispers, her chin wobbling.

"Hey, slow down." I swing my legs over the side of the bed, turning the note over in my hands. Magic tingles on my fingertips as I do.

Taking this to Auclair won't change anything. This wouldn't stop him from launching another attack. He won't care.

And maybe I shouldn't either. I shouldn't feel anything at all when I look at my mother anymore, but she looks so small in the picture. Curled into a ball in the corner of the bare room like she's huddling into herself for warmth. This woman who punished and reprimanded and tormented me my entire life.

This woman who saved me, probably even more than I realize.

"Please don't let her die," Adrienne whispers. "If you're going to do something, it has to be now. The attacks are never going to end unless we stop Westcott for good. So are you going to use that book or not?"

"Just..." I look from her to the note, a knife twisting in the center of my chest every time the picture catches the corner of my eye, so I turn it over. "We have to be smart about this."

"There's no time! There's no telling what Auclair and the others will do! They've already killed thousands of them without batting an eye. They could make some impulsive plan and attack any second—"

"Just give me the night to think about it, okay?"

"What's there to think about? I know you hate her, but she's my mom too. If you won't do it for her, do it for me."

"I don't hate her," I say quietly.

"If it's the sacrifice part of the spell you're so hung up on, just take that guy from the dungeon!" I balk, but she widens her eyes and shrugs. "What? He's going to die anyway! And he's a predatory douchebag! And this is—this is *Mom*." Her voice hitches, and she turns to the side, her nose scrunching the way it does when she's trying not to cry.

I smooth the wrinkles out of the paper in my hands, willing myself to feel surprise—disgust—at the suggestion, but the words land as if I've already thought them before, even if not consciously.

"Valerie," she pleads.

She doesn't understand my hesitation. It's not that I disagree with her. It's how easily I know I could justify it to myself. How easily I can imagine myself doing it. But crossing that line, I don't know if I'll come back from it.

"Your friends listen to you," she continues. "God, I wish I could do it, but I can't set this up alone—"

"You are getting nowhere near that spell," I snap.

"Then *help me*. You're the only one who can pull this off. Valerie, please. I never ask you for anything. Please."

When I don't respond right away, her face tightens, and she shakes her head, already taking a step away from me.

"Adrienne—"

"Hello?" someone calls as they knock gently on the door.

Adrienne and I exchange a look, and the door cracks open.

Quinn pokes her head inside with an unsure smile. "I'm sorry if I'm interrupting."

"No, no. Come on in, Quinn," I say. It isn't until I take in the serious look on her face that it occurs to me *why* she might be knocking at my door. "*Oh*, did you—"

She quickly shakes her head, her hand flying to something in her pocket. "I just came by to check on you. See how you're doing."

I stop short, my brow stitching in confusion.

"Oh, also"—she makes a big show of producing a sheet of paper, as if just remembering it was there—"Reid is resting. He's doing much better today, but the healers upped their dose of potions to get him back on his feet faster, so he'll be sleeping more, but he asked me to give you this note." I reach for the paper, but she doesn't release it. "Maybe read it in private. It seemed…personal."

"Okay," I murmur, not for a second believing this is from Reid. If he'd wanted to talk to me, he could have said something through the bond. And one glimpse inside the note verifies this is definitely not his handwriting.

She squeezes my hand, gives Adrienne a tight smile, then just as quickly as she'd come, turns and disappears through the door.

Valerie,

   Be careful where you read this and if you speak any part aloud. Your shadow self could be listening or watching even when you're unaware of her presence.

   You hold more power on this side of the veil due to your physical form. Should you venture too close to the darkness (a spell that requires a great deal of dark power, for example) her chances of overpowering you increase. But that would also be the most opportune time for you to force her back into the shadow realm.

   Reid tells me your mother has instructed you to perform a dark spell against Westcott. If you do, there are measures you can take to protect yourself. You can create a ward for a single person, usually bound to an object, like a necklace.

   A similar object can be created to help send your shadow self back. I've included the spell and ingredients you'll need below.

   Valerie, please be careful. For your sake, your family's, your friends', and selfishly, I'm asking you to think of Reid. I fear losing you is something he wouldn't survive.

Do what you must, but please, be careful.

Quinn

CHAPTER TWENTY-SIX

I DON'T SLEEP at all. I toss and turn for hours, my mind never slowing.

About Nathan. Westcott. V. Mom. Adrienne. The spell.

It was always going to come to this. I think a part of me knew that. But the finality of allowing myself to accept it sits so heavily in the center of my chest I can barely draw breath.

After another sleepless hour passes, I look past the text I'd sent Adrienne a few hours ago—*I'll do it*—and stare at the date at the top of the screen.

November 21.

Then I shove myself out of bed.

I leave on the tank top I'd been sleeping in and add some sweatpants, then I'm heading down the hall barefoot. It's the middle of the day, so most of the estate is asleep. I nod at the guards and servants I pass as I wind my way through the corridors, trying to muster a better mood for myself. This isn't how

I want to spend *today* of all days. For my sake and his. The problem will still be there come sunset.

A few servants linger in the kitchens, and they shoot me wary glances when I step through the door. After helping them finish their cleanup and explaining my plan, a few of the older women graciously step in. But once they help me find all of the necessary tools and ingredients, I insist on doing it on my own.

The staff scatters off with other duties, and the temperature in the room quickly rises as I preheat the oven.

"It can't be that different from making a potion," I assure myself as cloud of flour explodes in my face. I cough and wave a hand, trying to get it away from my eyes.

I examine the recipe on the counter, hands on my hips. It might as well be in a foreign language, but I am determined. Because the world is on fire and people are dying and plans are being made, and yes, it's all very important, but I refuse—I *refuse*—to let that get in the way of doing this.

I'm already sweating, and I haven't even gotten the damn thing in the oven yet. The servants earlier warned me I'd need to wait a good long while after it came out before adding the frosting. God forbid I fuck this one up and need to start over.

Because I am not walking out of this kitchen with a wonky-ass cake. It's going to be professional grade. The best damn cake anyone in this estate has ever seen.

THIS IS PROBABLY the worst damn cake anyone in this estate has ever seen. Four hours later, I make my way through the hall, practically holding my breath as I balance the plate in my hands.

The cake is two tiers, buttercream icing in the middle and in weird attempts at embellishments on the sides. The only food coloring option I had was blue, so I mixed it with the white icing to look like clouds—the sky during the day, something he never gets to see but I know that he wants to.

Well, that was the idea, at least. The top is caved in on one side, and the layers of icing are clearly uneven. There were also only two candles in that whole goddamn kitchen, so there's a shaky 26 in blue icing and the two candles awkwardly framing it.

It's a few hours before sunset, so he should still be sleeping, which is probably for the best. Then I can deliver my shameful little creation without having to see his reaction.

The closer I get to his room, the more depressing the sight of the cake becomes. Especially given the effort he'd put into my birthday in comparison. Circumstances were entirely different then, but yet...

Maybe I should turn back now. Save him from having to pretend like this isn't the most pathetic—

The bond twinges in my chest, and my steps slow as I blink hard, trying to keep the cake from falling. But now my vision is going in and out, and oh God—

The same familiarity I'd felt looking through the memories in Reid's head envelops me as his dream materializes in place of the hallway.

It's not the same as the memory itself, but the moment is instantly recognizable, even witnessing it from a different angle than the one I experienced it in.

Now, I stand by the door to Reid's bedroom. The rest of the space is a blur of motion as men swarm Reid against the wall and a past version of me is tied to the bed. I look away from myself, not needing a reminder of what happens next, focusing on Reid's face instead. It's twisted in anguish, though by the look in his eyes, it has more to do with what he's seeing than the physical pain of the stakes securing him to the wall.

"Reid," I breathe, pushing into the room. But even then, he sees right through me.

"Please just let her go," he wheezes, his lungs sounding like they're full of water. "I'll do whatever you want."

There are more men in the room than I remember there being during the actual incident, more stakes securing him to wall, and even more bloody wounds in his body from where he's torn some free.

He lets out a roar that's more animal than human, but I don't turn as I hear my own scream behind me.

"Reid, you're dreaming." I reach for his face, but my hands go straight through him. "Reid!" I shout, hoping he'll hear me somehow like he did when I was in the shadow realm. "You're asleep. *Wake up.*"

He struggles against the stakes, and rivulets of blood soak through his shirt. He manages to rip one arm free, but another man is there, stabbing a different stake into his shoulder.

"Take me instead," Reid pants. "Leave her out of this. *Leave her out of this.*"

There's another scream from behind me, this one blood-curdling and cutting off with a gurgle.

I stumble back a step, my shoulder connecting with a wall as I break out of the dream like bursting through the surface of ice-cold water. My fingers are in a death grip around the plate—it's a miracle I didn't drop the damn cake—and I close my eyes for a moment as I try to calm my breathing.

My chest tightens around my pounding heart. But it's not my chest, I realize. It's the bond, struck so tight between us it feels like it's on the verge of snapping.

He's still in the dream.

All common sense disappears as I reach his room and throw the door open.

But he doesn't wake up.

He's on his back in the bed, his chest rising and falling rapidly with his breath as his head twists against the pillow. Sweat plasters his hair to his forehead.

"Reid." Discarding the cake on the nightstand, I climb onto the bed and grab both sides of his face. "Reid, you're okay. You're dreaming. Wake up."

His head turns to face me, but he doesn't wake.

"Reid." I shake his shoulders. Is he still on those sedative potions to help him sleep? What if they're keeping him stuck there? What if I can't wake him up? "Reid, *wake up.*"

He gasps, then moves too fast for me to see. I hit the mattress on my back, and it knocks the wind from my lungs. He straddles my hips, his forearm pressing down on my throat and his fangs bared.

He blinks, realization dawning in his eyes, and yanks back, releasing me.

I gasp for air.

"Valerie," he says breathlessly. "I'm—I'm so sorry—"

"It's okay," I whisper, my heart sprinting at full speed as I cup the side of his face. "It's okay."

"What are you...?" He blinks a few times, like he's still trying to pull himself from the dream, and I push myself up to sit in front of him.

I probably shouldn't have come. I should go now that he's okay. I should, I should, but everything inside of me feels like an open wound looking at him in pain, and being in the same room as him makes my lungs feel like they can *breathe* again.

I take his face with both hands and inch closer. "It was just a dream. I'm okay." I wrap my arms around his shoulders, and he gives no resistance, immediately collapsing against me. His arms tighten around my waist, holding me to him like he's afraid I'll slip through his fingers.

"You saw that?" he murmurs.

I nod.

"I'm sorry if I woke you—"

"Shh." I run my fingers through his hair as he presses his forehead to my shoulder.

My heart feels like it's splitting clean in two. Because no matter what's happened, how much pain we've endured, I've never seen him like this. Not even close. The toll on both of us has been undeniable, but he's always seemed to bear it so much better than I can. But maybe that's just what he let me see.

"Reid," I whisper, tightening my arms around him while avoiding the bandages and bruises like I can physically put his broken pieces back together.

"I'm fine." He pulls back with a forced smile, blinking away the moisture in his eyes, that carefully kept wall closing between us again. And maybe it's not just me. Maybe he doesn't want anyone to see him need them. "Just a dream. You can…"

You can go is what he'd been about to say, though the death grip he has on my waist says otherwise. Even when it's so clear that he needs someone here for him, he won't ask.

"Would it be okay if I stay?"

His eyes snap to mine, the spark of light unmistakable. An eternity passes, or maybe only a few moments, but a million unsaid words pass between us.

I want him to say yes. I need him to say no.

Every time I look into his eyes, it feels like the first time. The endless blue is just as mesmerizing, the depth behind them boring deep into my mind, my heart, my soul. With one look, I know he's seeing more of me than anyone else ever has.

We haven't even spent that much time apart, not really. But maybe that's what makes this worse, why my chest is aching with an unquenchable thirst—to see him most days, but to not have him the way I want, the way I need.

He does a double take when he notices the cake sitting a few feet away.

"Is that a…?"

I snort at the sudden ridiculousness of it all, and he turns to me with an uncertain smile.

"Happy birthday? I know it's ugly, and it's lame, especially compared to what you did for mine. And I know things are weird between us, and the entire world is on fire, but I just—I just wanted to do something. And I have absolutely no practice with this kind of thing, which is why it looks, well, you know. It's supposed to look like the sky during the day. Those weird white things are supposed to be clouds, and yeah."

I snap my mouth shut and fold my knees into my body.

Slowly, Reid looks from me to the cake, and God I wish he wasn't so damn good at masking his emotions because I have no idea what that look on his face means. He looks…stunned.

"You made this?" he asks.

"Yeah." I scratch at the back of my neck.

"Just now? In the middle of the day?"

"Yeah."

He inspects the rest of the cake's details. Quietly, he says, "Thank you."

I nod, my throat too thick to respond.

Finally, he cracks a small smile, and I would give anything to keep seeing this look on his face instead of the broken emptiness that had been in his eyes a few moments ago. "You're not going to make me eat this alone, are you?"

"First you have to make a wish." I slide the cake off the nightstand to hold it between us, then prick my finger to light the two candles. His eyes soften as we look at each other over the cake, and he holds my gaze as he leans forward and blows the candles out.

"Happy birthday."

"Thank you, Valerie. Really."

"I know this isn't much—"

"It's perfect. No one's made me a birthday cake before. Let me go find some forks."

No one's ever made him a cake? I mean, I know he doesn't need to eat, but it's the principle of it. Even with my upbringing, I don't think my mother ever did, but Calla had, and so had my friends.

"Now I feel really shitty that *this* is your first experience," I mutter as I move to the table by the fireplace at the same time he returns and hands me a fork. He's moving around a lot better now—no more limping, at least.

I brace myself as he takes the seat across from me and digs out a bite. I wait for a wince, a gag, a shudder.

But he swallows and murmurs with his eyes closed, "That is the second best thing I've ever tasted in my life."

"Second best?"

There's a wicked glint when he opens his eyes, and my face floods with heat.

"You're terrible," I mumble, fishing out my own bite.

He presses his lips together, though it does little to hide his smirk, and the way he looks up at me through his lashes has that heat spreading to other parts of my body. I shove the cake in my mouth, hoping the horrible taste will draw my senses back to the present instead of the visual currently playing out in my head, and I pause as it melts on my tongue, the perfect mix of vanilla and chocolate. Well, that's surprising.

He's back to that soft smile as he watches me eat, and I cover my mouth as I swallow. The look in his eyes melts me from the inside out. Even now when I shouldn't let it. My gaze flicks back to the bandages remaining on his abdomen and the shadows of bruises lingering beneath his jaw.

"How are you feeling?"

"Better. Really." He digs out another bite of the cake. "Should be good as new in another night or two."

"Good. That's good. I...I should probably get going," I blurt out and rise to my feet, though it's the last thing I want to do. But the longer I stay in here with him, the harder it is to hold on to my resolve, to keep this much-needed distance between us.

He doesn't argue with me and stands to walk me out.

"Happy birthday," I say again, going in for a hug. His scent envelops me, and despite my better judgment, I give him a quick kiss on the cheek.

But when I start to pull away, his arms tighten around my waist.

I swallow hard. "Reid."

"Just…a little longer."

My body relaxes into his embrace like it has a mind of its own, the tension easing like I've finally come home after all this time.

But we can't stay here. The moment I walk out that door, reality will come crashing back. Pulling away feels like losing him all over again, reopening the jagged wound in my chest.

It isn't until he takes my face in his hands that I realize tears are running down my cheeks.

"Don't go."

"Reid…"

The intensity burning behind his eyes threatens to ignite us both. "I will call it off tonight," he says lowly. "I will do it right now if you stay. And whatever happens, happens."

"If you did—if you let all of those people die—you wouldn't be the man I love. And I wouldn't be the right person for you if I asked you to."

He brushes the tears away with his thumbs. "Just for once," he whispers, "I want to do the selfish thing. If it came down to them or you, I would choose you, Valerie. Over everything."

My breath hitches. "Reid…" Instead of putting more

distance between us like I know I should, my fingers find his chest and lightly trace up to his collarbones.

His eyes close at my touch. The contact tingles on my fingertips, just skin barely touching skin, but my breathing is already uneven.

I don't think it's the contact at all—it's everything else. Being close to him after so many nights of forcing ourselves apart, of trying to pretend it wasn't hard, of acting like there was nothing between us even as my heart screamed and begged for this, consequences be damned. My eyes fall closed too, and I feel him draw closer, the heat of his breath washing over me, but his lips don't brush mine.

When I open my eyes again, he's staring back at me, every emotion and thought and nameless sensation running rampant inside of me mirrored in his eyes. There's barely any space left between us, and I skim my fingers up his shoulders, his neck, until they find the sides of his face, fitting perfectly against him like they belong there.

"Valerie," he says, his voice a plea.

I wet my lips, the energy thrumming through me almost too much to bear. After so many nights of putting my own feelings aside, of doing the right thing...I'm so fucking tired.

So I close the rest of the distance between us, and I kiss him.

CHAPTER TWENTY-SEVEN

THERE IS no hesitation in the way Reid kisses me back. His tongue traces the seam of my lips, then mingles with mine, every movement slow and measured. I can't help the small whimper that slips out as he takes my face with both hands.

But then just as suddenly, he pulls back an inch. "If you regret this tomorrow," he breathes, "I'll never be able to live with myself."

"Reid." I hold tight to the back of his head before he can pull away. "I haven't regretted a single moment I've had with you. And I never will."

His forehead presses to mine, and his fingers trace a line from my wrist to my elbow, to my shoulder, into my hair. When they reach my face, he opens his eyes, staring directly into mine, into my soul, as he traces my jaw. Then, barely audible, he says, "I love you."

I pull his mouth to mine, and he backs me up a step, then

another, until the smooth stone wall surrounding the fireplace presses against my back.

Even as the kiss deepens, our breathing growing heavier and our hands wandering over every inch of each other, we make no moves to remove the layers between us, not yet. And I wonder if he's thinking the same thing I am. With how long it's been, and who knows how long it will be after reality sets back in with the night, I want this to last as long as it possibly can. I want to stay here cocooned in his warmth, my body vibrating with each stroke of his tongue and brush of his fingers.

I gasp as something cold spreads along the side of my throat. Reid smirks before he ducks his head and licks the frosting from my skin.

"You're defacing my cake."

"Repurposing," he counters as he hooks his hands behind my thighs and hoists me into his arms.

I can taste the sugar on his tongue as he carries me to the bed and gently lays me down. His knee pushes between my legs, and something between a sigh and a moan sounds in the back of my throat as he caresses my leg, my waist, his lips working slowly down my neck to my chest.

He hooks his fingers beneath the hem of my shirt and looks up at me through his lashes. I smile and run my hand through his hair as he pushes it up to my collarbones, exposing my breasts. My breaths quicken as he kisses my hip above the elastic of my underwear, then slowly up my ribs, beneath my breasts, on the sides, taking his time before finally taking my nipple into his mouth.

My head falls back against the pillow of its own volition, hand tightly wound in his hair.

"I love you. I love you. I love you," I breathe, unable to form any other words, as if holding it in all these weeks has been like water building behind a dam just waiting to burst.

His mouth seals over mine before I can say it a fourth time, the hard length of him pressing against my core as he leans over me. I grind my hips up and hook a leg around his waist. Hell to taking our time—I need him *now*. Judging by the low groan he makes, he feels the same.

"You are the greatest gift fate has ever brought into my life," he whispers as he helps slip my top the rest of the way off. "And loving you is the best thing I've ever done." He kisses his way back down my body until he reaches my hips, then removes my pants and underwear, pausing near my feet to kiss my ankle. "It's made everything worth it." My calf. "All of the terrible things that have happened, even before I met you, I would go through it all a hundred times over as long as I end up here." My inner thigh. "I was always supposed to find you."

"You make me so happy it scares me sometimes," I whisper as I shove his boxers down. "Because I think no one can be this happy for too long without something going wrong."

"I think we've already had enough things go wrong," he says against my lips as he holds my face between his hands like something breakable. "I think it's about time we get to the good part."

I lay my hands over his and turn my face to kiss his palm, tears breaking free onto my cheeks as I do.

He tightens his hold and brings our noses an inch apart. "We are going to get to the good part," he insists. He nudges my forehead with his, holding my gaze as his hand travels down my body and between my legs.

I already know what he'll find, seeing as I'm so ready I can feel the slickness on my thighs.

"Kiss me," I whisper.

His lips find mine at the same time his finger slowly glides inside of me, curling against my inner walls in a way that has my hips rising to meet him. I wedge my hand between us, finding him as hard as I am wet, and he exhales harshly against my lips. I feel like I might explode if I have to wait any longer.

"I need you inside of me, Reid. Now."

The same hunger is mirrored in his eyes as he guides himself to my entrance. I nod, hands clasped behind his neck as he pushes inside excruciatingly slow, inch by inch. I'm panting by the time he fills me, desperate for more friction but also for him not to move, to never move. His jaw hardens into stone like it's taking everything in him to hold back.

It hasn't been *that* long since the last time, but it feels like forever. He slowly pulls back, his gaze holding mine the entire time, and fire blazes through me as he continues with that pace.

It's slower than anything we've done together, even the times we've said we'd take it slow. And it's all-consuming. The extra space letting every sensation grow and expand, brushing every nerve, every cell. It feels like a language, the communication passing between us wordlessly in a way no one but the two of us could understand.

His hand never stops moving, the caress gentle but firm as he strokes my leg, my hip, my stomach, my breast, my arm, my face. It almost feels better than having him inside of me, feeling him everywhere all at once.

My hands create a similar dance on his skin, roaming from the flexing muscles of his back to the wide set of his shoulders, the flat planes of his chest, his abs, his hips, carefully skating around the bandages and bruises. He presses his forehead to mine, our ragged breathing filling the space between us.

A soft smile brushes Reid's lips, his hips pausing before he slows his pace again. I knot my fingers in his hair, giggling as his gaze flicks from my eyes to my mouth.

"What?" he asks.

I shake my head, unable to tame my smile. "You'll make fun of me."

He brushes his nose against the side of my throat before planting a kiss at my pulse point. "I won't."

That same sensation floods my stomach as he pulls back to look down at me.

"I just—I love that even after all this time, I still get butter-flies whenever you look at me like that."

His smile grows wide enough to crinkle the corners of his eyes before he leans down to kiss me. "For the record," he murmurs against my lips, "you do the same to me. All the time."

I giggle again as he kisses the corner of my mouth, my cheek, my jaw.

"We're so cheesy," I breathe. "I hate us."

His chest vibrates with his laugh. "Me too."

My laugh stretches into a moan as he grinds his hips

against me, pushing himself deeper, keeping the same slow, rhythmic pace. My heart feels like a stampede in my chest, my lungs struggling to pull in air.

There's pressure in my jaw—from clenching it?—but no, then in my gums, and then—

I gasp as I realize my fangs just extended. That's never happened during sex before. I look up at Reid, horrified. What is going on with me? I'm not even hungry. I've fed plenty since being here, more than enough since I've been trying to gain the weight back.

"Hey," Reid says, looking utterly calm as he stills. "It's okay. It's perfectly normal."

"It is? Oh!" I slap a hand over my mouth, even more horrified at how my words slur around the fangs.

"Yeah." Reid gently wraps his fingers around my wrist and lowers my hand from my face. "When vampires are romantically involved, plenty of them enjoy feeding on one another. It's just an instinct."

"Oh." I press a finger to the tip of a fang like I can force it back into my gums. They've come out before, of course, when I've fed, but they've always retracted quickly. Now, they're making themselves right at home. "But you've never, I mean, I've never seen yours come out."

He pulls the rest of the way out, and my body mourns the loss of him. He tucks a strand of hair behind my ear, expression thoughtful. "I've always tried to keep them back with you. I didn't want…I didn't ever want you to be uncomfortable. Or feel like I would…"

"I know you'd never hurt me, Reid."

His smile grows into something amused as he traces a finger along my bottom lip. "But so you know, I'm yours, Valerie. All of me. Anything you want."

"Have you done that before?" I ask, unable to look him in the eyes. I don't like thinking of him sleeping with anyone else, though I know there had to have been others before me. But for some reason, the idea of him feeding on them at the same time twists even deeper in the pit of my stomach.

"No." He cradles the side of my face and ducks his head, forcing me to look at him. "As you've seen, sharing blood with another vampire can create a pretty intimate bond, especially in this way. It also makes things more intense. It's not something I would do lightly."

"But you would do it with me?"

His lips curl. "But I would do it with you. If that's something you wanted."

"Just like you never wanted to turn anyone but accidentally turned me?" I tease.

His smile broadens into a grin. "You really do have me breaking all of my rules, huh?"

I run my hands up his chest, realizing my fangs are gone as I press my lips to his. "Now will you stop torturing me?"

I flip him onto his back, and he grasps my hips and grins up at me as I climb on top and push my hair behind my shoulders. He shakes his head a little, eyes blatantly tracing every inch of me as his hands skim up my stomach, my breasts.

"God, you're so fucking perfect."

We groan simultaneously as I lower myself onto him. He never takes his eyes off me as I start to move, but instead of feeling self-conscious under the weight of his gaze, it fills me up. I want him to see me. I never want him to look away.

"Come here," I say, breathless, and he sits up into my waiting arms, our torsos coming together. I wrap my arms around his shoulders and my legs around his waist, our foreheads resting against each other. The kiss is breathy and desperate and deep as he wedges his hands beneath my legs to help me move against him.

I whimper, and he wraps one arm around my back, the other guiding my hips as his lips hover near my ear.

"Just like that," he breathes. "That's perfect. There you go."

Heat builds in my core, my chest, my gums again. I pull back, clenching my teeth and hissing out a breath as the fangs reappear, but then Reid's hands are on my face, pulling me close.

"Go ahead. It's okay, love. Go ahead."

I search his eyes for any hesitation, and finding none, I let my instincts take over. My fangs sink into the space between his neck and shoulder. The taste of his blood is familiar, but the way it feels as it fills me is entirely different. There's more heat, more need, and it fuels the other heat already scorching my veins. My breaths shorten to pants, every muscle in my body wound as tight as it can go.

Reid strokes the back of my head, murmuring something beside my ear that I can't make out over the roaring blood. Then out of nowhere, I'm cresting the edge, the orgasm tearing through me strong enough that I wouldn't be able to stay upright if not for Reid's hold on me. I cling to his shoulders as wave after wave rolls over me, the sensation so much my body almost feels numb, like it can't quite register the intensity of it.

As if from a distance, I feel Reid tensing, hear his groan in my ear as he finishes with me. And the next thing I know, I'm on my back on the bed, Reid hovering over me as I struggle to catch my breath. He pushes the hair out of my eyes, his face flushed and chest glistening with sweat.

His smile is hesitant as he studies my face. "You okay?"

But as the world filters back in and that all-consuming heat ebbs away, an entirely different rush fills me.

Tears.

Reid's face falls, his eyes going wide. "Oh no, baby, no. I'm sorry. God, I'm sorry." His hands flutter around me like he's not sure what to do with them. "I never should have—"

"No, no." I wave my hands in front of my face, trying to swallow the tears, but that makes them run harder. "It's nothing. I don't know why I'm crying." My breaths turn into hiccups, and I press my hands into my cheeks like I can force the heat accumulating there away. "God, this is so embarrassing."

The concern on his face deepens. "No, Valerie…"

"I mean it. I just—" I search for a way to explain it, this overwhelming feeling expanding in my chest, filling my lungs and overriding my system. "I've missed you, I guess. I've just really, really missed you."

He strokes my cheek and studies my face as he brings our noses together, the heat behind his eyes simmering low like the last of the embers in a fire. "I've missed you too. Every minute of every goddamn day. Even when we're in the same room, I miss you."

The words don't bring comfort, just a deepening of the sadness already growing in my chest. Because everything has changed, and yet nothing has. It might, but not yet. And it hurts too much to pretend this is certain if there's even a chance I might lose it.

It's the one thing I haven't let myself say, haven't let myself *think*.

If this doesn't work out, I don't know how I'll ever get over it. I don't know how I'll ever move on. How I'll ever love someone else because I'll always know it's not as much as I loved him.

"I should go," I whisper.

"Valerie."

I shake my head, but he doesn't release my face.

"I can't do this, Reid," I gasp. "I can't—I can't lie here and pretend like I have you."

"You have me."

I shake my head again. Because I don't, not really.

"You have me," he insists, his eyes searching mine, the look on his face only growing more desperate as he doesn't find whatever he's looking for. His lips flatten in a tight line as he looks from me to something over his shoulder, then he releases my face and rises from the bed. "God, this—this isn't how I was going to do this. Just don't go anywhere."

After pulling on his boxers and digging through his drawers for a moment, he returns to my side, but this time, he lowers to one knee.

"I don't know else to show you how serious I am. How

certain I am. How much you have me like no one else ever could. I think about the future," he whispers, the words coming out in a rush, "and there's no version without you in it that I want. And not just as my Marionette. I want you as my friend, my wife. I don't want you standing behind me in that throne room. I want you sitting at my side."

Tears stream down my cheeks.

"I want to get a house somewhere. Anywhere you want. Maybe on a hill with a view. But somewhere close enough to a city so you can join an orchestra and play your violin, if you want to. That way, we won't have to be at the estate all of the time. And if we have kids"—his voice breaks—"we can raise them far away from all of this. We can do better than our parents did. We *will* do better. I'm sure of that." He gives me a small, rueful smile. "I'm hoping for at least two, but I'll take as many as you'll give me."

"Reid," I say, my voice sounding more like a choked sob.

"I'm so sorry for how everything has turned out. I'm so sorry for hurting you. And I'm sorry for not doing this the moment she showed up here. But please let me spend the rest of my life trying to make it up to you."

He flips open the small black box in his hands, and my breath catches at the ring waiting inside.

"Is that a...?"

I run my finger along the side of the ring, and sure enough, a small blade springs free.

"I know it's a bit much," he says hurriedly. "And if you'd rather have something simpler, I can—"

A small, delighted laugh breaks free, and the worry in Reid's face eases.

"I was hoping if you liked it, you might let me have this one back." He trails his fingers over the ring currently on my hand, then loosens the empty chain hanging around his neck, the one he'd used for my ring to keep it safe while I was gone.

"I've decided, so no matter what your answer is, I'm going to call it off tomorrow. There's a much better chance for negotiations with Anya now that her dad is gone. And this is my decision and mine alone. You will carry none of the burden, you hear me? I know there are a million things left for us to work out, but let me worry about them. I don't want you to think about anything other than if you want to spend the rest of your life with me. For you. And you alone."

There's no way he happened upon a ring like that. It must have been custom designed. How did he…? *When* did he…?

I realize upon closer inspection that amid the cluster of diamonds are a few other stones—a perfect match to the ones in his new crown.

"Valerie Josephine Darkmore." He pauses and smiles, like he likes the way my name sounds in the silence of the room. His eyes search my face, taking in every detail. "I am helplessly, endlessly, eternally in love with you, in this life and whatever others we may get. And there is no one but you I'd want by my side through whatever comes. You have my heart, my soul, my mind, my body, and everything I have to give." He inhales deeply, a flicker of uncertainty crossing the lines of his face. "Will you marry me?"

I press my lips to his before he finishes the question. "Yes," I breathe against his mouth. "Yes. A million times yes."

His smile is breathtaking, so wide and pure and genuine, the kind I never see when anyone else is around. He pulls back enough to slide the ring on, then hesitates when he's done, holding my finger like it's something breakable.

"Here," I murmur, reaching up to remove the chain from his neck. I slide off my old ring, loop it through the chain, then secure it around his neck. It falls beneath his collarbones, and I kiss his jaw, his cheek, his forehead, then let out a giggle as he climbs back into the bed beside me.

"What?" he murmurs as I tuck myself into his chest.

"You just proposed to me in your boxers," I say with another laugh.

He laughs too as he kisses the top of my head and laces his fingers through mine. "It wasn't exactly what I'd planned. I can do it again."

"It was perfect," I whisper. "I promise. I don't care about any of that stuff. I just want you."

He pulls me closer, and I close my eyes as we curl around every part of one another, as if having more points of contact will anchor us together.

"At least two kids, huh?" I murmur.

His fingers still in the path they're tracing against my back. "We can talk about it. If that's not something you want, I'm fine with that too—"

"I was thinking four. Too many?"

His arm tightens around me as his lips press to the top of my head. "Four sounds perfect," he breathes, a smile in his voice.

I smile back, tracing the pattern of freckles along his forearm and up his biceps.

His knuckles find my chin and tilt my face up. "I love you," he murmurs before bringing his lips to mine.

"I love you." I pull back and narrow my eyes at him. "Not anytime soon on the kids thing though."

He laughs and pulls me into his chest again. "Not anytime soon."

Hearing the steady rhythm of his heart urges mine to slow, and this time, sleep isn't difficult to find at all.

CHAPTER TWENTY-EIGHT

I WAKE to the weight of Reid's head resting on my chest. Eyes still closed, I run my fingers through his soft hair. It's long enough now the ends have a curl to them. It must have gotten hot in the day while we slept, because I don't feel the sheets wrapped around me, the open air raising the hairs on my bare skin.

Reid hums low in his throat, almost sounding like a purr, and nestles his face into my chest, his fingers tightening on my hip. He takes my other hand and brings it to his mouth, kissing my knuckles one by one, lingering on the new ring sitting on my fourth finger. He frames the finger with his own and gently caresses the sides.

A slow, lazy smile creeps onto my face as I pry my eyes open.

I gasp, every muscle in my body seizing.

Reid lurches up, cursing under his breath as he also takes in the woman standing at the foot of our bed.

His fiancée, to be exact.

She's smirking, her arms crossed over her chest. "Is this how American Marionette pairings work?"

Reid yanks the sheets from the bottom of the bed and tucks them around me.

"I did knock," she continues.

Reid leans forward like he's trying to block me from view. I'm frozen against the pillow, the shock rendering me useless.

This is all my fault. I never should have come here. I never should have stayed until sunset. All of this tiptoeing around each other for weeks, just for her to find out anyway—

"Well, what a relief this is!" Anya flings herself onto the foot of the bed like a child at a slumber party, her smile conspiratorial. She points at Reid. "And here I thought you were no fun."

Reid and I exchange a sideways glance, my pulse still frantically beating in the base of my throat.

"*So.*" Anya grins. "How long has this been going on? Tell me everything. Was this the first time? Just a hookup? Have you been sneaking around this whole time? Did this happen before or after you were paired together? *Oh!*" Her head snaps to the side to focus on Reid. "She's the girl, isn't she? She's who you're in love with!"

Reid rubs his thumb along my knee beneath the sheets like he's trying to comfort me, though neither of us says anything. Reid hasn't blinked, his gaze locked on Anya like he's waiting for her to pounce. We might be on decent terms now, but after finding out we've both been lying to her this entire time, it wouldn't be unreasonable.

"Why are you here, Anya?" he asks.

She sighs like she's disappointed he won't gossip with her. "I figured the two of us should chat, what with my father and brother being dead now." She says it so *casually*. Emotionlessly. Is it real, or is she just putting on a brave face? "Which leaves me as the next in line for the Vasiliev throne, and that puts the two of us in a much different position in terms of this betrothal. Which I'm sure you're happy about. Oh, don't look so worried, Valerie." She flicks her wrist and jumps back to her feet. I suppose with how upset she'd been in the library at the idea of Reid simply not liking her, maybe finding out this is the real reason he'd showed her no interest is some kind of relief. But it feels like there's more to it than that. "I'll step outside so the two of you can get dressed. Then we'll talk."

Reid and I say nothing as she slips from the room.

"You okay?" he murmurs.

Numbly, I nod.

He squeezes my knee one last time before pushing up from the bed and heading to his closet. After throwing on a pair of his sweats, I opt for the bathroom to brush my teeth.

My body moves like it's in a combination of autopilot and denial, but then the door creaks open and Anya's high heels clank inside, yanking me back to reality.

"Here I've been attending all of these boring political meetings, and you guys have been off having all the fun!" she says as I rinse my mouth. "I'll be honest, I'm a little hurt I wasn't included earlier. Like, I get it. My brother's friends tried to kill you. But still." Her eyes flick to me as I step out of the bathroom. "I thought we were getting along."

I ignore the questioning glance Reid gives me.

"You're not...mad?" I ask.

She scrunches her face up. "What, about you two?" She wags her finger between us. "No." She shoots Reid an apologetic look. "You're not really my type, no offense."

He presses his lips together like he's trying not to laugh and raises his palms. "None taken."

"A marriage is not the only way to form an alliance. This deal was outdated and barbaric anyway. Royals sending off their children like cattle." A wry smile curls her lips. "But you already knew that. Is that why you killed my father?"

"It wasn't Reid," I say immediately.

Anya's head swivels to me, her eyebrows raised, but her expression is simply curious. "No?"

I meet Reid's eyes over her shoulder.

How much are we telling her? How much of a choice do we have?

"Auclair has called an emergency meeting in a few hours," Anya adds, as if this piece of information is inconsequential.

An emergency meeting? Is this about Nathan or is he already planning another attack?

Spill any more of their blood, and I spill hers.

"Is this a bad time?"

My head whips up to find Kirby and Monroe lingering in the doorway. Thank God they didn't get here a few minutes earlier. They didn't come alone either. Daniel and Leif shift their weight behind them, along with Adrienne, who is currently avoiding eye contact—so that answers that about why they're all here.

To my surprise, it's Reid who says "No." He sighs before gesturing for Anya to take a seat too. "It's probably time we all talked."

ADRIENNE STILL WON'T MEET my eyes as she steps into the room, clutching her backpack to her chest for dear life. I don't know how I know, but that damn book is in there.

"What did you tell them?" I demand.

Finally, she looks up, her shoulders hunching toward her ears in guilt. "Nothing—just—"

"She said the two of you found a way to stop Westcott," cuts in Leif. "But we're running out of time to be able to do it. Cam's stuck in a meeting, but he knows we're here, and he's in too."

"You said you were okay with this," Adrienne all but whispers.

Yeah, but I didn't know she'd have an army breaking down my door in the space between me sending that text and waking up.

"And don't tell me I should have left them out of this. You and I both know we can't do that spell alone."

"What spell?" Kirby asks.

Adrienne stares at me for a moment, and when I don't move to stop her, she digs in her bag and pulls the book out.

There's a collective intake of breath as the book's power tinges the air in the room, dark and heavy. Adrienne flips to the right page, then hands the book to Kirby.

"Ah!" Kirby flinches as soon as she touches the book, then frowns. "This page is blank."

"Like the note your mom sent," Monroe says softly.

"Only Adrienne and I can see it." I sigh and rub the heels of my hands into my eye sockets.

"So what would the spell do, exactly?" asks Daniel. "How would it help?"

"It alone wouldn't be enough," says Adrienne.

"If we just get rid of Westcott, someone else will take his place, and his followers will turn him into a martyr," I say. "We need to control who steps up after him—someone we can actually reason with—and we need to make his followers think it's their idea to support this new person."

Leif snorts. "Have you met Westcott's higher-ups? They're all just as bad. Who could you possibly have step in—"

"Cam."

The room falls into silence at Reid's voice. "He's respected outside of the estates. I went looking for him when I was trying to find you, and everyone I came across knew who he was. He's well known, even if only for his reputation. He's recruited a good deal of Westcott's followers, worked with them for years. They see him as one of their own. He has experience with leading his pack. I think he's the best choice."

"And if they don't accept him? He's spent just as much time at the estates. They might not trust him anymore," offers Adrienne.

"Didn't you say his followers are all wearing those cuffs?" asks Daniel.

"What about them?" I ask.

He scoffs and spreads his hands like it's obvious. "Isn't that like a freaking candy store for an alchemist?"

"They might be able to use it to influence them," I breathe, "especially since we know exactly what they're made of. Cam's camp made most of them."

"The spell would give us control of Westcott," adds Adrienne. "So we can make it look like a peaceful transition of power. He can help talk his followers into it too. Make them more open to the idea of negotiating with the estates instead of just getting revenge."

"And if they're not interested in singing Kumbaya?" mutters Leif.

"Then we get the estates in on it," offers Monroe. "As backup."

"So, ambush them," corrects Kirby.

"The spell also requires a sacrifice," I cut in, the growing excitement and hope in the air making me nauseous. "And it..." I clear my throat. "They wouldn't die fast. It would be...*horrible.*"

The room sobers at that, but quietly, Adrienne says, "I think we should use Nathan. He's set to be executed in a few days anyway. And this could save thousands of lives, maybe more."

Monroe's head snaps up, and I wince as she meets my eyes. "You want to sacrifice Nathan," she repeats.

"I don't *want* to do any of this," I correct.

"And Nathan won't be the only one dying if you go through with this."

I straighten, the words of the others blurring to the background as I try to figure out where the hell V's voice is coming from.

"I can get Auclair and a few of the others on board," Reid is saying. "The estates are getting desperate to end this with Westcott. I can gather enough support."

"And if I throw my support behind it as well, that could help build some momentum," offers Anya.

Finally, I spot V lingering in the corner of the room. Her form isn't fully materialized, almost leaving her transparent as she props a shoulder against the wall and crosses her legs at the ankles.

"I agree with Adrienne," says Kirby. "I think this is our best bet."

"And what if it doesn't work?" counters Daniel. "Then we just butcher this guy for fun?"

"You don't know what he's done," Monroe says through her teeth.

"Then enlighten me! Is it enough to deserve this? And we're qualified to make that call how?"

V nods her head to the side before disappearing through the door. I take a step to follow her and meet Reid's eyes.

"I'll be right back," I murmur. "I need some air."

He nods, though I can feel him watching me as I step into the hall.

It's empty and quiet, no sign of V. I grit my teeth and pace to the end of the hall. "I'm really not in the mood for the games today," I mutter under my breath. "If you—"

"I'm trying to *help* you here, Valerie. You could sound a little more grateful."

I spin around to find her leaning against the wall right behind me.

"Then tell me what the hell you're talking about."

She gives me a slow, exaggerated shrug. "I was just surprised, is all. That you're not worried about your pack master. Ruthless, if a little cold-hearted. I like it."

She smirks like she knows exactly what she's dangling over

my head, but still, I take the bait. "What about Cam? If he steps in for Westcott, he can hold his own—"

Her eyes bulge comically wide. *"He's in Westcott's service until he releases him.* That's the deal he took on for you. Going *against* Westcott's best interest like, I don't know, plotting to kill him or make his following turn against him, doesn't seem like that fits the job description, now does it? If he helps with this plan in any way, there's a good chance he'd be going against his deal, which means—"

"Cam would die," I breathe.

"Of course there's no way of knowing if that would count as breaking his deal. But are you willing to risk it?" V's smile turns knowing, her eyebrows sky-fucking-high. "How much does the pack master's life mean to you?"

"He—we just won't include him in the plan."

"Oh, but he's already contributed, hasn't he?" She pretends to pout. "By telling you about the cuffs. He's helped already, dear Valerie. He's in it. So as long as he has your blood deal on his arm, if you go through with this plan, you'll kill him."

CHAPTER TWENTY-NINE

I DON'T KNOW where Cam goes after whatever meeting he's in, but it's not his room.

I would know. I've been sitting in it for two hours now.

Which, I suppose, has given me more than enough time to think.

To come up with a different plan.

In all the time I've been at Auclair, I've never seen where Cam's been staying. Despite how crowded the estate's been, he has his own room, though it's on one of the human floors, so it's small and furnished as a servant's room would be. Considering Cam's disdain for the estates' extravagance, honestly, he probably prefers it.

Maybe this was his request.

The door creaks open, and I jump to my feet.

Cam barely has one foot inside the room before I demand, "Where the hell have you been?"

He lurches back. "Christ, Darkmore. You scared the shit

out of me. I was—Leif was filling me in. What are you doing here?"

This is the first time I've seen him this close since the attack at Reid's coronation. I'd known he was okay, but Leif hadn't given me many more details. He has a fading black eye and a jagged mark down the side of his neck along with a dozen other healing cuts and bruises, and that's just what I can see.

The sight momentarily steals my breath, and I swallow hard, trying to force the sudden tightness in my throat away. "I need you to give me my deal back."

Slowly, he closes the door behind him.

"The blood deal."

"I know what you meant, Darkmore. I can't."

"I—yes the fuck you can. Because if you have that deal when we go through with this plan, it could go against the terms and kill you. So just give it back." I cross my arms over my chest and flick my wrist, though the words don't sound nearly as blasé as I intended. They're thin, strained.

His mouth freezes around whatever he was going to say, understanding dawning in his eyes.

"You're in his service," I continue. "He might not have specified what that meant with you, but going so blatantly against him…"

"Would likely go against the deal," he finishes. "Don't let that stop you, princess. This is the first plan I've heard around here that might work. Don't worry about me."

Don't let that stop me? Is he out of his fucking mind? I throw my hands up. "Of course I'm not going through with it like this!"

"Why not?"

I scoff and pace from one end of the bed to the next. "You know why not."

"I don't think I do."

"Cam, stop it. This isn't a game!"

"Do I look like I'm playing a game?" He steps into my path, and I jerk to a stop, breathing hard, and suddenly we're far too close. Close enough to breathe in his scent, to feel the warmth radiating off his skin. But I don't step back. Neither of us do.

"Tell me why."

I look away, the intensity in his eyes too much. *Tell him why?* Why I won't just let him die? Like he needs me to fucking spell it out for him. I could lie and say it's because the plan won't work with him dead, but I think we'd both see right through it.

I shove him by the chest, but he grabs my wrists, holding me there. "Tell me why," he repeats.

"Maybe because it's the right thing to do, not intentionally killing people."

"Yeah, I don't buy that."

I yank against his hands, but he holds firm, both of us breathing harder now like there's not enough air in the room.

"You're such an asshole," I whisper.

"Say it."

I glare at him. "What difference does it make?"

"Say it."

"I—because I will never get over it, okay! You want me to say it's because I care about you? Of course I do!" My voice wobbles, and I shove him again, and this time he lets me go. "If I do this spell and something happens to you, I will never forgive myself. For the rest of my goddamn life I will never get over being the reason you died. I'm the only reason you still have a deal with Westcott in the first place. So give me the deal back, Cam. Give it back."

Finally, the hard mask over his features cracks. "I can't—"

"Just give it back to me!" I scream and slam my fists into his chest. "Give it back."

He grabs the back of my neck and tugs me in, his arms coming around me in an unbreakable hold. His heart pounds beneath my ear as my chest heaves with my breath.

"I can't give it back to you, Valerie. A deal can only be transferred once. But even if I could, I still wouldn't."

I deflate against him, and he tightens his hold. The feel of it is too familiar, too comfortable. That feeling of safety that always comes with being close to him threatens to swallow me whole.

"This is bigger than me. You have to go through with it."

"I won't," I grit out through the lump in my throat.

"Valerie—"

"It's off the table. So either help me figure out something else or let me go."

How can both sides of this feel like I'm losing? I don't do the spell, my mother—and who knows how many other people—could die. If I do, I could lose Cam, and the things I'd have to do to Nathan to get there...

Cam pulls back, and I blink, startled to find a tear escaping down my cheek. Hesitantly, he cups the side of my face and wipes it away with his thumb.

For a long time, we look at one another. It's like I'm reliving every moment we've had all at once—the nights at camp he let me cry in his arms, when he told me about Rea for the first time, him saving me from Terrence by the lake, us arguing in the woods, the whip in his hand, the look in his eyes when he told me he'd take my deal for me. The girl in the memories feels like a different person, and I can't help but wonder what life would be like if I'd stayed her.

"Did you ever, even if just for a moment, consider it?" he murmurs, his forehead creasing like he's deep in thought. "Choosing me?"

The way he's looking at me, it's like he's expecting me to say no. Preparing for it. And it's probably what I should say.

A shaky breath passes through my lips as I whisper, "Yes."

And I have. More than once, and more than just for a moment.

If the answer brings him any comfort, he doesn't show it.

But then the weight of Reid's ring on my finger registers, and the feelings that fill my chest at thoughts of him are entirely different. And I know in the deepest parts of myself, no amount of history with Cam or fondness for him could ever override that.

"I want you to be happy, Cam," I murmur. "You deserve that."

The small smile he offers says he heard the unspoken part just as clearly. "Do me a favor, princess?" He takes my hand and taps the new ring on my finger. My eyes snap to his—I hadn't realized he'd noticed—but his expression stays the same. "Don't let him off the hook for this fiancée thing too easily, okay? Make him work for it."

I let out a small, watery laugh and step back, putting more

distance between us before the tears can start again. "There's another spell in the book. One that breaks blood deals."

"But?"

I shake my head and cross my arms over my chest. "I don't think I'd be strong enough to do both."

"Maybe we only need the one. If Reid can gather enough support from the estates to move ahead, and if I can get close enough to him without the deal, we could make this work."

"I might be able to control him long enough to transfer over power in front of his followers," I murmur. "It would just be through necromancy instead of the spell."

He frowns. "What's the difference?"

"The spell would require more power upfront, but the change would be permanent. Once I had control of him, I wouldn't be at risk of losing it. With necromancy, I'll need to hold my concentration the entire time. It's riskier, but we might just need a few minutes, right?"

"He'll feel it when the deal breaks," he says. "He'll know we're planning something. He'll be ready for it."

"So you should leave before I start the spell."

He nods, glancing at the window behind me. "I'll need to leave tonight to get there in time. He should be at his compound closest to Locklear. Are you sure you can get Auclair to agree to that spell? They're willing to execute that guy for breaking basically the same law—"

"I wasn't planning on telling him that part."

Cam's jaw works like he's holding himself back from saying something.

I startle as the door opens behind me, then do a double

take as my sister strides inside. Adrienne closes the door behind her, crosses her arms, and leans against it.

"What are you doing here?" I demand.

She lifts her eyebrows, looking from me to Cam. "If you're sending him, I'm going too."

Cam opens his mouth, but I snap, "What are you talking about? And how did you know where to find me?"

"I put a tracing spell on you weeks ago."

"You *what?*" A tracing spell? For it to be in continuous use, not just a one-time locator spell...*I* don't even know how to do that. I look at my sister, *really* look at her. Maybe I've been underestimating her even more than I realized.

She shrugs. "With your track record of going missing and getting kidnapped, can you really blame me? If you're sending him to Westcott, then I'm going too."

"Like hell you are."

"I'm not asking for your permission, Valerie," she says, somehow perfectly calm despite the absolute insanity currently coming out of her mouth. "For one thing, you need him to make it there alive and not get killed on sight. If I'm next to him, his chances are a lot better."

"I—"

"Two," she continues as if I hadn't spoken. "It can't be you who goes. You're needed here. For more reason than one. I'm not. Three, if Calla and Mom are really there with him, then I need to go."

I shake my head once, twice, knowing nothing I say will stop her if she's truly made up her mind about this. I have no authority over her. I can't force her not to. And she, annoyingly, makes a few good points.

I don't trust any of them at this point—Mom, Calla, or Westcott—but I don't think they'd let anything happen to Adrienne if she showed up.

Then again, I didn't think they'd leave Mom in a dungeon to rot. A simple spell to look through Adrienne's memories is all it would take to ruin this whole plan. I say as much aloud.

"By then, you'll have finished the spell, the estates will be at his doorstep, and Cam will have presented himself to Westcott's followers as the better alternative, so it doesn't really matter. But if it really came down to it, I could convince him I switched sides."

I scoff. "How? How could you possibly do that?"

"I could," she insists. "I can get him to believe me. I could spin some story about how you weren't there for me after Calla disappeared, that ever since then we haven't been close. Calla and I were always closer anyway, so if she's siding with him, she must have a good reason, and I trust her enough to hear her out. I could tell him how you've changed since getting paired with the prince and your feelings for him have blinded you, that you're willing to go along with the vampires' atrocities because of him—like killing Connor." She looks down at her hands. "Or how you attacked me in the bunker."

The following silence threatens to swallow me whole. I stare at my sister, her words ravaging my chest cavity with blades and barbed wire, leaving my heart raw, bloody.

A story to spin for Westcott it may be, but the words came from somewhere. Somewhere she may have been burying them for a long time, but how easily she could list them off, all the ways I've failed her. Hurt her. Betrayed her.

And she's not wrong.

Everything she said is true. I wasn't there for her. I let us grow apart. I hated the things I saw the vampires do as I went through initiation, but I went along with it. I *helped*.

Cam steps up beside me, and I don't know what he could possibly say. I can't even look at him, my face hot. At this point, I don't know if it would be worse to let her go or for her to stay. I don't want her anywhere near Westcott, but I also don't want her anywhere near this spell.

And she's made it abundantly clear what I want in this situation holds no weight.

"I'll take care of her."

My head snaps toward him, my mouth actually falling open in shock.

"I'll give you two a minute," Adrienne murmurs, slipping back into the hall.

"You and I both know there's no talking her out of this," he says. "It'll be a lot harder for me to keep her safe if I say no and she runs off on her own later. And if she can keep me from getting my head blown off before I even make it in the door, the least I can do is look out for her, okay?"

I know he's trying to lighten the mood, but the words make my throat tighten.

My shoulders deflate as it sinks in this isn't a battle I can win. "You don't even try to get through that door until—"

"Take a breath, princess." He offers a half smile, then claps his hands on my shoulders. "You're going to need some of that energy for our next stop."

CHAPTER THIRTY

"You can't go in there."

Two Marionettes sidestep to block the door in front of me, arms crossed over their puffed-up chests like they're expecting me to cower at the sight of them and offer a meek *sorry* before scurrying away.

"I need to speak with Auclair."

"You can't go in there," the one on the left repeats, emphasizing each word like I didn't understand him the first time.

"I really don't have time for this." The emergency meeting is in less than an hour, and this can't wait.

Unfortunately for this guy, his arrogance makes this a whole lot easier for me. Definitely settles my conscience, at least. I open my fist, blood already coating my palm, and they both drop to the floor in an instant.

"Damn, princess." Cam pokes his head around the corner.

"They're not dead."

Cam eyes their limp forms on the ground but says nothing.

I cut off the oxygen to their brains long enough to knock them unconscious, and I try not to dwell on how much easier it was than any time I've done it before.

The magic buzzes along my skin like it's waiting for another task. Eager for it.

"Come on." I nod for Cam to follow as I shove the large wooden doors aside.

I don't know what I'd been expecting for a monarch's office, but there's nothing impressive about this space. If Auclair weren't sitting behind the small oak desk in the back, nothing in here would point to this office belonging to him.

There are no windows, no decorations. Just piles upon piles of papers and books. His Marionette is so still in the corner he nearly blends in with the wall.

Auclair glances up from his reading as we enter, then eyes his other Marionettes on the ground before the doors close behind us.

"Valerie Darkmore. Camden," he murmurs, returning to the papers in front of him. "Was that really necessary?"

"You don't seem concerned," says Cam.

"If I thought the two of you wanted to assassinate me, we'd be having a very different conversation." Sighing, he leans back from the desk and folds his hands together on the surface. He's right, I'm not here to hurt him. But considering the circumstances, his confidence in that looks a lot more like arrogance.

Or stupidity.

I eye his Marionette in the corner again. No matter how bulky and broad-chested he may be, I could have him on his knees in a heartbeat. My magic tingles along my skin as if in agreement.

But I think I'd be hard-pressed to find one of the monarchs who didn't think themselves invincible, even after they've seen three of their own taken out, two of which had their bloody heads mounted on the wall like stuffed deer.

"What can I do for you?" he says.

"Actually, it's what I can do for you."

His brow pinches with a hint of wariness as I cross the rest of the distance between us.

"Can I show you?" I cut a line in my palm and extend my hand to him. "I just need a drop," I add, and his eyes cut back to mine, then over to Cam.

I don't turn to see whatever look Cam has on his face, but it eases the apprehension in Auclair's, at least enough for him to offer his hand.

He shows no reaction as I make a similar cut in his palm, then press our blood together.

At least in this position, I have control over what memories I offer, what I let him see. It feels entirely different than having someone else rifle through my head.

And we don't have time to pull punches or sugarcoat the situation—or for me to worry about his reaction to the choices I've made, if he deserves the amount of trust I'm about to give him. But the estate monarchs are becoming a dying breed, and he's the only one with enough power and authority to bring this plan to fruition.

So I do the only thing I can: I show him everything—the past, the present, the plan.

Transferring the memories probably takes only a few

seconds, but time slogs by as a glaze falls over Auclair's eyes and I concentrate on what I want him to see.

When he pulls back, there's a noticeable difference in the way he looks at me. If I didn't know any better, I'd swear he looked...afraid. His eyes shift from Cam to me, his throat bobbing with his swallow, the unspoken part of my message coming through loud and clear.

I'm trusting you with this. But now you've seen what will happen if you betray that trust.

"How are you expecting to pull this off?"

"We all agree we need to get rid of Westcott, but only if the person who takes his place is an improvement. And that can't be my mother, or my sister, or anyone else from the estates, for that matter. It has to be someone those people trust, someone who will speak for them. Who knows what it's like outside of these regions and who will be a genuine voice for them."

Slowly, Auclair's eyes trail to Cam as I speak. There's no mistaking the way he zeroes in on the blood deal mark. "How do you expect to accomplish that while you're indebted to him?"

"I can break the deal," I say.

Auclair inhales deeply and sighs as he leans back in his chair. "Half of the estates have been dying to kill Camden for years. No offense."

Cam shrugs.

"If he steps into Westcott's shoes," Auclair continues, "I imagine he'd be seeing his way out in the same way Westcott does just a few days later."

"That's where I come in." The door creaks open behind

us, and Anya's high heels click against the hardwood as she comes to stand at my side. I do a double take but try not to let my surprise show on my face. This is not what we agreed on.

Auclair purses his lips in thought as he steeples his fingers together on the desk. He looks from Anya to me to Cam. "I'm listening."

"He needs to align himself with the estates," says Anya. "Take over power with Westcott's followers *and* secure an alliance with us to show he's willing to work *with* us for this change."

The hint of amusement in Cam's expression quickly devolves into wariness.

"As we all know," Anya continues, "I am now the head of my estate. It would seem an alliance with the Carrington estate —the first of ours to have fallen—might not be the most prudent use of our resources."

If Cam's surprised by the suggestion, it doesn't show on his face. He's staring at his feet, his jaw rigid and brow furrowed. A million emotions war in my chest at the implication.

It's a terrible position to put him in, a choice no one should have to make, made even more complicated by Rea. She might be gone, but marrying someone else, especially someone strictly for duty, wouldn't mean nothing to him.

And also, selfishly, there's a spark of relief. For me, for Reid.

And tucked somewhere in a deeper layer of my heart is something else. Something darker and muffled, its cries forcibly being silenced at the thought of watching Cam marry someone.

Someone else.

I shake my head as if I can physically force the thought from my mind.

Auclair catches the movement and shoots me a questioning look. "You disagree?"

My breath catches as Cam turns to me. He searches my face for a moment, his expression giving nothing away. But whatever he's looking for, he must not find, because he turns back to Auclair with a stiff nod.

"If that's what it'll take."

"Cam," I all but whisper. "You don't have to do this."

A muscle in his jaw jumps, but he doesn't look at me again. Anya's expression is just as unreadable. After all that talk of *royals offering their children up like cattle,* here she is doing the same to herself? It's not a terrible plan by any means, but *why?*

"I'd have a few conditions," says Cam.

Auclair's eyebrows shoot up so far they disappear behind the band of his crown. "Go on."

"You can't really think we're getting out of this mess without agreeing to any of their demands. Sending me won't be an easy fix to smooth things over and let everything get back to normal. If you want me to step in as their new spokesperson, that's exactly what I'm going to be."

Auclair slowly leans back in his chair and crosses his arms over his chest. "So which of their demands are you suggesting we compromise on?"

"Equal representation in the government, for starters. Seats at the table for different species. A limit to the terms for the monarchs. Not shortening their lives," he says quickly as Auclair's mouth opens to protest. "Just their terms. And the blood donations."

"What about them?"

"They stop." Cam stands tall even as Auclair's expression threatens to turn him to stone. "No more forced donations or punishments for humans who don't give. The program will instead transition to a free market where the blood can be purchased, and those who give are fairly compensated."

A muscle in Auclair's jaw ticks, and he all but sneers, "It seems you've given this a fair bit of thought."

And I realize he really had thought Cam would jump into Westcott's role, calm everyone down, and nothing would have to change. As someone who's always been at the top of the food chain, compromising clearly is not in his repertoire. And judging by the way his lip curls back, a few altered policies will only be the beginning.

Because even if these changes manage to force the vampires to stop treating the humans like cattle, forcing them to bleed for them and killing them or enslaving them when they don't, in their minds, they'll still look at them as animals.

I squeeze my hands into fists at my sides, forcing myself not to say anything, letting Cam handle this. If he's really going through with this plan, if he's going to fill Westcott's shoes, he'll have to get used to it.

"Those are just to start," says Cam, spine straight and head held high despite the way Auclair is glowering at him.

And I can't help it. I smile.

I'd been more than a little doubtful about this plan. Everything seemed too messed up. The system broken beyond repair. That there was no possible end to this that wasn't ruthless and bloody and unjust.

But for the first time, looking at Cam, I see the potential for something else. Something better.

Auclair refocuses on me. "I can vouch for Camden with the other estates, though I've done so in the past, so I'm not sure how far my opinion will go. What do you need from me?"

I should be thrilled Auclair is even entertaining the idea. Our differences aside, we won't be able to pull this off without some support from the estates.

So then why does it feel like all of the air is getting sucked from the room?

Auclair raises an expectant brow.

Swallowing whatever this turmoil is inside of me, I ask, "How many alchemists do you have?"

CHAPTER THIRTY-ONE

"What was that in there?" I hiss through my teeth as Anya and I slip into the hall, Cam staying behind to discuss other details with Auclair. It's been less than an hour since we finalized the plans, and she's already making changes? It's complicated enough as it is with far too many opportunities for things to go wrong. Maybe I was too quick to trust her. If people start throwing in random—

"Come with me." Anya hooks her arm through mine and tugs me off course toward the back grounds.

Before we reach the doors, she nudges me right, shoving the two of us into a narrow alcove. Planting her hands on my shoulders, she towers over me and brings her face uncomfortably close to mine.

"Listen to me. It had to be this way. It wouldn't have worked without it."

"You don't know that. And you didn't have a problem with it before."

"Because I didn't *know* before. I didn't see it until the two of you had already taken off."

"See what?" I've gone over the details a million times. If there was some glaring hole, surely I would've caught it already.

Uncertainty knits her brow as she casts a quick glance into the hall, ensuring we're alone. In fact, everything about her demeanor feels off. The anxiety is practically vibrating off her skin as she fidgets and shifts her weight.

My next words freeze on the tip of my tongue as I narrow my eyes. "Anya, what do you mean by *see it*?"

She seems to decide something, because everything about her hardens—her jaw, the set of her shoulders, her voice. "We all have our secrets, Valerie. And we don't have time to get into it right now."

That response more than anything confirms it.

But that's impossible. For her to be a seer, she'd have to be a lunar witch. Or part of one.

She'd have to be a halfling like me.

But back at Magnolia's shop, she'd said she's been having trouble seeing lately. That there was something she couldn't see around, possibly another seer.

Was that because of Anya?

"What is this really about?" I demand. "All of that talk about royal marriages being barbaric—"

"They *are*—"

"Then why would you initiate this?"

"Because it doesn't work without it!" She throws her hands up, then rakes one through her hair with an exasperated exhale. "The other estates are going to have a hard time accepting a wolf to begin with. Some of them will never accept it—they'll just go along to stay in the alliance. Marrying me ties Cam to at least one estate officially. Without that protection, they'll make a move against him. Assassinate him before he even completes his first year as a monarch. You think I *want* to do this? You think I wanted the first vision I've seen in months to be of my own wedding that I didn't choose?" Her throat bobs as she swallows hard, but the fire in her eyes never wanes. "But I'm doing what I have to do. Just like you."

I stare at her, seeing far too much of myself in the fear behind the fire.

"Anya." I soften my voice. "We can try to come up with something else."

"Don't you get it?" she says, not unkindly. "You think I didn't look for alternatives? I ran every other scenario after that vision. It has to be this way. The Vasiliev estate has been one of the worst when it comes to relations with the weres. Almost as bad as the Carrington. *My* estate aligning with him will speak volumes. It's his only chance."

"Is that why you came to Auclair in the first place? Because of something you saw?"

She blinks at me, surprised. All this time I've been digging for the reason that really brought her here…of course I never found any answers if she doesn't know them herself.

"I know they weren't expecting you," I explain. "You stowed away on that plane. Why?"

She crosses her arms and lets out a slow exhale as she casts another glance around the hall, apparently accepting I'm not going to let this go.

"Yes. I don't know what it's like for anyone else who can

see like I do, but when I have a vision, I feel this obligation to fulfill it. I have this…this *knowing*…that something awful will happen if I don't. A few months ago, I saw, well, I saw what my brother's friends would do to you. I didn't even know who you were at first." She grimaces and gives me a half shrug. "And I saw myself stop them. That was long before these wendigo attacks started up again. Before any of this. I had no idea at the time there would be another purpose for me being here."

"Does anyone else…do they know…"

"About me?" She lifts her chin an inch. "No. And I'd like to keep it that way. Now are you going to trust me or not?"

A million other questions are on the tip of my tongue, but I know this isn't the time or place.

Has she always been a halfling, or did it manifest later in her life like it did for me? Is her magic limited to the Sight? How could she possibly have flown under the radar with her position? Was anyone else in her family like her?

Does she know that I'm like her?

I don't think she does. There's too much nervousness in the way she looks at me. Maybe it would help her feel like she could trust me with this if I told her, but in the end, I find myself only nodding.

"Good." Her gaze darts back and forth, but we're still alone. "There was one other thing I saw. But I don't know what it means."

"What did you see, Anya?"

She chews on her lip, her eyes unfocused as if she's seeing it in her head again, and for all I know, maybe she is. "I can't make anything out. It's dark and murky. But I saw this glimpse of your face. And your sister's."

"Adrienne?" I ask, my voice spiking up an octave.

She shakes her head. "The other one."

Calla.

"I just…I feel like I should tell you to be careful. I'm sorry. I wish I could tell you more." She looks around again and lowers her voice. "I don't see things often, Valerie. So when I do, I know they're important. I just thought you should know."

I search her face, and maybe I'm a fool to trust the sincerity there, but I do. "I need to go see Adrienne," I murmur.

She nods and steps back to let me pass, but I pause at the corner and look at her over my shoulder. "Did you see anything else?"

She hesitates, and I know immediately when she shakes her head that she's lying.

CHAPTER THIRTY-TWO

ADRIENNE'S already well into packing her bags by the time I make it to the room. Her shoulders tense as I step through the door, but she doesn't look up as I cross my arms and lean against the opposite wall.

She looks older somehow. Maybe she has for a while. I guess some people get frozen in your head at a certain age, and she's always been twelve or thirteen to me. The age she was before Calla disappeared and everything about our family changed.

She zips the bag closed and sighs when it becomes clear I'm not going to speak first. "If you're here to try and talk me out of it..."

"He'll try to charm you."

She stands up straighter, her brows pulling together as she finally looks at me. "Cam?"

"No, Westcott. He'll act like the doting father, full of warm stories and apologies. He'll try to lure you in. And Calliope..."

I shake my head. I don't know if it's worth bringing up Anya's warning, but without any context or details, I'm not sure how much good it'll do. "She's fallen for it. You can't trust her either, not like you used to. I honestly don't know with Mom. But you can trust Cam."

"You don't have to worry," she says quietly. "I know what they've done. Nothing they say would make me forget that."

"For the record, I hate this plan."

"I know." She gives me a humorless smile. "I know you think of me as a little kid, but I can handle this, Valerie. I promise. You just focus on getting everything ready over here."

Maybe that's why I'm not fighting harder to keep her from leaving. The only thing worse than sending her off would be to keep her here, to have her involved in what I'm about to do.

"That tracing spell you put on me…how does it work? Can you show me how to do it so I'll know you're okay?"

"Sure. It's easier to bind it to an object." I follow her gaze to my ring, or where it used to be. She blinks, confused at my bare finger—I usually never take the damn thing off—but that quickly clears as she notices what's on my ring finger.

"When were you planning on telling me *this*?" she demands as she crosses the room.

"Didn't seem like the most important thing right now," I mutter.

"Most important…Val!" She tugs me into a chokehold of a hug, and I let out a surprised grunt. "You're my sister and you're *engaged*!" She grabs me by the shoulders and holds me at arm's length. "It is Reid, right?"

I snort. "Yes. It's Reid."

"Just checking." She yanks me back into the hug. "I'm still

327

going to give him shit for another year or so, but I *am* happy for you. Good God, that ring is *huge!*"

I rest my chin on her shoulder and hug her back, rapidly blinking to fight off the tears. For a perfect, blissful moment, it feels *normal.*

"When did he ask you? How did he do it?"

I pull back, my face heating at the memory. We should probably come up with a different story to tell people. I wave my hands in front of my face. "We can talk about it later when we're not in a hurry."

She narrows her eyes but relents. "We can use this," she says, slipping her necklace over her head.

I cross my arms as I watch her lay the jewelry on the bed, tug a single strand of hair from her scalp, then collect the candles sitting on her dresser.

"We never learned anything like that at the academy," I say. "Especially not freshman year."

Her eyes flick to me only for a moment before refocusing on the knife she flipped out of her bracelet.

"Adrienne," I say, voice louder now as she lines the blade up with her palm. "Where did you learn this?"

"Like you've never taught yourself something outside the curriculum," she scoffs, and it sounds all wrong. Her pitch is too high, her gaze pointedly avoiding me now.

I grab her wrist before she can make the cut. "Where. Did. You. Learn. This?"

"From Calla, okay!" She shakes me off, presses the knife into her hand, then holds her bloody palm between us like a question. "Now are you going to let me help you with this or not?"

Blood drips off the sides of her hand as I peel my gaze back to her face. From *Calla*? But the last time she saw Calla, she was a kid, way too young to…

I take a step back, then another.

Anya's vision about Calla, had it been about this?

"Adrienne," I whisper.

"No," she snaps, and she clenches her bloody hand into a fist. "You don't get to give me that look. You don't get to decide how I feel about things. How I feel about her. She's my sister too."

I shake my head back and forth, back and forth, though I already know what she's going to say before the words leave her mouth. The spells Adrienne's been able to do that I never would have mastered at her age, her knowledge that was far too advanced for her, the things she had no business knowing…

"She's been helping me this entire time."

I barely hear the rest of her explanation, even as I ask follow-up question after follow-up question. *Since when? How? Why?*

Finding the note and Mom's nail in Adrienne's bed was no mistake.

It was just the only time I'd gotten there first.

They've been sending notes back and forth since I arrived at Auclair and told Adrienne the truth about Westcott and Calla.

"Why did you pretend you were as surprised by that note as I was?" I demand. "Why not *tell me*?"

"Because if I did you would have made me stop!"

"Of course I would have! Adrienne, you—"

"Can't trust her. Yeah, I've got that. You've only said it a thousand times. But she is still our sister. And she's with that psychopath. I'm sorry for what she was willing to do to Reid, I am. But I also believe her when she says there's more to the story. I believe her when she says she's trying to make up for it and she wants to help. Doesn't she mean anything to you anymore?"

I stumble back a step like she hit me.

The answer in the back of my head is immediate. *Of course she does.* But then just as quickly: *she would have let Reid die.*

"This is why you fought so hard for us to send you there with this plan," I say, my voice coming out hollow.

"I fought so hard for this because, like it or not, I am in this with you too, Valerie. I'm not a kid, and he's my dad too. This affects my mom, my sister, my home, my life. And I'm not just going to stand by and wait until you fix everything or die trying."

Who knows what Calla's been telling her the past few weeks. What ideas she's been filling her head with. She obviously wouldn't tell me the truth if I asked.

"You don't have anything to worry about," she insists. "God, Valerie, I know other people have given you reasons not to trust them, but I never have. You don't get to make me feel guilty for not blindly going along with whatever you say. I. Lost. Her. Too." Her voice cracks, and tears fill her eyes. I swallow hard, my own eyes getting misty. "You got to see her and make up your own mind about her. Can't you give me the chance to do the same? Or do you really think I'm so dumb that I can't put my personal feelings aside for what needs to be done?"

"Of course I don't think you're dumb," I whisper.

She throws her hands up. "Then what's it going to be, Valerie? Can you trust me or not?"

I CHEW on my pinky nail as the phone rings. I don't need further justification. Not really. But still, I find myself sitting on the edge of Adrienne's bed, doing the math in my head for the time difference.

Just when I think the call will go to voice mail, Avery's voice crackles through the speaker. "Hey, Val. Is everything okay?"

I cringe at the hitch of concern in her voice. It's not that we aren't on good terms, but we haven't really stayed in touch since her transfer to Botner. I can't blame it on the chaotic circumstances the past few months either—we've just never been the call-and-catch-up kind of friends.

But for this to be the first thing for me to reach out about feels shitty.

"Yeah, everything's okay, but do you have a minute? I need to talk to you about something."

There's a rustling noise on the other side of the line for a moment, then her voice comes through clearer. "What's up?"

"I need to know exactly what happened between you and Nathan."

Silence falls between us.

Maybe I should've built up to it more, softened the blow, but frankly, I don't have the time for subtlety.

Finally, she sighs. "Why? What did he do now?"

I explain the situation, starting with what Monroe and Kirby told me, then getting into the book from the shadow realm. I don't even have a chance to explain how this connects back to Nathan before she hums.

"So are you calling for my permission? Or are you wanting me to convince you that he deserves it?"

I open and close my mouth a few times, but nothing comes out. Neither. Both. I don't miss that she evades my first question, but I'm not going to push her on it.

"If you *are* going through with it," she continues, "can I ask a favor?"

"Of course."

There's another long pause, but when she speaks again, her voice is the strongest it's been since she picked up the phone. "Wait for me to get there. Because there's no way in hell you're doing this without me."

CHAPTER THIRTY-THREE

WE WAIT until the estate officials are in another meeting, this time coordinating how many people they're willing to spare to send as backup for the possible ambush against Westcott. To avoid overcrowding the room, only a dozen of the highest ranked Marionettes are inside with other teams stationed at the door and the surrounding halls. The distraction will make getting Nathan out of his cell less complicated, but not easy.

At least none of us are expected in the meeting.

Let me know if you have any trouble, Reid says through the bond.

I can practically *feel* how much it's paining him to be in that room and not help tonight. He and Anya both.

Maybe it's better.

Just because I've committed myself to doing this doesn't mean I want the man I love to see it. To see *me* like that.

It'll be fine. I have it handled.

I know you do. Just...I know you feel like you have to do this. But I want you to know you can still change your mind.

I know he means it, but he's wrong.

I can't afford to get squeamish or moral tonight.

Not if I want my mother and Cam to live.

"Are you ready for this?" Avery asks under her breath beside me. She'd been able to hitch a ride on the plane with reinforcements from Botner, getting here just in time. With Nathan's execution scheduled for tomorrow's full moon, tonight is our last—and only—chance at this.

Right about now I'd been expecting to feel some hesitation. Doubt. Guilt, perhaps? Maybe that'll come later.

A flash of pain flares up my jaw, and I force myself to unclench for the millionth time tonight.

"Are you?" I say in lieu of answering.

Avery lets out an audible breath beside me, and I squeeze her hand. She hasn't told me any more details since she got here, though she keeps looking at me and opening her mouth and then pausing like she wants to. If he'd done the same thing he did to Monroe and Kirby, I feel like she would've said *me too* or something on the phone.

We're a few halls away from the stairs to the dungeons, dressed in full Marionettes uniform, so if anyone sees us, hopefully it looks like we're patrolling. I resist the urge to check my phone for the millionth time. When the security cameras are down and we're in the clear, they'll let us know.

"I was drunk the night of my pairing ceremony," Avery says quietly.

I still, not even daring to breathe, like any movement or sound might spook her out of telling me this.

"It was a fun night," she continues, though her voice is monotone. "I was dancing with my friends. We drank and laughed because we were twenty-one and stupid and relieved initiation was over. And I'd just been paired with this cute guy who seemed nice and funny, and I liked it when he flirted with me because I was a flirty person too, so I thought he was just doing it for fun. I remember having to carry my shoes home because I couldn't balance in them anymore. And he offered to walk me to my room, and I'd actually thought, *Oh, what a gentleman.*"

A sickening coldness slithers down my spine as I know in my bones what comes next.

"The worst part was I didn't realize what was happening at first. I was that drunk. Maybe if I had...I could've reacted faster..." She pulls in a sharp breath. "Anyway. He helped me into bed. Put a glass of water out on the nightstand and everything. I really thought he was just being nice. I think that was the worst part. How much I trusted him. It wasn't until he climbed into the bed too... I didn't realize how much stronger vampires were until that moment. He's bigger than me, sure, but I couldn't move at all. He shoved something in my mouth to shut me up when I wouldn't stop crying and asking him to stop. I still don't know what it was. I think I blacked out somewhere in the middle. And then when I saw him the next day, he smiled and flirted with me like it never happened. I think he tried to glamour me to forget. But I've been wearing this since my mother gave it to me as a child. It's supposed to block them."

She tugs a necklace out of her shirt, a simple locket on a chain.

"Maybe it would've been better if he'd been able to make me forget."

I take her hand again, gripping her fingers tightly as the fire in my belly surges up so violently it steals my breath.

That's probably what's made him so cocky. He's been getting away with this kind of thing his whole life. Always the predator, never the prey.

He's in for a rude fucking awakening.

My phone buzzes in my pocket.

"Are you ready?" I whisper.

She's the first to take off down the hall.

A sickening wave of déjà vu washes over me as we descend the stairs to the dungeon, the memories from the last time I was in one—albeit on the other side of the bars—still fresh. Avery and I go alone, though a few of the others will join us shortly, once he's ingested Kirby's concoction. We mixed it with a blood bag, something he's bound to be so ravenous for at this point that if there's a taste difference, he won't even notice it.

The poison won't be enough to kill him on its own, though knowing Kirby, she left a bite to it. Just something to slow him down. Impair him enough that he won't cause any problems tonight. He hasn't been down here enough for his hunger to turn to decay—making him more of a liability than anything. If let out of his cage *without* feeding him, his instincts would take over and he'd attack anyone in sight.

The other cells we pass are empty, at least they appear that way. It's dark down here, full of shadows and spaces to hide. A shiver runs up my spine, but Avery struts confidently to his cell, tosses the blood bag through the bars, and waits with her arms crossed over her chest.

There's shuffling, then the sound of the blood bag tearing open, and desperate gasps and gulps. After a few moments, the sounds die down, followed by a soft "Aves?"

I have to bite back my scoff. He says it hopefully, like they're friends. Like she's coming to *save* him.

Even in the darkness, I can make out the cold, hard edges of Avery's smile. "Nathan. You don't know how happy I am to see you again."

"Yeah?" Apparently not the complete idiot, a hint of wariness seeps into his tone.

I step up behind Avery, and his gaze snaps to me, only now realizing the two of them aren't alone.

"They said...they said they'll kill me tomorrow," he says. "And I know, I know that I did it, but the longer I've been down here, the more I've thought about it, I can't remember *why*." He blinks up at Avery desperately, pleadingly, and I have to look away.

"Don't worry," Avery purrs, apparently not as affected by how fucked-up this situation is. "We're getting you out of here."

The effects of Kirby's poison are evident in the stagger of Nathan's walk. Evident to everyone except Nathan, apparently, because he's smiling and ogling Avery's chest as he walks with his arm around her shoulders, each step slower than the last as the poison spreads. Whatever was in the mixture must have dampened his senses as well, otherwise he'd hear the others coming.

The hall is empty as we slip upstairs and head around the corner, which means whatever distraction Daniel and wolves came up with for the Marionettes who were supposed to be guarding the exits on this side of the estate must have worked.

More footsteps fill the hall, and Saint and Jones take over for Avery. They grab Nathan roughly by each arm and yank him toward the door.

Avery's eyes darken as she falls into step beside me. I try to get a read on her. I have no idea what she must be feeling right now. If this feels complicated to me, it must be ten times worse for her. But if seeing Nathan again for the first time in almost a year is affecting her, she's not showing it.

"You're still sure about this?" I murmur.

Her response is immediate: "Do your worst."

CHAPTER THIRTY-FOUR

FREEZING rains pelts us from above as we make our way through the grounds, my skin stinging from the impact of each drop. We don't dare cross out of the safety of the boundary Auclair has erected, but we push it as far as we can on the property. The landscape works in our favor, the meticulously crafted lawns giving way to towering, lush trees once we pass the gardens, making the area feel much more private and secluded.

I help Saint and Jones with Nathan—now limp and unconscious—while the others cover our trail. Leif bounds ahead in his wolf form to ensure the coast is clear. Auclair may have agreed to our plan, but I left out certain details. Namely, breaking one of the vampires' most sacred laws against killing each other, especially on estate property.

But we don't have time to waste. The moon is already past its peak, and it would take too long to physically drag Nathan through the acres upon acres. Instead, we dump him in the back of one of the estate's trucks and take off into the darkness, leaving Kirby, Monroe, Avery, and Daniel to finish taking care of the Marionettes on duty and the security footage.

The property backs up to a vast body of water, and the trees cut off against intimidating cliffs.

And this is where we stop.

A figure waits for us at the edge of the cliff, silhouetted by the car's headlights. He turns as we open the car doors and climb out.

"It should all be here," says Feddei as he removes the bag from his shoulders. The light from the moon catches the angles of his face as he furrows his brow and hands it to me. The straps are soaked through like he's been standing here awhile. "She was already waiting with it by the time I got there."

Of course she was. Because Magnolia has known it would come to this from the beginning. I wonder how much she's been able to see moving forward, or if her sight is still being blocked whenever Anya is involved.

"Thank you for getting this, Feddei," I say. "Really."

He ducks his head in acknowledgment and side-eyes the truck as the wolves tug Nathan from the back and let his limp body plop into the mud.

"You don't have to stay for this part," I add, wiping the rain from my face. I was shocked Anya had been able to convince him to help in the first place. And with all the attacks on the monarchs, I wouldn't blame him for wanting to get back to her.

Feddei shakes his head and shoves his hands into his pockets. "I have a feeling we'll need as much power as we can get tonight."

As if in agreement, a bolt of lightning flashes behind his head, followed by the low, rumbling thunder.

I dig through the bag and compare the contents with the ingredients listed in the book as the boys drag Nathan's body closer to the cliff and Feddei gets started on the entrapment circle. My hands shake as I remove the two ward necklaces I spent the day making—one for me, one for V—from my pocket, slip them over my head, and tuck them into my shirt and out of view. Then I pull the containers out of Magnolia's bag and arrange them on the seats in the truck.

Snake venom. Rusty nails from a coffin. Wax. Rotting vegetables. Glass shards. Wood chips. Night nymph oil. Fresh grave dirt.

I don't even want to know where she got these.

I fill one of the empty containers with my own blood and watch through the windshield as Feddei chants and completes the circle of black salt around Nathan, who is currently lying facedown in the mud.

He deserves this, I remind myself. *This has to be done.*

But a stupid, small, traitorous part of me sees him lying so vulnerable on the ground, discarded like he isn't even a person...

A second pair of headlights cuts through the darkness, and the other truck pulls in behind us, its wheels kicking up mud. I turn as Kirby, Monroe, Avery, and Daniel climb out, their clothes drenched from the rain.

"You have everything?" Avery asks as she hunches next to me in the truck door.

I nod as she takes in the ingredients, pausing on the remaining empty vial.

"You need his blood?" she asks.

I nod, and she has the container in hand and is stomping toward Nathan in the next second.

I can't help but flip back to the other spells—the ones my mother wanted me to use. They're far simpler than the one we'll be attempting tonight.

"Valerie!" calls Daniel. "He's waking up."

Leif, Saint, and Jones are standing around the circle with their arms crossed as if ready to tackle Nathan to the ground if the spell doesn't work and he's able to get out.

Avery steps out of the circle with the vial full of Nathan's blood. He mutters inaudibly as he rolls onto his back and spits the mud out of his mouth. Rain hammers down on him, washing the rest of the muck from his face and plastering his suit to his body, the same one he'd been wearing at Reid's coronation. I don't know why the detail surprises me—of course they hadn't offered him a change of clothes for his execution.

"I want to see him burn as much as anyone," Monroe murmurs beside me, and I startle. I hadn't heard her approach over the rain. Her fingers brush the back of my arm. "But no one would blame you if you wanted out."

As she says it, the light from my phone screen fills the truck as Cam's name appears.

Made it a few miles outside of the compound. We'll wait here until you give us the go-ahead.

If I back out now, I just sent Cam to his death, or close to it. As long as he has that deal—*my* deal—if Westcott gets ahold of him, he'll never let him go.

If it weren't for him, I'd still be at that camp. I'd still be under Westcott's thumb. Hell, I might not even be alive.

I owe him this.

"Help me carry these over there" is all I say as I pile the ingredients into my arms.

Nathan has managed to sit up by the time I reach the edge of the circle, and he's hunched over his knees as he retches into the mud.

Kirby shrugs, not looking the least bit apologetic. "Pretty sure it wasn't me. He just drank the blood too fast."

Daniel snorts on her other side at the words *pretty sure*.

"I need these boiling," I say, handing the two vials of blood to Kirby.

"I'm guessing these go in the circle?" says Monroe, indicating the larger ingredient sacks.

I nod, and she and Avery get to it.

First with the rotting vegetables, which makes him retch harder, his arms covering his head as they pour them directly over him.

I ignore the twinge in my chest. I don't feel sympathy for him. I *won't*.

They throw the wood chips in next, then handfuls of dirt and the shards of glass.

By the time they're finished, Nathan's conscious enough to understand what's happening. He lurches back, hitting the invisible barrier of the circle, and he rebounds, landing on his hands and knees in the pile of ingredients. The scent of his blood fills the air as the glass cuts through his skin.

When he lifts his head, his eyes find Monroe first, and he has the audacity to look hopeful, like she might help him.

Kirby grabs Monroe's wrist and pulls her behind her like she can shield her from Nathan despite being half Monroe's size.

He pushes to his feet, his movements sluggish. According to Kirby's estimates, we should have another hour or so before the potion's effects wear off. Not that he'd be able to get out of the circle either way, but there are a few pieces of this spell that will get tricky if he has the strength to fight back.

"Roe," Nathan slurs, and her nickname on his tongue burns away any lingering sympathy. "What is this?" He turns to the guys, his nose wrinkling as he realizes they're mostly wolves, not even bothering to plead with Avery or Kirby, not bothering to look at them at all, like they're not even there.

"Get the fires started," I say.

Three points around the circle alight at once, one in front of Feddei, Daniel, and Kirby, the three of us who will center the spell, so to speak, as I manipulate the energy.

Nathan shrinks away from the flames, his gaze swinging to me as he realizes who's running this.

"Does your boyfriend know what you're up to?" he practically spits. "They'll burn you for this. All of you."

I dig the bags Cam left me from my pocket and step outside the circle's boundary. "Maybe. But you'll burn first." I toss Cam's blood and hair onto the pile of ingredients beneath Nathan's feet, and the concoction immediately goes up in flames.

He curses and lurches back, hitting the barrier of the circle again, then throws himself to the side, trying to get away from the heat of the fires, but they surround him and there's nowhere to go.

"I need his wrist," I say, my voice coming out hoarse.

Avery seizes his arm without hesitation, wrenching it the side until he cries out, and presents the inside of his wrist for me. He meets her eyes, the glow from the fires flickering across his face.

"Please," he says quietly.

But that just makes Avery tighten her grip until her nails break skin. "Funny. I remember saying the same thing to you."

She looks at me over her shoulder, giving a nod as the go-ahead, and right where my blood deal mark had been on the inside of my wrist, I position the rusty nails and hammer them in until they cross each other in an X.

If he screams, I don't hear it. But his mouth opens, so I think he must.

The rain pounds into the earth around us, violent and thrumming with energy as it's if a living entity bearing witness to this event. Part of me wishes I was still the host of the blood deal, then I'd be able to feel it transfer to Nathan before he dies so I'd know the spell is successful. What must Cam be feeling right now?

Using the wind, Kirby hovers the vials of blood over the fire, and Monroe adds the oil, sending plumes of thick, black smoke into the air.

A chill washes over me, so much colder than the rain, like the surrounding shadows are sinking through my skin. Then a current hums, starting at the soles of my feet and shooting up my spine. It almost steals my breath, the sheer power of it, how *endless* it feels. No matter how strong my blood magic is, I could always feel when I started pushing it too far, when I needed to ease back. But now the magic feels like it would never run dry, would never stop if I asked it not to.

"His mouth next," I say, and a shiver runs through me despite the heat of the fires.

More, the magic hisses inside of me. *More*.

Daniel stares at me for a moment, like he's arguing with himself. Burns and blisters coat Nathan's face, and he barely fights as Daniel finally steps forward, grabs him roughly by the jaw, and forces his mouth open. I pour the snake venom onto his tongue, and Daniel forces his jaw closed until he swallows, no matter how much he coughs and tries to wrench his face free.

"Don't let him go," I say, grabbing the wax next, letting it mingle with my blood as it melts and drips onto his mouth, sealing it.

I don't know what it says about me that this, more than anything we've done here, shakes me to my core. Maybe it's my body remembering better than my mind the feeling of having something forced into your body and your lips sealed closed.

"Val?" Monroe prompts, bringing me back to the present as Nathan writhes on the ground, hands futilely trying to free his mouth. Even if he claws the wax off, it won't matter. The magic has sunk deeper than that.

"What next?" asks Avery, her eyes shining in the light of the fire like she's eager for it.

Nathan lets out a noise that doesn't sound human against his sealed mouth, coughing and sputtering as he climbs to his hands and knees. Blood runs out of his nose, his ears. I force myself to watch, to not look away. I don't get to be responsible for this *and* turn a blind eye.

More. More.

Shapes form in the black smoke as it rises toward the sky, creatures with teeth and claws and features twisted beyond recognition. It could be my eyes playing tricks on me, but somehow I know in my bones that it's not.

More. More.

The cells in my body vibrate faster, the energy churning higher. The darkness calls to me, wrapping its arms around me in a cooling, velvet-soft embrace. My eyelids feel heavy, and I fight to keep them open, Nathan's next cry echoing around us.

More. More.

The necklace burns hot against my chest, hot enough that I yank it away from my skin and find a burn. The magic pounds against the walls of my chest—angry, screaming. I grit my teeth against it and feel a hot, thick liquid trickle onto my top lip. I try to lean into the magic, but all I feel is more blood dripping from my nose. The wind whips arounds us, sending rain into my eyes, and I swipe the blood away before anyone else can see.

The necklace. It's holding the magic back somehow. The protection comes from keeping me from getting too close to the dark, but I don't think I can complete the spell from this distance.

And this can't be for nothing. No one else can finish this but me.

I yank on the necklaces until the clasps break, then drop the protective one to the ground and keep the one meant for V in my fist.

The magic roars in my chest, rejoicing and racing through my veins like smoke with its newfound freedom.

"The oil," I croak. "The rest goes on him."

Avery and Monroe step up together, joining hands as they pour what's left of the vials over Nathan's back, and he goes up in flames.

Fire is lethal to vampires, though I've never used it on one still living. I always imagined the death would be quick. Perhaps under normal circumstances it would be. But this seems to stretch on forever.

More. More.

The light from the fire is so bright it's almost blinding. I see Saint and Leif out of the corner of my eye turn away, unable to watch any longer.

More. More. More. More.

"Well done, Valerie. I knew you could do it."

V's voice carries on the wind, all around me and nowhere. I blink, breaking out of the trance, and turn, looking for her, my fist clenched around the necklace. I just need to get it on her—

The last thing I see is the fire reflected in her eyes before she shoves me in the center of my chest, and I fall, and fall, and fall.

CHAPTER THIRTY-FIVE

IT'S DARKER HERE. So dark that *dark* is no longer an adequate description. And the air feels so much colder, thinner. Some instinct inside my body knows where I am before my mind catches up.

But unlike before, nothing looks familiar. Well, the trees look the same, but there are no lights in the distance. Not just for the estate but...anywhere. Like there's no civilization for miles. Only hollow echoes of the wind.

No. *No.*

I can't see or feel the others because even if they're standing in this same field, they're far away from here.

What had V said before? That I'd toed the line of the shadow realm with that spell, but I'd never fully crossed over. Well, I'm definitely here now.

If she stepped into my place, will they be able to tell the difference?

I never should have taken that damn necklace off. I'd

known she'd try something, but I'd been foolish and arrogant enough to think I could handle myself. She'd known all along what state I'd be in if I performed that spell. How weak I'd be.

How close I'd be to the shadows after using that much dark magic.

And she probably knew I wouldn't be able to pull it off unless I removed the ward. The perfect opportunity.

I turn a full circle, taking in my surroundings, though all I can see is darkness, fog, and trees. Each breath I pull in is shorter than the last, my head starting to swim from the lack of oxygen.

Whatever V has planned, I have a feeling this was only the start.

I have to get back. *I have to get back.*

I have to warn them.

Reid. He'll know right away that it's not me. He could feel the difference in the bond the last time I crossed to the shadow realm. But V would have suspected that. What if she's planning to hurt him? And the spell—did we complete it before she pushed me over? Cam—

"Valerie?"

My spine straightens at the familiar voice, and I whip around.

A single figure stands in the darkness. She's the clearest thing in this space, in full color the way she'd normally be, no shadows clinging to her form.

"Calla?" I take a step back and shake my head, immediately realizing it's not her. Not really. If she's on this side, then she's no better than V.

Her hand shoots out to grab my wrist before I can turn

away, her skin hot against mine, the only warm thing in this godawful place. And there's something…*wrong* in the touch. Something that feels like it doesn't belong here.

I look at her, *really* look at her.

"Oh my God, it's really you. It's me," she insists, tears filling her eyes. She yanks my hand to her chest and holds it there. Her heart beats beneath my palm. When I try to pull away, she tightens her grip, her eyes wide, pleading for me to understand.

What had Connor said? Shadow selves don't have heartbeats.

I search her face again as if the truth will be written there, but I learned the hard way that I can't read her anymore.

But if she's telling the truth…

"How long have you been on this side?" I ask.

Instead of looking hopeful at the prospect of me believing her, Calla's face falls. "A few weeks."

Weeks?

Weeks ago means while I was at the wolf camp—maybe by the time I'd reached Auclair—but not when I was at the compound.

So the things she did, the choices she made, those were all her.

Unconsciously, I take a step away from her, and she flinches.

"Why?" I ask tonelessly. "What happened?"

Weeks. My brain snags on that word again. If she's been trapped here for that long…

No. I can't afford that. I have to get back. I have to.

"Westcott wouldn't tell me anything after you left."

My eyes snap to her face at her calling him *Westcott*. She'd never shied away from calling him Dad before.

"And I was worried," she continues, wringing her hands in front of her. "I just wanted to know you were okay. Talk to you. Try to make things right. I hated the way we left things. And I felt like if I had more time to explain..." She clears her throat. "Anyway. No one would tell me anything. I could tell he was getting annoyed that I wouldn't stop asking. So I started looking for answers myself. But then I'd heard rumors about you being at Auclair. He told me to drop it. And when I didn't, when he found out I'd been trying to reach you..." Her jaw ticks as she squints at the darkness around us.

When he found out I'd been trying to reach you. The note. The nail.

So he must know about the book. About our plans.

"He said he'll bring me back when I'm no longer a liability," she adds with a flick of her wrist as if this is nothing.

I look around us again, at the darkness, the emptiness. Weeks. *Weeks* she's been here alone? A hint of my anger toward her burns determinedly in the pit of my stomach, but a second emotion I don't want to acknowledge grows beside it. "He...put you here?"

"He said he can't afford disloyalty, not right now. That I was becoming more trouble than I was useful."

"And your shadow self?"

She scoffs at that. "Jumped right at the opportunity if it meant she could take my place."

My heart comes to a complete stop in my chest. "She's there at the compound with Westcott? Your shadow self?"

Calla nods, chewing on her lip.

Adrienne. I already knew we were sending her into the lion's den, but *this?* My distrust with Calla aside, I'd thought Adrienne would at least have one ally on the inside.

"How many other people has he put over here?"

"Not many. At least, I don't think so. It's risky. Two versions of a person can't exist simultaneously in the same realm, so putting someone here would mean——"

"He'd have to deal with their shadow self."

She nods. "And as you've seen, they can be...unpredictable."

"Wait. You said he sent you here after you reached out to us. Adrienne said she's been talking back and forth with you this entire time."

Calla's face falls, and she wraps her arms around herself. "I know. I was gone by the time Adrienne replied to that first note, and I guess my shadow self saw an opportunity. There was nothing I could do to stop it."

"She's been teaching her spells," I say, my voice coming out hollow. "Things she has no business knowing at her age. Why even bother? What's in it for her?"

"I don't know."

"You have to know something," I insist. "You knew about it before I told you, so there must be a way to see what's happening from here."

"I can watch, but she's smart!" Calla throws her hands up and lets them slap against her thighs. "She *knows* I'm watching. So whatever her plan is, she's not letting me in on it. Don't look at me like that. What could I possibly have to gain from keeping things from you now? I'm sorry about Reid, Valerie, I am——"

I snatch my arm away as she reaches for me, Reid's name sounding all wrong in her voice, like she's lost the right to say it.

"I messed up, okay? I'm trying to make it right now, but you have to let me."

"If it were up to you, he'd be *dead* right now." I press my hands against my temples as a headache sets in. I'm wasting time talking to her. I have to find a way back. Who knows how much damage V has already caused.

Calla's mouth is open like she wants to speak, but her eyes are locked on my hand. On the ring. She looks from it to my face and back again, her expression crumpling.

"Oh, Valerie," she whispers. "I didn't—I didn't know how you felt about him. I didn't realize—"

I hold up my hands to stop her because there is nothing she can say that will erase it—the moment I realized she'd chosen Westcott over me, the moment I realized she didn't have my back since I showed up at the compound, the moment she led me to Reid's body on a metal table, knowing she'd contributed to putting him there.

"Honestly, Calla, I don't want to hear it. You want me to forgive you? Then *help me*. I have to get back. I have to get back to them. So you want to make this right? You want me to believe my sister is still in there somewhere? Then prove it. Show me how I can see what's going on over there."

She looks at me desperately, helplessly, because of course she doesn't know how to get me back. Otherwise she would've gotten herself out a long time ago.

But a hard kind of determination sets into her features as she stands up straighter and gives a single nod. "Okay."

CHAPTER THIRTY-SIX

I FOLLOW Calla to where she's been staying—the home of her shadow self.

"She goes by Popi, apparently," Calla informs me, her tone dripping with disgust as she shoulders the front door of a small townhouse open.

Popi, apparently, is a hoarder. I can barely make it through the threshold of the house, the floors covered in stacks of books, papers, clothes, crystals, and glass jars. I guess if she's supposed to be the opposite of my scarily organized type A sister, it makes sense.

"Jesus Christ," I mutter, stumbling over a pile of shoes as Calla fights to close the door behind us.

Popi also, according to Calla, hasn't been in contact with shadow-me or shadow-Adrienne since she was eighteen when she moved out. Calla hasn't seen any sign of V—seeing as she's been too busy weaseling her way in with me all this time —or shadow-Adrienne since she got here.

There's a clear path between the chaos, mountains of *stuff* piled on each side. Judging by the small metal bowls by the back sliding door, there's an animal around here somewhere.

"Are you hungry?" Calla asks, leading me through the narrow hall beside the stairs and to the kitchen. "I should warn you, everything here tastes like sawdust."

I make a face at the grayish apples sitting on the counter and shake my head.

A dog the size of a bear lets out a bark that's more of a roar behind me, and I nearly jump out of my skin.

"Oh, that's just Chicken." Calla shuffles around in her cabinets until she finds a bag of dog treats and tosses him one. He catches it out of the air, slobber flying from his mouth, then struts away into the shadows with his bushy tail held high. "Don't take it personally. He hates everyone," she adds.

Yet she seems at ease with him despite always being the one afraid of animals growing up. She heads back to the cabinets and pulls down two glasses, then heads to the fridge for a bottle of wine, clearly knowing where everything is, as if this is her own home.

Because she's been here long enough for it to feel like that to her.

This, more than anything else, threatens to sweep my legs out from under me. I fall onto a barstool, pushing off the stack of magazines sitting on it in the process. The weight on my chest grows heavier by the second until I feel like I can't breathe.

Am I stuck here? Really, truly stuck here? What if I'm already too late? Would I be able to feel it from this side, if something happened to Reid? Would I know?

"Breathe." The clank of Calla setting a wineglass on the counter in front of me pulls me back to my surroundings. I blink at her as she leans onto her elbows and swallows a healthy mouthful from her own glass.

I push away the wine and stumble back to my feet, unsure of where I'm going, but I can't just sit here.

"I know you're worried," Calla says behind me, her voice sounding distant, thin.

"You don't know," I snap, already heading for the front door. "You have no idea—"

"And you have no idea how to get back so just stop!" She grabs my arm before I reach the hall and turns me around. "I will help you. I told you I would. But that means you're going to have to accept that right now, you're here. And there's nothing you can do to get yourself back to our side. Not alone, at least."

Hot, angry tears fall to my cheeks. At least, I tell myself they're coming from anger. It's much better than this feeling churning in my stomach that's far too close to helplessness for comfort.

"How are you so calm about this?" I demand.

"Because I've been here for weeks," she bites out. "And I figured out early on that panicking wasn't getting me home any faster. I can't get you back right now," Calla says, her voice gentler this time. "But we will figure this out, and I *can* help you see what's going on over there."

I stop fighting her, my arm going lax in her grip. When it's clear I'm no longer going to make a break for it, Calla heads for the living room beside the kitchen and retrieves a small woven basket from inside the fireplace. She pulls the supplies

357

out and sets them in a line on the mantel. I recognize some herbs and crystals, though most of the items are entirely foreign to me.

"Fill this up with water," Calla says, extending a small bowl over her shoulder without looking at me.

I do as she says, then pause and watch her from the sink. She grinds a few herbs together and scatters them along the fireplace, but upon further inspection, I realize the fireplace is empty. It looks like it's never housed a fire in its lifetime. There's no wood, no ash, no gas mechanism.

Calla makes it look like a well-practiced routine, every item having a place, her movements fluid and easily finding a rhythm. Once she's finished situating everything, she raises an expectant brow at me over her shoulder, and I hesitatingly hand her the small bowl of water.

Without preamble, she tosses the water. But instead of the mess I'm expecting, the water moves in slow motion, coating the air in front of the fireplace as if there's an invisible wall there. My breath catches as the drops slowly trail down the surface. The air ripples like a tarp flowing in the wind, and my mouth runs dry as the sight scratches a familiar itch in the back of my mind.

I've never been a fan of scrying. It never came easily to me, and I never saw much of a use for it. Although this clearly isn't the same as what we learned sophomore year, but it must be something similar. The layer of water hovering in the air begins to shift, blurring and twisting until an image forms.

My legs feel weak beneath me, and I stumble back a few steps until I hit the couch. Calla remains standing a foot from the water, hands on her hips, as an image takes form.

It's difficult to see, the image murky and constantly moving —one of the things I always hated about scrying. It always felt like you were trying to see through moving water. But after a moment, it clears enough for me to recognize what I'm looking at.

Auclair stands at the head of the throne room, the floor below him filled with rows upon rows of Marionettes in uniform. They nod along to whatever he's saying as he paces back and forth on the dais. I squint, trying to get a good look at their faces, but I don't recognize any of them.

But of course I don't. If everything is going according to plan, then he should be briefing the alchemists and getting ready to send the reinforcements.

Watching from the shadow realm is nothing like I imagined it would be. Now much farther back from the threshold, there's no chance of interacting with the other side. To get people over there to feel us, hear us. Instead of a thin shadow of a cloth dangling between us, it's a mountain. A barricade.

We watch as if through a screen, watching a story play out instead of my own life.

I find myself back on my feet and drifting forward until I'm standing right beside Calla. "Can you see anyone else?" I breathe.

She nods and waves her hand. The image shifts along with her, blurring and spinning until I feel dizzy, but then another scene materializes.

It's much darker than the last, and I drift closer, squinting as I try to make out the figure hunched low in the corner.

"It's Mom," Calla says softly.

It looks like the same jail cell from the picture. The floor is bare concrete, and there's nothing else in there with her, the only light coming from a crack beneath a door in the distance.

"It's one of the dungeons in Westcott's compound," says Calla.

"Westcott put her—"

"No, no. Well, he knows about it." Calla clears her throat, her voice thick with emotion. "She caught on to Popi being in my place a few weeks ago. *She* put her there. They won't hurt her. They just don't want her in their way."

The figure in the corner—Mom—shifts. She's curled into a ball, her arms wrapped around her legs like she's trying to keep warm. I've never seen her look so small, so young...so *helpless*. A pang erupts in my stomach as I realize that's exactly what she is. She sacrificed her magic for me, and now she can't even fight back. She'd gone to Westcott thinking she'd be safe there, that it was the only place she'd be safe.

Calla waves her hand again, and the image disappears.

"How did you learn how to do this?" I ask. In appearance it might look like scrying, but we're not watching potential futures or vague messages. This is happening now.

"Everyone here does." She glances at me out of the corner of her eye. "How else would they keep an eye on their Mirrors —that's what they call us. Our decisions shape their lives. Guess I can't blame them for wanting a heads-up. I turned this place upside down when I first got here. Popi keeps all of her books and materials in the basement."

A shiver rolls through me. How many times have people on this side watched me without me knowing? Even if it was me watching, or a version of me, it feels undeniably invasive.

A familiar room emerges next, and my stomach bottoms

out. Reid is sitting at the foot of his bed, arms braced on his thighs, hands clasped together.

And V sits behind him, her legs on either side of him as she rubs his shoulders. Her lips are moving, so they must be talking.

My breath quickens as I search every inch of Reid's face, his body language. I can't hear what they're saying, but he looks…comfortable. At ease.

Like he thinks he's with me.

I stop with my face inches from the image, feeling physically ill from seeing V touch him. How can he not feel that's not me? I can't feel the bond at all on this side. He must feel that something's off. He's more in tune with his vampire senses than I've ever been. If what Calla said is true, he should at least be able to tell V's heart isn't beating. Unless she found some way to cover it up.

But does he really not…can he really not tell?

"Valerie," Calla says quietly.

I snap out of it and take a step back, then another. *He's still alive.* V hasn't hurt him. That's what matters. There's no room for my stupid pride right now.

"They should be able to tell she doesn't have a heartbeat, right?"

"Possibly. Unless she took measures to cover that up. I saw spells to mimic a regular pulse in the books downstairs."

"Can you show me Cam and Adrienne?"

If the alchemists haven't started yet, then they should still be waiting outside the boundaries of Westcott's compound. But Cam was expecting me to give them the go-ahead once it was time. How long will he wait before he realizes something is wrong? Knowing Cam, he won't wait long.

The next image is so bright from the snow on the ground that it burns my eyes. A wolf paces into view, mostly hidden within the trees, but he keeps poking his head into the open like he's looking for something.

"Where's Adrienne?" I whisper.

Calla shakes her head, squinting just as hard at the image as I am. "I...don't know."

"What do you mean, *you don't know*? Find her."

"I'm...trying." Calla's face contorts as she says it, like the effort of the spell is starting to physically pain her.

A loud knock on the front door reverberates through the house, and the image in front of us disappears altogether as Calla loses her concentration.

"Are you expecting visitors?" I ask dryly, but the concern that burrows itself between her brows stops me from saying anything else.

She holds up a finger to stay quiet as she pads toward the door and peers through the peephole. A sharp intake of breath is her only reaction, but she keeps looking outside for several moments as if waiting for something.

Finally, she opens the door—

—and reveals Westcott standing on the other side.

CHAPTER THIRTY-SEVEN

My instincts take over. The fangs come out first, and I don't remember cutting myself, but warm blood trickles down my fingers. Just as quickly, I lose the air in my lungs as I slam into the wall.

There's a voice calling somewhere. Distant. I think it might be saying my name. But then a pair of eyes comes into focus, so similar to mine they give me vertigo.

There's a hand around my throat, holding tightly enough to keep me subdued, but not enough to harm. Once the haze clears from my vision and I come back to myself, the hand loosens another degree.

"I really am sorry about that," says the man in front of me —*Westcott.*

But now that he's standing mere inches away, I know in my bones that's not him. And after a moment of straining my ears for a heartbeat I never find, the pieces click into place.

"You're Westcott's shadow self."

He nods, dropping his hand and taking a step back from me. "You can call me James, if you'd like."

"What are you doing here?" Calla asks, arms tightly crossed over her chest as she looks him up and down.

But he doesn't respond to her. It's like he doesn't hear her at all. His smile widens as he takes me in, looking nothing like the way Westcott smiles. There's no hidden spark in his eye, no threats thinly concealed beneath the surface. For a shadow version, he's so full of...light.

His hand lifts like he wants to reach for me, but he lets it drop to his side, his smile turning sad. "I'm so sorry to meet you under these circumstances. And how strange this must be for you. This place. Me."

I exchange a sideways glance with Calla, and she steps up next to him, but still, he doesn't turn.

"I said *what are you doing here?*" she demands, but her voice loses its bite by the end as he continues to pay her no mind. Slowly, she reaches a hand forward and waves it in front of his face.

He doesn't react.

"I'm sorry. I don't mean to..." He clears his throat as he continues to stare at me, his eyes growing misty. "I'm a stranger to you. I know that. But I've, well, I've watched you grow up. And I've been so proud of you and the choices you've made." He winces and tilts his head to the side. "It's made the version of you over here...well, you've met her."

It made them the opposite of us. Cold. Hateful. Unforgiving.

But then that would mean this man standing in front of me is the opposite of everything our father turned out to be—

ruthless, selfish, cruel. That would make this version of him…
well, the father I'd wrongly built Westcott to be in my head.

He gives me a sad smile like he can tell what I'm thinking,
like he can see all of the missed possibilities too.

When I turn to Calla, her face is pale.

"You can't see her, can you?" I whisper.

Slowly, James looks from me to where Calla stands, but it's
clear his eyes don't focus on her. "See who?"

Calla covers her mouth with her hand.

"Calliope is standing right next to you."

His eyes scan the space around us, like she'll suddenly
materialize.

"You really can't hear me?" she asks.

His silence is answer enough.

"What does that mean?" I demand. "Why can you see me
but not her?"

"How did she get here?"

"Westcott forced her."

"I saw what happened with you, Valerie. Saw it the
moment you crossed over. But Calliope…" He tilts his head as
if something's occurring to him. "He would have anticipated
that," he murmurs, more to himself than to us.

"What is he talking about?" asks Calla.

He blinks as if coming back to himself. "Your father. When
he sent you here, he must have done something to cover your
cross to this side. Shadow selves or not, we're blood, and we
can feel it when one of us passes through. In the same way I
imagine you have a feeling, a knowing, when someone you love
is gone on your side. But when you came here, I couldn't see it,

and I felt nothing. Your father must have cloaked you some-how. He didn't want anyone here to see you, to hear you."

"Why would he do that?" I ask.

James shrugs. "He must have put her here for a reason. Didn't want to leave it up to chance that someone from this side could help her get back."

"Could you do that?" I demand. "Could you help us get back?"

I turn to Calla, but the spark of hope igniting in my chest fizzles when I see the suspicion on her face. Because of course she's suspicious. We both should be. I was fooled by our version of Westcott once before, allowed myself to start to believe him, to trust him.

I won't make that same mistake twice.

"That's why I'm here. Those girls." He shakes his head, the softness of his expression quickly disappearing. Those girls —*his* children, technically. "They never should have crossed to the other side. The world should never have to know their evil. I couldn't just sit by. I had to help."

"Help?" Calla repeats, not even bothering to hide her skepticism.

"We don't have much time," James says, his earlier senti-mentality apparently gone as he hurries through the hall and beelines to the basket Calla had been using moments before he arrived. He digs through the contents and lets out an impatient breath through his nose. "Does she still keep her supplies in the basement?"

"That's where Calla said she found those."

I'm barely finished with the sentence before he's moving

again, heading straight for the door across the kitchen, and then he disappears down the stairs.

Calla and I exchange another glance, unsure if we're meant to follow him, if we should even be considering this in the first place. The last two shadow versions we've met had ulterior motives and clearly no regard for the well-being of their counterparts—who's to say this one is any different?

"Now, neither of you have been here long." His voice drifts up the stairs, followed by the hollow thuds of his boots as he returns with his arms full of various jars and containers. "So you may not have noticed the effects of them being on the other side yet, but you will. Their actions will start to mold you —your thoughts, your choices, your actions. It's not as obvious as it may sound, that their lives dictate yours. You'll think it's your idea. That you're the one calling the shots over here."

A shiver runs up my spine as he sets out his armful near the fireplace again. Have the effects already started and I haven't noticed?

"How does this work?" I ask and follow Calla numbly as she joins James in the living room and inspects the new ingredients.

"I've been trying to find a way out since I got here and haven't come up with anything," says Calla, who looks at me until I repeat it aloud for James to hear.

"Because there are no one-way tickets," he says. "Not to here. Not to there. There always has to be balance. A life for a life."

"So you'll have to pull them back here," I say.

James nods his head to the side, which isn't a yes, but it isn't a no.

"Now that they've had a taste of that side, they'll dig their heels in." James pulls two small plastic bags from his pocket to add to the growing pile of ingredients on the mantel. I take a step closer, trying to see inside the pouches, and he holds them up. Very clearly inside sits two clumps of dark hair.

Belonging to V and Popi, if I had to guess.

He sets the third pouch—Adrienne's shadow self's, probably—off to the side.

"I'll need one of you girls to take it from here. I'll tell you what to do." When neither of us moves, he adds, "I have no magic of my own."

It's easy to forget with how Westcott turned out that he was once only a vampire. But this version of him never stole powers and collected them like trophies.

Calla steps forward to take over, nodding along to his instructions even though he can't see her. The spell looks eerily similar to what she'd done before, all the way down to throwing the water and having it latch on to an invisible wall, though no image appears this time. The water ripples in the air, growing darker by the minute like some kind of portal.

I eye James warily as he sets the two bundles of hair in the center of the rest of the ingredients. There's no way it's that easy—otherwise our shadow selves would've ripped us through that portal and taken our places a long time ago. V wouldn't have gone through the trouble of waiting until I'd crossed over, then trying to get me to trust her enough to give her a stronger foothold.

"How do you know all of this?" I ask.

James dusts off his hands as he rises to his feet, still looking a little shellshocked as he takes me in, like he's trying to memorize every detail. "Your father's quest for power turned into my quest for knowledge. I didn't want to lead or change. I wanted to learn. To know as much as I could about those who came before, how things came to be. I've spent my life researching and teaching at one of the universities here. The intricacies between the realms has always been an interest of mine.

"Now, I won't lie to you and say it'll be easy going back. Your shadow versions won't go out without a fight. But you both can't exist on the same plane simultaneously, so you'll return in your body—the one they currently inhabit. The only one who can cast them out is you. You'll have the upper hand. Your body will recognize you, and the darkness will call more to them. I trust they trained you to fight off possession at the academy? Perhaps to resist a glamour?"

Calla and I look at each other, my own anxiety mirrored in her expression. That was a topic for senior year.

A year neither of us completed.

When we turn back to James, I see the first flicker of uncertainty in his face, but it disappears just as quickly.

"I can teach you," he decides.

"We don't have time," Calla says. "For all we know, Adrienne is already in that compound with Westcott and my shadow self. She needs us." Quieter, she adds, "Mom needs us."

"We're short on time," I say.

"It won't do either of them any good if you're unsuccessful." James's voice is firmer than it's been since he walked in the door. Almost sounding like a...father.

"And what would happen if we were unsuccessful?" I ask.

There's a long beat before he responds. "Whichever

version gets overpowered, they wouldn't just return to this realm."

"It'll kill them," I conclude.

"It's the only way," says James. "They won't risk getting too close to the veil to simply pull them back."

"Why would you help us over your own kids?"

"I know it's hard to understand." His smile turns sad, wistful. "And it's probably hard to believe that you girls have always felt more like mine than they have. Things are different on this side, when your lives aren't your own. When you watch your children grow into your worst nightmares and there's nothing you can do to stop it. They're angry—V and Popi. Bitter. Resentful of the two of you and the role you've played in how their lives have turned out. What I could never teach them was how many choices they *did* have. That it *is* possible to do more with your life on this side. But now that they've crossed into your realm, they will spread nothing but that hatred and darkness."

"Hello again, James."

I gasp at the voice behind me and whip around. The front door hangs open, the darkness from outside seeping across the threshold in tentacle-like fog. And in the middle of it all stands the shadow version of Rosemarie Darkmore.

CHAPTER THIRTY-EIGHT

"You've always been an embarrassment," she spits. Each step she takes is menacing and deliberate, like a predator preparing for the kill. "But to choose *her* over your own kind? Your family?" She juts her chin at me—apparently not able to see Calla either—her lip curled back in a sneer like I'm something filthy lying on the side of the road.

It's not entirely foreign to how our mother has spoken about me, but this seems to validate what she told me in Reid's memory, that it wasn't real. It was a role she was forced to play to protect us. Because if she was lying, this version of her would be the opposite.

James steps between us, and for the first time, I take in the ring finger on his left hand, how it's bare. Even in the shadow realm, their relationship hadn't panned out. His shoulders tense, and a subtle tang of fear fills the room.

He's afraid of her. The only reason Westcott is so powerful on our side of the veil is because of the magic he stole. But this version of him hasn't done any of that, leaving him a vampire with no magic of his own, only knowledge.

"I should have known you were behind this," he says lowly.

"I'm trying to give *our* girls the best life they can have." With a flick of shadow-Mom's wrist, crimson red blood slashes across the floor in front of James in a perfect line. "The power to make their own choices." The blood goes up in flames. "Because unlike you, I haven't given up on my own children." The fire spreads toward us.

Calla grabs my wrist from behind, pulling me back as black smoke climbs toward the ceiling.

"Go," urges James, spreading his arms like he can physically keep the fire back from us, the flames reflected in his wide eyes.

"Tell him to come with us," says Calla.

He bares his fangs as shadow-Rosemarie takes a step forward, her mouth twisted in delight as the shadows of the flames dance along her face. More blood drips from her palm, but she freezes at the sound of a low growl.

The dog stands in the doorway, its hair standing straight up and its teeth bared.

"Did I forget to mention how much Chicken hates her?" Calla whispers. "I had to hide a picture with her in it my first day here. He wouldn't stop trying to attack it."

The dog and James lunge at the same time.

"*Go*," James roars as he pins her to the ground by her throat and the dog circles them, snarling. The fire jumps to the curtains, the furniture, the heat in the room amplifying to an unbearable degree.

Calla's face twists in the way it does right before she starts to cry, looking anguished at the idea of leaving him to whatever fate here, and I'd be lying if I said I didn't feel a hint of that too. All but a stranger, but someone who has fought for us more than our real father ever did.

I interlace my fingers with Calla's and force her to look at me.

She shakes her head as a tear falls onto her cheek, her rising panic palpable, and she takes a step away from the portal. If we cross back and fail, we'll die there, but there's a chance we'll overcome them. Here, our fate wouldn't be any better.

I grab her by the shoulders before she can take another step away and tell her, "Fight like hell," right before I shove her through the threshold.

The fire roars behind me, but I hear it the moment shadow-Rosemarie overtakes James, his body making a loud thump as she flips him onto his back and pins him by the throat. I spare a single moment to look over my shoulder. He's already looking back at me, silently pleading with me to run.

It's senseless, this wave of emotion threatening to drown me over a stranger. And maybe it has little to do with him, but rather, all the possibilities. For a life I'll never have, but maybe I could have if we'd had this version of him in our lives instead. The chance for an actual family. A relationship with my father that wasn't built on lies and manipulation.

Shadow-Rosemarie plants her hand in the center of his chest, her nails digging into flesh. Chicken snaps at her, forcing her to pull back. James shoves her away, rolling to the side before she can regain her balance.

I feel like I should have final words to say. Something meaningful. But in the end, James meets my eyes one more time, and we exchange a nod.

Then I follow my sister into the dark.

CHAPTER THIRTY-NINE

EVERYTHING IS ON FIRE. It isn't the flickering orange flames I see first, or the heat that I feel. It's the taste. The smoke is so thick in the air it coats the back of my throat, and the burn in my lungs is immediate.

At first I think I'm still in the townhouse. That I waited too long and the portal closed without me. But no, the world is in blindingly bright color once more, and that is most definitely the Auclair estate engulfed in flames.

You're even dumber than you look, says a voice in my head, and I can hear the smile in it, like this was exactly what she'd been hoping I'd do.

The roaring fire stretches toward the night sky, covering the main structure, the buildings behind the estate, the gardens. The surrounding land fills with noise and bodies as people evacuate, their movements panicked, frantic. Their mouths are open in screams or cries, I'm not sure, since I can't hear them over the fire. What the hell happened here?

I don't direct the question to V, but she must hear it because she says, *Isn't it magnificent?*

My physical body registers next. I'm standing barefoot in the dirt behind the tree line, arms crossed over my chest. I try to take a step forward, to turn my head to look around, but my body doesn't obey my commands.

Because I'm not in charge anymore.

Tsk, tsk. Thought you'd put up more of a fight than that. You don't even know how, do you?

I search for the presence of her in my body, feeling around, but she's everywhere and nowhere all at once.

"There she is!" barks a voice in the distance.

Uh-oh, V singsongs as a group of people breaks through the trees. The first is Wes. I can't tell if his face is that red or if it's the reflection of the fire, but he's coming toward me fast, his eyes wide, wild.

"Wes!" Daniel appears next, hands extended like he's trying to hold Wes back, but he keeps slipping through his fingers.

Another two, Warren and Laura—Daniel's and Wes's partners.

More branches crack, but I don't see whoever joins us next, because then Wes's hands are around my throat, and he throws me to the ground. It steals the air from my lungs, and I sputter internally as my instincts to fight back rage but my body doesn't respond.

For some reason, V doesn't even bother trying to stop him, though I know she could.

Instead, she starts to laugh. It's a full, deep laugh that sounds nothing like my own and is somehow unperturbed by

Wes cutting off our oxygen.

"Let her go, man," says Daniel, pulling at Wes's shoulder.

"Let her *go?*" he scoffs, tightening his hands. "Why don't you say that to Beth?"

Beth?

Wes's hands shake as he tightens his hold, tears forming in his eyes now.

What did you do to her? I demand.

V waves a hand, blood glittering on her fingertips, and Wes flies off of us, crashing into the dirt several feet away on his back. The others hurry to help Wes as V makes us sit up, sigh, and redo our ponytail.

"Just tell me why you did it," Wes demands through his teeth, tears streaming down his face now. "Why her? She never did anything to anyone."

The truth sinks to the pit of my stomach like a rock. *Did.* Past tense.

You killed her?

V shrugs internally—a strange sensation. I can feel her intention to do so, but our body remains immobile.

The gap-toothed bitch was smart. She figured me out almost immediately. Can't say the same for the rest of these idiots.

My eyes burn like I need to cry, but of course, no tears can form. Beth. *Beth.* I've only been gone for what? A day? Maybe longer? And I'm already too late.

The bushes rustle as another person surges into the clearing, and the center of my chest warms in a distant, murky way. It must be the bond, suppressed beneath the extra layer of V in here with me, but still intact.

Oh good, sighs V. *Prince Charming.*

He freezes once he clears the trees, gaze intense as it sweeps over me sitting on the ground. V cocks her head to the side, grins, then stretches her legs forward and crosses one ankle over the other as she leans back on her hands.

Reid shows no reaction to this. Just keeps staring at her— our—face like he's looking for something.

V bristles, and I feel her magic stirring inside of me, twisting into something dark and thin, then extending in Reid's direction.

It's clear the moment it reaches him because the muscles in his face relax and he crosses the distance between us and offers his hand to help us back to our feet.

She's been controlling him. That's why he looked so calm in the scene I saw earlier. He knows damn well that's not me, and she's been pulling his puppet strings to keep him quiet.

Very good, Valerie. Do you want a gold star?

Ignoring her, I search for that feeling in my chest again. Can he feel the bond now that I'm back? If I can communicate with him through it…would V be able to hear that?

I need to get her out of this body. But how? It feels like she's filling every inch of it and I'm shoved in the corner barely keeping my head above the water.

I wait for anyone else to join us—Kirby and Monroe, maybe—but the woods are quiet now.

Did you kill anyone else? I ask, my voice shaking even in my head.

Oh, plenty.

I focus back on the raging fire in the distance, and she laughs in my head.

Stop worrying so much. You're giving me a stomachache. Your friends are fine. They'd be no use to me dead.

But you killed Beth.

Okay, so she *had use to me dead.*

"You're all just going to let her get away with this?" Wes demands in a way that sounds like he's been talking this entire time and V's been tuning him out.

"We don't know that it was her," says his Marionette.

"Of course it was fucking her!" Wes rips his arm out of his partner's grasp and takes a step back. "I bet she started the fire too. None of the elementals can get it under control—say the magic is like nothing they've ever felt. Who else could have done that?" He turns to me now, the anger on his face twisting into anguish. "How could you? She was your friend. *She was your friend.*"

Each word hits me like a punch to the stomach. I might not have dealt the killing blow, but I invited V in. Which makes this as much my fault as it is hers.

Reid steps between us before Wes can come any closer, and I can't tell if he did it on his own or if V is moving him around like a chess piece.

But then I notice our hands clenching into fists, our shoulders tense like she's straining. Reid's fighting her. Her magic fills our body, dark and cold and nothing like the way my magic feels. I tentatively reach out to it, letting it rush over my fingers in my mind's eye like water, and it responds immediately like it's my own.

It doesn't know the difference between me and V.

I'm willing to bet my magic would react the same to her

then, so before she can figure that out, I tighten my grip on her magic and pull.

She physically falls back a step, and I yank harder, imagining I'm scooping the very essence of her out of my body.

What the hell do you think you're doing? she hisses.

I tighten my grip, adding my magic and letting it mingle with hers, drawing strength from my blood, but also up from my shadow the way she taught me, letting all of the different magics twist and weave together until they fill my body whole. It feels hot and cold and dark and light all at the same time, so overwhelming I almost can't bear it.

"Valerie." Reid turns, and I can see the clearness in his eyes. He's broken through her hold.

V lets out a roar of frustration and extends a hand toward Reid, her fingers curved like claws. He lets out a sharp breath, then clutches a hand to his chest.

No, I shriek as he falls to his knees.

Then behave. She twists her wrist, and he lets out a pained groan.

But instead of scaring me back into my corner, it makes the magic burn brighter, singing in my veins, funneling toward the shadows pushing me into the darkness inside my own body while V takes center stage.

I don't know how to do this, but somehow I know I can trust that this magic *does.*

You will never hurt him again, I say, letting the magic wrap around her essence, encasing her in chains of power. *You will never hurt anyone ever again.*

You think you're so much better than me? You think you would have turned out any differently had the roles been reversed?

Her voice echoes in the empty chamber of my body as if she's being pulled farther and farther away. I don't bother responding, not even as she shoots her—our—hands up to the sky, and the trees around us catch fire, the flames as black as the night.

"*Valerie.*"

Reid says my voice like a prayer, but I can't see him, can barely hear him. Can hardly hear or see anything at all.

At some point I ended up on my back, and distantly, I feel my arms and legs spasming against the ground, fighting back, fighting against the magic purging everything inside of me that does not belong.

"You can fight her," urges Reid.

"They're coming." Daniel—Daniel's voice somewhere in the distance.

"We have to go." Another voice I don't know.

"Valerie." Reid's hands on my arms, my face. My body continues to convulse against the ground.

The magic wraps around my throat, my chest, my hips, squeezing and burning and threatening to consume me. I keep my hand wrapped around it like a leash, too afraid to keep holding on but too afraid to let go.

The last thing I hear is the echo of V's scream.

CHAPTER FORTY

"No one touches her."

"She's a fucking liability."

"Then what are you proposing? That's my best friend—"

"*And Beth was my girlfriend!*"

"We're all sorry about Beth, Wes—"

"No, you're not. Because you're protecting her murderer as if that's still Valerie in there when we know it's not. She fooled you all once and now Beth is dead. You're going to give her a chance to do it again? Whoever is next—their blood will be on your hands. All of you."

I keep my eyes closed as I listen, failing to keep track of who's saying what, though I know it won't be long until they realize I'm awake. The pain in Wes's voice burrows deep into my bones. In all the years I've known him, I've never heard him sound like that.

I try not to think of that night we'd all met at the diner, but it shoves itself into my mind anyway. The way he'd smiled so wide it looked like his lip ring would pop right out. How he'd held Beth's hand on top of the table, like he was proud to show everyone that she was his. She'd blushed and batted her eyelashes at him, nothing short of adoration in the way she'd looked at him. They were a couple none of us expected, but as soon as they were in front of me, it made sense.

And now she's gone. The girl who used to share her crayons with me in preschool and always smiled and waved at me in the hall even when I didn't deserve her kindness.

And it's all my fault.

It's quiet inside my body now. I wait to see if V's voice will appear too, but I don't feel her presence anymore.

Is she really gone?

The world vibrates and jolts beneath me. Are we in a car? It feels too smooth for that. A plane? I'm lying on my side on something soft.

"It is Valerie now." The voice is quiet and much closer to me than the others had been. Reid.

"So you say," Wes mutters. "You want it to be her so bad you'd believe anything."

"Why do you think they let us go?" asks a small voice— Kirby. It sounds like she's in the front seat.

"Who let us go?"

There are a few audible gasps as I shakily push myself into a seated position, only now realizing I'd been lying on Reid's lap. He keeps one hand braced on my back like he's afraid I'll fall over.

Around me is a sea of blue velvet—couches, reclining

seats, compartments for luggage overhead. *The estate train.* I'm on one of the sideways-facing couches with Reid, the others scattered through the rest of the train car. It's dark as pitch outside the windows, no city lights in sight.

I can feel Reid's gaze on the side of my face as I take in the others—Monroe, Kirby, Daniel, Wes, Leif, Saint, Jones—but it's Wes I choose to look at, as if he'll be able to see the difference in my eyes now, to see that I'm as anguished about this as he is.

But his lip curls in disgust and he turns away.

"The wendigos," Reid says beside me. "They were gathered around the boundary at Auclair. As everyone started evacuating, we worried they'd attack or that the fire would extend to the barrier and they'd be able to get through. But we passed right by them, and they barely looked at us."

I know all too well if the wendigos let you get away, it's because they want you to.

"What…what happened? How long was I gone?"

"Nearly a week," says Daniel.

A week? It hadn't even felt like a day in the shadow world.

"And the estate? The fire—was Westcott—?"

"We don't think so," says Reid, tension weighing on his features.

"This was all V?" I whisper.

This was all because of me.

"But why? Why the fire? What was she trying to do?"

"She wasn't exactly forthcoming with her plans, but it seemed like she was trying to sabotage any attempts at peace with Westcott's people. Valerie, I—I'm so sorry."

My head snaps up at the crack in Reid's voice.

"I fought her off as often as I could," he whispers. "And I can't remember everything she made me do, but I know she had access to information she shouldn't have." He rubs at his eyes. "I think I can remember her making me give an order—but I can't remember for what or to who."

I shake my head even though he isn't looking at me anymore and squeeze his leg. "Of course I don't blame you for that, Reid. But I don't understand. What would she get out of sabotaging our plan?"

"Isn't it obvious?" Monroe turns around in her seat at the front, her brows knit as she studies my face like she's waiting for V to reappear at any moment. "She wanted to be *you*. And if she was able to get the Anya betrothal out of the way, that left room for *her* to marry Reid instead, to become queen of the first region. And if nothing changes, if Westcott and his people were all massacred—"

"She'd get to rule at the top of the food chain with a puppet for a husband," offers Leif. He glances at Reid over his shoulder. "No offense."

I suppose it makes sense. The version of me who felt powerless to *my* decisions wanting to flip the script and put herself in the most powerful position of all.

And I helped her do it.

I inhale sharply as Reid's hand cups the side of my face and tilts it, inspecting me. I stare back, not sure what he's hoping to find, and the bond expands in my chest as if it's searching too. I don't know what I'll do if he doesn't believe it's me. If none of them do.

He searches my eyes for a moment and asks, "Is she gone for good?"

Swallowing hard, I nod, and I hope to God it's the truth.

I'VE NEVER TAKEN the HSR trains before, more commonly referred to as the *estate trains* since they mainly transport important personnel between neighboring estates. They run between a few of the different regions, and seeing as I'd never left New York before a few months ago, I'd never had a need. They're much nicer than the train that runs between the academy and the estate. Sleeker. Faster. And the inside is clearly built for clientele who expect luxury, not the everyday public transportation crowd. The fact it's still running is a miracle itself.

Or maybe it's a testament to how much of a bubble we've lived in. Westcott's attacks have made the entire world feel like it's burning to the ground—but all that space outside the regions, all of the people who have never set foot in an estate, maybe life is exactly how it's always been for them.

Would things have been different if I'd taken Connor up on his ideas to leave the region all those months ago?

But I know the answer is no. Maybe things would've been different for me—maybe we'd be happy and oblivious somewhere—but Westcott would still be trudging forward with his plans, putting everyone I know and love in danger. Closing my eyes so I wouldn't have to see wouldn't stop it from happening.

The plan was to take the train as close to Westcott's compound near Locklear as we dare. There's a spot a few miles out where what remains of Locklear's Marionettes will meet us and help transport us the rest of the way. The backup numbers Reid and Auclair managed to rally aren't quite what we hoped, but they're enough to fill a dozen train cars behind ours, which will have to be enough.

Even going over two hundred miles per hour, it's a long ride. As far as I can tell, it's British Columbia outside the windows, leaving Yukon and the entirety of Alaska left.

When I was younger, I always thought one day I'd get out in the world to see the rest of the estates. But now I'll never get to see what Locklear was like before the attack. According to reports, it's all but destroyed now. I don't let myself linger on the thought for too long.

Calla was nowhere to be seen when I came back to my body. Because if Popi was working with Westcott, she'd already be at one of the compounds. Same with Adrienne and Cam—both of whom no one has heard from since they set out.

But the alchemists completed the spell before the fire started, so the plan *should* be moving forward as expected, but that brings little comfort when there's no way to confirm it. And besides, their role was merely a stepping stone.

We pass through a lot of open space. There are some towns and cities outside of the estate regions, but we never get close enough to see them. Even for someone whose only experience with life outside the regions was tainted by Westcott and the wolf camp, it seems unnaturally quiet out here.

Reid switched to the carriage behind us shortly after I woke, the same one the rest of the vampires and higher-up Marionettes are in since it's equipped to protect the vampires while the sun is up.

I move to one of the regular seats instead of the couch. The others shoot glances at me over their shoulders when they think I'm not looking, but Jones is the only one to approach.

At least he's not as angry with me as some of the others, having never met Beth, and he shoots me an uncomfortable smile when takes the seat next to me. He and I were never particularly chatty to begin with, but it's a comfort, having someone, *anyone*, in that seat.

Apparently traveling back and forth from the shadow realms is incredibly taxing, and I lose my fight to stay awake more often than not, drifting in and out of sleep with my face pressed against the cold window.

I dream of fires and shoving my sister into darkness and my blood deal slithering from my arm to Cam's, of the humans strapped to metal tables in Westcott's labs and bloody lashes across backs and a mindless Queen Carrington lunging at me before turning to ashes at my feet.

"Princess?"

I gasp, the air feeling like ice against my skin as I turn around in a dark space. The floor is cold and gritty beneath my bare feet. Low in the corner there's a figure crouched—no, two. Chains rattle as one of them stands and steps forward into a pocket of light from the moon.

Cam's face is covered in dirt and dried blood, looking thinner than I remember him to be. He seizes my upper arms, but I barely feel him.

"They know. They *know*—"

When I lurch awake in the train, I'm covered in a cold sweat. Monroe and Kirby are on the couch facing me, that wary look still in their eyes.

I blink, shaking off the dream—or *had* it been a dream? It felt different. The second person...was that Adrienne? But Cam and I have never shared that kind of connection before.

Well, except for one time. When he felt called to that tarmac to save my life.

What if this…?

"I think something's wrong," I start, and then all the lights in the train go out.

CHAPTER FORTY-ONE

THE STOP IS sudden and violent, barely giving the train a chance to slow. I fly forward, my face hitting the seat in front of me. My mouth fills with the coppery taste of blood, and my seat belt digs so deeply into my waist it feels like it might cut me in half. My ears ring as loud crashes and groans surround me.

The lights flicker overhead. A bulb near the back of the car bursts, followed by a scream. My vision slants and swims as I lean back against my seat, my face pulsing with pain. Shakily, I unclasp my seat belt.

Jones is unconscious beside me, slouched forward with his seat belt holding him up. He looks like he has a broken nose at least, but when I check his neck, I find a pulse and let out a sigh of relief.

"Is everyone okay?" I call, my voice sounding weak and strange.

A few groans answer me, but not enough voices for how

many people are in this car. Slipping around Jones, I sway on my feet once I reach the aisle and steady myself on a nearby chair as I look around.

Splatters of blood mar the ground, the walls. Plumes of smoke catch my eye out the window. I need to get to Reid. Are we being attacked?

"Valerie." Leif climbs out of a row in front of me, the left side of his face covered in blood and one of his arms hanging awkwardly at his side. His face twists as he straightens, his body hunching to compensate for the injury. "I think it's just out of socket," he grits out, jutting his chin to his shoulder. "Can you pop it back in?"

I nod, taking stock of the others. Kirby is lying prone near the front of the car, her hair spread around her, looking more red than pink with the blood. But Monroe is seemingly okay enough to tend to her. Daniel and Wes are both moving a few rows behind us, so that's a good sign.

I get into position to help Leif, and he lets out harsh breaths through his nose as I gently take his arm in my hands and feel around the joint, making sure I'm not going to cause more harm than good. It feels like a clean dislocation.

"Are you hurt anywhere else?" I ask.

"I don't think—*ah!*"

"Better when you don't see it coming," I mutter, stripping off my sweatshirt to tie around him as a sling.

"Is Saint okay?" I ask, peering at the row Leif left.

He nods and winces as he adjusts the sling on his shoulder. "Breathing." His eyes flick from me to the back door. "I'll hold down the fort here if you want to go check on them."

"Thank you." I squeeze his good wrist and take off toward

the other car. When I slip through the door, it's a little less chaotic than ours. There's blood and vampires everywhere, but everyone seems to be conscious and moving around, their injuries healing rapidly.

"Valerie." Reid steps around a heap of bags. "Your face…"

"I'm fine," I say, though I don't know if that's true. The reminder brings the pain back with a vengeance, and the taste of blood is strong in my mouth. "But we need to get everyone out of here. I think this is—"

Every window on the left side of the train shatters, followed by a deafening, screeching sound. Reid's hand is in mine, but then it's not. Dozens of bodies surge into the small car, and a pair of arms circles my waist, squeezing my bruises and broken ribs and whatever else is in there. I let out a pained gasp as a cloth covers my face, forcing me to breath in the ether-like odor that pulls me back into the dark.

It's cold when I wake, and a wave of déjà vu washes over me as I take in my surroundings. Dirt floor, rusted bars, no roof. A cage of some sort.

Or a prison cell.

"Valerie."

I startle. When I turn, chains rattle, limiting my movement to a few inches.

"Adrienne?" I call, my voice spiking up an octave. "Is that you?"

"Valerie." It comes out like a sob, then more chains rattle and she throws her arms around me in a suffocating hug. I tense, expecting pain from the injuries I sustained on the train, but it's a dull ache now. My body must have already healed the worst of it.

I take her face between my hands as I pull away, her skin cold. Tears cut lines down the dirt on her cheeks, and she gives me a watery smile.

"Are you okay?" I ask.

She nods, holding my face just as tightly. Soft metallic tings rustle around us, and I stiffen as I realize we're not alone.

"It's okay," she says quickly. "It's just Cam."

I blink, my eyes adjusting to the darkness, and Cam comes into focus. He's sitting a few feet away with his back propped against the wall, arms slung over his knees. He nods, though his forehead is deeply creased, his jaw hard.

"The others?" I ask, looking around the rest of the cell.

"Others?" asks Adrienne.

I push to my feet, and the chain around my ankle pulls taut, preventing me from taking more than a few steps. I flip the blade of my ring, but Adrienne lays her hand over mine before I can make the cut.

"Your magic won't work in here. There's red salt in the shackles."

Of fucking course.

"They didn't bring anyone else in with me?" I try to see through the bars if there are other cells.

"Just you," says Adrienne.

"Where are we?"

"What's left of the Locklear dungeon," comes Cam's gravelly voice behind me. "Must have run out of room in their own," he adds in a mutter barely loud enough for me to hear.

"What do you mean? What happened?"

Cam and Adrienne exchange a look.

"It worked—your alchemist plan," Adrienne says slowly. "Westcott's followers started to turn on him. He caught on quickly, forcing people to remove them, but the damage had already been done. He started imprisoning traitors within the compounds. He's kind of…"

"Out of his goddamn mind?" Cam offers. "He's got hordes of his wendigos patrolling the perimeter now—that's how they found us."

"Have you heard from Calla?" I ask, terrified of being hopeful, but there it is in my chest just the same. If I managed to break free of V's hold, there's no reason she couldn't do it too.

Adrienne's expression darkens. "She's the one who put us down here."

"But when was that?" I push.

Adrienne shrugs, looking to Cam for help.

"A few days ago?" he says.

Before the real Calla and I crossed back then. So there's still hope.

"Has Westcott come to see you?" I ask.

Adrienne shakes her head.

So much for that family is everything *bullshit he was feeding me.*

"Who brought me down here?"

Cam shrugs. "Didn't see his face."

None of this makes any sense. Keeping me and Adrienne

down here, I guess I can understand that. Especially after Calla told me he'd done the same to Mom. He thinks we're a threat but doesn't want to kill us...yet. But then why is Cam here?

I meet Cam's eyes. "Did the spell work?"

He rolls up his sleeve, exposing his bare forearm. "Seems like it."

I dig my brows in. "Do you think Westcott knows that?"

"Your guess is as good as mine."

"Well, we can't just sit here and wait." I throw my hands up. "Tell me you have a plan."

"We've tried everything," says Adrienne. "You can't break the shackles. They're bound with magic. *Our* magic doesn't work. And I called for help until I lost my voice the first night —there's no one else down here."

I look around the empty cell, cringing at what must pass for a toilet in the corner. "Food and water?"

"It's been dropped off twice since we've been here," says Cam.

"Okay, what did you see? Who brought it? Which way did they come in?"

An expression entirely foreign to Cam falls over his face. Sad, resigned. He says nothing, just looks up at the gaping hole over our heads.

They dropped it down here.

My chest constricts, and I pace as much as the chain will allow, refusing to let the panic in. I haven't made it this far to only get this far.

Are you there? I send through the bond. It feels tight and thin, like he's far away. He might be too far to hear me.

If Westcott has any sense left, he would've known to do something to keep us from communicating. But at the very least, I can feel the bond. If Reid were hurt—or worse—I'd be able to feel that.

I wait, holding my breath, but no response comes.

CHAPTER FORTY-TWO

As THE SUN RISES, I huddle into the only part of the cell with shade, my gums throbbing. To my surprise, when there's a drop later that day of water bottles and protein bars, there's also a bag of blood. They fall from above as if from nowhere —no sign of who dropped them. Not a shadow, a glimpse, the crunch of a footstep. I'm not dumb enough to see the blood as a kindness. If Westcott's keeping Cam and Adrienne safe down here for whatever reason, me sinking my fangs into them would throw a wrench in his plans.

Though I'm beginning to think *plans* is too generous of a word. I saw firsthand that something wasn't right with West-cott, then Mom's warnings in Reid's memories, and Cam's. Maybe he's not acting like the strategic leader who has meticu-lously crafted his plans over the past century that his followers know him to be.

He's someone losing himself from absorbing the powers of

too many others running scared and desperate now that his back's against the wall.

Which might make him sloppier, but also that much more dangerous.

I check the bond obsessively, looking for a sign that Reid's closer, that he's okay. But it feels the same as it did yesterday.

I startle as Cam's hand brushes mine. I hadn't noticed him coming over to join me in the shade. Adrienne's curled up on the opposite side of the cell fast asleep, which is probably what I should be doing.

"How are you holding up?" he asks.

I shake my head, pull my legs into my chest, and wrap my arms around them. "I hate just sitting here."

"I know. Me too."

I stare at Adrienne on the ground, grateful at least that we're in the same place so I know she's okay.

"My shadow self took over after I did the spell. Shoved me into the shadow realm and took over my body here. She killed people. *Friends.*"

It's the first time I've said it out loud. I don't know why I'm telling him this, how much it matters now. Maybe I'm not saying it to him so much as trying to work it out myself. Everything's been so crazy since the moment I got back. I haven't even had a chance to process it.

It's clear from the blank look on his face that he has no idea what I'm talking about, and growing up in the barrens, why would he? *I* hadn't even known about the shadow realm until a few weeks ago. I give him the briefest explanation I can manage.

There's a long beat of silence before he says, "I figured

something must have gone wrong when I hadn't heard from you. But you're back now. How'd you manage that?"

Stupidly, my eyes fill with tears, and I scrunch my face to keep them from falling. "Westcott's shadow self helped us cross back."

Cam barks out a laugh and leans back on his hands. The rest of my words register a moment later, because he leans forward again. "Us?"

"Calla was there too. Westcott did it when he realized he couldn't control her anymore."

Cam looks from me to Adrienne. "So the version who put us down here…"

"Shadow self." I nod, then grimace. "She goes by Popi."

"Popi," Cam scoffs the name, then frowns as he scrutinizes the side of my face. "Does that mean the regular version is back in her body now? You think she would help us?"

"If she can," I all but whisper. "Getting back was only half the problem. Pushing V back out of my body—" I clear my throat. "I hope Calla managed to do it."

I can't bear to entertain the alternative.

"You Darkmores are forces to be reckoned with. I'm sure she'll be fine. But I have a feeling there's something else that has you so worried."

I blink up at him, surprised, but he isn't looking at me. His eyes are locked on the diamond ring on my finger.

"He was with me when I was taken," I say hoarsely. "I don't know how many of Westcott's people were in that ambush, but they outnumbered us. Westcott's already tried to kill him once." And the thought of it happening while I'm trapped here and can do nothing to stop it…

I let out a frustrated breath through my nose, trying to force the image of Reid in that body bag from my mind, him staked to the floor, the Russians pinning him to the wall… Why do I feel like I'm always on the brink of losing him?

Cam takes my hand in his, intertwining our fingers, and squeezes. "He'll be all right. Your sister too."

A loud screech of metal on metal fills the air, and I cringe. Cam's the first to his feet, getting as close the bars as his chain will allow to see where it's coming from.

"What's going on?" Adrienne stirs, still sounding half asleep, and I hold up a finger for her to be quiet, my heart steadily beating faster in my chest as I stand and join Cam.

Dust swirls in the air in the pockets of light.

"Ugh!" Someone coughs, and high heels click against the cement, drawing closer. "It's dis*gusting* down here."

I stop breathing at that voice.

Oh my…oh my *God.*

"Is that…" Cam mutters.

Anya steps in front of our cell, squinting in at us with her nose scrunched. "Oh, it's even worse in there." She grabs the bars with one hand and yanks it clear from the wall. Cam and I back up as chunks of dirt and cement explode from the walls and rain down from the ceiling.

Anya tosses aside the bars, and my shoulders slump, that surge of hope quickly souring in the pit of my stomach.

"Anya…"

She beams at me, not realizing. The bars were never what was keeping us in.

She glances at the shackles around each of our ankles. "Oh, are you worried about those?"

She probably thinks she can break those too. But if they're bound with magic, no amount of strength will be enough. But then she does the unthinkable. From the dainty white purse hanging off her shoulder, she produces a set of keys.

"Where did you—how?" I ask.

"These"—she jangles the keys before getting to work unlocking Adrienne—"were easy. The guards up there went down without much of a fight. There were half a dozen when I first scoped the place out, but it's down to three right now. So Westcott must have pulled them back for something."

"The train—the others...?"

"There was so much chaos. I made myself scarce. Turns out all those years of stowing away paid off. There were a lot of them. Way too many to take on myself, especially with how quickly they had everyone unconscious. I don't know what kind of magic it was, but it was *powerful*. I don't think I've ever felt anything like it. They left a lot of the backup Marionettes behind and unconscious. But then they were taking you somewhere different than the others, so I followed. Figured I'd have a better chance with their jailbreak if I had some backup."

"You know where they took them?"

She nods as Adrienne's chain rattles against the ground as it drops, then she moves on to me. "The compound. All still alive, as far as I could tell. The security is intense. But he wouldn't have killed them yet. Not with..."

She trails off as she starts to work the key into Cam's shackle.

"I've got it," he murmurs, his voice lacking all of its usual edges, and Anya stares at him for a moment before handing him the key.

"Not with what, Anya?" I demand.

She swallows hard as the last of the chains hits the dirt, glancing from Adrienne to Cam to me.

"They've been erecting these structures in front of the compound since the moment we got here. It looks like they're preparing for a public execution."

CHAPTER FORTY-THREE

IT DOESN'T TAKE LONG. The remains of the Locklear estate are only a half-hour drive away from Westcott's compound. I watch out the back of the car—one Anya stole from a guard, if I had to guess from the smear of blood on the steering wheel —as we drive away. There's a body splayed out a few feet above a hole in the ground that must lead to the dungeon cells. Most likely the unfortunate former keeper of the keys.

The estate beyond is mostly intact, though it clearly sustained some damage. But it's the feeling in the air I can't shake. Like the spirits of everyone who died in the attack are lingering behind.

We stay hidden on the way to the compound, ditching the car once we're a few miles out and following Anya's lead, but the closer we get, the less that seems necessary.

Because Westcott clearly has plenty else on his plate.

There are crowds everywhere. People are screaming and holding signs, and it takes a moment for me to realize they aren't rallying, they're *protesting.* There must be hundreds of them. At the front of the crowd is a line of wendigos like some kind of security, but they leave the people be no matter how loudly they yell or how charged the energy in the air gets.

I see what Anya was talking about too. In the middle of the courtyard, a stage has been erected with thirteen posts stretching toward the sky.

The compound itself looks untouched from Auclair's earlier attack. The surrounding ground is scorched from the fire, but the structure looks the same.

If I look closely enough, I can see faces behind the windows watching this all unfold. What's left of his following that hasn't turned on him? There's some out here too.

The crowd roars louder as the people on Westcott's side move about. They duck their heads as if physically trying to retreat from the jeers, carrying various supplies in their arms, all walking like they're in a hurry.

Our group stays back within the tree line on a hill, watching it play out.

"Witches, vampires, humans, werewolves…" Adrienne says, eyes locked on the crowd. "They're all down there."

"Anya, after the train ambush, was there any sign of the Locklear team?"

She presses her lips into a thin line and shakes her head. "But we were a few miles out from our meeting point. They could be nearby now."

"I've never been inside this compound, but I imagine the layout is similar to the ones I have seen," says Cam. "If they're keeping everyone in a holding cell, it'll be several levels below. I think we should split up."

"What?" I demand. "We should stay together."

"We had a plan, Darkmore," Cam says lowly, back to surveying the crowd now. "There has to be someone leading this."

"Cam," I gasp as he takes a step forward like he's planning on going down there and joining them.

His eyes flick up, not to me, but to Anya. "Can you get them inside?"

She scoffs like she's insulted by the question. "Of course I can."

"Then you take care of the others." He swallows hard and meets my eyes one last time, and I can see him make up his mind. "And I'll take care of Westcott."

"Cam, what happened to a peaceful transition of power?" I demand.

"You willing to give him more time go through with those executions?"

I follow his gaze to the posts, imagining far too clearly everyone I love up there.

Quieter, he says, "Plans change." Then he shifts into his wolf form before I can protest and takes off down the hill, shifting back just as he reaches the crowd. A few people at the back turn as he approaches, and the transformation happens from one blink of an eye to the next, taking him from Cam to pack master as he shakes hands with each person and starts talking.

"Maybe you two should wait here while I scope the place out," says Anya.

"We can come with you," insists Adrienne, but I lay a hand on her shoulder.

"She'll be faster without us," I say. I have a better chance of keeping up with her speed with my half-vampire side, but there's no way I'm leaving Adrienne here alone.

"I'll only be a few minutes," says Anya before disappearing through the trees.

The silence feels thicker in her absence. Adrienne diligently watches the protest, her eyes flicking back and forth with every movement below.

My heart beats a little faster in my chest as I watch her. I've been meaning to talk to her ever since that speech of hers, but it's never felt like the right time. Especially since we haven't had a chance to be alone.

"Adrienne," I blurt before I can talk myself out of it. "I'm really sorry."

She blinks up at me in surprise. "For what?"

"The things you said in Cam's room…"

"I—Valerie, I didn't mean it. I was just trying to show you that I could convince Westcott—"

"I know, I know. But you were also right. I wasn't there for you after Calla, and I should've been. I should've tried harder."

To be honest, I don't remember much from those first few months after it happened. Mom was AWOL, and Kirby and Monroe were trying to be all sincere and get me to talk about my feelings, which I had no interest in doing, so I latched on to Avery and her older friends. That summer was full of smoking and drinking and numbing until I didn't have to feel like a person anymore. I can't even recall a single conversation Adrienne and I had during that time, if there were any.

My stomach sinks as something occurs to me. No wonder

she'd been so hypervigilant when I started spiraling after the attack on the tarmac. It was a side of me she was already too familiar with. The version who shuts down and forgets anyone else exists.

She doesn't say anything for what feels like a long time, just goes back to watching the crowd below. But then quietly, she says, "We were all doing the best we could. And it's not all your fault, Valerie. I didn't let you be there. I needed someone to blame, and I couldn't be mad at Calla because she was dead, so you were the next best thing. And that wasn't fair."

I step up beside her, my gaze trained on the protest. Cam has completely disappeared within their midst now. I take her hand in mine and squeeze.

"I won't ever check out on you like that again. I promise."

Her eyes are wide and vulnerable when she turns to me, but as she opens her mouth to respond, the trees behind us rustle, and then Anya reappears.

"Something's wrong," she says breathlessly.

Two security guards are attaching chains to the posts on the stage and yanking on them to ensure they're strong enough.

My heart stops in my chest. Is this happening right *now*?

"We have to do something," I say.

"I know you're out there!" The compound door bursts open, and out flows a stream of people led by the man of the hour. Even with how far away he is, I can picture the look on Westcott's face perfectly. The smug smile. That dark glint in his eyes when he thinks he's won.

I suck in a sharp breath, every muscle in my body going rigid as he drags Kirby along by her hair, yanking her onto the platform and leading her to the first post. Calla is behind him, pulling Monroe. More of his guards continue the trend, bringing Daniel, Leif, Saint, Jones, Wes, Avery, Feddei, and Reid onto the structure, along with Kirby's and Wes's partners. I eye the remaining post.

"Oh my God," Adrienne breathes as the door flies open a second time, and two guards drag Rosemarie Darkmore behind them.

She's thinner than I've ever seen her and covered in dirt, her hair a tangled mess around her shoulders. But still, she fights. She clearly has no intention of making this easy for them as she kicks and thrashes in their arms, all the way up to the moment they chain her to the final post, then she spits on the guards' faces before they can walk away.

"Calla," Adrienne murmurs, her voice wobbling.

Westcott stands at the front of the platform now like he's preparing to address the crowd, and Calla stands calmly at his side, her arms crossed in front of her body.

It's such a stark contrast between her and the others—fresh clothes, clean skin. Very clearly not a prisoner.

Adrienne lets out a choked sob beside me as she comes to the same conclusion. "She couldn't do it," she whispers. "That's not her."

The anguish is sharp and deep. I take Adrienne's hand in mine again, offering what little comfort I can. Because the grief is twofold. Mourning the loss of her now, and when we'll inevitably have to kill her along with Westcott. Because if Calla hasn't broken through now, she's not going to. All that's left inside is Popi.

"I know you're out there, Valerie!" Westcott calls, but the

crowd doesn't quiet. "I hope you know you're the reason it's come to this." He paces along the edge as he speaks, his movements manic and nonsensical.

"He's out of his goddamn mind," mutters Anya.

"And you all!" Westcott points and throws his arm in a wide arc around the crowd. "How foolish, how *naïve* could you possibly be to think there would be no loss, no bloodshed in this war? How fragile your loyalty must have been to turn so easily. Maybe you don't deserve what you seek if you're fickle enough to make me your hero in one breath and your villain in the next."

My feet take me forward of their own accord, slipping in and out of trees and behind bushes as I make my way down the hill. Judging by the crunching leaves and snow behind me, the others are following.

There's no time for a more thought-out plan. Not when he has that many hostages *right there.* All it would take is…

And I refuse to be too late.

Cam might think he can deal the killing blow, but his chances are much better if I can subdue Westcott first. And for that, I'll need to be closer.

The bond feels stronger in my chest with Reid this close, but I can't feel him the way I normally do, not enough to communicate. They must have given him something to cut off the connection. But he has to feel it too, that I'm closer now. That I'm coming. That I won't let this be the end.

"Our purpose will live on for those with bravery in their hearts and logic in their minds. Not deserters who flee at the first sign of struggle."

We're halfway there now, the voices of the crowd growing

louder, stronger, enough for me to pick out some of their words.

Traitor.

Coward.

Selfish.

Unfit.

You let them burn.

I inspect the thirteen on the posts as I get closer, but despite their disheveled states, none of them seems injured. As my eyes flick back to Westcott, I freeze when I realize Calla is staring right at me. I've made it to the back of the crowd now, hoping to blend in with the hundreds of other bodies, but she's somehow already picked me out. We hold each other's eyes for one beat, two. My heart hammers in my chest. If she alerts Westcott—

—but then she blinks and turns away.

I exhale shakily. Had I imagined it? Maybe she hadn't been looking at me at all.

Or maybe…

"What's truly saddening is that you have all known struggle before! It is what drew us together. What bonded us. You've seen hardship and cruelty, and yet you seem to forget who the true enemy is so easily!"

I can feel the magic in the air as I shoulder my way through the crowd. So many witches here. After a moment, I realize why none of them have tried anything with Westcott so close. There's a shimmer in the air, barely visible, cutting off the platform from the crowd behind the wendigos. A magical protection barrier, if I had to guess.

I look around for Cam but don't see him. Adrienne has

one hand fisted in the back of my shirt and she shuffles along behind me so we don't get separated.

"He's holding the barrier," she says in my ear, and I follow where she points to a witch standing beside the platform. I squint at him, trying to figure out how she can tell, when Anya splits off from us, disappearing into the crowd in his direction.

God, I hope no one recognizes her.

"What's the plan, Val?" Adrienne asks.

I don't relish the idea of getting any closer to a wendigo than I have to, but the more I look at them, the more I realize how much they're for show. Compared to the number of people in this crowd, they alone would never manage to subdue them if a riot broke out. They're here for intimidation.

Wescott is counting on that barrier not coming down. If that's gone, we might not have to do much. The energy in the air buzzes louder with each passing second, the anger palpable. These people are ready to tear him limb from limb.

They probably had families in those compounds he let burn. Parents, friends, children.

And instead of acknowledging their pain and grief, he's talking down to them. Questioning their loyalty, their character, and ranting up there like a madman, giving them more reason to question his suitability as their leader.

"Does this not remind you all of what we've been fighting for?" Westcott steps beside Reid and yanks his head back by his hair.

I freeze. Reid barely reacts to this. His hands and feet are chained down, and he doesn't try to fight his restraints. His jaw is hard as he stares back at Westcott.

"The crown prince of the Carrington estate—no, their *king*

now! A region many of you fled! A region where many of you endured abuse and threats and injustice. They bled you dry like animals or threated you like vermin if you didn't join their ranks. Some of you weren't welcome within their borders at all."

The chatter of the crowd dims, like they're listening to what he's saying for the first time since he stepped out here.

"If we turn on each other now, we're letting them win. We're handing the power right back to those privileged vampires who have never struggled a day in their lives. Is that what you want?" Westcott yanks Reid back another inch. "Or do you want to send what's left of them his head?"

I lose all of the air in my lungs, a breathy "No" escaping me.

Adrienne's fist tightens on my shirt, not urging me forward, but holding me back. If I thought for a second exposing myself would spare Reid, I'd be charging through the crowd. But I know that wouldn't stop him.

I look around wildly, willing an idea to form.

"We'd rather have yours!"

I still, recognizing the voice immediately, and search the crowd for him. Cam is near the front, only his profile in view.

What the hell is he doing?

If Westcott's surprised to see him, he doesn't show it. "Camden," he says on a sigh, then smiles as his fangs extend. "It'll be a shame to lose such an asset. But not even you can stop this. Calliope. Would you do the honors?"

The world moves in slow motion as Calla takes a step forward, a stake in her hand. Westcott remains beside Reid, his hand fisted in his hair and pulling his head as far back as it can go against the post. At some point I start running because I feel Adrienne lose her grip on me.

I shove my way through the crowd and dig my nails into my palms until my hands are coated with blood, the magic I don't know what to do with surging through me. But I have to get that wall down. I have to get to Reid.

Calla raises her arm, that serene, doting smile on her face as she looks at Westcott.

"No!" I scream, my magic reaching for her arm, trying to freeze her muscles, but it can't cross the barrier.

Reid's head jerks out of Westcott's hold at my voice. His eyes find mine, and the resignation in his face pulls a choked sob from my chest.

I reach for the other kind of magic, letting its darkness funnel through the soles of my feet until it fills me. The stake cuts through the air, getting closer and closer, and with a roar, I let every ounce of power burst through me and into the shield—

—as Calla pivots at the last second and sinks the stake into Westcott's chest instead.

CHAPTER FORTY-FOUR

THE BARRIER SHATTERS LIKE GLASS. Sparks fill the air as its pieces scatter to the wind. The crowd turns into chaos—shrieking, ducking, and covering their heads from the explosion.

I take off at a sprint toward the platform, that coldness from the magic lingering on my skin, but instead of feeling depleted, it hums with joy, waiting to be used again.

I'm not the only one taking advantage of the opportunity. Others from the crowd charge forward, and the wendigos swarm, trying to fend off a hundred times their number.

Leaving the perfect opening for me.

"He's not dead!" Calla calls as I reach the platform. There's a trail of blood at her feet, but Westcott is gone. She points into the crowd.

I grab her arm and pull her close, peering into her eyes and checking her wrist for a pulse. "Is it really—"

"It's me," she insists, fishing a set of keys from her pocket. "Where's Adrienne?"

I whip around. She was right behind me, but now all I see is the chaos of the crowd, turning more violent and restless by the moment.

Calla gives me a small push. "Go. I'll take care of them."

She slides the key into Reid's restraints first, the rest of the world dimming as I meet his eyes.

He nods. "Go. I'll be right behind you."

"Get me out of this thing!" Leif yanks at his chains and bares his teeth. "I can help. Get me out!"

"Calla, are there more keys?"

"Got some!" Anya jumps onto the stage, dragging a limp and bloody man in Westcott's guard's uniform behind her, and twirls his keys around her finger.

"Cam?" I ask.

"Went after Westcott," says Anya, getting to work on Leif's locks.

I search the crowd for any sign of them, but it's impossible to see. Some members of the protest are fleeing, some are fighting off wendigos and Westcott's guards. It's a mess of teeth and claws and blood—but there, in the thick of it, the crowd is streaming in a single direction like they're chasing someone. The wendigos are flocking to that area too. Likely to protect Westcott.

"Valerie."

Calla's hand seizes my wrist before I can step away. Why is she stopping me when she just told me to go? She juts her chin toward the estate. Through a window on the second floor there's a line of girls—literally *children*—holding hands, their eyes locked on the fight and mouths moving in sync. They look so similar it's hard to differentiate one from the next—same dark hair, dark eyes, light skin…

Oh God.

Calla's chewed so hard on her lower lip she's drawn blood. "This is about to get really ugly," she says.

"What are they doing?"

Calla shakes her head, but the panic in her features hardens into determination. "I'll take care of it."

"Calla—"

"I'll handle them. You handle things out here."

I cast one last glance at my friends over my shoulder. They all stare back with the same solemn, determined expression.

With a nod, I plunge into the crowd.

The wind roars and whips around us far too forcefully to be natural. It nearly knocks me off my feet. Ducking my head, I push forward. Shrieks surround me as heat fills the air, and I look up in time to see the trees surrounding the clearing go up in flames so tall that I can no longer see the sky.

Another gust of wind cuts through the crowd, lifting people off their feet and throwing them several feet back. An elbow clips me under the chin and I drop to my knees, trying to avoid the other airborne bodies as blood fills my mouth.

I brace my hands on the earth to push back to my feet, but my fingers meet something warm and wet. When I yank it back, my hand is covered in blood. I follow the stains to the body lying a foot away—a woman splayed on her stomach with a piece of her skull missing. Her eyes are closed, her mouth open in a silent scream. People step directly onto her back as they rush past her.

I try to shove down the nausea surging up from my stomach.

But then the woman's eyes fly open.

They're glassy and unseeing, and her movements are jerky as she climbs to her hands and knees, then pushes to her feet.

I shove myself back as her eyes lock on me, and there's absolutely nothing behind them but darkness.

This is what Westcott's other daughters are doing up there.

"Shit," I breathe, using the power from her own blood against her to freeze the muscles in her legs before she can come any closer.

But she folds at the waist until her fingers dig into the ground, then she starts to drag herself forward. A man lying behind her with his spine and arms bent unnaturally stirs, his head popping up next.

Dirt kicks up as a wolf darts past me, then two. *Leif?* I don't turn to the platform to check. I scramble to my feet and follow. Anyone I take down in this crowd will likely come right back. I need to get to Westcott.

The crowd thins—from Westcott physically blowing them back or their own departure, I'm not sure. But then something brushes the inside of my ankle, and I shriek as a horde of mice sprints past me.

There's a clear line ahead of me now, where Westcott stands with his guards, his complexion tinted red as he bellows something lost to the wind. But as he finishes, more people in the crowd disappear. At least, that's how it first seems, the space they occupied suddenly empty. But then I notice more mice scurrying across the ground.

He's transforming them.

The same way he transformed himself from a mouse to a man to *him* a million nights ago as I rotted in a cell and he locked me into the deal.

Just one of the many powers he stole. Of course any man who absorbed that many different powers would be powerful, but I'd never seen it firsthand until now.

His shirt is soaked through with blood from where Calla stabbed him, but if he's feeling any negative effects from the injury, it's not showing. He whips around as a werewolf lunges for him and grabs the creature by the throat. Then just as quickly, he seizes a hind leg and rips the wolf in half like it's nothing.

Blood and gore pours onto the ground, and Westcott roars, the moonlight reflecting off his fangs and the crazed look in his eyes.

"Valerie!" someone screams, or maybe it's the wind.

People stream back and forth, knocking into my shoulders, blurring my vision. My ears ring from the noise, my senses overwhelmed by the number of smells, sounds. I think I see blurs of black Marionettes uniforms. The estate rein-forcements?

I'm almost to him now. Dark magic floods up from my feet, and I cut into my palms, letting the blood magic join it.

A flash of black fur catches the corner of my eye, and I'd recognize him anywhere. Cam bounds closer, and my stomach flips at how easily Westcott tore apart the other wolf. He needs the element of surprise.

"Hey!" I shriek, funneling my magic into my voice, and it echoes around the field.

Westcott's head jerks up from a body he'd been feeding on,

his eyes landing on me as blood pours from the corners of his mouth.

I can feel the blood's magic emanating from here. It must have been a witch. I seize it like a thread in the air, adding it to the growing pool inside of me.

Westcott smiles, nothing about it warm. Nothing about it looking like my father.

Which alleviates whatever guilt I may have felt as I tighten my hand into a fist. Westcott stiffens and jerks like he's trying to move but can't. Once I have a solid grasp on his muscles, I move to his organs, his heart, his lungs, the very blood pumping through his veins.

The guards behind him notice a moment later, their mouths moving as they shout to each other and turn toward me, but then one by one, they're taken out. A wolf tackles the one on the far right. The one beside him is blown back several feet and then encased in thick vines that sprout up from the earth. Anya leaps on the one closest to me, ripping his throat open with her fangs.

"You can't really think you can beat me, Valerie," Westcott grits out, and I feel each word pulling and forcing itself through my hold on him.

"You're killing off your own followers," I say, taking a step closer. "They don't trust you anymore. They don't believe in you. You've already lost your family. Without them, you have no one and nothing. *You* can't really think there's a way out of this."

His mouth twists into a smile. He's stalling me.

I dig my nails harder into my palms, trying to regain my

hold on him, but it's harder to grasp now that he's made cracks.

An unnatural coldness washes through me. The world turns gray at the edges, fog creeping in along the ground.

I should've noticed sooner. How could I not have noticed?

With all the chaos, I'd focused so hard on not losing sight of Westcott. I'd seen the wendigos when I first joined the crowd, but there hasn't been a glimpse of them since.

An inhuman roar rips through the air, breaking the last of the hold I had on Westcott. The force of it slams into my chest and throws me back into a pair of arms. *One of the others?* That split second of hope fizzles out just as fast as I feel the claws, the cloak.

Fight back and they'll die, echoes a voice in my head.

"If you surrender now, you will be shown mercy!" Westcott bellows as the wendigo drags me forward, its hold on me firm, but not painful. Clearly meant to subdue, but not harm. I desperately look for the others and try to take in my surroundings through the fog, but suddenly there are wendigos everywhere when there were none before. Have they been here all this time, waiting on the other side of the veil, perhaps?

They each carry a body forward—Monroe, Kirby, Avery, Anya, Feddei, Daniel, Leif, Wes, Saint, Jones, Cam, Reid, Calla, Mom, and Adrienne. Once the wendigos have convened in a circle, they drop us to our knees and hold us there.

No. *No.* Not when we were this close. But there's so many of them, and their claws are poised beside each person's throat. One wrong move and...

Westcott leisurely paces the inside of the circle, taking in each person one by one. When he reaches Calla, Mom, Adrienne, and me, he looks at us as if we're strangers. As if we're nothing to him.

Maybe we always have been.

Despite the smug look on his face, there's an obvious limp to his walk, an exhausted slump to his shoulders. That display of his powers had been gaudy, frivolous. And it's taken its toll.

Can you hear me? I ask through the bond, trying to catch Reid's eyes across the circle.

He lifts his head an inch. *Yes.*

He's weak. Tell me you have an idea. I can try to use my necromancy on him, but it won't do any good if the wendigos attack.

Reid subtly glances around the circle. If any of Westcott's followers remain, I can't see them past the wendigos—one for each of us—but there's also a group amassed on the outside of the circle, seeming to stretch on forever in every direction.

"I'd be doing you a favor, wouldn't I?" Westcott purrs, trailing his fingers under my mother's chin. She stares right back at him, unflinching, exuding every ounce of power she did before despite having no magic to back it up this time. "How many people have you pissed off enough over the years to want you dead?" he whispers. "I think I'd be kinder about it. They'd make sure you suffered. They'd enjoyed watching you die slowly. But then again, maybe *I'd* enjoy watching them tear you limb from limb."

Slowly, the pressure on my arms eases, and I suck in a sharp breath as the wendigo behind me releases its hold. Daniel makes a similar surprised sound on my left, and I look at him out of the corner of my eye.

What the hell are they doing?

"Don't touch her," Calla snaps beside Mom, and Westcott turns his attention to her.

"And *you*, my dear Calliope, you may be my greatest disappointment. I saw so much potential with you. I suppose it's not your fault that you got more from your mother than you did from me."

The wendigo behind me slips into the circle first. Westcott's back is to us, but he stands up straighter as the wind shifts, then turns. His gaze shoots to me, like I'm somehow controlling the wendigo, looking more unamused than surprised.

But then the rest start to move.

First it's just the layer of wendigos behind each of us, but then it's all of them coming forward.

My muscles brace themselves for some kind of attack, but they pass each of us as if we're not even there.

No, they are purely focused on Westcott.

It's not until his scream pierces the air that it occurs to me these wendigos, they were once his followers too. They trusted him enough to submit to his experiments.

How much of their humanity is left in there?

Enough, apparently, to think for themselves.

And now they're fighting back.

But one by one, as they make a move for Westcott, the wendigos collapse into dark heaps on the ground. Slowly, their forms fade until they're reduced to ash.

The experiments, Cam said they required something similar to a blood deal. Going against Westcott, it's killing them. Yet they keep drifting forward. They keep trying, as one by one, they fade like dust on the wind.

The fog grows thicker until I can't see anything but flashes of black capes and claws. As each wendigo falls, another is there just as fast to take its place. Daniel grabs my hand so he doesn't lose me in the darkness, and I reach for Leif on my other side.

There are sickening wet sounds as claws rip through his flesh.

As quickly as they'd swarmed him, a small patch disperses enough to reveal Westcott in the center of them all. The ground beneath him saturated with his blood. Not only are chunks of his flesh missing, but what's left is peeling, decayed, like he's rotting from the inside out, looking more skeletal than human. He bares his teeth, his focus entirely on the wendigos as they approach.

They knew they couldn't finish this. But they can distract and weaken him enough so we can.

I pace forward at the same time Calla, Adrienne, and Mom do. We join hands as we step through the opening of wendigos.

Magic buzzes through our joined palms, our different strands collecting and coiling together. I know the moment it's ready, the heat coursing through me burning almost to the point of pain.

But we wait until Westcott turns his head.

So the three of us are the last things he sees before he dies.

CHAPTER FORTY-FIVE

IRONICALLY, once Westcott is gone, his followers are incredibly loyal—to one another. No injured or dead is left behind, and everyone helps each other as much as they can. Those who stayed inside the compound while this was all happening immediately open the doors, ushering the injured to the medical wing, several doctors flooding into the field to give help to the more severe cases. The remaining Marionette reinforcements jump in, working alongside them.

I can't help but side-eye the people who continued to support him, but I try to remind myself that they could've been too afraid to stand against him.

What was left of Westcott disappeared along with the wendigos when it was done. The darkness had parted like a curtain, the fog wrapping around them until it became indistinguishable from their cloaks, and then they were gone.

There's a moment of panic after the calm, when I search the crowd for my friends. The tightness in my chest doesn't relent until I've verified with my own eyes that everyone's okay. Bloody and dirty and bruised, but alive.

I search for Reid through the bond when I don't see him, and it gives a strong pull, as if letting me know he's all right. I follow the feeling until I spot him across the field offering whatever aid he can. He meets my eyes for a moment with a small smile and nod, then gets back to work.

"You did it." Kirby takes my face between her hands, her own stained with blood from a cut hidden somewhere in her hairline. "How are you feeling? Are you okay?"

Monroe joins us and crushes us into a hug before we can respond, tears streaming down her face. "Thank God you're both all right."

"Can I get some help over here?"

I follow Daniel's voice and take off at a run. Wes is on the ground, his partner at his side. Daniel kneels by Wes's head, pushing the bloody hair back from his face.

"He has a pulse and he's breathing," says Daniel. "But I can't wake him up."

"We should get him inside," I say, falling to my knees as I search Wes for any visible injuries.

"I've got him." A figure appears, momentarily blocking the light from the moon, and I crane my head back. Leif bends to scoop Wes's limp form into his arms, lifting him with no visible effort. His eyes cut to Daniel, scanning him for injury. "You all right?"

Daniel nods.

"The other wolves?" I ask.

"They're all good," says Leif, heading for the compound.

Dried blood coats the side of his head, and there's a slight limp to his walk. "Leif, are you—"

"I'm fine," he insists as we slip through the door and follow the stream of people already heading toward the hospital.

The infirmary buzzes with noise and movement as we step inside, but we manage to find a bed for Wes near the back corner. As we settle him on his back, his eyes crack open. He extends a hand, and I glance around for the others, but they must have gotten lost in the crowd on the way here.

Despite probably being the last person he wants to see, I take his hand and pull a chair beside his head. I prepare myself for him to yank his hand away, for that same disgust I'd seen on the train to fill his face, but he just stares at me, his eyes a little wide.

"You're okay," I murmur. "We've got you."

He squeezes my fingers, and tears sting my eyes.

"Wes, I can't tell you how sorry I am about Beth."

"I know," he rasps.

"We should try to flag down a doctor…" I trail off when I realize Leif isn't beside me anymore. I search the room. Maybe he went back outside? But then I notice Cam on the opposite side of the hospital. I frown, rising to my feet to see what drew him over there, and freeze when I realize it's Anya.

She's sitting up in her bed, a bag of blood hanging on an IV stand beside her head. Cam stands with his arms crossed tightly over his chest, a scowl firmly in place, but every time Anya moves an inch, his gaze cuts back to her.

"Sorry—sorry. I'm here." Daniel appears through the crowd, and I step away so he can take my seat. "Oh good, you're awake. Val, your sisters were looking for you in the hall. Don't worry, they were both fine."

"Thanks, Daniel." I squeeze his shoulder before heading that way.

But when I break through the sea of people heading for the hospital, it isn't my sisters I find.

My mother stands by the windows with her back to me. There's a perfect view of the field from here, and she stares at the platform, specifically, the post she'd been chained to. Her arms are loosely holding each other in front of her stomach in a stance that looks far too...vulnerable for her. She doesn't move as I approach. Even as I step up beside her, her gaze remains on that post.

The post the father of her children chained her to and had every intention of watching her die on.

My father was not a topic up for discussion after he left. What I knew about him growing up mostly came from others and my own memories warped with time. She couldn't even stand to hear me play the violin, which was why I'd gotten so used to practicing in the gardens. For a while, I'd thought it was because she was angry about the cheating. That she'd never been a particularly emotional or sentimental person anyway, so talking about the past was a waste of time to her.

But looking at her face now, I can see how wrong I was.

For better or worse, she loved him, at least at one time. But even now, I can see it in her eyes that she never expected him to turn on her, to be willing to *kill* her. She'd thought she would be safe with him.

"Did you know who he was when you met?" I don't know who's more surprised by the question, me or her.

What's even more surprising is she answers.

"No. I didn't know about his past as Westcott at all until after Adrienne was born, until after the scandal was out. He went by William Adler when I met him."

"What was he like?" I whisper.

She cocks her head to the side, and her voice comes out soft as she says, "Charming. Kind. I didn't make it easy for him either, but he never gave up. Kept pursuing me. Kept insisting I was the one. He didn't turn out to be the man I fell for, but believe me when I say this, Valerie." Finally, she turns, and her eyes are glassy. "No matter his lies and manipulations, I would do it all again to end up with you three girls."

I stare at her, too stunned to respond. We don't talk like this. We don't *care* like this. She made those expectations as a Darkmore clear very early on.

But if what she'd said in Reid's memory was true, that she was protecting us, all the while reeling from the betrayal of the man she'd thought was the love of her life…

The one thing that has me swaying toward believing her is what I saw in the shadow realm. If *that* was the opposite of her, then at least some of the past twenty-two years must have been an act.

But act or not, every second of it felt real to me. And I don't know how to reconcile knowing the reasoning behind it and remembering experiencing it.

I take a step away, and uncertainty pinches her brow like she's just as confused on how to navigate this.

"Are you…?" I clear my throat. "Are you okay?"

"I'll be fine."

I rub at a spec of nothing on my shirt so I don't have to

maintain the eye contact. But when I look up, she's not staring at me—she's staring at my ring.

"I'm happy for you," Mom says, and I can't help but wonder if Reid and I ever would have happened without her. She'd orchestrated so much behind the scenes to keep me alive, to bring us together, so many little pieces that had to fall into place for us to end up here.

Against my better judgment, I throw my arms around her shoulders. She's slow to hug me back, her touch light and unsure when she does.

"I'm not ready to forgive you," I say. "But I don't want to spend the rest of my life hating you either. I'm glad you're okay. And I want to thank you for everything you've done for me. If there's a way for me to give some of this magic back—"

"No," she insists, her arms tightening around me. "You keep it."

"Mom?"

I pull away at Adrienne's voice, stepping aside as she hurries in for a hug.

Another pair of arms circles my neck at the same time, crushing me against my other sister's chest. "Thank God," breathes Calla. "I was so worried about you."

I hug her back, my eyes falling shut. "You scared me pretty good at the beginning there."

"I'm sorry I couldn't tell you sooner. If Westcott knew, he would've thrown me in the hole with you and I would've been no help to anyone. I had to keep up the act."

"No, that was smart. The others, the daughters, did you…"

"They're fine. A few of Auclair's Marionettes helped me

subdue them. We put some of those red salt cuffs on them for now, just in case, but they didn't really seem to understand what they were doing. Val, I—" She chokes on a sob. "I'm— I'm *so* sorry about Reid and everything."

"Shh. I know." I squeeze her tighter and rest my chin on the top of her head.

Because the fact of the matter is, I spent years thinking she was dead and wishing to have her back, a prayer I never thought would be answered. And then it was, for a moment, until I saw her on that stage and thought only Popi was looking back. And I felt that soul-crushing grief all over again.

But now she's here and standing in front of me, and I'm not willing to waste any more time.

I pull away with a smile and squeeze her shoulders. "You just saved all of us today, you know that?"

She smiles as someone calls my name behind me.

"Go on." She releases me and joins Mom and Adrienne's hug.

"Can I have your attention?"

The surrounding chatter quiets, and I step to the side so I can see through the doorway to the hospital. Cam stands at the end of the room on top of a desk, Kirby at his side, using her magic to project his voice.

"For those of you who don't know me, my name is Camden Farley. I've spent the last ten years as a pack master in the barrens. And through a blood deal, I was also in Westcott's service for the majority of that time."

Heads turn in his direction, and he stands tall beneath the scrutiny, like he belongs up there.

"I know you've all been through so much. So I'm not here

to tell you what to do or who you should follow. Instead, I'm going to offer you a plan for how we move forward from here. And it'll be up to you to decide if that's something you want to be a part of."

I chew on my lip, watching the crowd as he continues. We can't force them to accept him taking Westcott's place, but if they don't, I can't see us finding peace anytime soon.

But through the exhaustion and pain and skepticism in their faces, one by one, as Cam lays out his plans, something else starts to break through. Something I haven't seen in a long time.

Something that looks a lot like hope.

CHAPTER FORTY-SIX

A FEW WEEKS LATER

"Does this make you wish we'd had the big wedding?" Reid murmurs beside me.

I chuckle. *Not in the slightest.*

He's summoned to the front of the ceremony before I can respond. He plants a quick kiss to my temple then joins the rest of the estate heads as the older monarchs explain how this will work. It was Anya's idea to combine the wedding and Cam's swearing into the alliance for efficiency, making the royal vampires look slightly ridiculous standing in a semicircle beneath an arch of white flowers.

For the most part, the wedding is tame. Anya's not even in a wedding dress, just a full-length gown sporting Vasiliev's colors—crimson red and gold—and the same ceremonial sash as the rest of the royals. Because today she's the bride...and one of the estate heads swearing in her soon-to-be husband.

The entire thing is bizarre.

But I plaster on a smile just the same as I shift my weight

in my wooden chair, my high heels sinking into the grass each time I put too much pressure on them.

Cam's not out here yet. They'll summon him once the ceremony begins, and I fight the urge to go check on him. The wolves are already waiting inside with him, and he's Cam. He's fine.

I'm probably the last person he wants to see today anyway.

Which makes my front row seat doubly unfortunate.

All things considered, it's a good turnout. We'd been prepared for more of the estates to fight the idea. But all eight in the alliance are in attendance—even Olofsson and Jógvan, who agreed to renegotiate now that changes to turning protocols are back on the table.

They're not all happy. That much is clear from the sneers and eyes shooting daggers at any wolf that gets too close to some of them, but they're *here*.

I'd been expecting more bad blood after three of their monarchs were butchered, but most seem content about having members of the younger generations fill those seats. Considering some of the monarchs have held their positions for over a century, it must be refreshing.

It's a clear night, the stars shining brilliantly overhead, so much brighter than in the city. They let Cam choose which of Westcott's compounds he'd prefer working out of, and being the first monarch—though he's insisted he will *not* be using that word—who isn't a vampire, his location is the first to not be limited geographically to optimize minimal sunlight.

It made sense that he'd prefer the one in Eastern Canada, the original one I'd stayed at. It's in the middle of nowhere, surrounded by beautiful mountains and woods, the climate familiar to him. The perfect place for someone who detests the extravagance of the estates and intends to spend the majority of his time outside.

We're set up in the field behind the compound, framed on either side by the mountains. Under different circumstances, it would be a romantic, picturesque wedding.

But Anya is no blushing bride, and Cam is no doting groom.

Anya looks all business as she nods along to Queen Suksai's instructions. The wedding part of the ceremony will come first, after which they'll jump to swearing Cam into the alliance.

I'm just glad I'm not part of the ceremony. Reid had tried to talk me into it—*as my wife, you're just as much the head of the Carrington estate now as I am*—but the other estates have only one representative up there.

The rest of the monarchs' partners are sitting in the front row with me, none of whom I know, though I recognize several of their faces from my studying. The woman next to me is the closest to my age, but I don't remember her from the books. She must be with the new head of Locklear who took power a few weeks ago.

Every one of the white folding chairs set up is filled— wolves, vampires, witches, humans. Some from the estates, some from Cam's past, some of Westcott's following. There are clear lines drawn—the estate vampires sitting together, an entire wolf pack in the corner—but they're all in one place and not trying to kill one another, so that feels like progress.

My friends are here somewhere, but I can't see that far back. All the better though. The second they saw me with this crown on they wouldn't stop bowing and curtsying and calling me *Your Majesty* like broken windup toys caught in a loop.

Seeing the size of the crowd makes me all the gladder Reid and I didn't do this. Standing up in front of this many people —which we would've had to do, no such thing as a small estate wedding—looks miserable. It would have been an all-night affair, and I would've known less than five percent of the people attending.

A quick signing of the papers and a celebration for just the two of us was perfect. I was never someone who dreamed about my wedding since I was a little girl. What came after— the life, the partner, the family—*that's* what I want.

I trace over the ring with my fingertips, a smile pulling at my lips. A warm sensation floods the bond, like Reid can feel it too. I still haven't gotten used to the word *husband* when thinking about him.

He stands at the head of the group of monarchs, looking entirely at ease, like he's always belonged there. Everything about him looks perfect—the polished shoes, the three-piece suit with golden embroidery to match my dress...everything but his crown that's slightly askew in his messy hair. I swear he never manages to get that damn thing on straight.

A hush falls over the crowd as orchestra music fills the air and Anya steps up to her place, the rest of the monarchs falling into the traditional places of bridesmaids and groomsmen.

I press my lips together to keep from laughing as Cam makes his way down the aisle, all heads turned in his direction like he's the bride. One of the wolves lets out a loud whistle, and Cam shoots him a death glare.

The ceremony itself is fast—no vows, no flourishes. Merely a sworn agreement and a signing of documents. They don't even kiss. It's cold, detached. Just business. If Anya's upset she ended up in a political marriage after all, she doesn't let it show. And she'd been right—the marriage alliance had been the key factor to getting all of the estates to agree.

And I can't help the overwhelming relief that it's not Reid standing across from her.

It's over as quickly as it started, and Anya falls into place among the other monarchs as they form a semicircle around Cam and begin the tedious swearing-in process, comprised of lots of reading of duties and rules and history.

But when all is said and done, after every oath is made, it's Anya who steps up and announces, "We hereby declare the Farley estate of Quebec the eleventh estate and the ninth member of the alliance."

Despite the tension in the air, the crowd applauds as the rest of the estate heads take a step back and Cam is left in the center. He looks like he's scowling as he faces the crowd and gives a minuscule bow of acknowledgment, but the slight flush in his cheeks gives away his discomfort. When his eyes land on me in the front row, I give him a cheesy grin and thumbs-up, and for the first time tonight, he smiles.

REID and I teleport out early the following evening to make it to New York in time for the food drive happening downtown. The city has been slow coming back to life since the evacuation. The restoration of the estate itself has been much faster, but Reid was adamant about setting up stations throughout the city with food and supplies to help the humans as they rebuild too.

Crouching beneath the plastic folding table, I collect the rest of the water bottles in my arms as yet another person flags Reid down, asking questions about his plans for the region moving forward. Even though he's given the same answers a million times over at this point, Reid's tone is nothing but patient as they talk, and others crowd around to listen. A few members of his new security detail orbit the scene, close enough to jump in if needed but trying to give Reid the illusion of space.

I set the water in a neat line at the end of the table beside the boxes of food and medical supplies, then brace my hip against the building beside us, smiling as the line moves forward smoothly. It's gotten longer throughout the night as word spread we were here. We'll need to send a team out to restock supplies again soon.

"Is it one per person?" a woman asks as the baby propped on her hip tugs a tiny fist relentlessly against her blouse.

I shake my head. "Take as much as you need. Here, we have bags."

My gaze trails over her head like a magnet constantly being pulled to where Reid stands a few paces away. Even in his attempts to blend in—a simple white button-down shirt and slacks—I could pick him out anywhere. He doesn't need the crown or fancy clothes to remind people of his station. It's the way he stands, how he holds himself. He shakes the hands of the group of men he'd been talking to before returning to our table. He catches me watching him and smiles.

"How are you holding up?" he asks as he braces his hands against the table on either side of me, pressing his chest to my back and his chin to my shoulder.

"I could ask you the same thing. That was a long talk over there."

He nods. "They were asking about blood donations. It'll take some time, but I'd like to transition to Cam's idea to reimburse donors, but I think the blood farm locations will need to be renovated first. I don't want people to have to—"

"Remember those when they go?" I offer quietly.

He nods again. "I'd like them to have a nicer space for it."

I lay my hands over his on the table and intertwine our fingers, looking out at the sea of people before us. After seeing little more than a ghost town the last few times I was in this city, my heart feels full seeing the streets crowded with people again.

There's still so much work to do. If I let myself think about it for too long, my brain starts to shut down, terrified that we'll never manage it.

But people even being willing to come back to this place, I suppose, is a start.

"They like you."

He chuckles softly, his breathing stirring the hair at the base of my neck. "Anything would've been a step up from my mother."

I glance at my watch and nudge him in the ribs. "You'll have to get back for—"

"The trade meeting, I know." He sighs and presses his forehead to my shoulder.

He's put on a brave face for it all so far, but there hasn't been a moment of peace since he took that crown. Another meeting, another crisis, another duty. Another problem only he can solve.

I rub my thumb along his hand. "You're doing a good job, Reid."

He tightens his fingers around mine. "It never feels like enough."

"You"—I spin around in his arms and take his face between my hands—"need to learn how to take a compliment."

His smile turns rueful as his gaze travels from my eyes to my mouth.

"So let's try this again. Reid, you're doing a good job."

He leans down to kiss me, his lips brushing mine as he murmurs, "Thank you."

CHAPTER FORTY-SEVEN

"Where did you even come up with a spell like this?" Monroe mutters beside me.

"Shh!" Kirby hisses as she skips around the grass, lighting the white candles surrounding us as she goes. "Keep your bad vibes out of the circle."

Smirking, Monroe raises her palms in surrender, the softness in her eyes as she watches Kirby never wavering.

The deep orange and pink hues of the sunset fade in the distance behind the Carrington estate, and I lean back on my hands as I close my eyes and breathe in the fresh air, full of floral notes from the garden that's been slowly coming back to life as we've begun rebuilding.

"Yeah, Roe," I say. "Stop harshing my mellow."

She elbows me in the ribs, and I sit up straight again, laughing.

Kirby stops in the middle of the circle of candles with her

hands on her hips and a slight pout to her lower lip. "You're both making fun of me."

"I'm not!" I insist. "I think this is a great idea. I'll take all the good fortune I can get."

Exactly what she's hoping to accomplish with this ritual is unclear—rid us of the heavy, negative energy from the past several months, bring in good luck, that kind of thing. It all sounds pretty similar to York Academy's blood moon rituals, to be honest.

The smile falls clear off my face at the thought, remembering how much Beth loved the blood moon. Being a lunar witch, the rituals always seemed more meaningful to her.

As if she can read my thoughts, Monroe reaches over and squeezes my hand.

"I saw your sisters earlier," she offers.

I bob my head. Calla and Adrienne have been attached at the hip since the moment we got back, the same way they'd always been before Calla disappeared, like nothing's changed in the past three years even though everything has.

"We're all having dinner together tonight. With my mom. And Reid."

Monroe makes a face. "Is that weird?"

I snort. "Very. It was Reid's idea."

"Aw."

I raise an eyebrow.

"Oh, come on. He's trying to get along with your family— and no offense, that's no easy feat. It's cute."

"So you're saying you won't create a fake emergency to get me out of it?"

She bumps her shoulder against mine. "You're on your own with this one, kid. He's *your* husband."

I shake my head. "I'll never get used to that word."

She grins. "Me either. But I love it. Our little Valerie is all grown up and *married*."

She pinches me in the ribs repeatedly until I swat her hands away.

"You are such a child."

"All set!" Kirby plops on the grass in front of us, then extends her arms for us to join hands. I give Monroe a warning look not to try anything else, and she presses her lips into a thin line to keep from laughing.

As we lace our fingers together, a soft current of power passes through my palms at the connection.

"Now close your eyes," instructs Kirby. "And think of something happy. Maybe something that hasn't happened yet. Just something good."

My mind goes blank for a moment, but then I think about a conversation I'd had with Reid earlier. I've moved into the royal accommodations at the estate with him, but he's assured me it won't be a permanent solution. That he wants to find a place of our own. We won't be able to leave the estate full-time with his duties, especially with how hectic this transition's been, but a real home to escape to from time to time sounds plenty good enough for me.

I try to picture it in my mind, somewhere quiet and with a beautiful view. But simple, unlike the estate. Nothing gaudy or luxurious. Just something that feels like *us*.

"Good," Kirby murmurs. "Now hold on to it. Hold on to that feeling."

She switches over to soft chants in Latin, and the warmth between our palms grows until all I can see behind my eyelids is softly glowing white light, and something about it feels like home.

EPILOGUE

WHEN I WAKE, the bed beside me is empty. My hand searches through the sheets for a moment, but Reid's side is cold. I pry my eyes open. Judging by the faint outline of the curtains, the sun is still up. The music downstairs filters in next, and I wrap a robe around myself as my bare feet hit the floor. Despite how many nights we've spent here, I keep expecting the floor to be cold with how the weather's been, forgetting that it's heated. I let out a content sigh as I shuffle through the master bedroom and head for the stairs.

The days we get to spend in this home make all the difference. It feels like an escape from it all, like we're in the middle of nowhere and not forty minutes outside of New York. When the weather's right, you can see the city from our spot on top of the hill, as well as the lake beneath us. But other than that, it's just trees and peace and quiet.

More than half of our time is spent at the estate, and

maybe that's what makes the time we *do* get here feel so special.

The music grows louder as I descend the stairs, a soft jazz record on the player, but there's no sign of Reid. Not in the front room with the fireplace, or the music room—I freeze when I catch sight of him in the kitchen.

He's staring out the glass doors that lead to the deck, the sun setting in the distance and painting the sky vibrant shades of pink, orange, and violet.

The windows here offer a much better view than at the estate. Not just because of our positioning on the hill, but instead of the old UV-blocking technology the estates use, we *borrowed* some of Westcott's technology from his compounds, the kind they used in the nets that let vampires out in the field during the day. It doesn't darken the windows nearly as much.

I wrap my arms around Reid's waist from behind and rest my head on the center of his back.

He layers his hands over mine and lightly traces his thumb on the inside of my wrist. "Sorry if I woke you."

"What are you doing up so early? Couldn't sleep?"

"No, I just..." He trails off, and a long stretch of silence follows. Then so quietly I almost can't hear him, he says, "I never realized sunsets looked like this. It's so...bright."

My heart twists at the reverence in his words. The wonder. It had been the whole reason I'd wanted to alter the windows here in the first place. After twenty-six years in darkness and a longing to see the sun he never dared to voice, I thought it was well overdue.

I keep one hand on his waist as I come to stand at his side. "Have you been sneaking down here every night all alone?"

A faint blush touches his cheeks as he ducks his head. "I didn't want to wake you."

"Reid," I sigh, and the shyness in his smile is adorable. "Wake me." I cup his face with my hands and give him a little shake. "Wake me."

His eyes soften as he tucks a lock of hair behind my ear, his gaze slowly tracing over my face.

"What is it?"

He shakes his head, his smile growing into the kind that makes my chest ache to look at. "I've never gotten to see you in the sunlight. You're always beautiful, but seeing you like this is my favorite."

Now it's my turn to blush. I tuck myself against him, my back pressed to his chest, and he winds his arms around me as we watch the sunset together, the clouds in the sky making it all the more beautiful. He presses a kiss to the side of my neck, then leaves his chin resting on my shoulder.

There are a million things we need to discuss, a million problems to solve now that the weight of the region is on our shoulders, and everything is changing on a day-by-day basis. But we made a deal when we got the house on the hill that work would never cross that door. When we're here, we're still just us. So I force it all from my mind with an exhale and turn around in his arms, smiling up at him.

"Dance with me?"

He has one hand on my waist and the other in mine before I finish the sentence, like he'd already been thinking the same thing. I laugh as he spins me around the kitchen, then we fall into an easy rhythm as I rest my head on his chest. It feels so much like a dream that I'm afraid to open them again. But after so many months of danger and uncertainty—a lifetime of it, if I'm being honest—a few months of peace feels like a fluke, not the new normal.

A soft tail winds around my ankles, and Reid chuckles as he tightens his arms around me to keep me from tripping.

I sigh as Pepper lets out one pitiful meow after another until Reid finally releases me and leans down to pick her up.

Jealous little furball. She curls up on her back, letting him hold her like a baby as he scratches her belly, and her eyes cut to me as if to say *ha*, purring like an engine all the while.

We met her the first day we came to the house—a stray who liked to hang out on the porch. Her all-black fur had her blending in with the night, and it wasn't until she strut right to the door and waited for us to open it like she was expecting us that we even saw her.

No matter how many times we let her outside, she keeps coming back.

"So much for cats don't like you," I mutter.

Reid grins, his entire face lighting up as he looks at the cat. For someone who'd been so against keeping her—if I didn't know better, I could have sworn he was *afraid* of her at first—he sure switched his tune fast.

He got tired of me just calling her Cat, so he picked the name. I'm not convinced Bell Pepper—Pepper for short—is much of an upgrade. Though I have to admit, watching her sneak across the counter and steal all of the peppers the first time he cooked me dinner here was pretty cute.

At least this will occupy him for a while so the baby conversation won't come up again. *That* isn't happening for another few years, at least.

I try to hold on to my scowl, but the damn cat is adorable rubbing her face all over Reid, flopping around so much he can barely keep a hold on her. Finally, she climbs his arms and comes to sit across his shoulders.

"Looks like you two would like to be left alone," I say. "I'm gonna go grab a shower."

Reid catches my hand before I can go, pulling me in and pressing his lips firmly to mine. "I'll join you," he says.

"The cat cannot come," I say flatly.

He smiles against my lips, then gently sets Pepper on the ground. Unperturbed, she sticks her tail straight up in the air as she struts to the front corner of the house where her food is.

I shake my head, watching as she walks away. Aren't animals supposed to favor the people who feed them? *I'm* the one who takes care of her, but she worships the ground Reid walks on.

Reid kisses the side of my neck again, his fingers loosening the tie on my robe.

"You can't be jealous of the cat." He pushes the robe from my shoulders until it pools at my feet.

"I'm not," I insist as he kisses down the side of my throat, my shoulder.

I definitely am.

I'm almost tempted to suggest we get a second one, but if *that* one liked Reid more too, my poor ego couldn't take it.

I turn in his arms and press my lips to his, not wanting to talk about the cat anymore. Not wanting to talk at all, in fact. He grins as he scoops me into his arms and heads for the stairs.

"I really do have to get ready," I mumble between kisses. "I promised Daniel I'd help with his move up to the compound today."

Everyone else has taken to calling it the Farley estate, but it feels too weird to say. But now with Cam taking over power, the other monarchs insisted he have a Marionette of his own, no matter how much he tried to protest.

Daniel's partner died in the Auclair fire, so he offered, which Cam was slightly more open to since he wasn't a complete stranger. Maybe him being a skinwalker feels close enough to a wolf to him, who knows?

It's not that Daniel particularly needs my help, but I was planning to head to the compound anyway to take care of some business, and he and I haven't had the chance to spend much time together since I "came back from the dead."

Lots of members of the Carrington and Auclair estates have been relocating as we rebuild. It's bittersweet. It'll be weird not having Daniel in New York, but it's not too far. A few hours by plane, and an easy enough distance to teleport if I'm not planning on using much more magic that day. There have been talks of adding a trainline too.

But I figured we'd lose Daniel to be closer to Leif anyway since, unsurprisingly, the wolves are sticking with Cam. Daniel would never say that's the reason he's going. I still can't get a straight answer out of him whenever I ask about Leif, but he gets the most obvious goofy grin and blush on his face when I do. Which means Wes also decided to go, though I think that may have to do with needing some space after everything that happened with Beth.

The one who surprised me the most was Connor, though in retrospect, I should've seen it coming. He's been desperate for a fresh start for years. And the compound is full of people like him—people who left the estates, who can relate to everything he's been through.

Kirby, Monroe, Adrienne, Calla, and Mom though, at least they're staying.

Seeming to sense my shift in mood, Reid sets me on my feet outside the bathroom and smooths his hands over my hair until his hands cradle the back of my skull.

"Are you sure you don't want me to come with you today?"

I shake my head. "You have that meeting with the academy staff. One of us needs to be there to get things moving if we want it reopened before next semester. I'll be fine."

He presses his lips to my forehead and rests them there. "With how often you'll see them, you won't even notice they're gone."

I nod. Even with how short of a time I've known the wolves, I think I'm going to miss them just as much.

"You want me to be the bad guy and decline their transfer requests? We can find a different partner for Cam."

I laugh, shake my head, and interlace my fingers behind his neck.

"The only thing I need," I murmur, my lips brushing his, "is for you to take off all your clothes."

He smiles against my mouth. "That I can do."

TURN THE PAGE

For exclusive bonus content.

CALLA

I COULD JUST *STRANGLE* VALERIE. You'd think after twenty-two years she might grow up a bit and stop thoughtlessly diving into things headfirst, but no, it's clear that part of her personality is never going to change.

I reach desperately for her arm—to take her with me or pull myself back, I'm not sure—but the darkness sucks me in before I can make contact. The heat from the fire disappears immediately, replaced by perfect, serene nothingness.

That peace lasts only a moment before I'm thrust into a bright light, and I feel myself lurch upright.

I blink, my hands coming up to my chest, my face, but not from my command. They're moving like someone else is pulling the strings.

I don't recognize the bed I'm in or the surrounding room, but judging by the silk pillows, fine sheets, and general extravagance, it's one of Westcott's compounds.

Gaudy would be the best word for it—everything gold and

cream. Sheer curtains are draped over the far windows, letting the sunlight spill through.

How the hell did you get back here? demands a voice in my head that sounds like my own but also not. She annunciates poorly, and there's more gravel lurking beneath the surface than I could ever manage.

Popi.

I don't think we've had the pleasure of meeting, I reply.

She scoffs internally. *It doesn't matter anyway. You do realize this doesn't end well for you, don't you? You should've just stayed there.*

In case you've forgotten, this is my *body.*

She throws our legs over the side of the bed and stands. *Not anymore.*

The floor is cold beneath our feet as she heads to the bathroom, and even though no signals I send to my body seem to go through, I still feel every movement acutely, maybe even more so than when I'm calling the shots. Every muscle, every bone, every breath, every blink—I feel them all.

Popi stops in front of the vanity mirror and smiles as she looks into the reflection of our eyes, and I know it's meant for me. We're in some cream silk pajamas set I've never seen before, our hair done back in messy French braids. She hums under our breath as she takes out the hair elastics and fishes through the drawers for a few skincare products.

Even though she's no longer focused on the mirror, I can still see the reflection in our peripheral vision.

Can still see the outline of something in her shorts' pocket. Something small and round, and even though I can't move my hands to investigate, somehow I know exactly what it is. Can feel it.

I hadn't thought much of it at the time. After Valerie appeared in the shadow world, she dropped something. I picked it up before leading her back to Popi's house, too preoccupied trying to get her to calm down to get into it, so I shoved it in my pocket for later. I'd barely given the necklace a second glance, but I could feel the power when I picked it up, so I figured it might be good for something.

But why—*how*—did this cross back into this realm with me when nothing else I was wearing did?

The more I focus on it, the more the magic in my blood warms, like it recognizes it. *Valerie's magic.* And somewhere beyond that there's a deeper knowing.

"What's got you all serious?" muses Popi aloud. She meets her—our—*my*—eyes in the mirror with a faint smirk, then digs out the necklace from her pocket. "This trinket?"

Electricity shoots through my veins as soon as she makes contact. Judging by her sharp intake of breath, she feels it too. Which means she's probably only a fraction of a second away from figuring it out.

A fraction of a second.

That's the only chance I'm going to get.

I follow the natural path my magic wants to take, pushing myself to the surface. It's like a vacuum, like trying to break through the atmosphere.

Popi's hand is outstretched with the necklace, frozen, like she can't release her grip on it.

Numbness tingles through my extremities as I fight my way through her hold. Our eyes widen slightly in the reflection until finally, *finally*, when I speak, my mouth obeys my command.

"Get the fuck out of my body."

I tighten my fist around the necklace as a tremor starts somewhere deep inside my chest, deep enough that doesn't feel like it's coming from me.

You're too late, growls Popi. *You can't stop this.*

"We'll see about that."

There's a knock on the bedroom door, and I jump.

"Calliope?" calls an unfamiliar feminine voice.

Popi's essence is fading, but I can still feel her holding on. I press the necklace against my chest as if getting it closer to where I feel her will force her out faster.

"Calliope?" calls the voice again. "Are you in there?"

A thin line of blood drips from my nostril. "Just a minute!" I call back, my voice coming out high pitched and all wrong. I sway on my feet and steady myself against the counter.

You have no idea what you've done, hisses Popi, but her voice is fainter now, distant.

I fall to my knees on the tiled floor, panting and clutching the necklace against my chest for dear life.

"Is everything all right?" The voice outside the door is now edged with panic, and the person knocks again. "Calliope... I...I'm coming in!"

Don't you know what happens to people who don't have a shadow self anymore?

Nothing. Nothing will happen. She's just desperate and willing to say anything right now. If there had been anything else to know, James would've told us. For someone so obsessed with knowledge, if anyone would know the consequences, it would be him.

And you're that certain you can put your trust in him? asks Popi. *He's* my *dad. Not yours.*

The door to the bedroom creaks open, followed by light footsteps on the hardwood.

I tighten my fist around the necklace and send what little magic I have to spare alongside its power. *Definitely more that I can trust you.*

I feel it the moment she leaves my body. When I inhale, the tension in my lungs is gone, granting me a full, satisfying breath. My hands shake as I push up from the floor.

"Your father wants to see you," calls the woman, followed by a gentle knock on the bathroom door. "He says it's urgent."

I glance in the mirror and quickly scrub the blood away from my nose. I feel like I could sleep for a week straight, and that was *with* the help of whatever this necklace is.

Oh, God. Valerie. She has nothing to help her. What if she can't break through?

I have to believe she can. I have to.

"Is everything okay in there?"

I pull in a deep breath and count to three before swinging the door open. The woman's eyes widen—someone I've never seen before in a servant's uniform—and she backs up a step.

"Of course." I force a smile. "Everything's fine."

SEE WHAT HAPPENS NEXT

Thank you so much for reading *Ruthless Ends!* If you enjoyed it, **it would mean so much if you left a review!**

Want to see what happens next? This may be the end of Valerie's series, but for news on Cam and Anya's story, you can sign up for my newsletter at katiewismer.com. Book one is expected to release in 2025.

Good news! I also have a bonus scene **from Reid's point of view**, available through my newsletter. Find out why Valerie and Reid were *really* paired together.

ACKNOWLEDGMENTS

Is this the acknowledgements or just a love letter to my readers? I'm not sure.

I can't thank you all enough for seeing this series through to the end with me. This being my first series I've completed, I can now confidently say I had absolutely no idea what I was getting myself into when I started outlining book one in 2020. I had no idea where these stories would take me, on and off the page, but I know I'll always look back at these books as something really special. So thank you for taking a chance on my weird little vampire stories, and thank you for loving these characters as much as I do. (But, mostly, thank you for putting up with my cliffhangers.)

Also, a huge shoutout to everyone who participated in The Marionettes Deluxe Content Kickstarter. I had so much fun playing around with bonus content for the series, and seeing the support and enthusiasm was incredibly heartwarming.

Valerie Galderisi, Heather Keller, Kellie N., Jesica Bertrim, Katie Todd, Amanda la, Mary Partain, Kylie Rodriguez, Jamie Rice, Leah Coker, Sarah, Cecily Hager, Maggie Thompson, Amber Rodriguez, Sherill, Astra Carter, Beverly Adams, Ashley Bettencourt, Selah Ella, Shauna Golden, Heidi R, Allie Seale, Courtney, Josee Smith, Christian Shipp,

Vanessa, Agnes Mullett, Nikole C., Michaela, Rossella Lopez, Fatimah Abdul Rashid, Sara P., Kim Peer, Amanda Lynne, Maria Mejia, Christina Cassoday, Emily Stewart, Jordyn Roesler, Makenzie Bell, Samantha Bourbon, Samantha Traunfeld, Bonnie Minatra, Annabel S., Krystal Santiago, John saxon, Alyssa Radle, Kaylani, Alexandra V. Thiel, Jessi N, Alyssa aka Nerdy Nurse Reads, Jojo Rodas, Gemma Roman, Joseph Noll, Sarah Tracey, Rebecca K. Sampson, Alexandra Larch, Angela Ruth, Katie H., Lauren, Nijeara "Ny" Buie, Maria Arell, Allison Post, Ashley, Sky Armstrong, Bobbi Lackey, Andie Vargas, Skyler Ramirez, Corrine, Opt out, Laura Schmidt, Irina R, Sam Kubichek, Cassandra Coca, Rissa Feliciano, Sarah Simonson, Stephanie McKaskle, Lilith Darville, Vada, Angel Jackson, Lauren Green, April Shea, Mariel A., Shaughnessy Duke, Jen Harrington, Lisa H, Rebecca Gregg, Danielle Castañeda, Jovanah Watkins, Gena, Erika Gudino, Heyley Ingram, Madi, Stephanie Borden, Cal Hale, Dana Hebel, Laura J Smith, Rhiannon Bird, Kirsten, Penny Pascolini, Gerald P. McDaniel, McKenzey Smith, Hannah Rush, JC Chapman, Ellie Ward, Danielle Gillen, Kayla Cotrell, Anna Muh, Ashley B., Ingrid, Danielle Cage, Emilie Garneau, Ayre Wilson, Lorenzo G, Denniz Ehn, Vanessa Mohr, Leslie, Morgana Perez, RosieD, Winona Reitzer, Brooke Peterson, Elly Walter, Brittney Eastwood, Moala, Teresa Beasley, Alexa, Linda Richards, Erica H, Kaleigh Smith, Kierstin Martin, Shaylyn L., Alex Merritt, Beth Mischler, Precious Mangosing, Ivelisse Colón, Davinia K., S Meredith, Alex, Kat, Sebastián Urrutia, Cheyenne, Natasha McGrath, Zoe Whittfield, Diane Provost, Anny Mahlum, Carla Savelberg, Qavee, Catherine (Cat) M., Brittany Nock, Summer Hill, ☠Stephanie Cerda☠, Laura Jensen, Christina W Nichols, Makayla Payne, Tasha Armstrong, Kenyon Wensing, Amanda Guertin, Naemi, Court, Ruthenia (RAD), Sekhmett, Ali Fitzpatrick, Ashley Smith, Cherelle H, Britt Andrews, Kirk Righetti, Ashton Smith, Kevin Varner, jenn_loves_2_read, Corinne Posar, MicaelaL, Maryn Corkran, Sarah A. G., Jessica Wandvik, Ann Stansbeary, Emily wood, Lizeth, Madie Roberts, Tabitha Wilson, Nicole Haarstad, Vanessa Ramirez, Sofia Forsström, Carson Frame, Vicki Hsu, Tony W, Christina White, Julia Morgan, Renee Cheytanova, Rochelle Moore, Make zie, Grace Major, Allie Alvarez, Grace Derr, Kaitlyn Mehrtens, Serena M, Stephanie Clark, JB (Janelle Brockman), Kaela Munson, Keisha, Jensa Fish, and Emily J Craft.

And thank you to Bonnie, Laura, and Sam (Belle) for participating in the second "name a character" tier of the Bloodless Ties Kickstarter! I hope you enjoyed seeing yourselves in the book! :)

ABOUT THE AUTHOR

Katie Wismer writes books with a little blood and a little spice (sometimes contemporary, sometimes paranormal...and sometimes even poetry.)

Be the first to know about upcoming projects, exclusive content, and more by signing up for her newsletter at katiewismer.com. Signed books are also available on her website, and she posts monthly bonus content on her Patreon (including a Patreon-exclusive book!)

When she's not reading, writing, or wrangling her two perfect cats, you can find her on her YouTube, Instagram, or TikTok.

patreon.com/katiewismer

tiktok.com/@authorkatiewismer

instagram.com/authorkatiewismer

youtube.com/katesbookdate

goodreads.com/katesbookdate

amazon.com/author/katiewismer

bookbub.com/authors/katie-wismer

Printed in the USA
CPSIA information can be obtained
at www.ICGtesting.com
LVHW092044131023
761069LV00001B/1